Mending Dreams

Mending Dreams

Bonnie Schroeder

ISBN: 979-8-9857529-0-8

Library of Congress Control Number 2022908353

CREDITS

Cover photo: itakdalee/iStock

Cover design: Paula L. Johnson

Proofreading: Flo Selfman/Words à la Mode

FIRST EDITION 2014

SECOND EDITION 2022

Printed in the United States of America

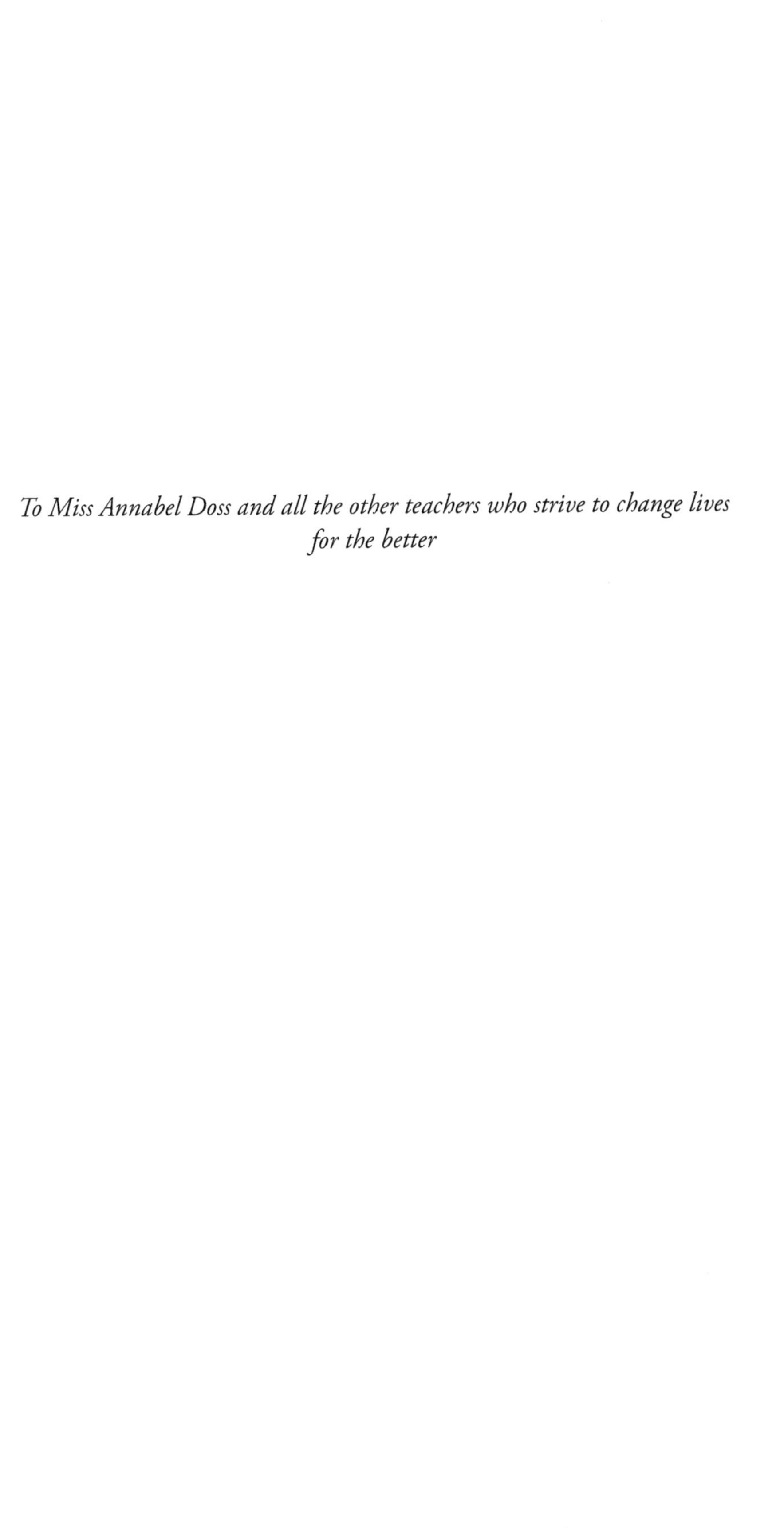

*To Miss Annabel Doss and all the other teachers who strive to change lives
for the better*

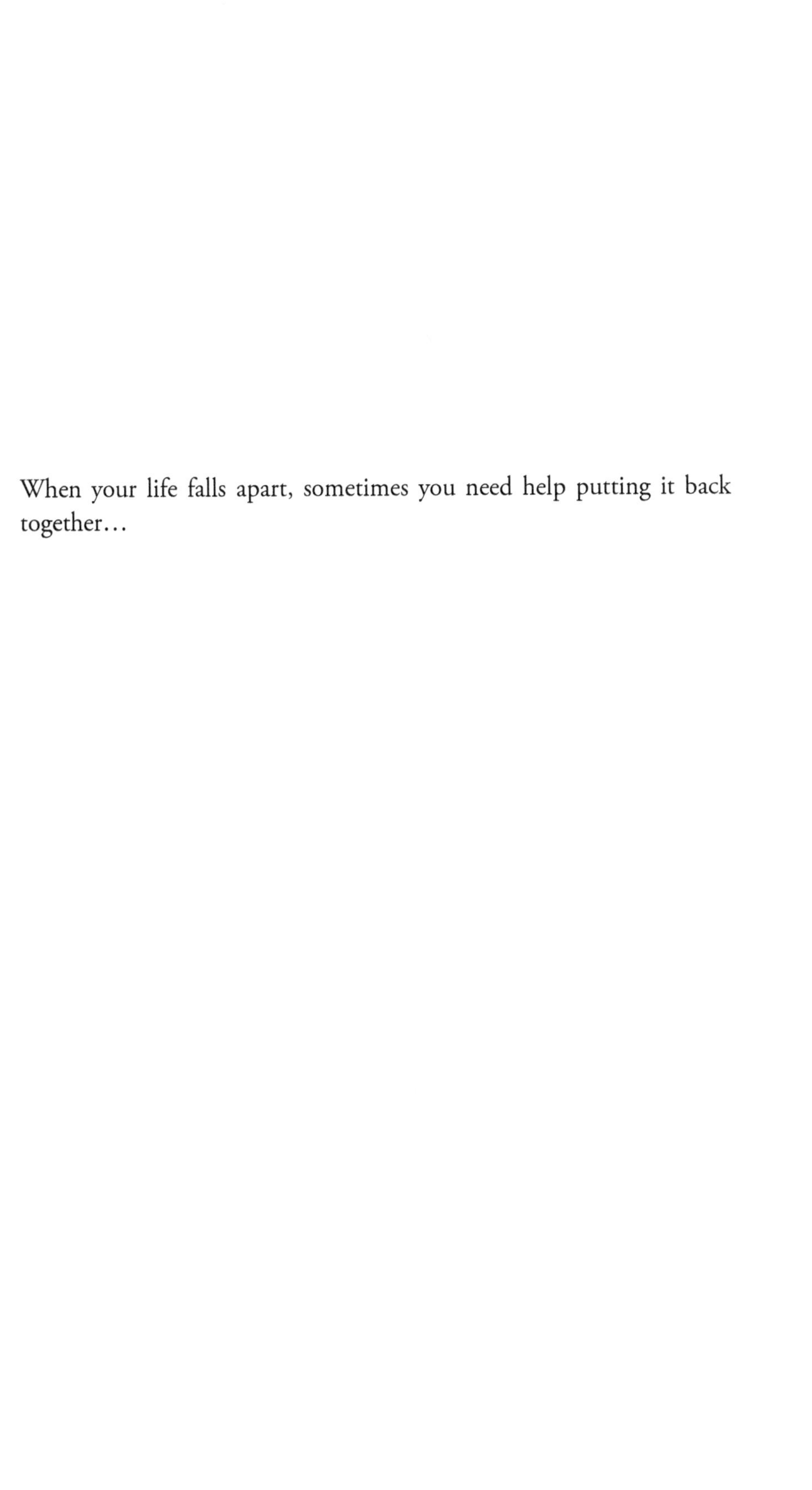

When your life falls apart, sometimes you need help putting it back together…

Chapter 1
A Narrow Escape

Did you ever have one of those days that was so bad you thought, *Well at least it can't get any worse?* And then you realized, *Oh, yes, it could. It most certainly could.*

That August Monday started out hot, humid, and as wretched as Los Angeles can be. Somehow it always surprises us, the people who live here. "Where's the ocean breeze? Why is it so *hot*?" Because we live in a desert, that's why. It's been greened over with stolen water, but it is what it is.

The muggy weather came courtesy of Hurricane Isabel, which had devastated a bunch of towns along the Gulf of Mexico, and then brought her havoc further inland, even as far as California. Thick clouds held the heat in, and we baked, simmered, and stewed. A malicious pink sky tinged everything the color of thin blood.

Mechanical devices misbehaved. Traffic lights suddenly went dark. Internet servers spontaneously disconnected. Air conditioners strained and threatened to die.

I was late to work, thanks to some moron's car in the no-park zone of Glendale Blvd. When I finally arrived, caffeine-starved and out of breath, disaster awaited.

Over the weekend, I'd logged on to my office network and picked up my emails, even as "workaholic" hissed around in my brain. Jacobs Laboratories had sure been getting its money's worth out of me. I'd flown home late Friday night after five fun-filled days at our Dallas plant, and on Saturday I barely had time to take in my dry cleaning, mail my mom's birthday present to New Mexico, and restock my refrigerator. My houseplants begged for water, and so did my elderly neighbor's front lawn, which I'd helped take care of since she fell and broke her hip. Unpaid bills lurked in the pile of unopened envelopes scattered across the floor beneath the mail slot.

And I was desperate to get to the gym. Those days of enforced inactivity and hotel food had taken their toll. Maybe I was overly paranoid about my weight, but I'd been on diets since I was ten years old, and I'd finally learned that exercise helped silence the nagging little voice—my own or my mom's, I was never sure which—that whispered "fat, fat, fat" whenever I saw my reflection.

Not until Sunday did I even get time to catch up with my friends. Noah, the man in my life, was camping with his son in Yosemite. He'd left a message on my answering machine to welcome me home (as usual, I'd forgotten to turn my cell back on after the flight) and in some ways that was better than having him there in person.

* * *

My first clue Monday wasn't going my way at work came as a voicemail from my assistant, the inaptly named Angel Fairweather.

"Susan, I hate to do this, but I caught one mother of a summer cold," her recorded voice said between sneezes and coughs. "I know you'll be buried with work, but maybe one of those lazybones down the hall can help out. I'll try and be back tomorrow. Sorry." Another sneeze for good measure before she hung up. Her message had been time stamped at five o'clock Monday morning, and she sure sounded miserable—but Angel was an aspiring actress, and a couple of times before, she'd phoned in sick to go to an audition.

"Damn," I muttered as I booted up my computer and connected to the Jacobs intranet.

My email inbox was relatively clean, thanks to my weekend check-in. But sitting in the middle of my desk was a note from Derek Bord, my boss, asking for a time-consuming report on my year-to-date expenses compared with my budget. Double-damn. I went to the break room for coffee, and by the time I got back, I'd received three new emails, all way more urgent than Bord's request.

A few minutes later, Bord himself stomped into my office. He was a small man with dyed-looking black hair and eyes that didn't quite line up.

"Ah, there you are, Susan. Good."

I put all my energy into a smile and pointed at the computer. "Derek. I'm researching the expense data right now."

This was a lie, but he wouldn't know the difference. Bord's computer skills were somewhere below a first-grader's.

He waved a manicured hand. "Forget that. We have bigger fish to fry."

I bit my lip. "Fine. What's up?"

"I need a list of everyone in Benefits, how much they make, how long they've been here. And I need it right away."

I peered into his beady little eyes and wondered if he'd somehow forgotten that my job description—Manager of Corporate Compliance—didn't include keeping personnel records on individual work groups. I had enough of a challenge making sure the company maintained a semblance of ethical corporate conduct.

"Val should have that at her fingertips," I said without thinking. Big mistake.

My friend and co-worker Val Desmond managed Personnel, which also reported up to Bord and included recordkeeping. I overcame the urge to point out that last detail.

Bord's face scrunched up like a squirrel passing an acorn. "I'm not asking Val. I'm asking *you*. I have my reasons—and please don't cause another scene about this."

Another scene?

"I don't understand," I said, trying to figure out what had Bord wound up so tightly.

Again the squirrel face, accompanied by a heavy sigh. "I don't have time to explain it to you. I need the information, I need it *now*, and I need it done discreetly. If it's beyond your capability, I'll get someone else to—"

I held up my hands in surrender. "I'm on it."

He still blocked the doorway, studying me. I shuffled some papers to show I meant business. "Anything else?"

He shook his head. "An hour, Susan. I need it in an hour."

I went to work. The data wasn't that hard to come by, but the research kept me from what I considered more important matters. Every time I glanced at my email inbox, the number of unopened messages had grown.

I sent my query to the database, and an obnoxious little box popped up in the middle of my computer screen, informing me that the system was "WORKING … PLEASE STAND BY." While I waited, Ginny Loring tapped on my door. Ginny was Val's assistant, a pale, freckled woman with curly red hair and a bizarre sense of style manifested in the yellow sundress and purple sandals she wore that morning.

"No one's answering your phone," Ginny said.

I frowned. "I know. Angel's out sick, and I'm on a rush project for Derek. Just let 'em go to voicemail."

"Okay, but NitroLitho's calling—they really need—"

"Not now. Take a message. Thanks."

Back to the computer, where rows of data appeared on the monitor. I scrolled down to see if the names looked right. Wait—there was one I didn't recognize. Was it a mistake, or someone who'd just been—

Tap, tap, tap. Ginny again.

"What?" I snapped.

She flinched, and I felt a twinge of remorse, but I could practically hear Bord snorting for his damned report.

"Do you want your mail, or should I leave it for Angel to open when she—"

"Leave it! Please."

Ginny actually whimpered as she turned away. Belatedly, I called out "Thanks" as her sandals slapped down the hallway. I sighed and made a note to apologize later, when things calmed down. Even if she had a poor sense of priorities, Ginny meant well.

I found my place in the rows of data, found the unfamiliar name. A new hire. Okay. I downloaded the list, still trying to figure out what that little prick Bord was up to.

Lilah Cantrell, Bord's own personal Dragon Lady, glared at me as I approached, report in hand.

"Mr. Bord is on the phone," she told me.

I cursed the day I'd opposed Bord bringing Lilah with him when he was hired. She had to know about it, judging by the way she treated me. None of the other managers on Bord's staff got the chilly reception I did. Sure, I was just doing my job when I recommended he take one of the existing assistants rather than bring in an outsider, but I don't think Bord had explained my reasoning to her. Not that Lilah would have cared anyway.

I ignored the ice in her voice. "He asked for this report ASAP," I told her, fluttering the papers.

She held out a red-taloned hand. "I'll see that he gets it."

Yeah, right—in another hour or so.

"I'd rather give it to him myself. In case he has any questions."

She pressed her thin red lips together and glanced toward the heavy wood door that closed off Bord's inner sanctum. With a belabored sigh, she got up and knocked softly, then went in and pulled the door shut behind her. A moment later she emerged. "You can go in."

Still on the phone, Bord motioned me to a seat in front of his heavy walnut throne. Me, I'd have gone for a smaller scale in furniture, but I guess he thought it made him look important.

After a leisurely end to his phone call, Bord peered at me over his reading glasses. "What've you got for me?"

I handed him the report and he paged through it, frowning. No "thank you," no "good work, Susan." Just the Bord scrutiny.

"I don't see any ages on here," he said finally.

I fought down a wave of annoyance—at him for the belated request and at myself for not anticipating it.

"You asked for names, salary, and length of service," I said.

He shook his head with a well-crafted look of disappointment. "I expected better of you, Susan."

"It would help if I knew what was going on, Derek. I'm working in the dark here."

Bord looked at me blankly. An awkward moment passed.

"How soon can you get me more complete information?"

I checked my watch. "Fifteen minutes."

He gave me back the report, like it was too contaminated for him to keep. "Do it."

I went back and rewrote the query to ask for age data—plus gender and minority codes for good measure. That should give the little creep more information than he knew what to do with. I sent the request and then retrieved the voicemail messages that had piled up while I worked on Bord's pointless project.

As the query results began coming in, my phone rang. I picked it up without looking at the ID display, sure it was Bord wanting to know how long he had to wait.

"Hi there."

It took a second to place the voice, coming at me out of context like that.

"Bad time to call?" he continued when I didn't answer right away.

Is there ever a good time for a call from your ex-husband? Frank Krajewski and I had somehow forged an edgy truce in the shattered aftermath of our marriage, and even if he did still tell me every time he saw me that I looked just like actress Angie Harmon, *only better*, it didn't mean I was happy to hear from him. Oh sure, I kept his name after the divorce, despite the inconvenience. It's pronounced Cry-YES-ky, but I lost count of the times a sales clerk cheerfully addressed me as Mrs. Kurh-JOO-sky. My maiden name was Stafford, but I'd used Frank's name professionally for six years, and it was just too much trouble to change back.

Besides, the Stafford name was about all my father gave me. I never knew him, but I was pretty sure I liked Frank better. That's not saying much, though. Months of therapy and gallons of tears had worn away the sharp corners of my feelings, but sometimes I felt like my anger toward Frank was all that kept me going.

"No, it's fine," I said in answer to Frank's question, proud of how easily the lie came. "How are you?"

A pause. "Okay. I was wondering if maybe you'd like to have dinner at Emilio's tonight? Haven't seen you for a while."

Something in Frank's voice made me uneasy. I twirled my stainless steel letter opener and then pressed its sharp tip into the report Bord had rejected. Behind me, the computer hissed softly. A black plastic tray full of incoming mail sat on the far corner of my desk, and it wasn't going to magically disappear on its own. One of the fluorescent lights in the ceiling started to flicker and buzz; I scribbled a mental note to call Building Maintenance.

"Susie?"

"I'm here. Just checking my schedule. Ummmm, yeah, I can do that."

"Great!" He sounded relieved.

"How's Clayton?"

Fine—he's up at Davis for some kind of training."

Aha, that explained it. Frank was on his own and bored; he never handled solitude well. We agreed to meet at seven. I went back to Bord's little emergency and put Frank out of my thoughts. Almost.

* * *

This time the Dragon Lady didn't even bother to look up at me. "Go on in."

Bord studied the report, lips pursed. He set it down and shook his head. *Oh great, he's going to find something else wrong.*

"A lot of people," he said, looking at me across four feet of gleaming walnut.

I nodded. "Anything else?"

Bord leaned forward and lowered his voice, even though the connecting door was closed. "This is highly confidential, but you're going to have a role in it eventually, so we may as well get you started."

I dug my nails into the padded leather chair arms. *Terrific—more pointless work.*

If you're beginning to think I didn't have much respect for Derek Bord, you're right. I wouldn't have liked him in the best of situations, but it so happened he was hired to replace my favorite boss of all time,

Paul Dumas. Paul had been tough on his people, but when they delivered, he wasn't stingy with praise. Or bonuses. Paul and I worked well together—until he dropped dead of a heart attack at the age of fifty-three. That had been two years earlier. When Paul died, Jacobs was in the midst of acquiring a medium-sized processing plant in Washington State; we needed to merge their workforce into ours without delay. As Vice President of Human Resources, Paul had been working twenty-four seven on the merger, which is probably what killed him.

Pressed for an immediate successor, Jacobs had opted for an outside hire with supposed credentials in the area of blending workforces. Enter Derek Bord.

And at that moment Bord was giving me an imitation of a benevolent smile from behind his desk, sure of his place in the Jacobs hierarchy. "We have decided to outsource our benefits work," he said.

We who, Derek? You and the rat in your pocket?

"What for?" There I went, speaking without thinking. But the idea sounded stupid, even for Bord. Our Benefits group was small and, except for a marginally competent manager, pretty efficient—too efficient to warrant outsourcing. In my opinion anyway.

Bord scowled. "There are a lot of reasons, but I don't have time to explain it all right now. The thing you have to keep in mind is that people will be … released. And we'll need to avoid the appearance of discrimination when we decide who to keep and who to let go."

He paused and cocked his head as if waiting for some sign of agreement from me. When I didn't offer any, he added, "That's where you come in."

Still trying to absorb the news, I nodded.

"So you need to be thinking about who's expendable and who's not. And I want you to think outside the box here, Susan."

"Outside the box?" I repeated like a moron. Was he asking me for ways to circumvent our normal Equal Employment Opportunity practices?

"Yes. For example, Jeff Tate. Jeff's a fine manager, but I'm not sure we'll need *his position* when the outsourcing's done. However, Jeff's skills are transferable—we could, say, move him into Personnel and—"

"But that's Val's—"

I didn't have to finish my sentence. Val and Bord had clashed several times when he tried to cut corners in the hiring process. This outsourcing would give him a prime chance to weed out the people who'd stood in his way, the ones he didn't like or want. Maybe even the Compliance Manager, if she gave him an excuse.

"Of course we have to obey the rules," Bord continued. "I'm not suggesting any wholesale disregard. Just … be creative. Think of ways we can *flex* the rules."

I got up and pretended to study the view. Bord's office had a nice set of windows, and I could see the glass cylinders of the Bonaventure hotel to the north. On bright days the reflection might blind you, but those thick, murky clouds had smothered the sun. I looked back at Bord's desk and his shiny brass name plate, and I pushed away an image of me bashing him over the head with it, blood splashed all over his crisp white shirt and gray silk tie.

Finally I trusted my voice enough to speak. "I'll see what I can come up with."

He nodded. "This is top-secret, Susan. I know you and Desmond are friends, and I'm counting on you to be discreet."

"Don't worry, Derek. I'm good at keeping secrets. I know where a lot of bodies are buried—figuratively speaking."

I hoped that sounded mysterious enough to make him wonder if I had anything on *him*.

I sprinted back to my office, closed the door, and leaned against it. My desk was exactly the way I'd left it, but I felt like my whole world had changed. Val was my friend. Should I warn her of Bord's plan? What good would that do? Was I next? Bord didn't like me, and maybe he knew how much I disliked him. And what about the other people who would lose their jobs? People with kids in high school, a mortgage, doctor bills.

Somehow I found my chair and sat down, hard; then I made myself inhale and exhale until I could feel my skin again. My hands shook so much that I spilled coffee when I tried to take a sip, but I didn't care. I just watched the pale brown stain, almost the color of dried blood, spread over my copy of Bord's report.

Then I decided the best antidote to Bord's toxic news was the comforting familiarity of my regular work. Among my unopened emails was one from NitroLitho, our printer. The subject line read "URGENT!!!" The message forwarded a draft of Jacobs' new employee handbook. They wanted comments by close of business. No wonder they got Ginny to bug me. Thankful for any distraction, I started editing.

Val tapped on my door just before noon and poked her head in. "Welcome back. Lunch?"

Val didn't look a day over thirty, but I knew she'd just turned forty-three. Compact and energetic, she had the mischievous grin of a teenager—always ready to laugh, and when she did, she put her whole body into it. She had straight, shiny brown hair, and her green eyes smiled with the rest of her face. I knew Val looked forward to lunch. She enjoyed her food but never seemed to gain weight, lucky duck. All that laughing must have vaporized the calories.

I marked my place in the handbook draft and shook my head, trying to avoid those smiling eyes and grateful for an excuse to pass on lunch. "I'm buried here. Rain check?"

"You got it. Want me to bring you anything?"

"Thanks, but I'm not real hungry. I'll survive."

I sent NitroLitho my comments on the handbook, answered eight other routine messages and returned all the phone calls. Things were looking up, except for the big, gloomy cloud Derek Bord had dropped on my world. I found some stale rice cakes in my desk drawer and washed them down with another cup of coffee, then decided I needed a stretch and a pit stop.

As I passed a bank of vending machines, the Snickers and Milky Way bars on display started calling my name. Damn, I was hungrier than I thought. Snickers had peanuts in them—that meant protein, right? *You deserve it. No, you don't. You don't deserve shit. You can hardly fit into your clothes now. Yeah, but it'd taste soooo good.*

The dialogue was tiresome but familiar. I gritted my teeth and kept walking. Some women would have caved, but not me—not that time, anyway.

As I reached the door to the women's restroom, Ginny Loring's voice came through from the other side.

"She's such a bitch," I heard Ginny say as I swung the door open, "I don't know how Angel—"

Ginny and Alice DuValle, another assistant, were washing their hands; Ginny had raised her voice to be heard over the water flow. She stopped mid-sentence as I came in, and the freckles on her face almost disappeared in the red flush that rose on her cheeks.

"… how she can wear those pointy-toed shoes," Ginny finished, carefully not looking at me.

Alice cringed, but I ignored both of them and locked myself in a stall. Only when the door hissed shut behind them could I let out my breath.

The women's restroom walls were a dull, sickly yellow, and the overhead lights put shadows on your face in places they didn't belong. Even drop-dead gorgeous Angel looked slightly jaundiced in there. The mirrors had dulled with age and abuse, and I think the idea was to discourage loitering.

I knew all this, but when I emerged from the stall I still flinched at the sight of my worn-out, scared reflection. Two weeks overdue for a trim, my normally flattering chin-length hair had morphed into a muddy brown fright wig with curls poking out in all the wrong places. My face looked like every one of my thirty-five years had told a story on it. And where did I get the idea I could wear black? It did nothing to hide the unwanted pounds I'd picked up during the funfest in Dallas.

When he saw me, Frank would probably shudder with relief that he didn't have to look at me across the dinner table every night. Would he still compare me to Angie Harmon? Not tonight—I'd lay odd against it. I smeared on some lipstick and fluffed up my hair, but that didn't help.

"The hell with it," I muttered, and then I went back to work. Some days you can't do much except grit your teeth and try not to notice how bad things are.

The rest of the afternoon swept past in a blur of messages, responses, and interruptions, but by the time I left work just after six-thirty, tired and famished, I'd done a decent job of clearing my desk. I hoped Frank was on time and ready to eat.

* * *

Emilio's Ristorante was the consummate Southern California Italian restaurant—big windows, lots of warm wood offset with marble and terrazzo, cozy glass-topped tables flanked by grapevines on the shaded patio. Interesting choice on Frank's part—our first date had been at Emilio's. The restaurant hadn't changed much over time except that the old neon sign had been replaced with discreet lettering in the window, the final "e" curling into the shape of a lush red rose.

I spotted Frank's silver BMW in the parking lot—at least I assumed it was his from the rainbow license-plate frame. I eased into a space next to the Beamer, took a deep breath, and tugged my dress into place as I walked toward the entrance.

The clouds had finally lifted, leaving a heartless blue sky that bounced a shaft of sunlight against the chrome trim on Emilio's front door, temporarily blinding me as I pushed into the dim lobby. Time warp: the burnished walls mimicked the inside of a cave—cool and dark. I could almost hear water dripping over rock. Even though smoking had long been outlawed inside Emilio's, as it had almost everywhere in California, decades of nicotine had saturated the dark paneling with a lingering tobacco smell.

How long had it been? Six months, at least, since I'd seen Frank.

I took one last glance at myself in the gold-veined mirror behind the host's lectern. The view was a little more forgiving, but I still hated my hair. Oh, well. I licked my lips and headed for the bar, where I knew I'd find Frank.

He was talking to the bartender so he didn't see me come in, and I had a chance to study him. Slouched over, right hand cupping his highball glass, he was, for just a second, still My Frank: the first man I ever loved. Frank was handsome, in the classic sense—a good, straight nose, black curly hair that he always wore just a shade longer than most men so it spilled onto his forehead and the back of his neck. Blue eyes so pale they sometimes seemed transparent. And artist's hands: long, slender fingers, capable and strong.

Violin music played softly from the dining room, and candles flickered in stubby little glasses along the bar and on the round tables by the window.

The bartender looked my way, and so did Frank. His face broke into a smile like sunrise over the desert. He slid off the bar stool and turned to me, arms open wide.

"Hey, Susie," he said, "you look terrific. Great dress—I was hoping to see those killer legs."

Suddenly, the extra pounds, the lousy hairdo, the shitty workday dissolved in a fizz of pleasure.

"Thanks. You're looking good yourself."

"Liar." He said it with a little laugh to take the bite out.

I hugged him and was surprised at the feel of his body. Frank had always been slender—a cosmic practical joke on me because he could eat his weight in M&M's and not gain an ounce, while I put on a pound just thinking about candy. But that night I felt his bones through his soft white shirt, every knob and junction of his spine. Had he always been that lean, and I just hadn't noticed? Or was Clayton wearing him down to nothing?

He kissed me, quick and close-mouthed. Too bad.

Damn you, Susan, don't go there.

I held him at arm's length. He looked okay, but something didn't feel right. He seemed pale, especially for the end of summer, the skin around his eyes and cheeks more deeply furrowed than I remembered.

The bartender put a tall vodka-tonic next to Frank's bourbon without being told; I pried my eyes away from Frank's face, slid onto a bar stool, and picked up my drink. So did he, and we clinked glasses.

"Cheers. Good to see you, Suse."

I took a hefty pull on the vodka and smacked my lips indelicately. Frank laughed.

I should say right now that Frank Krajewski was not the worst ex-husband in the world. And one thing that had drawn me to him from the start was that he made me feel like a woman. He noticed stuff— my perfume or my clothes or my hair. Thinking back, that should have tipped me off, but oh, no. And isn't it just the mother of all irony that he left me for a man, not another woman? But before and even after our breakup, my coarser habits, my height, my laugh—which some have compared to a donkey's bray—never fazed Frank. He took the whole package, and he never criticized me with one of those "Oh please!" looks designed to wither a person's soul. That wasn't in his repertoire.

When Frank told me about Clayton, I threw up. Really. Oh, not at the very minute. At first, I'd thought he was joking. And when I'd realized he was serious …

What kind of woman was I, that my husband would walk out on me for a man? And how stupid was I, to never have had a clue? I mean, I'd been so happy that he was interested in me. It's not like I had a hundred guys trying to date me. Being almost six feet tall kind of narrowed the field. My mom had seen to it that I never got really fat, but I'd never truly been cover-girl material either. I couldn't believe that tall, handsome, funny Frank Krajewski wanted to be with me. Too good to be true. Oh, yeah.

I looked around the half-empty bar: not like the old days when you had to be there by five o'clock to get a seat. Crowds change. Tastes change. I took another sip of my vodka.

"Are you starving?" Frank asked.

I shook my head. "We can drink a while first."

He smiled and took hold of my hand, brought it to his lips for a quick kiss. This was not normal behavior.

"So—how are things?" I asked, expecting to hear about Frank's job, Clayton's veterinary practice, their yard, their house. And maybe he'd drop the other shoe, the one hovering in my mind ever since he called.

Frank took a deep breath, drained his bourbon, and signaled for a refill. I passed. The vodka had gone straight from my empty stomach to my brain in a giddy rush.

"Not so good—truth be told."

Uh oh. I was afraid of this. Something's going on. Maybe he and Clayton are breaking up. Maybe he finally realized I was The One after all. Ha ha.

"What is it?" I tried to sound low-keyed but concerned.

The bartender slid a glass of bourbon with very little ice in front of Frank, and he took a swig before answering.

"I've been feeling kinda lousy lately, so I went to the doctor. He did some tests."

Oh my God. Clayton has given him AIDS.

Frank looked down at his drink. "I'm sick, Susie. I've got lung cancer."

His voice gave out, and he covered his eyes with one hand and grabbed onto me with the other.

Tiny dark sparkles erupted behind my eyeballs and for a few seconds I couldn't see Frank, or much of anything. I shook my head, the way you do when you get water in your ears, like maybe I'd heard him wrong.

I put my arm around him and pulled him close to me. "Jesus! What—how—when did you find out?"

He sat back and swiped at his face. "Sorry. I swore I wasn't gonna bawl like that. Friday. I found out Friday. Doc sits me down across from him and tells me—bam! Just like that. You've got cancer, Mr. Krajewski. Late stage, not much they can do. Just like he was reading me the menu in a restaurant, just that cold."

"Maybe you should get a second opinion."

Frank shook his head. "He was the second opinion."

"God, Frank. I don't know what to say."

I still didn't believe it. Oh, I knew he wasn't kidding, but sometimes you hear something so horrible, so unthinkable that you just won't let it into your head. Maybe, I thought, if I don't really hear it, if I don't believe it, it won't be true.

"Susie? You're not gonna pass out on me, are you? I'm the one who's sick, but you look like hell."

Breathe, Susan. My body felt like it belonged to someone else, but somehow I managed to inhale a few sips of air. There. The buzzing in my ears subsided. I took a hasty gulp of vodka to loosen my vocal cords.

"Oh, Frank." That's all I could say. Big-time comfort.

Frank rubbed my back. "I should've quit when you did. But no, I had to be the stubborn asshole, didn't I?"

I quit smoking the year Frank and I got married. It was the hardest thing I've ever done. Only the mercy of Prozac kept me from dissolving into tears and/or rage, and each day I grimly applied a nicotine patch to my upper arm, fearing that if I smoked with the patch in place, I would overdose on nicotine and die.

"Can't they operate, or—"

He shook his head. "It's late stage. He kept saying that. Late, late, late. Too late to cut it out."

"Chemo?"

He scowled. "I'm not gonna spend the last few weeks of my life bald and puking. The oncologist—can you believe it? They have their own special name! Anyway, he says I'm too far gone for chemo to help much anyhow."

All I could do was stare at him. My mouth probably hung open like an idiot's, but it would have taken too much concentration to close it.

Frank went on, "I could try some experimental drug, but that's not very promising either. The tumor has already spread to my back. That's how I noticed something was wrong—back pain. All the time."

"So what happens?"

He drained his glass and slammed it on the bar. "Nothing—yet. When it gets worse I'll go into the hospice program."

I wasn't sure exactly what that meant and, honestly, I didn't want to find out. Frank told me anyway.

"They set you up at home, keep the pain under control—they say —and ..."

He waved his hand in the air.

And they let you die on your own?

"Did you tell your mom?"

He shook his head. "Not yet—haven't had the guts to. I don't want her roaring out here and taking over, dragging me to every quack in the country to find a miracle cure. No, thanks."

I couldn't think of a single helpful thing to say, no matter how much I rummaged through my mental collection of comforting phrases. Maybe none existed for this.

"I'm sorry, kiddo," he said. "I just kinda dumped this on you, huh?"

I rubbed the back of his hand. "I'm in shock."

"Yeah, I know the feeling. But for me the shock is wearing off, and I'm getting majorly pissed off."

He took a deep breath and then seemed to pull himself together a little.

"Is there anything I can do?" I had to ask.

"Yeah—find me a new body."

Back when we were married, that had been his stock response to my offers of help when he had the flu or a hangover or any other minor ailment.

Frank's "ain't-life-a-bitch" smile was as lopsided as ever; his mouth curved up more on the right than the left. "Sorry to bring you down, Suse. But I wanted you to know, and I felt like I needed to tell you face to face."

He turned on his bar stool, and I felt a twitch in my chest, that magnetic pull he exerted. Even then. Even when he was dying.

He put down his bourbon and signaled the maitre d' that we were ready for our table. I had no appetite by then and considered pleading a sudden stomach upset and fleeing. But I couldn't abandon Frank that abruptly, so I let him put his arm around me and lead me into the dining room.

I took a deep breath. "So—how is Clayton handling this?"

"Not real well. He's pretty much freaking out." Another drink arrived, and he took a sip. "Clayton is *emotional*—you know?"

I nodded, although I didn't "know"—not really. Aside from the fact that he'd taken my husband away from me, I knew little about Clayton Selden except that he was a veterinarian, he liked to grow roses, and he was a terrible cook. These informational treasures came from a few forcedly cordial encounters in the four years since Frank and I broke up. I no longer bore Clayton ill will, any more than I did Frank. What happened, happened. I accepted it and moved forward with my life. For the most part.

Frank took another hefty swig of his bourbon and shook his head. "Yesterday I found him in the garage, bawling his eyes out. He says, 'What am I going to do without you?'—like he hadn't made it through the first thirty years on his own. But that's Clayton. He doesn't handle trouble well. Not like you."

"Yeah, I'm such a beacon of strength."

"You are."

Yeah? But not strong enough to make you change.

I kept my thoughts to myself. Frank had enough to cope with. We ordered another round and studied our menus.

"Well, you *look* good," I said. *Let's try and redirect this conversation.*

Frank shrugged. "I feel okay, actually—except for the back pain. Most of the time I can't believe I'm sick."

"Are you going to take some time while you still feel up to it and do stuff you've always wanted to do? Travel, or sky dive, or anything?"

Frank put his menu down and took my hand. "I've pretty much done what I wanted all my life, now haven't I?"

Yeah. Come to think of it, he had. Including walking out on me when he met Clayton Selden.

* * *

He told me on a Thursday, and I've hated Thursdays ever since. I thought things were okay between us. Sure, I'd been putting in some long hours at work; the Department of Labor had been crawling all over our employment statistics, like they did every couple of years. Jacobs was a federal contractor and had to document fair treatment of its workers. But as the audit wrapped up, I looked forward to some quiet time, alone with Frank; maybe we'd go down to Mexico for a long weekend.

Instead I got the verbal equivalent of a kick in the gut. He'd met someone, he told me. He was in love. He was moving out. Leaving me. Oh, P.S., the someone was another guy.

"How could you not *know* you're gay?" I'd shrieked at him during one of the soul-scorching yelling matches that followed his defection.

He'd come back for some of his books and CDs a few days afterward. It was midafternoon, the house full of sunlight and the sweet smell of roses, strong enough to break your heart. Frank had probably expected me to be at work, but I'd phoned in sick ever since he left, lying on the living room sofa watching television without seeing it, eating Milky Ways without tasting them, and crying until my eyes were practically swollen shut.

He started packing the boxes he'd brought, while I glared at him from the sofa. I wanted to rip open his skin, shred his flesh with my fingernails. I wanted him to stop filling the boxes and admit he'd been playing a bad joke. Frank couldn't make eye contact with me. He looked so damn good. The bastard had on a turquoise shirt I'd given him for his birthday, and he had the sleeves rolled up above his wrists, a cruelly sexy look. New gray slacks—no doubt Clayton had picked them out. I still wore my pajamas.

He'd flinched when I yelled at him and then finally he looked at me. His eyes were a little red, so maybe this wasn't all sunshine and happiness for him after all, I remember thinking.

"Susie, it's something I fought my whole life, something I tried to pretend wasn't there. But when I met Clayton, I just—I couldn't keep on pretending. I was too damn tired."

I'd thrown an ashtray at him. I missed, and it rolled all useless across the floor. He'd finished loading up his stuff and left without saying anything else.

* * *

"Susie? You in there?"

I blinked away the memories. "Sorry."

"You haven't asked the big question yet."

I had no clue what he meant, and it must have shown.

"How long?" He wiggled his eyebrows. "How long do I have?"

"Oh." Jesus, when did I turn into such a brilliant conversationalist? "I didn't want to—"

"It's okay. You can ask me anything, kiddo. Anyway, the doc says three to six months. Everybody's different, blah de blah."

Those goddamn sparkles came back, pushing in between Frank's face and my eyeballs, and I felt like my head was about to explode. Three months? Three *months*?

Frank kept talking, and finally I could hang on to his words again.

"… but the tumor's gonna grow, and spread, and they'll put me on morphine. Right now Vicodin does the job. Vicodin and Zoloft. Yum."

When the waiter brought our drinks, I pointed to his bourbon.

"Should you be drinking?"

Frank laughed. "I'm probably doing irreparable damage to my liver."

To my horror, I laughed along with him.

We ordered dinner. Funny the things you remember: he got the salmon and I got the sea bass—accompanied by Emilio's famous pasta, of course. Alfredo for him, Marinara for me. Just like always.

He skipped on to other subjects, but I had a nervous feeling one more bomb was going to fall. I crunched on a thick slab of bread to drown the alarm bells, as my thoughts jumped all over the place. So Clayton was panicking, and Frank was looking at a slow and miserable death. Hospice or no hospice, he wouldn't be able to take care of himself, and he didn't want his mom's interference. Who was left? And wouldn't that just be the shittiest outcome in the world, if that's what he was leading up to? Now, after all that had happened, was he going to ask *me* to be his caretaker? Hey, like an idiot, I'd even offered my help.

Please don't ask for it, Frank. Please please please. I wouldn't be able to do it anyway, I have my job, my life, Noah … I practiced excuses with half my brain while the other half talked with Frank about mutual friends, his garden, my work.

He brought me up to date on my former in-laws, who lived in Chicago, Frank's home town. His sister Zoë and her husband Henry had a daughter now to go with the son who'd been born while Frank and I were married; his mother Elise still ran most of the family business; and his grandfather was still going strong at eighty-plus—which pleased me because Grandpa Krajewski had always been kinder to me than the rest of Frank's family.

And, oh yeah, Frank and Clayton had a dog—a Max look-alike, he said. Not that any dog could ever replace the late, great Max, who had died the summer before at the ripe old age of fourteen.

* * *

Frank had always loved dogs. When we started dating, I was surprised the first time he took me home to meet Max, a Golden Retriever mix Frank had rescued from the animal shelter. Lucky for me, Max and I hit it off. Frank later confided, and I think he was only half-joking, that I'd passed an important test when I picked up a slobbery tennis ball and threw it for Max to fetch. Again and again. And again. I'd been a non-animal person until then, but I grew really fond of Max, with his dark unjudging eyes and sloppy pink tongue. I liked the way he'd lean into me as if this simple physical contact was enough to make him totally happy.

I never dreamed that Max would cause the greatest disaster in my life, though.

Here's what happened: the dog, a prodigious glutton, had a yen for people food. Late one afternoon, he gobbled up a whole dish of cellophane-wrapped chocolate mints that Frank, oh careless man, had left on the coffee table. An hour later, Max started convulsing. I was still at work, so Frank took him to the emergency veterinary clinic on his own.

Clayton Selden was the doctor on duty, and while he pumped the dog's stomach and reassured Frank that accidents happen, my sweet, proper husband fell in love with him. Right there in the treatment room. Max survived, but our marriage did not.

* * *

Normally, I'm a pretty hearty eater, but that night at Emilio's I scarcely tasted my food. Frank pushed his salmon around on the plate, but I didn't see him take many bites.

The voices around us blurred into one wide murmur, like a swarm of bees. Our forks clinked against our dishes. Otherwise, we ate in silence. I chewed and swallowed and tried to think of something clever to say, something positive and comforting. Words had always been my forte, my weapon of choice, but they let me down, badly, that evening.

Finally the wretched meal was over, and I practically leaped up the minute Frank remarked that it was getting late.

He walked me to my car. "Thanks for coming, Susie. I've been missing you."

I tensed. He wanted something else from me; I could *feel* it. What? *Out with it, Frank!*

He hugged me, and he smelled of bourbon and cigarettes, just like I remembered. Frank was still pretty strong, and he held onto me so tight that I feared he might crack a rib. When he let go, he was crying, and I stroked the tears away.

"Thanks for listening," he said. "It helps to talk about it."

Okay. He just wanted to tell me the news, he doesn't want anything else from me. Thank God. I'm safe now. I'm safe.

Then why did I feel the teeniest bit disappointed? I *wanted* to do something to help Frank, but I sure didn't have a cure for cancer up my sleeve.

"No problem."

"You're the best, Suse. You always were."

A quick kiss on the cheek, and he let me escape.

After I started the car, the sparkles came back and blocked out my view of the instrument panel. I sucked in a big lungful of air and let it out in a whoosh. The sparkles intensified for a second before they dissipated. Frank was standing by the Beamer, head cocked. I waved and backed out of the parking space.

Over and over on the way home, I swiped at the tears trickling down my cheeks. It didn't seem possible. How could he be dying? I cringed at the memory of all the times I'd wished calamity on Frank for abandoning and humiliating me the way he had. Before I moved past it all, I'd torn up most of the photos of us together or scribbled "Eat shit and die" on them. And now . .

I comforted myself by thinking of the fate I'd escaped. To watch someone you love die, piece by piece. That had to be the worst thing in the world. Thank God I wasn't married to Frank anymore. Thank God I wasn't in love with him anymore.

I was so deep into these thoughts when I turned into my driveway that I almost forgot to open the garage door. Zeus, my neighbor's cat, a big tom the color of night, liked to sprawl on the cement apron flanking the garage. Normally the opening door's rumble startled him into motion, but since I didn't push the remote until I was two-thirds of the way down the driveway, he was blinded by the oncoming headlights. I saw his eyes flash green as he leapt up, not knowing which way to run.

I hit the brakes, hard. Zeus escaped by a whisker.

"One down, eight to go," I whispered as he scrambled over the fence.

Chapter 2
Noah

Two days later, Noah came back from Yosemite and invited himself to dinner. I didn't mind because my kitchen faucet was leaking, and I knew Noah would fix it for me. Noah liked to fix things.

Sure enough, right after a long, wet hello kiss, he went to work on the faucet like a kid with a new toy. I left him in the kitchen and went outside to put steaks on the grill. By the time they were half done, he came out, wiping his hands on his shirt hem, face registering the satisfaction of a challenge overcome.

And a handsome face it was, too, if not in the classic sense of the word. At thirty-nine, Noah had deep creases around his eyes and mouth, and ruddy skin that told of days spent outdoors without benefit of sunscreen. Brown eyes so dark I couldn't read anything in them. In a Marlboro Man contest, he'd have come up the winner any day of the week. Oh, yeah. A whisper shorter than Noah, I usually wore low-heeled shoes around him, in case the height thing bothered him. He never said, but I didn't want to risk it.

I handed him a glass of cabernet. "Thanks for playing plumber."

I'd had a head start on the wine, and when I leaned into him for a quick kiss, I didn't mind at all when he kissed me back, longer and harder. His body pressed against me, and if I hadn't been working up the nerve to tell him about my dinner with Frank, I might have let the steaks burn. My roses, creamy white and pink Double Delights, were in full bloom, and the balmy evening breeze washed the patio with their heavy perfume, enough to make you dizzy. Noah's free hand skimmed my t-shirt, and I knew he was ready to tear it off with the tiniest bit of encouragement.

But I had to tell him I'd seen my ex-husband. I wanted to get it over with, even though I knew it would lead to an argument. Although he'd never met Frank, the mention of his name darkened Noah's expression like a solar eclipse. The first time I casually told him I'd had drinks with Frank was the first time Noah had raised his voice at me. "I don't want you seeing him, okay?"

"That's not fair," I'd protested. "You see June almost every week."

June: the ex-wife. The mother of his only son.

"Big difference. We had a kid together. And that's the only reason I have anything to do with her."

Knowing Noah, I would have bet my life that he told me the truth.

I didn't flaunt my defiance, but I kept on seeing Frank from time to time. I considered Noah's jealousy irrational and pointless, and if there's one thing I hate, it's being told what I can and can't do.

As we kissed by the dying light of the summer sun, everything tinted a romantic shade of rosy peach, I considered keeping my latest visit with Frank a secret. No, this was too important. Frank was dying. Maybe Noah would feel more secure if he knew Frank wouldn't be around much longer to pose even an imaginary test of my loyalty.

Noah's temper rode close to the surface, and it didn't take much to set it loose. But once he let it out, his anger passed quickly. I, on the other hand, collected grudges like beach pebbles from summer vacation. Which meant that after we fought, Noah moved on, and I stayed behind.

I eased away from him and drained my wine glass. Before my cabernet courage wore off, I told him, all in a rush, about my dinner with Frank. While he absorbed that information, I added the terrible news about the lung cancer, and I braced myself.

The Malibu lights surrounding the patio winked on just then, but still I could hardly see Noah's expression. The rose scent almost choked me, and the evening breeze turned sharp. I shivered and reached for the wine.

Noah took the bottle from me and filled my glass.

"Bummer," he said. "Good thing *you* quit smoking."

He clinked his glass against mine and sipped. His reaction stunned me into silence. Was that it? No explosion? No yelling? No sulking?

Noah set his glass down, wrapped his arms around me, and nibbled at my neck. He was squeezing the breath out of me. I tugged free.

"They'll burn," I said, and lifted the lid on the grill. A smoky cloud flowed out, and I fanned it away from us. The steaks sizzled nicely over bright orange flames. I turned down the fire and closed the lid. Noah stayed right behind me, rubbing my back. I moved away, smoothed my hair, and took another drink.

Noah hovered just inside my comfort zone. The smoky air stung my eyes, and I blinked away watery tears and swallowed.

"Hungry?" I asked him.

He nodded. I went inside to check on the potatoes in the oven. Noah was standing on the edge of the patio when I returned, and I held back a few seconds, just watching him. With his strong, compact body, Noah was what my mom would have called a "manly man." When he took off his shirt, I liked to see his muscles move. He had his share of scars, physical mementoes of his profession: a wide shiny zigzag around his right hand, another across his left shoulder. A little one on his left temple that he claimed came from a flying wood chip but that I always suspected resulted from a barroom fistfight.

He faced the darkening sky, but I doubted he really saw it. Noah Davis had never shown any signs of appreciating nature's beauty.

* * *

He may not have known it, but Noah saved my life. When Frank left me, I vowed to show the world it was *his* problem, not mine. I dated feverishly, whoever I could find. Men I met in line at Starbucks or the bookstore. Old boyfriends who were still single, or single again. Blind dates with a friend of a friend. I went out with a civil rights lawyer fixated on conspiracy theories dating back to the Kennedy assassination, a cute computer technician who informed me on our first (and last) date that he was looking for "a woman" to take care of him, and a bipolar poet whose homicidal tendencies surfaced when he went off his lithium.

Then Noah entered my life. After a rainy winter, I noticed a big section of dry rot in the boards along the west side of my house. Things like that totally freaked me out, and one day at work as I whined about the traumas of home ownership, my friend Val Desmond handed me Noah's business card.

"He's not cheap," she told me, "but he'll do it right the first time."

I expected a grizzled old coot with a couple of missing teeth, but the man who drove up in a shiny white Chevy half-ton was about my age, with nice straight teeth and thick, curly red-brown hair. He had a voice so deep and gruff that at first I thought he was pissed off at me, but I soon learned that was how he talked—as if in a hurry to finish the conversation and get out his hammer and nails.

He studied the damaged siding and ran his thumb along the peeling edge of a board. Then he opened his leather-bound notebook, scribbled for a minute, and handed me an estimate—an estimate for a lot of money, but I remembered Val's recommendation, and something about Noah instilled confidence.

We agreed on a start date, and he didn't ask for a deposit.

"You look like you're good for it," he said, and smiled for the first time. Then he shook my hand and drove away. I stood on the porch, praying I'd made the right decision.

Had I ever. Noah finished the siding replacement right on target, cost- and time-wise. As he was picking up the last nails and wood debris, he told me I had a faulty sprinkler head that had contributed to the wood rot.

"It's hitting the boards, and you don't need that," he said with a rare and priceless smile. "I'm going to change it out. When I give the word, turn on the sprinklers, so we can test it."

I stood by the control box, and I heard him say "okay" so I

turned the switch on. Water erupted in a rainbow arc right in Noah's face. He yelled something I couldn't hear and twisted his screwdriver in the sprinkler head until the flow was going where he wanted it, while I stood watching like an idiot. By then he was pretty well soaked.

"I am so sorry," I said. "I thought you said to turn them on …"

"My fault," Noah told me. "I did say 'okay' but I was talking to myself. Forgot to give you the code."

He laughed as he peeled off his soaking-wet shirt and shook it out. I tried not to stare. Same curly red-brown hair on his chest. *Yum.*

"Can I get you a towel?" I asked. "Or a dry shirt?"

He laughed again. "It'll dry soon enough," he said, "but I wouldn't turn down a towel."

He didn't turn down my offer of coffee either, so we sat at my dining table while I wrote out a check for the siding work. Noah draped a big blue bath towel over his shoulders while his shirt dried on the porch railing.

From the corner of my eye, I noticed him studying the room like he was looking for something. More work to do? I tore off the check and handed it to him.

"Thanks," I said. "I've heard all kinds of horror stories about contractors, and now I don't believe them."

"Oh, there're a lot of crooks out there, but my dad didn't bring me up to cheat people out of their hard-earned money."

He didn't seem to be in a hurry to leave, and I had no urgent plans, so I asked him about his dad and how he learned his craft. Half an hour later, I'd learned that he grew up in northwest Oregon, where his father owned a construction company, but the wet weather had been murder on Noah's sinuses, so he headed to Los Angeles, hooked up with a fellow who'd apprenticed under his father, and had been working nonstop ever since.

"I can see why," I told him. "You're good."

He smiled. "I bet you are, too. What do you do, if you don't mind my asking?"

I refilled our coffee mugs and told him how I'd started in the clerical pool at Jacobs while I got my business degree in night school, how

I'd moved up to a supervisor's job in Personnel and then into the Compliance Manager's position.

"Right place, right time," I said.

"And a lot of hard work to go with it," he replied. "Must be tough on your personal life."

"Sometimes."

He fiddled with the coffee mug, then stretched and stood up. "Guess I'd better get out of your way," he said. "Thanks for the coffee. And the towel."

He retrieved his still-damp shirt and stood on the top porch step while he pulled it on.

"Well," he said, "I don't think you'll have any more trouble, but if something doesn't look right, you give me a call, okay?"

"I will. Thanks again. It's been a pleasure."

He started down the porch steps and then stopped and turned toward me. "You have a nice place here. And you keep it up. That's good."

"I do my best," I said with a shrug. I didn't know why, but I didn't want him to leave.

Noah's smile seemed a little uncertain. "Look, slap my face if this is out of line—but would you have dinner with me sometime?"

Good thing I'd been resting my hand on one of the posts that supported the porch roof, or I might have fallen over. Was he reading my mind? Had I been that obvious? Did I care?

"I'd like that," I said, as lightly as I could.

* * *

Noah was full of surprises. Instead of the Chevy, he drove a two-seater Mercedes when he picked me up for our first date. We went to a nice steak house in Burbank, and we had a great time. I'd worried about what we'd have in common to talk about, but I needn't have. Although his formal education ended with junior college, Noah liked to read. A lot. Anything and everything. The *Los Angeles Times*. *Forbes*. Steinbeck. Faulkner. Irving. He didn't claim to always understand what he read, but it gave us plenty to discuss.

He swore like a sailor, but that didn't bother me much because I did too. Sometimes a good "fuck you" is the only satisfying response. Aside from that, Noah had perfect manners. He held doors open for me, and he wasn't afraid to pay compliments; Noah was the first man after Frank to call me beautiful, and I think he meant it.

The perfect boyfriend? Not quite.

Noah had a couple of drawbacks. The main one was his son, whom I privately referred to as Hellboy. Jason had been in and out of trouble since age eight, cutting school and setting fires. He moved on to smoking pot and swiping his mother's prescription painkillers and got caught shoplifting a fifth of vodka when he was twelve. He graduated to stealing a CD player, some radios, and a small domestic car.

Jason had undergone plenty of therapy, and Noah and June had really worked at helping the kid, but it seemed as if Jason was programmed to self-destruct. I couldn't figure it out: as straight-arrow as they come, Noah clearly loved his son and had tried to give him a good life.

We'd been dating for several weeks before Noah told me about his troubled son. I didn't know what kind of comfort to offer, so I just let him talk. Sometimes I'd ask him how things were going, and if he wanted to tell me, I listened. But I didn't push. Once I asked him to bring Jason over for dinner, but it wasn't a lot of fun. The boy mumbled short answers to questions his dad asked but otherwise remained mute, and he picked continually at a scab on the back of his left hand. The one time he looked directly at me, I had an uneasy feeling he was sizing up my necklace and earrings to see if they were worth stealing.

Jason had finally gone into a drug rehab program, and maybe it had worked. He'd been clean and sober for ten whole months, but I knew Noah was holding his breath and waiting for a relapse; in Jason's sixteen years there had been many relapses. I did my best to be supportive, but there were times when I thought the best approach would be to lock up the kid and throw away the key.

* * *

As I stood watching Noah stare up at the sky, dark and sprinkled with twinkling stars, I wondered if his thoughts were on Jason. Or on Frank. I cleared my throat and went up to him, kissed him lightly on the cheek. "Let's eat."

I'd prepared a simple meal: steak and potatoes—Noah's favorite. Nighttime insects began to swarm, so we ate inside. I lit a big red pillar candle and dimmed the overhead lights.

"Thank you," I had to go and say just as Noah sliced into his steak.

He looked at me as he chewed the first bite and nodded his approval.

"For understanding about Frank," I continued.

Oh, just shut up and eat. Let it go.

Noah stopped chewing. "I don't. And I don't like your seeing him. But it's done. Just stay away from him now. Let me know when he's dead."

"Oh, come on—don't you have any mercy in you?"

Storms clouds began to gather on his face. "I don't want you catching anything. Stay away from him."

"It's cancer."

"So *he* says."

"It is. He wouldn't lie to me about something like that!"

Why did I have to go poking a sore spot?

Noah put down his fork. "Hey, baby, if you want to believe that asshole's sob story, go ahead. But I don't buy it. I think he's too chickenshit to tell you he's got AIDS."

"You're being ridiculous."

"And even if it is cancer—tough shit. Boo hoo, poor old Frank. He finally gets what's coming to him, and *now* he wants you to hold his hand. But where was he when you needed him?"

"Why can't you let that go? I have."

"I haven't."

"I know, and it's crazy. There's nothing for you to be jealous about with me and Frank. I'm over him. If you don't know that by now, then—"

"I'm not worried about you screwing him," Noah said, and took another bite.

"So what's the big deal?" I asked.

He just glared at me as he swallowed.

"I forgot the butter," I said, grateful for an escape, however brief. I leaned over for a quick kiss on my way to the kitchen, and he grabbed my wrist.

"Don't be mad," I pleaded. "My heart, and the rest of me, belongs to you anyway."

Noah kept a gentle hold on my wrist as he stood up and finished our kiss, his tongue pushing against my lips. I opened my mouth to him.

He started unbuttoning my blouse. "Prove it."

The physical attraction between Noah and me had stayed at fever pitch. I loved how he never tried to hide his lust. I always knew when he wanted to make love, and what he wanted.

He backed me against the wall and found the snap on my jeans. I forgot about the steaks cooling on the table and started on his shirt buttons. My heart thudded well above its target rate.

The damn phone rang, and I let the answering machine take it. Frank's voice came through the speaker loud and clear.

"Hi there. It's me. Hope I didn't bum you out too much the other day." A pause, then he went on, "You asked if there was anything you could do. Well, there is—so please, call me when you get a chance, okay?"

Noah's hand withdrew and he pulled away from me. I scrunched my eyes closed.

"What's with that shit?" he demanded.

I opened my eyes. Noah was glaring at me, the anger on his face designed to reduce me to disobedient-child status. I took a breath.

"He's dying, he's scared. Maybe he needs me to—"

"You see what I meant? Now he's gonna ask you for a little 'favor' and before you know it, you'll be—"

"Be what? What could I possibly do with Frank? What kind of idiot do you think I am?"

He leaned against the wall, arms folded across his chest.

"If you had a friend in trouble," I went on, "you'd do the same thing, no questions asked."

"Fuckin'-A I'd help out a friend. But this guy is no friend of yours. He used you and then threw you away like a piece of trash when he—"

"Now who's being an asshole? You don't know anything about this, and you have no right to judge me or—"

"You know, you're right, Susan. So just go ahead, do what you want. Do whatever you damn well want."

He stomped past me, and on his way out he slammed the door so hard the windows rattled.

Noah had driven the little Mercedes that night, the car he prized so highly that he'd yelped in pain the one time he let me drive it and I ground the gears. But that night he burned rubber as he sped off. Was he racing out of my life forever? Did it take that little to drive him away?

The candle had gone out, and a smudgy odor from the smoldering wick competed with the smell of cooked meat. Although the dining room had gone dead-quiet, I could still hear our pissed-off words echoing.

I shoved the dimmer switch back to high, picked up our ruined dinner, and tossed it in the trash. Then I poured myself another glass of wine and dialed Frank's number.

"Hello?" His voice was muffled at first. "Sorry," he said, more clearly. "Clayton and I were just having an intense talk."

Must be something in the air.

"Oh. Well, when you finish—"

"No, it's fine, honest. Thanks for calling me back."

He paused, like he needed time to work up enough nerve to tell me what he wanted. I started to worry. What was he going to say?

"I have a huge favor to ask," he went on, and I felt my whole body tighten.

"Go on."

"The trust," he said. "When you and I split up, Grandpa K changed it so that if anything happens to me, my share goes to Zoë. I need you to talk to him about it going to Clayton instead."

Wow. I wasn't expecting that. Compared to other possibilities, it came as almost a relief.

"You're kidding, right?"

"I'm serious, Suse. Serious as a heart attack. I mean, I love my sis and all, but she's got Henry to look out for her. Clayton won't have anyone. I want him to get the money. And you are the one person on earth who has a shot at convincing Grandpa to do what's right."

"So he knows you're … he knows about the cancer?"

"He will by now. I called Mom and told her right after I saw you. Figured I might as well get it over with."

"Oh shit—that had to be hard."

"To put it mildly. I did convince her to stay put in Chicago, though. For now. She said she would, but I'm not sure I can trust her."

Yeah, his mom was used to doing things her way. I learned that hard lesson early in our marriage.

"Have you tried calling him yourself?"

"He won't talk to me, Susie. He pretty much wrote me off when … when everything happened. I think he would've left me out of the trust altogether, but I bet Mom stopped him."

"So wouldn't she have a better chance of getting him to do what you want?"

"Hah. Mom would sooner cut out her heart. I mean, she's okay with Clayton, sort of, but no way does she think he's *family*."

"God, Frank, I don't think I can do it. I mean, I haven't even talked to Grandpa in ages."

"Yeah, but he likes you. Doesn't he still send you a card every Christmas? With a check?"

Why did I have to go and tell him about that?

In truth, Grandpa K's checks were an embarrassment. Regular as clockwork they arrived the week before Christmas. Five hundred bucks. Hell of a Christmas present. The first one, the year Frank and I divorced, I assumed was a mistake, so I called the old guy to thank him and remind him I was no longer married to his only grandson.

"I always liked you, Susie," Grandpa Krajewski had replied. "You have guts. And even if you're not with Frankie any more, you still matter to me. You take that money and use it well."

I invested the check in a no-risk CD, and each year afterward I added to it with Grandpa K's Christmas check. I thought he'd approve, although he never responded to the thank-you note I always sent. My only communication from him was that annual Christmas card—always a brisk winter scene with trees and houses, and no people. Inside he'd write in shaky script, "Hope this was a good year for you, Susie. Love, Grandpa K."

That hardly constituted a relationship strong enough to persuade him to change the terms of a trust he'd set up before Frank was born. Grandpa K, aka Joseph Krajewski, Sr., had grown a small real estate office into a healthy commercial brokerage that had made more money than he or his descendants could spend in two lifetimes. He was a smart, gruff old buzzard, and I suspected that he liked me mainly because Frank's mother didn't.

"Jesus, Frank, I wouldn't know how to begin to ask him something like that. How would I explain even knowing about the—"

"I understand. I know I don't have any right to ask you. I'm just … I'm scared, Suse, and I'd like to be able to provide for Clayton. It's not right that Zoë and her dipshit husband get the whole thing when I'm gone. Clayton's been a part of my life for—"

"It's not that I don't want to help him," I told Frank, and I meant it. "But I'm not good at persuading people to do what I want. You should know that better than anyone. I'd just mess it up."

I poked the cooling candle wax with my index finger and wondered if I was just being a coward about the whole thing. How hard would it be to give Grandpa K a call? What's the worst that could happen? The chair where Noah had been sitting remained pushed away from the table at a sharp angle. The world outside the windows was heavy and dark.

"It couldn't get any more messed up than it is right now. All I'm asking is for you to give it a try. Please."

I gulped my wine and tried to think of a good, strong excuse for denying Frank's request. There wasn't one.

"I'll think about it, okay?"

"Thanks, Susie. You're the best."

I dropped the phone in its cradle, drained the wine glass, and fell into bed. Sleep came fast, but it wasn't a good rest.

* * *

Morning arrived with a price tag. Even before I opened my eyes, I felt it—a red wine headache and a dull anxiety that I didn't place at first. Then I remembered the fight with Noah.

I swallowed two Tylenols, and they had pretty much done their best by the time I got to work. Angel had returned to her post, and the sight of her curly blonde hair cheered me momentarily. She was talking on the phone, but she smiled and mouthed "coffee's fresh" as I passed by her workstation. She'd unlocked my office and turned on the computer, which sat waiting for me to enter the secret combination of letters and numbers that would connect me to the Jacobs Labs intranet.

I got myself some coffee and scanned my incoming emails. Nothing critical. Same with the snail mail in the black plastic inbox. I'd just gotten my hopes up for a decent day when the phone rang, and I saw Derek Bord's name on the caller ID display. *Shit.*

But it was just Lilah. She liked to use Bord's phone line because she knew you'd answer if you thought the boss was calling.

"He wants to see you." Lilah's crisp, unfriendly voice held no hint of what was going on. Naturally.

Less than two minutes later I reported to Bord's lair, to find him talking on the phone, of course. Lilah wouldn't let me into his office until he finished, so I had to stand by her desk like a dork, trying to figure out what the little bastard was up to. So far he hadn't given me any sign that I'd made his hit list, but I couldn't know for sure what went on behind his opaque, oily eyes.

I thought I'd done a pretty good job of hiding my feelings for Bord. We'd clashed overtly only once, right after he'd been hired. He'd insisted on bringing Lilah with him from his prior employer, and after Val Desmond did the usual pre-employment screening, she phoned me because we were on shaky ground, Equal-Employment-Opportunity-wise. Lilah hadn't passed a basic computer-skills test that most job-hunters aced, and the position with Bord would have meant a promotion for several of the secretaries at Jacobs. Secretaries with real skills. I'd gone to Bord and tried to reason with him about the EEO risks.

"You're saying I can't hire Lilah, then?" he'd asked, his beady eyes glinting.

"I just want to point out the potential problems it might cause," I began, cautiously. The man was, after all, my new boss, and I didn't want to start off on the wrong foot.

He nodded and stroked his chin. "I see. Well, thank you for being so diligent. I appreciate it."

No concession or commitment, just a quick dismissal. I learned fairly quickly that Derek Bord played dirty. Arthur Trent, Senior VP of Operations and the man who had hired Bord and who signed off on all big events in Human Resources, phoned me the next morning and reined me in. Derek needed Lilah, and Arthur was convinced that she merited the risk. She understood Derek's work style, she was a proven performer, blah de blah de blah.

But Bord must've told Lilah that I'd opposed hiring her, and she got even in petty ways, like "accidentally" losing my expense reimbursement requests. Usually I overlooked the payback and tried my best to show courtesy and respect to Lilah and her boss. Or so I thought.

I stood as patiently as I could, waiting for Bord and watching Lilah ignore me and pretend to be busy. She studied a fat blue-bound report in front of her, dragging those scarlet fingernails down page after page, her face wrinkled in concentration. Then her phone rang, and when she turned to answer it I caught a glimpse of the report's title. Reading upside down is an underappreciated skill. *The Emotional Ramifications of Workforce Restructuring.* Oh brother. I looked away before Lilah caught me spying, and then Bord finished his call and beckoned me in.

"I want you to take a look at something."

None of the usual how-are-you's for Bord. He handed me a fat blue-bound report like the one on Lilah's desk. I checked it out. Yep, same title. Created by one Myron Streitzler, PhD.

"Okay," I said, hoping my distaste for this reading assignment didn't show. I figured Bord would elaborate on its purpose, and the little pissant didn't let me down.

"Dr. Streitzler is a respected expert on Change Management," Bord explained. "And he's offered to help lead us through the outsourcing, from a human perspective. He runs seminars for companies like ours, and he's offered to let us sit in on one and evaluate its potential. I want you to study this report and go to the seminar."

"Of course," I said, relieved he wanted something that easy. But I had a nagging feeling there was more to the story.

Sure enough, Bord added it. "Dr. Streitzler has reserved a block of rooms at the hotel, so that won't be a problem, and of course you'll have to book your own flight. Right away."

"When? Where?"

He jabbed his finger at the report. "Tuesday. Chicago. The details are in there."

I started to protest that I hadn't quite recovered from my last out-of-town trip, but I knew it was useless with Bord, so I nodded.

"Anything else?"

"Be open-minded, Susan. And give me a one-page summary the day you get back."

"No problem."

He made that squirrel face—why, I wasn't sure—and sent me on my way.

I put Angel to work booking flights while I juggled a couple of appointments I'd set up for Tuesday. Silly me to think I had any control over my own schedule.

A freak late-summer rainstorm rolled in that afternoon, complete with thunder and lightning. The walls of my office rattled with every thunder clap, and although the light show outside was awesome, I knew the drive home would be hell. As office doors clicked shut and people called out their good-nights, I decided to let the traffic thin out and get a little work done without any interruptions. But after a while the storm started to spook me, so I headed for the gym to exercise away some of my fears and frustrations.

* * *

An hour of pounding the treadmill and working the free weights left me sweaty and sore, but rid of the tension I'd been carrying around.

Although rain pelted the pavement when I left the gym, it felt warm and comforting. I made my way home through less traffic than I would have faced earlier, so I didn't mind the rain as much. No neighbor's cat in the driveway. I pulled into the garage and took a deep breath. Sanctuary at last.

As I walked toward the house, someone approached me. The rainy darkness hid age and gender, so I swung my gym bag to show I had a weapon. A few steps more, and I recognized Noah, umbrella in one hand, a bouquet of roses in the other. In the reflection of the garage light I saw reconciliation in his eyes.

He held out the roses. "I was a jerk," he said. "Again."

I dropped the gym bag and took his peace offering. The velvet red petals smelled sweeter than anything I could recall. I leaned over them awkwardly and kissed him on the lips.

"Can I come inside?" he asked. He sounded like a little kid.

"Of course you can," I told him. "Of course you can."

I needed a shower in the worst way after my gym workout, so I left Noah opening a bottle of wine in the kitchen.

I had just lathered up when I heard the shower door open behind me and felt Noah's hand on my soapy belly.

"I brought you some wine," he whispered in my ear.

I turned, and he held the glass to my lips; I got in one sip before he took it away.

"First I have to make sure you get all clean," he said

I turned into his naked body. He pulled me close as shower spray drenched us both, and his skin gave off a rich, husky man-smell, sweat and salt and sunshine crushed together. His mouth tasted of wine. His dark unreadable eyes focused on me, and he smiled just a little as he stroked me from head to toe, sudsing and then rinsing every inch of my skin. I leaned against the shower wall and let him explore, gasping steamy air as he found all the right places. The pulsing in my body drove its way into my brain and left no room for thought, just feeling, and Noah, just Noah, and the only words I heard were not spoken.

Mine. You're mine. Mine.

And, in that moment, he was.

Chapter 3
Girls' Night Out

"See?" my friend Judy said as I gaped at the mountain of cardboard boxes in her living room. "I told you it was a damned mess."

She pretended to yank out a clump of her curly black hair.

"It's not so bad," I lied. "Let's get some rock & roll going, and start unpacking."

Judy stabbed an accusing finger at the untidy pile. "I don't know where to *start*! And we can't even have music, because my stereo is somewhere in all of *that*."

She took a crumpled pack of Marlboros from her jeans, pulled one out and lit it, waving the smoke away from me.

"Get that away from here," I said.

She held her breath, ran to the window, and exhaled into the night air.

"Shit," she said, "I miss my balcony."

"You're nuts," I said. "This place is way nicer. And you should quit anyway."

"Not today," she said. Her face was a little kid's pout, but she put out the cigarette.

"Quit whining." I said it in a teasing voice, but I was only half kidding. I'd sacrificed my Friday night to help her get settled in her new apartment, and this was more than I'd bargained for. "If you'll help me find the CD player, I can hook it up for you."

Her big dark eyes got rounder. "You can do that?"

"Yeah, no problem." I scratched my head. "But first we gotta find it."

Judy poked at one of the boxes like she expected a cobra to leap out. "I know it's here somewhere."

"Yeah, right next to Jimmy Hoffa."

She pursed her lips and glared at me. "And of course you'd have been way more organized."

My annoyance dissolved. "Not necessarily," I admitted. "But how hard can it be to find those big-assed speakers?"

Not hard at all, fortunately. I spied one lurking near the far edge of the cardboard fortress and pushed some of the rubble aside to unearth the player and the other speaker. Then I studied the layout of the living room and pointed toward a bookcase on the north side.

"How's about I set it up there?"

"Terrific! It'll be—"

The doorbell sounded, and Judy sprinted away. That would be Margaret Deschanels. She and Judy and I often got together on Friday nights—usually for dinner and a movie, not slave labor. But that's what friends are for, right? To help each other.

While Judy let Margaret in, I set the sound system components in place and went to work on the speaker wires—child's play, really, with their color coding, and a cinch compared to my desktop computer and printer.

I was in a pretty good mood, even with the chores that lay ahead of me. In between unpacking and electronics-connecting, I planned to tell Judy and Margaret about the latest developments at Jacobs; they'd reinforce my shaky belief that I, at least, had nothing to fear from the outsourcing. That's what friends are for, right?

Margaret's voice reached me from the entryway, and I smiled as I listened to her admire the apartment. Every word rang true: it *was* a pretty place, especially compared to the dump from which Judy had just moved, but I'd been so overwhelmed by the boxes I hadn't taken time to remark on the wood-trimmed doorways and high, bright ceilings.

"Susan's putting my stereo together," I heard Judy say, and then Margaret's astonished, "She *is?*"

Another voice chimed in. Who was that? I didn't know Judy had called on anyone else for help. I pushed a button on the receiver, and Fleetwood Mac blasted out of the speakers just as Judy, Margaret, and a thin, pretty blonde came into the room. I lowered the volume and dusted my hands on my jeans.

"You did it!" Judy cried, clasping her hands under her chin like a kid seeing Santa Claus for the first time.

"No problem," I replied, giving Margaret a welcome hug.

The blonde held out her hand to me. "Hi. I'm Jen."

"Hello."

Her grip was firm for someone so thin. She had clear, pretty skin and looked barely twenty-one, except for her big blue eyes. Her eyes were at least thirty.

"Jennifer is an interior designer," Margaret told me. "I asked her to come along and give Judy some tips."

I nodded. "Great."

And where did she come from? I knelt down and went back to work, wrapping the speaker wires in tidy bundles and tucking them out of sight. I hadn't expected a stranger, and even though I hardly knew her, already I didn't care much for pretty Miss Jennifer. Behind me I heard the three of them carry on about the tile around the fireplace, the crown molding, the integrity of the hardwood floors. It made me want to puke. No apartment was worth all that fuss.

Jennifer the Interior Designer's high heels clattered down the hall. She sure hadn't come dressed for drudgery. Probably didn't want to snag her perfect fingernails.

A minute later I felt a hand on my shoulder, and I looked up: Margaret. She was about my height, but very thin, almost hard-edged, with steel gray hair, piercing blue eyes, and French ancestry evident in the angle of her nose. When she smiled, however, the edges dissolved and her face brightened with color, as if by magic. Most days I wanted to be her.

"Are you all right?" she asked. "You seem troubled about something."

Normally I'm pretty good at masking my feelings. One time at work I overheard Val warning a co-worker, "Susan keeps her feelings under wraps. You may never know if you've pissed her off, so be careful."

I liked the idea of being considered vaguely dangerous, and later I'd stood in the bilious glow of the women's restroom, studying my expression: pretty neutral, all right. I'd tried to summon angry feelings to see if my reflection changed, but with nobody there to provoke me, I couldn't get mad. So I took Val's word for it.

But this was Margaret, who could read my moods better than I could. And I didn't have to put on an act with her—except that I felt really petty for being annoyed by the unexpected addition to our threesome.

I stacked the last of Judy's CD collection next to the receiver and got to my feet. "It's been a rough week. And this is not my idea of fun."

My confession undermined the vague nobility I'd felt at offering to help Judy get settled in her new home, but I was definitely feeling underappreciated for my sacrifice.

Margaret smiled and patted my hand. The therapist in her couldn't help it.

"Think how good you'll feel in the morning," she said with a smile. "And how happy Judy will be to wake up in her new home without having to spend the weekend unpacking."

"You're right," I replied. "As usual."

"I hope you don't mind that I invited Jen."

"Not at all," I said, a little too fast. "So where do you know her from?"

"Her office is next to mine, and we have lunch together sometimes. She's full of good advice—and very talented."

Funny Margaret had never mentioned her before. I thought we pretty much shared all the important stuff about each other's lives. I'd known Margaret for seven years, and she was probably my best friend in the world. She had a PhD in Clinical Psychology from Stanford University and was a practicing therapist, with two young daughters and an often-absent husband, when I met her in a night school classroom. I'd never used her professional services, but I didn't hesitate to share my troubles with her. Although she was only twelve years older than I, in some ways she'd become my surrogate mother—the real one was stashed away in Santa Fe, New Mexico, so our lives didn't intersect the way Margaret's and mine did.

Margaret had a knack for listening. She didn't interrupt or judge—just let you talk until you worked your way around a problem and maybe—*maybe*—figured out a solution.

"I thought as long as we were doing good deeds, we might try for a twofer," Margaret continued.

I didn't get what she meant, and—other opinions to the contrary—it must have shown.

Margaret lowered her voice. "Jen's been very down in the dumps this week—something to do with a bad boyfriend. And I thought an evening with us might cheer her up. I know being around you and Judy always makes *me* feel better."

"Who's feeling better?" Judy asked as she and Jennifer thundered back into the room.

I pointed at her television set. "You'll be, if I can get some help hoisting that onto the stand over there so I can hook it up for you."

Judy stood over the TV, hands on hips. "Let's do it."

Jennifer and Margaret stood by while Judy and I lifted the television. Actually, she did most of the lifting.

"Hey, Muscle Woman," I joked as we straightened the TV's base on its perch. "Been hitting the gym?"

Judy smirked. "All those years tossing kids around the classroom are paying off."

Judy taught third grade. Yes, chain-smoking, gutter-mouthed Judy put on another persona entirely every weekday and became demure Ms. Fairstein at Buena Vista Elementary School.

"You guys go decorate," I said over my shoulder as I unwound the cord wrapped around the VCR. "I'll just continue to pretend I know what I'm doing here."

Judy began dismantling the cardboard mountain, and Jennifer

went to work unpacking dishes and silverware in the kitchen. We assigned Margaret the task of putting sweaters and lingerie away in the bedroom dresser, although she claimed, "You'll never be able to find matching stockings again, I warn you. Just ask Claire!"

Ah, Claire: Margaret's younger daughter—eighteen going on thirty. Deirdre, at twenty, was the Perfect Child, in her junior year at UCLA, an honor student who wanted to go into public service when she graduated. She played violin, worked part-time in a lawyer's office, and volunteered at the Los Angeles SPCA, grooming homeless dogs to make them more adoptable. But Claire—Claire seemed hell-bent on creating problems. She protested loudly and often that Margaret was ruining her life by forbidding tattoos, piercings, and sleepovers at her boyfriend's house.

Lucky I never had kids—imagine how I could've screwed that up. Then again, Noah and his ex had probably started off like Ozzie and Harriet, and look what that got *them*.

I turned my focus back to something I could handle: the dumb television. Although an older model, Judy's set did have color-coded plugs for the VCR and cable box input/output, so in no time I had a rerun of "Law & Order" playing on the screen.

It was worth giving up my Friday night to see Judy's fabulous smile when she realized she was back in touch with NBC and HBO.

"You are so amazing!"

I laughed. "What next?"

"Want to hang my mirror? You're so tall you don't need a ladder—which I don't have anyway."

"Hammer and nails?"

She picked up a red toolbox. "Right here."

She actually had different sized picture hangers. Impressive. I hefted her beveled-edge mirror and moved toward the fireplace.

"Oh, not there!" Jennifer called out, coming in from the kitchen. "All you'll see is the ceiling."

I put the mirror down and winced at the "thunk" it made. Oops. "Okay—where?"

She stood in the center of the living room, pivoting on those dainty high heels, hands on her skinny hips. She pointed to the wall by the outside window. "There."

"There?" It seemed a waste of the mirror to tuck it away in a corner like that.

Jennifer nodded. "There."

I picked up the mirror, relieved to see I hadn't cracked it, and held it against the wall.

"Not so high," Jennifer said.

So you need cheering up, eh? Does ordering me around make you feel better?

This time I lowered the mirror gently to the floor and propped it against the wall, then handed Jennifer the hammer.

"You know more about this than I do. Be my guest."

My voice had more of an edge to it than I meant, and something between surprise and hurt flicked across Jennifer's pretty face.

Judy stopped flattening a pile of boxes and looked over at me. I felt like I'd been caught kicking a lost puppy.

"Here," I said to Judy, "this I can do."

I nudged her out of the way and stomped on the empty boxes. It felt good. Behind me I heard the tap of the hammer and then a satisfied "ahhh" from Judy. I turned around. Damned if Jennifer wasn't right: the mirror looked great in its new spot.

* * *

Half an hour later we'd mostly finished. Judy did a little victory dance on the pile of flattened boxes. "Time for a toast," she announced.

We gathered in the kitchen, and I had to admit Jennifer had done a decent job of organizing the stuff in the cabinets. The wine glasses were on a bottom shelf ("In case there's an earthquake they won't have far to fall"), and I lined up four of them on the counter while Judy took a bottle of chardonnay from the refrigerator, which otherwise looked pretty empty.

"Gee, I thought you'd have some nifty casserole in there to feed us," I joked as Judy filled our wine glasses and we clinked them together.

She wiggled her dark eyebrows at me. "Better," she said.

Almost on cue, the doorbell chimed, and Judy raced off to answer it. She came back with a huge Domino's box. "Dinner is served."

She set the box on the counter, scowled at me and whispered, "Don't start with me tonight—WW talk is off limits."

Judy and I became friends through Weight Watchers. I joined in a pathetic attempt to stay lean, mean, and sexy for Frank, even as I had to acknowledge that marriage didn't always stop the sudden, aching urge to overdose on chocolate. Judy was about my age, but compared to her, I was a binge amateur. I laughed *and* cried when she described gobbling down a take-out order of taquitos as an appetizer before moving on to a main course of fried chicken and garlic mashed potatoes, topped off by an entire Mrs. Smith's peach cobbler, à la mode, of course.

When I first met her, Judy carried around a good thirty extra pounds that looked like more on her short body. She'd worked off most of the weight in the five years we'd known each other and had begun to look downright attractive with her smooth, creamy face— now minus a couple of chins—set off by all those dark curls. She'd started dressing in snug jeans and t-shirts and looked ten years younger and light years happier.

Judy's determination helped me during some of my rough times as I shaved off fifteen pounds, which should have been easy compared to her struggle. It wasn't. But I'd say to myself, "If Judy can get through the Girl Scout Cookie gauntlet without giving in, I can too." I could. I did.

And when Frank left me for Clayton, I dragged Judy to movies, walks in the park, book-signings I'd read about. Anything to keep us out of Ben & Jerry's parlor of delights. And she almost always went along willingly. I owed her big time, which is why I hadn't hesitated when she called me for help moving into her new place.

She had fought with her former landlord about cigarette smoking. Imagine that! She typically lit up on her small second-story apartment balcony, and her next-door neighbors had complained to the landlord about the smoke drifting in their bedroom window; they had a seven-month-old baby. When the landlord asked Judy to stop, she gave him a pure-Judy response: "I don't complain about their kid wailing all night, so they can just get used to my smoke." That didn't sit well with any of the parties, and when Judy missed her rent due date by a few days, the landlord threatened to start eviction proceedings.

"Fuck you," Judy had said. "I'm out of here!"

When Judy made up her mind, her momentum ground most obstacles to dust.

So I kept my mouth shut about Weight Watchers and drank my wine while Judy dished out pepperoni pizza on her good stoneware plates.

"You guys are the best," Judy said through a mouthful of pepperoni and cheese. "Don't think for a minute I'm not super grateful to you for giving up your Friday night to help me."

Margaret's smile edged dangerously close to a smirk; I saw her lips twitch, but she kept her eyes on her plate. "You'd do the same for us," she murmured.

Judy licked tomato sauce from her fingers and turned to Jennifer. "And I don't even know you, but—wow—thanks!"

Jennifer shrugged and drained her wine glass, which Margaret quickly refilled. "I was glad to be included. Margaret's told me about her great women friends and how much fun you guys have. And to be honest, I'm feeling kinda lost these days—I just broke up with my boyfriend."

"Ouch," Judy said. "I'm sorry."

Jennifer smiled. "He was a jerk. But he was *my* jerk."

"Been there," Judy said. "I know what you mean."

Margaret turned to me. "Speaking of boyfriends—how's Noah?"

Margaret and Judy had never met Noah, but they knew the ups and downs of our relationship. Especially the downs.

I chewed a chunk of pizza crust and swallowed. "He's good."

"He didn't give you any static about tonight?" Judy asked.

One time Noah had pitched a fit when he wanted to go out on a night when I'd already made plans with Judy and Margaret, and he couldn't understand why I wouldn't bail on them to be with him. I'd made the mistake of telling them about his tantrum, because I thought it was funny. Neither one of them laughed. Judy had pointed out that he seemed to like to be free and clear when he wanted to play Dad with Jason, but the scale didn't tip the other way.

I shrugged. "Nope. I think he's taking his son to a baseball game anyhow."

I saw the look that passed between Margaret and Judy; I'd seen it before. Margaret had as much as told me she thought I deserved better than Noah. And although Judy never let me forget that at least I was dating, she usually chimed in when Margaret got on my case for letting Noah slip away from any kind of commitment. I insisted I was happy with such a "flexible" arrangement, and most of the time I halfway believed myself.

I reached for the wine and came up with an empty bottle. Margaret had given the last to Jennifer.

"I have more," Judy said, popping up from the table before I could stop her.

"Would either of you be interested in going to the main library with me Tuesday night?" Margaret asked, looking from Judy to me. "Jennifer's giving a talk about feng shui."

Jennifer ducked her head and smiled with a modesty that looked fake to me.

"Count me in," Judy said. "My social life is pretty dead right now."

"I can't," I said. "I have to go to Chicago."

"Chicago?" Judy said. "Yuck. It's going to be Humidity City right now. Why pick August?"

"I didn't. Derek did. He's sending me to evaluate some stupid seminar."

"Derek the Dickhead?" Judy giggled. "Be careful he hasn't booby-trapped the plane!" She poked an elbow into Jennifer on her left. "Susan works for this creepy guy who's always picking on her, and—"

"But he doesn't want to *kill* me!" I surprised myself by how loud I said it.

Judy dabbed a napkin across her lips. "Sorry!"

"No," I said, "*I'm* sorry. Things are a little tense at work right now, and I'm taking it out on you."

I quickly summarized Derek's outsourcing scheme, and just as I figured, my friends were pissed off at him and supportive of me.

"They need you more than you need them," Margaret assured me. "I doubt he's stupid enough not to know your value, but plenty of other companies would leap at the chance to hire someone with your background."

"Yeah," Judy agreed. "If you didn't have a mortgage to pay, you could tell them to go fuck themselves. They couldn't run that place without you."

"Yeah, they could. Not as easily, but they'd manage."

"Your boss must like you, though," Jennifer said. "It sounds like he trusts your opinion."

I wasn't about to let her appease me. "Actually, I think he's punishing me for missing his sacred staff meeting last week—never mind that I was off in Texas doing my job. I think he forgot that part. Anyway, yeah, the weather is going to suck—and to top it off, I'm gonna have to see Frank's grandfather while I'm there."

I hadn't meant to say that. I still wasn't sure that I'd actually get in touch with Grandpa K once I got to his home town. And I didn't want to bring Frank into the room with my girlfriends.

"What does Frank's grandfather have to do with Jacobs?" Margaret asked. Reasonable question.

Oh, shit, here we go.

"Nothing. I have to … Frank asked me for a favor, and I don't want to do it, but he—"

I honestly thought I could tell them all calm and matter-of-fact, but those damn hot salty tears ambushed me. I hate the way I look when I cry. My eyes get all rabbity, and my face turns blotchy red. But there I went, bawling like a five-year-old with a skinned knee, right in front of Little Miss Blonde Perfection.

"Frank's dying—he has lung cancer. And …"

My vocal cords froze and a frog-like croak was all that came out. Judy got up and put her arms around me.

"Oh, God, Susie, I'm so sorry. You have all this shit going on, and here I dump my troubles on you. And you're such a good friend, you came and helped me anyway." I recognized her Comforting Teacher voice, and I didn't mind.

Judy's dining table was a smooth, sturdy pine with just a little gloss to it. She'd set out some bright green and purple woven place mats that matched the painted flowers on the rims of her stoneware. I fingered a raised section of flower petal, a pansy or petunia—I always mixed them up—and tried to compose myself.

All three of them were looking at me like I'd grown a second head. My lips moved, but my tongue was stuck to the roof of my mouth, and I felt like somebody had shoved a wad of gauze in there. My hand shook a little when I picked up my wine glass and took a sip; a few drops slopped onto my arm and I concentrated on wiping them off with my index finger. Then I swallowed, and my lips made a stupid little smacking sound as I worked up some moisture so I could talk.

"Jeez, I didn't mean to melt down like that. Shit—I wasn't even going to say anything about it, but—"

Where did the damn tears come from? This was supposed to be one of those "look how I dodged the bullet" moments, but instead I started to bawl again, like a kid whose teddy bear got swiped by the schoolyard bully. I took a deep breath, blotted my eyes with Judy's nice linen napkin, and left a mascara smudge behind. "Okay. I'm okay now. Honest. Shit—I don't know why I even care what happens to him."

"Because you're human," Margaret said and then explained to Jennifer, "Frank is Susan's ex-husband."

"Susan's gay, cheating ex-husband," I blubbered. Might as well make this a farce.

That got Judy laughing, and she let go of me. There: all better.

"But he's dying, and you're sad about it. Wow." Jennifer smoothed a stray blonde lock. "When Steven—my boyfriend—left me, it was for another woman, and I thought *that* was the end of the world. I hate him, though, and I wouldn't care what happened to him." She took a drink. "When he told me he was leaving, I yelled at him that I wished he was dead."

And that put a stop to our conversation. We munched and avoided each other's eyes for a minute, but Judy couldn't endure silence for long.

"So you have to tell Frank's grandfather he's dying?"

I shook my head. "It's about the family trust."

I told them about the Krajewski fortune and what Frank wanted done with his share. And, damn me anyway, I knew by then I'd have to call Grandpa K during my trip to Chicago and try to persuade him to change the trust.

"So Frank's an heir," Judy mused. "Who'd have thunk it?"

"Ya never know," I said.

"Wow," Jennifer remarked, "he has some nerve, expecting you to help his … his *boyfriend*"—and here she made a little face—"get his hands on the money."

She twirled the pretty gold bangles on her wrist.

"It's not like I'm giving up anything I might inherit," I said. "That train left the station already."

"You're fucking nuts to go one inch out of your way for him," Judy said. "He dumped you. For a *guy*."

"I think we've pretty much established that, but thank you for reminding me," I said.

I scraped my thumbnail over the mascara smudge on my napkin to avoid their eyes. "Anyway, I just feel it's the right thing to do." *Pretty lame, Susan.*

"Because you're a good person," Margaret said. "Who likes to help people out. Like you did tonight."

"Little Miss Helpful, that's me."

My eyes were still burning, and I sure didn't want to look in a mirror. I took a gulp of wine. "Let's talk about something else, can we? Jude, let's talk about you, and *your* love life."

Judy chuckled. "Oh go ahead, remind me I'm the Dateless Wonder. Sometimes I think I should eat my way back to 160 and give up."

"Don't you dare! You're just going through a dry spell," I said. "We've all been there."

"I don't remember your dry spell," Judy said, "but if you say so."

I helped Judy clear the table and put the plates in the dishwasher while Margaret and Jennifer discussed window treatments and hung the two Rousseau prints that constituted Judy's art collection.

"All I have to do is make the bed, and I'm home," Judy said, smiling sweetly as she took in her new surroundings.

"I'll help you," Jennifer said. Making herself right at home, wasn't she?

She and Judy went off giggling like teenagers at a slumber party.

Margaret smiled. "It's good to hear Jennifer laughing."

"You like her, don't you?"

"She reminds me a little of myself at that age. So vulnerable," Margaret said with a broad, Gallic shrug.

"You?"

"*Moi*. But I got over it. Jen will, too."

I didn't know how to respond to that, so we just sat nursing our wine. Finally Margaret said, "So he's leaving you a second time, isn't he?"

I hadn't thought of it that way. Or had I? "Hey, no head-shrinking tonight, okay? Besides, you don't work on your friends, remember?"

She nodded. "It's all right to have feelings for him. I just want you to understand that."

"I do. I'm sad, sure—and I guess I'm a little pissed off, too. The first time was bad enough, but now—and I don't much like doing this favor for him, but I can't exactly refuse a dying man, can I?"

"You could, but you won't. It's not in your nature." She cocked her head and studied me for a minute like she was trying to make up her mind about something. Then she leaned over and whispered, "You don't turn love off like a water faucet. You can't. You shouldn't."

She was right, of course, and her words sucked the air from my lungs.

"Yeah, well, I'm not good at letting people go. You know that already."

Friendly light spilled down on us from the chandelier in Judy's dining room, warming the wood trim around the doorway and bringing out the grain in the table where I rested my elbows. It felt quiet and safe in there, sitting with my best friend, the one who always found the good in me when I'd given up on myself. My wine glass had left a little ring on the table, and I wiped it away and then drained the last of the chardonnay, which had definitely given me a buzz. My earlier teary outburst still burned in the skin of my face, but just looking at Margaret, at her blue silk t-shirt that intensified the light in her eyes, I felt soothed. I felt like I'd be okay.

"And that's a great strength. People can count on you. It's a gift."

"More like a curse."

"Not always. You're a strong woman, Susan, and people sense that. That's why they come to you for help. Judy. Frank. But you're not indestructible. Remember to take care of yourself, too. Don't let this—"

"It won't," I said. "I'm not exactly made out of glass."

"I know that. But if this does get overwhelming, will you get help? Promise me you will."

"Sure. I'll go back to Dr. Francis. Wouldn't that be a hoot?"

Dr. Francis, the therapist I'd consulted after Frank left me, was a middle-aged man with a halo of fuzzy brown hair and a hoarse voice that made him sound like he was perpetually coming down with a chest cold. His basement office always smelled faintly of cigar smoke. Margaret had referred me to him, and I always thought him an odd choice—way too confrontational for my taste—although he did help me rebuild my shattered self-esteem and revise my expectations of the world.

One time he told me I had a strong, unsatisfied need for unconditional love.

"Who doesn't?" I snapped back.

He chuckled and then said, "You know it doesn't exist, though —right?"

And I nodded, but I didn't know, not really. Frank had come close to loving me unconditionally—he never put me down for being who and what I was. And what a big fat irony *that* was, because his love ended up having the biggest condition of all: he stopped loving me because I was a woman. Whenever I beat myself up for losing him I had to hang on to that fact—the one thing about myself that I couldn't change was what did us in.

Margaret's hand on my arm drew me back into Judy's dining room. "Just promise you'll ask for help if you need it."

I did my best eye-roll. "Yes, Dr. Deschanels."

"And try to work on your affirmations," she said.

Margaret thrived on affirmations—those little positive sayings you're supposed to repeat over and over until they come true. "I am beautiful and strong. My life is filled with prosperity. My life is filled with joy." That kind of stuff. To tell the truth, I did sort of believe in them. The few times I used them, I thought I felt a little better, even if my life continued to suck, which it often did.

"I will," I said, trying to remember where I'd left the list of "power thoughts" Margaret had once given me.

Laughter drifted in from Judy's bedroom; it sounded like she and Jennifer were having a pillow fight. Maybe Jennifer wasn't quite as prim and proper as I'd thought; I began to like her a little bit more.

"I care about you," Margaret said. "I want us to grow old together. I want you to dance at Deirdre's wedding and console me when my first grandchild is born. You see, I rely on you, too."

I didn't know what to say, so I picked up our wine glasses and put them in the dishwasher. Margaret followed me into the kitchen and put her strong arms around me. I didn't resist, just soaked up the comfort and let myself feel protected and valued, and unconditionally loved.

Chapter 4
My Kind of Girl

It's not too late to back out, whispered my Inner Coward. I paused six inches from Grandpa Krajewski's front door. *Yeah, it is.* After all, he was expecting me. I'd called him from my lonely cell at the Hyatt, and instead of letting me take him to dinner, he'd insisted that I come to his place for a home-cooked meal.

He flung the door open an instant after I rang.

"Susie Q," he said, enveloping me in a big, warm hug and planting a wet kiss on my cheek. He smelled of Old Spice and clean cotton.

For some weird reason, I wanted to cry. But I didn't, I just savored the sweet comfort of his hug until he let me go. We appraised each other with affection; he looked wonderful. Well into his eighties, Grandpa K stood tall and straight, and when he led me into the living room he walked with a younger man's gait. Sure, his hair had eroded to a white fringe, and his skin was weathered, but those blue Krajewski eyes twinkled at me with an energy I wished I could transfuse into my own weary spirit. He had on a simple brown plaid cotton shirt and khaki trousers, and he wore them with as much elegance as he would an Armani suit.

Grandpa K lived on the fiftieth floor of a ritzy high rise right on Lake Michigan. I'd been there before, when Frank and I were married.

Still, when he led me into the living room, I had to stop from gasping like some country bumpkin. It looked even more interior-designer elegant than I recalled, or maybe he'd redecorated since my last visit. My feet sank into plush light green carpet, a color echoed in the chenille sofa and big comfy-looking easy chairs. Smooth ivory walls set off three nice Edward Hopper prints—at least "Nighthawks" was a print; the other two could have been originals for all I knew. Across from the Hoppers, a bank of floor-to-ceiling, wall-to-wall windows presented a breathtaking view of the lake, its shoreline just beginning to twinkle with lights against the pink stain of sunset.

"This is gorgeous," I said, and wished for a better word to describe it.

"Take a load off, honey. I'll get you a drink—what's your pleasure? I'm sticking to wine these days, but I have hard stuff if you want."

The wine, a rich cabernet from the central California coast, glided down my throat.

Grandpa K flopped down next to me and squeezed my hand.

"You're looking good, Susie Q." His wink held no trace of lechery, and I felt absurdly pleased by the compliment.

"Thanks. You are too. I've missed you."

I didn't realize the truth of my words until I spoke them.

Outside the windows, the lake darkened and filled with bright pinpoints of glittering diamonds. I fought off an unexpected craving for a cigarette. Must have been the jet lag, and my nerves. I felt comfortable there, but I was, after all, on a mission.

"Hungry?" he asked.

Not just hungry, I was ravenous. "You bet. Can I help you cook?"

"Come keep me company while I grill the burgers. You *are* still a meat eater, aren't you?"

I laughed. "That I am."

"My kind of girl."

I parked myself on a high padded stool and watched him work. He sang a tuneless, nonsense stream of "Lo… lo… lo… la… de… dah" as he plopped the beef patties on the stovetop grill and took a gulp of wine. For a second—maybe it was the way the light struck his face—the resemblance between him and Frank was so strong that I shivered.

He grinned at me as he flipped the burgers, and the similarity evaporated. Frank's lopsided smile had always held a touch more cynicism than Grandpa K's. "Okay if we eat in here?"

"Terrific. I'll set the table."

His kitchen was bigger than my living room, with a sturdy oak table at the outside edge, alongside more plate glass panels overlooking the lake. He dimmed the chandelier above the table so I could take in the view.

"You want something else to drink?" he asked, wine bottle in hand.

I nodded. "That's good stuff."

He winked and refilled my glass.

He'd baked some French fries to go with the burgers, and it was one of the best meals I'd ever had. I told him so, and he chuckled and blew off my compliment, but I could tell it pleased him.

While we ate, I updated him on what I'd been doing in the four years since his grandson and I divorced, and he brought me up to speed on his life. He'd mostly given up driving a car, but he still jogged three mornings a week—just slower than he used to—and played tennis on the days he didn't jog. He confirmed what Frank had told me: he'd pretty much turned the family business over to Frank's mother Elise, widow of his son Joe Jr. However, he still oversaw a few things himself—mostly a charitable foundation that Winnie, his late wife, had induced him to set up. The foundation channeled some money to worthy causes like the Red Cross and the Humane Society, but it mostly focused on shelters for victims of domestic abuse.

When I replied that I knew, vaguely, about the foundation but hadn't realized the extent of its reach, he winked at me.

"There're a few things about me you don't know, Susie Q." He put down his fork. "Winnie always said we were lucky to have as much as we did, and that if we spread our good fortune around, it'd just come back to us one way or another."

"Smart lady."

His fingers slid across his chest, pointing to his heart. "You kinda remind me of her—backbone, brains, and beauty. That was Winnie."

My cheeks burned from the compliment, and I focused on my

plate as I scraped up a dab of ketchup with my last French fry. Then I leaned back and patted my stomach, exhausted and stuffed.

"You are just amazing," I told him. "You know you're my role model."

He cocked his head in a funny way that reminded me of a parrot. "Why d'you say that?"

His kitchen was quiet except for the refrigerator's low mechanical hum. Grandpa K's reflection smiled at me in the window glass, and from the lake a big boat's spotlight shone through his image, right in the middle of his plaid shirtsleeve. My own transparent likeness looked messy and content, dark sweater blending with the night so my head floated, detached. I pushed my unused spoon around on the smooth oak tabletop and pondered an answer that would allow me to segue into the trust and what Frank wanted him to do with it.

"You're so—so alive. In control." I meant it, too. "Me, I'm usually at the mercy of whatever comes down the road, and I just flop around. But you: you always seem to know what you're gonna do. I wish I was more like you."

Grandpa K drained his wineglass and put it down. "And is that why you haven't gotten married again, Susie Q? You following my bad example there?"

"Is it? Bad, I mean."

Grandpa K had never remarried after Winnie died—some ten years before I met him. A good-looking man, wealthy and educated and personable, he must've had plenty of chances to take on a trophy wife. But he never did.

His brown-spotted hands were a little rough; I could feel every callus as they closed over mine. "Depends on what you're looking for, honey. I never looked real hard for another woman like Winnie. But you're so young—don't give up the search."

I felt my face turn hot again. "I haven't. Actually, I've been seeing one guy in particular."

He made a sound halfway between a snort and a chuckle. A snockle. "I hope this one knows what he wants."

"Oh yeah," I said. "Noah knows what he wants, all right."

"You gonna marry him?"

I didn't mean to pull my hands away, but I did. Grandpa K leaned back and crossed his arms in an "aha!" pose.

"We have some differences to work out first."

"Everybody's got differences, Susie Q. Don't let that keep you from doing what you need to do."

"I know. We're working on it."

Neither one of us said anything for a bit, and I was getting nervous. How could I bring up the trust when he only wanted to talk about me and my so-called love life?

Then out of the blue he said, "So—you see Frankie lately?"

"As a matter of fact, I did. We had dinner last week."

"Then you know about the cancer."

"Yeah," I said.

Grandpa K shook his head. "Terrible thing. If only the dumb little shit had quit smoking."

He stood and picked up our dinner plates. I grabbed the ketchup and empty wine glasses and followed him to the sink.

"Yeah, he should've. But I know people who got cancer and they never smoked. Sometimes you just catch a bad break."

He opened the dishwasher and turned around. His blue eyes looked sad and wise. "You're still sticking up for him after all that happened."

"Hey, I still care about him. Just because we're not together anymore doesn't mean we can't be friends."

Grandpa K snorted. "Friends."

He started loading the dishwasher, and my thoughts drifted off to the first time I saw Frank, standing in my office doorway. He'd just taken over the territory for NitroLitho, Jacobs' main printer, and had come by to introduce himself. My immediate reaction was *What a handsome guy*. He leaned against the doorframe, and his crooked little smile went all the way up to his eyes. He had on a double-breasted navy blue suit that only a tall, slim man can look good in, with a blinding-white shirt. A beam of late-morning sun slanted in the window and lit up his face and that wonderful dark hair. He'd taken my breath away, and I'd had to clear my throat and hang on to the edge of the desk to keep from evaporating.

Grandpa K was staring at me. "Did I lose you, Susie Q?"

"Sorry," I said. "Jet lag. And good food."

He smiled and closed the dishwasher. "I'm glad you and Frankie can be friends. But I wish you'd move past him. Your Noah doesn't stand a snowball's chance in hell as long as you've still got Frank so big in your heart. There's no room for anybody else."

Unexpected anger rose up in me. "I have moved past him! Why is that so hard to believe?"

Grandpa K clasped my hand and patted it tenderly, which pissed me off even more. "Who're you trying to convince—me or you?"

I pulled away. "I know what I feel." I rubbed my hand and tried to calm down.

"You want some coffee, honey?" he asked. "Maybe some decaf?"

"That'd be great. Here—let me do it."

I rode the momentum of my aggravation.

"So," I said, over my shoulder as I poured water in the coffeemaker, "Frank's real worried about what'll happen to Clayton when he's gone."

Grandpa K set out a couple of coffee mugs. "Not our problem, Honey."

I took a breath and plowed in. "No, it's not. But I'm puzzled by something."

He crossed his arms and leaned against the counter, waiting.

"And maybe this is none of my business, anymore—but Frank said you've set up your trust so Zoë would inherit his share."

He didn't say anything, so I nudged him a little more. "And I remember that when Frank and I were married, you had it going to me."

"Damn right. But you two aren't married now, and I mean for it to stay in the family." Another snockle. "But I've provided for you, too, if that's what's bothering you. I'm not leaving you out in the cold."

I was horrified that he thought my motives were selfish. "Oh no, Grandpa, that's not what I'm getting at, honest. You've always been generous to me, and I appreciate it—and I totally understand about family. But I was talking about Frank and Clayton. It's your money and all, but I know Frank would be so relieved if you gave Clayton at least someth—"

His expression turned all business, hard and cold. "Did that little coward put you up to this?"

The transformation astonished me. And what could I say? He'd busted me.

"I thought so! Little bastard, sending you to do his dirty work. Not that I'd change anything if he showed up here himself, wearing high heels and a ball gown."

I bit my lip to keep from laughing at the image he conjured. The situation was deteriorating badly, and I had no clue how to turn it around.

"You give me one good reason of your own, Susie. You tell me, in your heart of hearts you think it's right for me to turn over a chunk of what I worked for, to someone who's not even in the family."

"To Frank, Clayton *is* family, just as much as I was, as much as ..." I couldn't remember Zoë's husband's name for a second. Harry? Herb? "... as Henry is."

Grandpa waved his hand dismissively and made a "faaah!" sound.

I filled the mugs and handed one to him.

"I know this is hard to talk about, but—"

"It's just wrong, Susie, what Frankie did."

"Look, if I don't hold any grudges, you sure don't need to."

He sat down and shook his head. "That's not what I meant— although I did want to throttle the little yutz for throwing away the best woman he'll ever have. No—it's wrong. Two men—faaah!"

His expression tightened, and his eyes held no trace of affection. Oh, great. I'd managed to alienate the one Krajewski in-law who still had any fondness for me. I had nothing else to lose, so I plunged into the argument. I didn't even know where the words came from. They just poured out.

"Grandpa K, listen to me for one minute. You tell me not to deny what's in my heart, but don't fool yourself about what's in *your* heart. Frank's your flesh and blood, and you're shutting him out of your life like he's some kind of felon, and that's wrong. Really, really wrong. He's still Frank. Sure, you don't like what he did. That's your right—

you don't have to approve of it. You don't understand it, and neither
do I. But we're talking about *Frank*—our Frank. And I know you still
love him, even if you can't admit it."

I didn't dare look closely at Grandpa K's face because I'd lose my
courage. So I kept on talking. "Sure, I may not be the logical one to
defend Frank and what he did, but I do know a couple of things
about love. And I know that Frank and Clayton love each other. And
I know that Clayton will be the one to take care of him, to watch
him die and hold his hand at the end—and if that's not love and
commitment, if that's not being family, then I don't know what the
hell is."

Would my words only provoke him? I couldn't tell from his expression as he let me rant on, trying to salvage something from the disaster
I'd created. And I didn't even know why I cared so much. At that point
I'd stopped worrying about the damn trust. Clayton made a good
living; he'd survive just fine. But I didn't want this decent old guy to
reject his only grandson because of some pin-headed prejudice. If the
trust was a lost cause, maybe at least I could reconcile Frank and
Grandpa K.

When I stopped for breath, he didn't say anything at first. *Maybe I
should get the hell out before I make it any worse.*

But evidently Grandpa K wasn't totally pissed at me, because his
face finally relaxed a little. "You're a good woman, Susie Q. But you
need to get your head on straight."

"It's on pretty straight, whether you believe it or not. And I'm
sorry you feel the way you do. I hope you'll at least think about what I
said."

"I will, honey. I will."

Yeah, sure you will.

He stretched and yawned, and I took the hint. I picked up my
purse and turned to face him, still mortified by the way things had
gone. I managed not to cry. In fact, I summoned my best smile for
him, pecked him on the cheek, and said a sincere thank-you for
dinner.

When I was out the door and on my way back to my bleak little
hotel room, I consoled myself with the knowledge that I'd given it my

best shot. I'd tried, and I'd failed, and if Frank's mother had been watching, she'd have smirked and said, "I told you so. She's useless."

Sometimes, I had to agree with her.

* * *

"How many of you feel passion for your work?" Myron Streitzler demanded from the lectern.

Give me a break. My head throbbed, and so did my right knee, which had collided with a hard metal support when I'd squeezed myself into place at one of the flimsy tables. The chair felt like its padding had been reinforced with cement.

No one responded, and Streitzler put his hands on his hips and peered around the room. He looked about forty, tall and fit, dressed in a well-cut gray business suit, pale pink shirt, dark gray necktie. Conservative stuff, except for his shiny blond hair, pulled back into a ponytail, and glasses tinted the same shade as his suit. Clearly, Myron Streitzler had a bohemian streak, or so he wanted us to think.

"By the time we leave here today," he went on, "every one of you will answer 'yes' to that question. I'm going to describe to you a paradigm shift so radical that it can change forever the way you do your work."

He was a Big Gesture guy, accentuating his words with hands that swooped and slashed, while his pony tail swung from side to side.

"What I'm going to ask of you now, people, is that you put aside your doubts, open your minds, and take in my message. It will change your lives. That's a promise."

Chandeliers dripped crystal prisms around the room and bounced off Streitzler's hair. He preened as if he felt the light's caress. A blast of air conditioning brushed the back of my neck; I shivered and took a swig of rancid hotel coffee.

I turned to the guy on my right. His name, I'd learned, was Larry, and he hailed from Houston, Texas, with those wonderful manners Texas women instill in their sons. He'd scooted over to make room for me, then offered water from the big drippy pitcher in front of him.

"This is going to be a long day," I whispered.

Larry nodded. His smile looked genuine and warm, his wavy red hair clean and freshly trimmed. He must have been as bored as I was, for his notepad was covered with doodles of armadillos playing saxophones. For some reason this cheered me immensely. He shifted in his seat, and I caught a whiff of crisp, woodsy fragrance in the space between us: Chrome, maybe. Frank used to wear Chrome, mostly because he liked the bottle.

"Think of how you've done your work until now," Streitzler told us. "Human Resources work. Important work. And if I asked any one of you why you're in the people profession, you'd tell me it's because you want to help others. Isn't that right?"

Heads bobbed up and down. Streitzler's voice droned on, and I jotted a few notes to put in my report to Bord. Larry kept doodling. I glanced at my watch, sorry but not surprised to see that only twenty minutes had passed.

Streitzler took off his glasses, revealing a pair of contact-lens-green eyes. "And how many of you have had to say those dreaded words, 'You're fired!' How many of you have seen another human being overcome with tears, or rage, or pure incomprehension?"

Several hands went up around the room.

"And how did that feel? Did you enjoy it? Of course you didn't. You were probably filled with compassion and frustration. Have I got that right?"

Oh, like this is some big revelation. I was tempted to start doodling myself, just to stay sane.

"When this day is over," promised Streitzler, "you'll go back to your workplace armed with the knowledge, and the skills, to address that frustration, to do your job in a whole new way, a way that brings you the results you always wanted and were never able to actualize. All you have to do is follow the simple steps I'm going to outline for you."

Oh really? Is that all there is to it?

"We're going to shatter some paradigms today. And it's up to you what you'll take away from the day's learnings. I am here to show you how to lead the way."

Oh, brother. I took a deep breath and drained the last of my coffee.

I'll give him this much: Streitzler sounded and acted like he believed every word he was feeding us. And maybe he did.

* * *

Eight hours later, however, I still had no clear-cut idea of how to Manage Change in Turbulent Times—the subject of his workshop. I hadn't learned a single new skill for softening the "You're Fired" message. And it wasn't for lack of trying.

We had to complete workshop evaluations before he set us free, and in my best corporate-speak, I wrote, "The presentation lacked specificity. I did not gain any real-world ideas for guiding employees through workplace upheaval and providing them with survival tools."

I picked up my notebook and was halfway out the door when Larry called out, "Hey—California. Some of us are going down to the bar for a little liquid refreshment. Want to come?"

The notion of sitting in a crowded hotel bar and being addressed as "California" for the next couple of hours was slightly more appealing than pacing my room until I succumbed to fatigue. And so, a few minutes later, I sat in a sticky vinyl booth between Larry and a guy named Cliff from Boston. The noise level in the bar, between the rowdy drinkers and the big screen TV that blared a baseball playoff between the Cubs and some team I'd never heard of, made conversation tricky. However, it didn't discourage my new best friend Larry.

My vodka tonic was frosty and strong; lucky for me, someone ordered a few appetizers to soak up the booze.

"So, California—how long are you in town?" Larry yelled over the racket.

I shouted back that I had to leave at the crack of dawn, and his face puckered in disappointment. We had vaguely described our work situations during the too-frequent breakout sessions at the seminar. Larry worked for Excal Energy, a superpower of the oil business which had gobbled up his previous employer. Larry told me he'd dodged the layoff bullet for over twenty years, and he didn't look a day over forty.

"Too bad," he hollered, leaning a little too close to my ear. "I'm gonna play tourist while I'm here. Thought maybe you'd like to do a little sightseeing with me."

I smiled my regret and wondered if Mrs. Larry—and from the ring on his left hand, I knew there was a Mrs. Larry—knew what her hubby was up to.

Two rounds later the Happy Hour crowd around us thinned out, and the Cubs won the ballgame, so things quieted down. There were six of us left in the booth: Larry, Cliff and me, plus two women and a man whose names I hadn't caught. I was tired and looking for a gracious way to leave.

Larry's beer bottle clanged down on the table. "Well," he said, "I'm gonna bail on y'all. All that learnin' has worn me out."

I seized the opportunity to follow his lead and fished a couple of twenties out of my wallet.

Larry's hand closed over mine. "Your money's no good here, California. This is on me. Or should I say, on Excal. Think about it the next time you pay five bucks a gallon at the pump."

"No, really, I can expense this, too, and—"

"Hush now. Let me be a gentleman. Please."

I thanked him, waved to the others and wished them good luck, and followed Larry out of the bar.

The elevators seemed incredibly slow. While we waited, Larry whistled and looked around the lobby, which still bristled with travelers.

"So—you get anything useful from the workshop?" he asked with a funny little smirk.

I shook my head. "Not really." I lowered my voice and added, "My boss is getting ready to outsource a big chunk of the department, and he seemed to think Dr. Streitzler would have some ideas for dulling the pain."

That got a loud laugh from Larry. "Oh, yeah, like there's any way to do that."

I nodded. "I know. I am *so* glad I don't have to deliver the message to anyone. I don't think I could handle it."

"Oh, you'll get dragged in," Larry assured me. "Everybody does. You think you're exempt, but you're not. And just wait—it'll get plenty ugly. You'll see sides of people—and things about yourself—that you never expected to see."

I shivered. Larry took a business card out of his pocket and pressed it into my hand. "If you need to talk to somebody about what's goin' on, I'm your guy. So call me—okey dokey?"

"Okey dokey," I said. "Thanks."

And on that folksy note, the elevator finally arrived.

I pressed the seventh floor button as four other people piled into the car; each of them wanted a floor below seven. Larry hummed and studied the ceiling, hands in his pockets.

"So," I said when the last of our fellow passengers had exited and we were on our way up again, "what d'you mean, I'll get dragged into it? How can I get around that?"

The elevator had mirrors on the side walls, and I could see myself and Larry, our reflections repeated endlessly, growing smaller and smaller. The overhead light, a dim, sickly yellow, reminded me of the women's rest room at Jacobs—every bit as unflattering. I still had Larry's business card in my hand; it had a big "EX" and a smaller, more flowery "cal" going diagonally across, and then his name and title: Manager, Human Resources Services. Good generic title.

My reflection in the mirror looked tired; my pants were wrinkled. Larry, somehow, still looked tidy and crisp. His pale blue shirt could have come fresh from the cleaner's, and he had his jacket hooked over his shoulder in a casual, jaunty way. He wasn't a bad looking guy, I decided, with a quick stab of envy for Mrs. Larry. And funny, too. I hoped she knew how lucky she was.

"Oh," he said with a laugh, "that's just me talkin'. I talk too much. You'll be fine. You've got the right stuff. I can tell things like that."

The elevator stopped at seven. I started to bid him goodbye, but he smiled and said, "This is where I get off too, California."

We stepped into the empty corridor. It took me a second to figure out the way to my room. I turned to Larry and held out my hand.

"Hey, it was nice meeting you. Thanks for helping me stay awake in the workshop."

He took my hand and kissed it. I had a sudden urge to cancel my flight back home, to stay in Chicago with him, tour the Field Museum and the Sears Tower, eat pizza, and watch the sun move across Lake Michigan, holding hands and—

Stop it! What the hell is wrong with you anyway?

Larry reached out and brushed a strand of hair back from my face. I knew, or I thought I knew, that if I made one slight move in his direction, our lips would meet. What would it feel like to kiss him? Would he be soft and gentle like Frank, or fierce and hard like Noah? Would it feel different to kiss a married man, someone who belonged to another woman? Would he like kissing me?

"You be careful now," he said, with a little wave as he turned and walked off down the corridor in the opposite direction from my room.

"You too," I called out softly. Then I turned and hurried away before I did something utterly foolish.

* * *

Once inside my room, I fastened the deadbolt and the safety lock and took a deep, shuddering breath. What had I been thinking?

My cell phone chimed, and I almost jumped out of my skin. Had I given the number to Larry? Had he realized the signals I'd been sending? The number on the display looked familiar, so I answered.

"Hope it's not too late to call," said Frank.

"No," I said. "I just got in."

"Are you okay? You sound out of breath."

It might have been bad form, but I was still rattled, so I told him about nearly making a pass at Larry in the hall.

I think I could have heard Frank laugh even without the phone.

"Oh, Susie, thanks—I needed that."

"So glad to be of service," I murmured, but I did feel a little better. It wasn't anything so horrible after all. I relaxed, and for a minute it was just two old friends sharing a funny story. Then it occurred to me: "You know I'm in Chicago?"

"Yep. I phoned your office today, and Angel told me."

Damn it, Angel, you shouldn't have done that. But I'm glad you did.

"I put two and two together and thought maybe you'd see Grandpa while you were there."

"Pretty sneaky—but it's okay. Yeah, I had dinner with him last night."

I heard the unmistakable flick of a lighter.

"Frank Krajewski, if you're smoking a cigarette right now I don't know—"

"All right, all right, I'm putting it out. So—what happened?"

I took a deep breath. "I'm really sorry, Frank. I tried. But I screwed it up. He's pissed at you and now he's pissed at me. I think I made it worse."

"No way could it be any worse. Is it the gay thing?"

"What else?"

I left out the part where Grandpa said he wanted to throttle Frank for "throwing away the best woman he'll ever have." Instead I lowered my voice a few octaves and proclaimed, "It's just wrong, Susie Q. Two men—faaah!"

I didn't want to hurt Frank, but I wanted him to know how strongly Grandpa K opposed his lifestyle.

"He said that?"

"He did. And he implied that I'm out of my mind for trying to help you. He probably thinks I'm condemned to hellfire along with you and Clayton. So … no go. Sorry."

"Hey, you gave it a shot. I appreciate that. Sorry the old guy got on your case. He'll probably stop the Christmas checks now."

"If he does I'll just cross your name off the gift list."

He laughed, softly. "Are you okay? That Larry guy can't get in, can he?"

"No way. The door's triple-locked, and from the looks of him he'll be sleeping off a booze overload until long after my plane takes off."

"Safe travels, Suse. And thanks again."

"For nothing."

"For a lot."

At times like that I really did wish I was still married to Frank. But I wasn't in love with him, I just wanted the calm safety of belonging to him. If I'd been married to Frank, I'd never have had an irrational urge to make a pass at someone like Larry. Would I?

* * *

For most of the flight home, I chewed on my thumbnail and tried to find something positive to include in my report to Derek about Streitzler's seminar. Finally, I gave up and decided to be utterly honest, repeating much of what I'd written on the evaluation form I'd turned in after the workshop. It seemed like the best approach. If I didn't tell Bord the truth, he might hire the loser and then later on blame me for the waste of money.

As soon as I got off the plane, I powered up my phone so I could tell Noah I was safely back on the ground. He almost never took calls when he was on the job, so I left a message and then phoned Angel. It was midafternoon by then, and I felt no great need to show my face at the office if I didn't have to.

"Wow," she said, "you missed a good one. Derek and Val Desmond had a big screaming fight."

"What about?"

I could almost hear Angel shrug. "It was something about people switching jobs. *You're* not going anywhere, are you?"

So Bord had started his little purge.

"Not as far as I know," I said, surprised Angel even cared. We got along well enough together, but I knew my reputation among the rest of the support staff. Overhearing Ginny Loring just confirmed what I long suspected: they'd voted me Queen Bitch of the Universe.

"Good. I—hell, I don't want to work for any of those other bozos. Especially Jeff Tate."

I played dumb. "What's up with Jeff?"

"He and Val were supposed to trade jobs or something, but Val didn't go for it. You know her—she doesn't take any shit. Especially from Derek."

"So what happened?" I asked.

Angel giggled. "She banged his door open so hard the doorknob dented the wall! And she called him an arrogant fool."

"Was that before or after he fired her?"

"Oh, he didn't fire her, exactly. He put her on admin leave."

Administrative leave. A harmless-sounding phrase for what

amounted to disciplinary suspension, usually as a prelude to being fired.

"How did you find all this out?"

Again the giggle. "You couldn't help but hear them yelling. And poor ol' Lilah, she didn't have a clue as to how to put someone on leave. She had to ask *somebody*, and … well, lucky me."

"Lucky you," I agreed.

I ended the call and thought about phoning Val at home to offer support. No, I needed to check out the scene of the crime first and find out what was going on. She was probably meeting with her lawyer anyway. I retrieved my car from short-term parking and headed home.

* * *

The sun had almost set by the time I unpacked, and I waited until I'd had a glass of wine before calling Noah again. Still no answer. He'd started a big remodel job that week, though. Noah was pretty compulsive and tended to work to the point of exhaustion, so maybe he was still at the site, doing whatever he could to speed the work along.

I left a cheery message telling him I missed him, and then I started getting ready for bed. I'd just brushed my teeth when the doorbell rang.

Noah stood on the porch, looking grimy and tired. "I noticed your lights were on," he said without explaining why he'd driven twenty miles out of his way to notice them.

He smelled of perspiration, lumber dust, and something oily, like turpentine or gasoline.

"Welcome home," he whispered as he pushed me against the wall, one big arm almost lifting me off the ground. "I missed you, too."

He'd missed me, all right. I could feel how much. I tried to kiss him back, but as his tongue probed my mouth I pushed him away. I couldn't breathe.

Noah let me go. "You okay?"

I shook my head. "Sorry. I … I'm really tired."

It sounded so dumb, but how could I have explained it any other way? I didn't understand it myself, but his unexpected visit felt like an invasion. At the same time, the rational part of my brain cried out that I shouldn't feel that way about someone I loved.

Noah's expression darkened. Soot had collected in the lines of his face, emphasizing the frown that started between his eyebrows and spread out.

"So excuse me for coming between you and your rest," he said in a tight, quiet voice.

He turned and started for the door.

Now, I told myself. *Stop him. Grab him!*

My hands stayed at my sides, though. I was frozen. Finally I freed my voice.

"Noah—wait. I'm sorry. I just … you surprised me. You know I don't handle surprises very well."

He stopped. At least he stopped.

"And I *am* really beat," I continued, on a roll now. "I had a rough day. I didn't get much sleep, and—"

He turned, slowly. I didn't want him to leave mad, but I did want him to leave.

"Can we do this over?" I asked, trying to sound playful. "Tomorrow night? I promise I'll be better company then."

The frown lines were still there, but not so deep. His big "who cares?" shrug was just for show, and I knew it.

"I guess," he said. He didn't try to kiss me again, just tromped down the steps and into the night.

I shut the door, turned the lock, and took a deep breath. Then I trudged off to bed. Alone.

What the hell do you want, anyway? I wondered just before I fell into the mercy of sleep.

Chapter 5
Luscious

Even without Angel's warning, I would have guessed something was wrong when I walked into Jacobs' HR Department the next morning. No one loitered in the break room to critique last night's television shows. No laughter. The secretaries were all at their desks, tapping on computer keyboards, frowning at monitors. Their bosses were either talking on phones in hushed voices or clicking away at their own computers. Several office doors were closed.

Angel, at least, looked happy to see me. "Welcome back."

"Thanks. Any more explosions since we talked?"

She shook her head and set in motion the curly gold halo around her face. The cheerful bounce of Angel's hair contrasted painfully with the atmosphere around us.

"But Derek's not here yet," she told me.

Typical Bord—he set his own hours, at his own convenience. If that meant he strolled in at nine but needed you there for two hours after quitting time, so be it.

"Probably getting fitted for a Kevlar vest."

Angel grinned. "I'll get you some coffee."

Unusual behavior for Angel: although competent and loyal, she'd never been into the personal-services side of secretarial work. I decided to enjoy it while it lasted. Besides, I needed to finalize my report to Bord.

I'd just emailed my evaluation of the so-called Change Management seminar to Bord when the man himself passed by my doorway, cell phone glued to his ear. He didn't wave or otherwise acknowledge my existence.

*　*　*

I'd pretty much cleared my inbox when Lilah summoned me to Bord's office. He was sipping coffee and shuffling papers when I entered.

"Close the door," he said, not looking up. "Have a seat."

I sat and waited. Finally he peered at me over half-moon reading glasses.

"So you didn't like Myron's seminar, eh? That's disappointing."

"I assumed you wanted my honest opinion."

Bord tapped his fingers on the desk top and scowled at me. "Yes, I did. I did indeed."

Bord's hair was beginning to thin a little, and this proof of his mortality reassured me. His squinty eyes were fixed on me, though, and I knew something was going on behind them, something that spelled trouble for me. Bord rolled his Mont Blanc pen—he was a Brand Name Man all down the line—between his hands. His nails were buffed to a glossy sheen, but his fingers were short and stubby, and he looked like a little kid playing with Daddy's toys. Sunlight spilled in the windows; I felt a slice of it on my back. Despite the air conditioning, sweat trickled down between my shoulder blades, but I stayed put.

"But I expected you to go there with an open mind," Bord continued.

"I did."

Bord released the pen and leaned back in his chair. I amused myself with a picture of the chair going back further and further, until Bord tumbled to the floor, a little overturned insect with flailing feet. But no such luck in real time.

"This," he said, waving a set of papers that I assumed was a printout of my report, "is not the work of an open mind." He jabbed his finger onto one of the pages. "'Despite the presenter's claim that his conclusions are earthshaking, in fact the simple principle of learning to listen to one's constituents is taught in every business communications class in America.'" Bord looked up and glared at me. "That sounds like character assassination to me."

Oh, come on. "Derek, I regret that you're disappointed in the outcome. If I'd known you had an agenda going in, I could ha—"

"I didn't have an agenda! But I have a job to do, and I am getting very tired of you fighting me every step of the way."

I cleared my throat and fought to stay calm. "How am I fighting you?"

"I expected you to bring back some useful ideas for managing the transition we'll be going through."

"I wanted to, believe me. But he didn't offer any. Look, there are a lot of people working for you who already know the stuff he was dishing out—Val Desmond, for instance. If you'd get her involved, she could help. Save yourself the consulting fees, Derek."

"I see. A transparent attempt to save your friend's job. That's exactly what I should have expected from you."

"It's not—"

Bord stood. "You can go."

I knew a lost cause when I saw it, so I got up and started toward the door.

"Oh," Bord said as my hand grasped the doorknob, "one last thing."

I turned around, braced for the worst. "Yes?"

"Lilah is taking some vacation right after Labor Day. I'd like Angel to fill in for her."

"Angel? Doesn't Ginny Loring usuall—"

I stopped myself. *I get it. Payback.*

"I'm sure she'll be delighted." I almost sounded convincing.

"Talk to Lilah, set up a training schedule."

And just what am I supposed to do for help while Angel arranges your golf games and manicures?

If the Dragon Lady had eavesdropped on our conversation, she showed no sign when I opened Bord's office door. I summoned a friendly voice from God knows where.

"Hey," I said, "Derek says you're taking vacation—good for you."

She stopped typing and looked at me, but she didn't smile. "Yes."

"Going someplace fun I hope."

"Michigan. Family reunion."

"Oh. Great."

"Not really."

"Okay, then—when do you want to start training Angel?"

Lilah squinted at her calendar. "Tomorrow afternoon. I'm working up a schedule right now. If she catches on fast, we can cover the important things in two or three days."

Oh, give me a break! To do your job? Angel could handle it on her coffee breaks if she wanted.

"Fine, I'll ask her."

Lilah's dark eyes shone with hostility. "This isn't optional."

"I know," I said, "but nobody likes to be ordered around, now do they?"

"You think I'm useless," Lilah continued, biting off each syllable and spitting it at me, "but there is more to this job than you realize. I'll thank you to let Angel know that it's going to be a challenge. And I'd appreciate it if you'd speak to her about dressing up a bit."

Holy shit! Who do you think you are anyway? Angel would look better in a gunny sack than you would in Oscar de la Renta.

"Maybe you could elaborate on that when she's here for training, Lilah. I'm not certain I'd give her the best advice."

Lilah didn't disagree. As I walked away, she hurled a parting shot at me. "I see you didn't like Dr. Streitzler's workshop."

Of course she'd seen my report; she got copies of all Bord's emails.

I took a deep breath and turned around. "I was a little disappointed in it, yes."

"That's a shame. And surprising, too. From the way Mr. Bord talks about him, I just knew there'd be a lot to learn."

"I understand that Mr. Bord is a big fan of his, but we all have differ—"

"He's not a 'fan,' Susan. He and Dr. Streitzler are old friends. I thought you knew that."

That verbal gut-punch left my mouth hanging open, but I managed to close it and not stagger from the blow. I couldn't feel my feet, but I could smell Lilah's heavy floral perfume. The fluorescents threw harsh shadows on her face, which would have looked hard and lined even in kinder light. Lilah's printer whirred, puncturing the stark silence between us. *Well, duh! I should've seen that one coming! Idiot!*

"No. I didn't."

Lilah swiveled in her chair, retrieved the page from the printer and shoved it in my general direction. "Here's the training schedule."

She threw one last smirk at me before she turned back to her computer monitor. I clutched the paper in my right hand and dug my fingernails into my left palm to keep from saying anything that might have gotten me fired.

* * *

As I could have predicted, Angel kicked up a fuss about subbing for Lilah.

"That old sow," she said. "Why does he even need a replacement for her?"

"He thinks he does, and that's what counts here. Look, I'm sorry, and I know you hate doing it and I hate sending you over there, but we don't have a choice."

Angel gave me a funny look.

"What?" I asked.

She shrugged. "Nothing. I just wondered ... it seems like everyone's running scared these days. Like we have to do whatever he wants. Or else."

"He is the boss."

She tugged on a blonde curl. "Yeah, yeah, I understand. But that doesn't mean I like it."

"Me neither. Anyway, it'll be a change of pace, and maybe it won't be as horrible as we think."

I didn't mention Lilah's suggestion about dressing up; let the

Dragon Lady deal with that, and if Angel dumped coffee on her after being insulted, it would serve Lilah right.

Angel got up and went to the doorway, looked both ways and closed the door, then sat back down with a serious expression on her pretty face. "Look, I want you to level with me: is Val being fired? Are you? I mean it, I won't work for Tate, he's an idiot and his breath stinks besides."

I couldn't hold back a laugh, but Angel looked so worried I quickly sobered up. So Bord hadn't announced the outsourcing to the rest of the department yet. Fine. But he hadn't repeated his "this is top-secret" warning to me either.

"This is confidential, okay?" I said.

The gold curls bobbed up and down. "No problem."

No, it probably wouldn't be. Angel did her best to stay on friendly terms with the rest of the support staff, but she clearly didn't consider herself one of them. The job was just a pit stop on her way to stardom.

"Okay then: Derek, genius that he is, has decided to outsource Benefits."

A silent nod.

"So Jeff Tate and his crew will be out of jobs eventually," I went on. "And I think he's trying to get rid of Val so he can rescue Jeff."

Another nod, and her dark blue eyes opened wider.

"So far I don't think he's found a way to get rid of me," I told her, "but I think he'd like to."

Angel bit her lip. "Yeah, when he tells you to jump, you don't ask 'how high?' on the way up—but Jeff does."

"You got it. So—does that help?"

"Sort of."

"Look, nothing's for sure anymore."

"I know, I know. And I could always bail and get another job, it's not like I'm doing brain surgery or anything here. No offense."

"None taken," I said, not quite truthfully.

"But I like working for you. You're fair, and honest. And if it even looks like he's gonna try and get rid of you, I'd—"

"You'll be one of the first to know," I promised.

Angel tilted her head. "Just don't let him scare you into being a Jeff clone, okay?" She snapped her fingers. "You could get another job like that."

I smiled at the innocence of her assumption. If only it were that easy.

* * *

Once Angel went back to her desk, I decided to call Val Desmond, so I got up and closed my door again. With all the hushed tension in the office that day, no one would wonder about it anyway.

I halfway hoped she wouldn't answer, so I could leave a prepared message of support, but she picked up on the first ring, like she'd been waiting for a call.

"Hey," I said when I heard her voice, "it's me. Susan."

A flicker of a pause followed.

"About damn time."

"About damn time," I agreed. "I didn't know what to say. Still don't."

I heard a long, slow exhale. "It's okay. Neither do I."

"He'll get his. Someday. I just hope one of us is around to see it."

"Sure."

"So how are you doing? Really?"

"Really? I am so pissed off I can't sleep. I'm scared. And I don't know what hit me, or why I went off on him like that."

"You went off on him because he's a slimy little creep who was trying to nudge you out of your job."

"Nudge, smudge," said Val. "He was trying to make me hand it over to that moron Tate."

"So what really went down? I hear you left a nice dent in his wall."

"I wanted to leave one in his head but I couldn't find anything big enough to throw at him."

"I know that feeling," I said, tingling with my own evil urges toward Bord.

"He gave me the usual bullshit line about cross training and job enrichment, like he thinks I didn't invent some of that crap in the first place, and when I wouldn't back off he started blabbering about how maybe I'd be happy in a 'more structured environment' and that he'd be glad to help me look somewhere else for a job."

"That little prick," I said, loud enough that anyone trying to eavesdrop could hear. I clamped my hand over my mouth to muffle any more outbursts.

"Yeah," Val said. "As if he could get rid of me that easily. Anyway, you know how I get, I pretty much told him I was on to his little scheme and I wouldn't put up with it, and he couldn't take away my job just like that, not without good cause, and that's when he got all puffed up and said he was sending me home to cool off."

I longed to come up with a way to make Bord reinstate her, some obscure clause in the labor law books, but even that probably wouldn't help. He'd find a way around it, and management would back him, just like they did with Lilah. I'd only succeed in putting my own job in jeopardy.

You're a lousy friend, Susan.

"They better be paying you at least."

I heard her sigh. "I never thought about that."

"They better," I said again, wondering if somehow I could ensure that Val got paid, wondering if that, too, was a dangerous move on my part. I thought about counseling her to use the time off to look for another job, but she didn't need that. Not yet. Maybe in a few days …

"So," I went on, "what'd you tell Mark and Ronnie?"

Val's husband, Mark, sold residential real estate fairly successfully, so I knew they were in no danger of starving, even if Val ended up being fired. On the other hand, his commission-dependent income would feel the strain, especially since their son Ronnie, in his junior year of high school, had his hopes on Cal Poly—not cheap.

"Mark's trying hard not to freak out. Ronnie … well, he's a *teenager.* He doesn't want to be bothered."

"Let me know if there's anything I can do, okay?"

"Thanks, sweetie. And thanks for calling. You're the only one who did. It's like people are afraid I'm contagious or something."

"They probably don't know what to say. But I never let that stop me from opening my mouth."

"You be careful, Susan. Things are a lot different there since Paul died."

"Yeah, don't I know. Don't worry, I'm keeping my back away from Bord."

I hung up, relieved at having done my duty and even more pissed off at Bord and the needless upheaval he'd created. Jeff Tate was a lousy candidate to run the personnel department; my neighbor's cat Zeus could've done it better, and with two paws tied behind his back.

* * *

The rest of the day passed Bord-free and productively enough to remind me of why I liked my job—at least when Bord let me alone long enough to actually do it. I helped the head of Computer Services review applications for a technical support job, and we narrowed the field to five candidates of diverse gender and race. I consulted with the General Auditor about a demand from an ex-employee's lawyer for all the personnel records of everyone who worked in the department over the last ten years.

When I told her we didn't have to comply with the full request, the G.A. said, "Thank God—do you have any idea how much it would cost to copy all those files?"

I wish that was my *biggest worry.*

I stopped at the market on the way home and was lugging my groceries in from the car when the phone rang.

"There you are!" my mother's voice sang out when I answered.

She probably didn't mean it as an accusation, but I felt my defenses rise up anyway.

"Hi, Mom. I just got home from work," I said as I began transferring yogurt and chicken breasts into the refrigerator. I hadn't talked to Mom for a couple of weeks, and I didn't expect the call to be short. "What's up?"

"Not much, but we haven't talked for a while. I just want to be sure my baby girl is okay."

Your baby girl?

* * *

My relationship with my mother, although a loving one, had a sharp edge to it. Dr. Francis, the therapist who had helped me work through my feelings after Frank left, insisted that I needed to root around in my childhood, even though I had no desire to relive my youth. He kept at me until I went into some of the big stuff: the way my father ran out on us when I was a kid and how hard my mother had worked to give me a nice home and new clothes for school.

Mom was not a June Cleaver-style homemaker—good thing, because we would have ended up starving in a cardboard box in the park. She always had my best interests at heart, although sometimes she was a little more businesslike about it than I would have liked. I told Dr. Francis how my mother put me on a diet at age ten because she didn't want me to be "one of those fat, unpopular girls." I lost most of the weight—my first adventure in dieting. Mom praised me for getting skinny and acted almost as happy about my weight loss as she did about the A's I brought home on my report card.

Dr. Francis had interrupted my tale. "Her love felt pretty conditional, didn't it?"

I'd heard the term before, but it wasn't until he said it that reality clicked into place. His eyes were huge brown pools of kindness, so even when he said mean things they didn't sound hurtful—at least not until I had time to absorb their meaning. His basement office felt like a warm, secure cave from which I'd emerge, mole-like, after enduring the lacerating flow of emotions that he pulled out of me every week. I suspected him to be a closet smoker, because he gnawed continually on a Number-Two Venus Velvet pencil which he used infrequently to scribble a note on the pad by his chair.

It had taken a few weeks for me to feel safe there, to trust him enough that I could show him my Evil Twin, the one who wanted to mangle and maul Frank and Clayton and then hurl my own body off a bridge. We tamed her, Dr. Francis and I, over a long, tear-filled year. I'd started to hope that life would not always hurt so much—until we did the little trip down Memory Lane, and he dared suggest my mother didn't love me blindly and completely.

"I never thought about it," I'd said in reply to his question, and had felt the tears on my cheeks before I realized I was crying. Then I started bawling so hard I couldn't talk. My stomach clenched into a searing knot.

Dr. Francis had handed me a Kleenex box and chewed on his pencil until I composed myself.

"That was a shitty thing to say," I'd told him when I could speak again. "She was just doing what she thought was good for me."

He'd held up his hands in surrender. "I never suggested she wasn't."

I did love my mother, a lot. She always gave me what I needed, even if it wasn't exactly what I wanted. And I felt that I could go to her and say something like, "Mom, I just murdered five people with a hatchet," and she'd tell me, "Well, dear, I'm sure you had a good reason for it."

Even so, when Frank left me, I'd dreaded telling her because part of me worried she'd think it was my fault. But Mom came through for me, big time.

"The asshole!" she'd hissed into the phone. "I never thought he was good enough for you." News to me, but it helped restore my savaged ego. "Somebody wonderful is out there waiting for you, Susan. Just you wait and see. Think of it—I would never have met Jack if your father had stuck around."

She'd met Jack in a Santa Fe jazz club the summer she relocated there. They never married, but she moved into his house within months, and they'd stayed together ever since, impossibly happy after ten-plus years. I would have liked Jack even if he didn't treat my mother like the Queen of England. A sturdy little guy with a thick brush of white hair, sparkly brown eyes, and a quiet but acute sense of humor, Jack owned an art gallery in Santa Fe and had a massive knowledge of music, painting, and movies. He'd gone to art school with Robert Rauschenberg and had known the late R.C. Gorman well enough to tell stories about cooking him dinner when he came to town.

*　*　*

A mental picture of Mom and Jack hovered in my mind as I shoved the refrigerator door shut with my hip. "Your baby girl is hanging in there," I said, "but I have some sad news I was gonna call you about anyway."

Her voice changed right away. "What's wrong?"

I felt a stab of guilt. "I'm fine, Mom," I said, "but Frank's not."

She knew that Frank and I had stayed friends, although I think it really puzzled her. She'd written my father out of our lives the day he abandoned us, and she never even spoke his name if she could help it.

"Oh?" she asked, and I could tell she had to work at the neutral sound of that one syllable.

"Yeah," I continued. "He's got cancer, Mom. He's dying."

"Oh, God, that poor man," she said. "I'll never forgive him for what he did to you, but I wouldn't wish that on anyone."

"I know," I said. "It really sucks."

I decided not to tell her about the stuff at work. We had kind of a silent agreement not to unload too much on each other at any one time. She'd had a breast cancer scare two summers earlier, and after that crisis had a happy ending, I learned the art gallery had been teetering on the brink of bankruptcy at the same time. Jack pulled off a brilliant save on that one with a sold-out show by some old friends from California, and they were back in relative financial safety by the time Mom told me the story.

"Give him my sympathy," Mom said.

We chatted a few more minutes about life in Santa Fe, her cactus garden, and the cooking class she was taking. When I hung up the phone, I realized I'd forgotten to stash the ice cream in the freezer, so I had to trash a perfectly good pint of Ben & Jerry's Peanut Butter Cup. *Just as well—she saved you from yourself.*

Five minutes later, the phone rang again. *Now what?* I thought as I said "Hello?"

"What are you wearing?" Noah asked.

It was a standard joke between us, and normally I laughed and said something like, "My red lace Vicky's Secret bra. Nothing else."

That night he just annoyed me. "A sweaty old pantsuit," I said and left it at that.

"Uh oh. Someone's had a bad day."

"A shitty day."

"Ready for company?"

Oh hell—I promised him, didn't I?

I softened my voice. "Only if you give me time to change clothes."

"Deal. Put on something easy for me to take off."

That was the thing about Noah: when he was playful and charming and available, there was no one better. By the time he rang the doorbell, my mood had lifted. I'd showered and changed into a skimpy sundress and sandals and felt more like having company. I even lit a scented candle in the bedroom.

"Hey, cutie," he said, nuzzling my neck. "I brought a little something to revive you."

It turned out to be a six-pack of Corona. Given my mood, a cold beer was better than roses and candy. I popped a couple of them open and handed one to Noah. We clinked bottles. The beer fizzed deliciously down my throat, and I put the frosty bottle against my face.

"Things are looking up," I said, and gave Noah a big kiss.

He touched the side of his bottle to my chest, and cool little trickles slid down between my breasts. Noah licked them off. He stroked my arm with his free hand.

"Tense," he whispered. "You need a good rubdown."

"No argument from me," I answered. He took my hand and led me into the bedroom, which smelled pleasantly of roses and warm candle wax.

Noah let me have one more swig of Corona before he pulled off my dress and guided me face-first onto the comforter. He gave heavenly back rubs. For someone who spent his days in manual labor, he had surprisingly well-tended hands. As they stroked and kneaded, I felt myself unclench.

"So what'd those pissants do to make my girl so tense?"

I turned my head to one side so I could give him a summary of what had gone on with Val.

"Nasty," Noah murmured. "See, that's why I don't work in an office."

"You're smart. Man, I wish I could get that little jerk, though. Find a way to turn things around on him and get him fired."

"Be careful what you wish for," Noah said. "He's a creep, but at least you know his game."

I rolled over and pinched his cheek gently. "My, my, we're feeling philosophical tonight."

He grinned. "Sometimes, babe, I actually have a thought or two—strange as that may seem."

He turned me back around and went on caressing my back with those strong, capable hands.

"So," he said softly, "any more news from your ex-husband?"

He might have been able to feel my body's response if I lied to him, so I took a chance and told him about my visit to Grandpa K in Chicago and how that had gone. Noah didn't alter the rhythm on my back, but he leaned over and kissed my neck.

"You're a good woman," he whispered into my hair. "That asshole didn't deserve you."

"Yeah, but I don't think he deserved to get cancer either."

"Coulda quit smoking."

Noah, as far as I knew, had never smoked, so he had no notion of the difficulty of quitting. I made my best attempt at a shrug from my horizontal position.

"Anyway," I said, "I don't think I'll be seeing much more of him. So we'll have to find something else to fight about."

He laughed softly. "Hey, I'm trying hard not to be an asshole about you and Frank. You feel you need to keep in touch, keep in touch."

"Wow," I said "did you have a talk with Dr. Phil or something?"

He gave my butt a soft swat. "You need to do right by him. It's who you are. And I'm trying to be cool about it. I just don't like to see you get hurt."

"I won't."

"And I hate what he did. I mean, I don't get being gay in the first place. But how could he give you up? You're so luscious."

I rolled over again. "Luscious?"

"Yeah," Noah said, his index finger tracing its way across my collar bone. "Luscious."

I stretched toward him, and took his hand. God, I wanted him. Who could not want a man who thought you were luscious?

* * *

Afterward we lay panting and sweaty.

"Hey," he said, "want to run away with me?"

I laughed. "Sure. How far d'you think we'd get?"

Noah looked so perfect with the damp yellow sheet twined around his waist. The color brought out the red in his chest hair, and I rubbed my hand lightly over him, savoring the soft tickle of his hair on my palm.

"About as far as Napa," he said.

I propped myself up on one elbow. "Why Napa?"

He grinned and pulled me closer. "Because I made reservations for Labor Day weekend," he whispered, his breath warm in my ear. "That is, if you can tear yourself away. Can you do that?"

I pretended to think about it. "Hmmm, I'll have to check my schedule."

"Oh yeah?" He threw the sheet aside, grabbed me and started tickling, first under my arms, then the soles of my feet. "You're not sure you can spare the time?"

My whole body tingled at the touch of his hands, and I squirmed and squealed like a three-year-old.

"Well, I'm pretty sure now," I said when I caught my breath.

He kissed the inside of my arm, then nibbled the skin just above the bend in my elbow, sending shivery shock waves all along my arm. "Hungry?"

I tugged his hair with my free hand. "No," I said, "but it looks like you are."

"I wouldn't turn down a sandwich."

I could've curled up next to him and nodded off, but I got up and slid into my robe. Food sounded like a good idea anyway. Otherwise I'd wake up starving in the night.

Chapter 6
Labor Day

The week before Labor Day, our weather turned wretched—hot, sticky, and thick with tension. Lilah consumed way too much time training Angel, who returned from each session rolling her eyes and giggling at the minutiae Lilah expected her to remember: Bord liked black coffee in the morning, tea with honey in the afternoon. His favorite lunchtime spot was Lunette on Sixth St., where he practically had his own table. Angel had to dust his furniture every other morning, and remind him, at least three days in advance, of any family birthdays or anniversaries.

When Angel reported all this to me, I could only sputter in disbelief. "Good grief! When is Lilah going to explain the *work*?"

Angel shrugged. "Maybe there isn't any. Maybe that's her secret."

While Lilah monopolized Angel, I had to open my own mail and let voicemail take my phone messages. Sure, I could've asked for help and probably ended up with Ginny Loring or her pal Alice DuValle, but since they both hated my guts I thought it wiser to just suck it up and take care of myself.

Jeff Tate moved into Val's office and pretended to know what he was doing, but he didn't fool me. Val hadn't called since our phone visit, but I didn't have the heart to get in touch. Truth be told, I was afraid to. I visualized her in her bright, silent kitchen, reading a book about career transitions and editing her résumé.

Frank didn't call either, and again I took the coward's route and let it lie. I told myself he'd call if he needed anything, and I didn't want to hear details about the cancer's progress. My imagination did a good enough job, but I knew it couldn't compete with reality.

I kept myself as invisible as possible at work and hoped for the best, counting the hours until Saturday morning and our Southwest Airlines flight to Oakland, where Noah had rented a car for the drive to Napa.

On Friday night I laid my suitcase on the bed and started pulling clothes from my closet while I tried to decide how little I could get away with packing. I tended to travel as light as possible, even when I had someone like Noah to hoist my carry-on into the overhead bin.

Noah called just after eight, and his voice sent a little flutter of pleasure along my nerve endings.

"I'm almost packed," I said. "Am I anxious to get out of here or what?"

The pause before he answered should have warned me, but I was too busy feeling good to notice.

"Look," he said finally, "there's no easy way to say this. I've got bad news."

All the color drained out of the bright paisley comforter, out of the red and blue blouses draped over my suitcase, out of the glossy Napa guidebook I'd picked up at the bookstore. The phone was a rock in my hand, heavy and useless except to do harm.

"What's up?" I asked. My tongue felt thick and stiff.

"June's in the hospital."

"Uh oh. How bad is it?"

Noah's ex-wife was diabetic. Juvenile onset, the really nasty kind.

"She'll live."

"Good," I said.

Noah continued, "Her blood sugar went out of whack—happens sometimes for no reason."

Was she maybe sneaking a Hershey bar?

"Bummer."

"Yeah. Anyway, she was puking and got all dehydrated, and—well, she's gotta stay in the hospital over the weekend."

"Okay. And you're telling me this because …?"

"Because now I have to stay in town and look after Jason."

I knew it was coming, but still I didn't believe what he was telling me. The tranquil white walls of my bedroom seemed to waver and advance, suffocating me in their creamy indifference. The bed looked very far away, my suitcase even farther. If I blinked, it might disappear.

"There's nobody else who'd look after him for a couple of days?"

Noah's sigh came through so loud it hurt my ear. "Hey, believe me, I don't want to do this, but I don't see any way we can—"

"Bring him with us then."

Another brief pause before he answered.

"That'd be hard. We can't exactly share a room, and they're probably all booked up by now."

I didn't trust myself to say anything. My fingers hurt from clutching the phone.

"Besides," Noah continued, "He has a soccer game tomorrow. It's the only thing he seems to enjoy these days, so—"

"I understand," I said.

"Do you?"

Do I have a choice?

"Yeah. He's your son. I'm disappointed, sure, but you need to do what you need to do." I took a breath. "The wineries will probably be packed this weekend anyway. We can go later, when it's not a holiday."

"I really wanted this trip. You know that, don't you?"

"Yeah. Hey—how's about I tag along to the soccer game? We can yell ourselves hoarse and then go to a—"

"That's real sweet, Susan, but we'll probably go check in on June after the game, and it would be—"

"Awkward. I get it. Okay, fine. No problem, I've got plenty to keep me entertained. Call me when you can."

I hung up before I choked on my nobility.

I started to put the phone back in its base, but my hand wouldn't obey my brain. Instead, like I was watching a movie, I saw the black handset fly across the room. Plaster dust flew as the phone bounced off the wall, left an ugly dent, and thudded to the floor.

I left the phone on the floor and headed to the kitchen. If I couldn't go to Napa, I'd bring Napa to me; I opened a bottle of Sterling Sauvignon Blanc and filled a stemmed glass so full a few drops of wine slopped onto the counter. I ran my thumb over the spill and licked it before I took a big swig, taste buds puckering as the crisp wine flooded my mouth.

So what was the big deal? I hadn't exactly given up other great plans for the weekend. This would give me time to catch up on some reading, maybe work in the yard a little. No big thing. Then why did I have to start crying?

Don't be such a baby, I told my pathetic reflection in the kitchen window. *Grow up. Just grow the hell up.*

I took my wine into the bedroom and unpacked my bag, and as I lifted it onto the closet shelf, I noticed the phone lying like a big beetle on the floor. I picked it up and smoothed away the edges of the shattered plaster just above it. My automatic thought was, *Noah can fix this.* Then I remembered. *Damn. Okay, tomorrow I'll go to the hardware store, get some plaster patch, and fix it myself.*

The phone chirped just after I put the handset back in its base. For a second I thought it was scolding me for my tantrum, but then it rang again. I grabbed the receiver, desperate for good news from someone. Anyone.

"Hi, there," said Frank when I answered.

I flopped onto the bed. "Hi."

"What's wrong?"

Damn—how does he do that? How can he always tell?

I sighed. "Just feeling sorry for myself. Noah and I were supposed to go up to Napa for the weekend, and he bailed on me."

"Bastard."

"It's not entirely his fault," I said. "He has to babysit his son because his ex is in the hospital."

"Bummer. How old is the kid?" Frank asked.

"Sixteen, but he acts more like six. He has issues."

Frank's laugh sounded muffled. "I bet. So—you wanna come drown your sorrows over here?"

If I hadn't already been lying down, the invitation would've floored me.

"I appreciate the offer—but I've already started drinking. Don't think I should drive."

"I could come get you."

"Nah. But thanks. I'll survive. It's probably good for me."

"I wish we could take off to Napa—we'd have a blast, and Clayton really knows his way around the wineries, he's obsessed with—"

A coughing spasm cut off the rest of his words. I had to hold the phone away from my ear, it was that loud.

Listen, you selfish bitch—he's dying and you're the one whining. Get a grip.

A minute or so later he quit coughing and cleared his throat. "Sorry."

I didn't know what to say, so of course I asked the world's dumbest question. "Are you okay?"

He cleared his throat again. "Pretty much. Damn cough is worse at night."

I heard him suck in his breath. "Anyhow, I actually did have a reason to call. Clayton has this half-baked idea that with my birthday coming up, we should have some kind of shindig because … well, you know, it's probably the last one."

I couldn't think of a suitable reply beyond "Oh, Frank," so that's what I said.

"Sorry, Suse—that didn't come out right."

Is there a prettier way to put it?

"Anyway, you're gonna get an invitation, and I hope you'll come."

"Uh, sure—I'll try. When is it?"

He told me the date, and I started thinking up excuses right away. This was one party I wanted to avoid. What a hideous idea: Frank's Last Birthday. If that wasn't a good enough reason to stay away, add the fact that I wouldn't know anyone, and I'd feel like yesterday's wife, on display for their morbid curiosity.

"You sure you're okay, Suse?"

"Yep. I'm fine. Just a little ticked off about the Napa trip. You know how well I handle disappointments."

I hadn't meant it to come out like an accusation, but it sounded that way.

"Yeah, well, you've had your share, kiddo."

"Not really, a lot less than—"

He started to cough again. I heard another voice in the background, and then the phone must've changed hands.

"Susan, hi, it's Clayton. Sorry, Frank can't talk anymore until I give him his meds."

"Sure," I said, "and tell him thanks for calling, will you?"

"I will."

I lay on the bed and stared at the ceiling and felt like the Asshole of the Year. Frank couldn't even hold a conversation and there I was whining over a canceled trip. Hell, at least I could still go places if I wanted to, even if I had to go on my own. At least I *could*.

I polished off the Sauvignon Blanc and went to bed.

* * *

The next morning brought overcast skies, and I woke to a sense of dread, knowing something was wrong but unable to recall precisely what. Then it came back to me. I staggered to the kitchen for coffee.

The empty hours loomed over me like a death sentence. *Get over yourself. It's just three days. You have plenty of stuff to do.*

That much was true. I'd brought home my usual briefcase full of weekend work, even though I hadn't planned on touching it. Now I could. The Jacobs plant in Washington State had sent me a draft of its first-ever Affirmative Action Plan for review, and I'd put it off for three weeks already. No better time to go over it.

First off, I watered my elderly neighbor's lawn. Even with the overcast skies, Mrs. Murphy's grass was crisping up, and I felt a tug of guilt for neglecting my one neighborly duty. She'd never complain, of course, but I'd promised to do it, and I hadn't. It wasn't even that big a deal; all I had to do was turn on the sprinkler valve, wait a little while, and then shut it off. While the sprinklers shot shiny jets of water into the murky air, I tackled Washington's AAP, which actually turned out pretty good. Maybe all the coaching I'd been doing was paying off. Then I shut off Mrs. Murphy's sprinklers, full of self-satisfaction at doing somebody else a good turn.

Just that little bit of work soothed me and helped counteract the spooked, lonely feeling nipping at my heels. Everyone else in the world was off doing something fun while I tackled a stack of periodicals with exciting names like *HR Today* and *Personnel Journal*, but at least they burned up the empty hours. Half the day gone, and I could hear the kitchen clock ticking, that's how quiet it was inside my house, as the second hand marked off fractions of my lonely, useless life. The air crackled with emptiness.

Go to a movie, then. You can go by yourself! Nah, I'd look like a pathetic loser. Which I am. Stop it! Quit whining and make yourself useful. At least give your fat ass some exercise.

So I did—I hauled my fat ass to the gym, but even sweating through a workout didn't quite make me feel right. On the way home I stopped at Home Depot and bought some plaster patch. Nothing like a little home improvement to make a girl feel competent.

* * *

I spread the plaster patch around and smoothed out the edges; it was kind of like frosting a cake—not that I'd ever been fabulous at that, either. The new surface looked a little bumpy, but I figured that when it dried, I'd be able to sand it and cover the evidence with paint. Meanwhile, more empty time taunted me. *Damn you, Noah.*

So I took a long, hot shower, filed my fingernails, and poured a glass of wine. Why not? The clock read 4:20—way past cocktail time on the East Coast, and practically tomorrow

morning in England. No more work, I decided. Maybe I'd find something good on cable.

The program guide listed nothing but reruns and movies I'd already seen. And I'd done enough reading for one day. Tick, tick, tick went the clock. I suppressed a murderous urge to smash it, or at least bury it in the trash can out back. Over and over I told myself how stupid I was being: it was only a weekend, plus one day, not a lifetime of solitary confinement. Not like I'd never spent time alone before. Not like I wasn't capable of amusing myself.

But the empty time dredged up so many memories. I hadn't been all that popular in high school—mainly because I was at least two inches taller than most of the boys, at least until senior year. And by then the damage was done. I'd spent more than my share of Saturday nights alone. My mom had moonlighted as an "event planner"—which meant overseeing banquets and parties almost every weekend—leaving me to amuse myself with the television and a few good books. Not horrible—unless you're sixteen, and the rest of the world has paired off.

Okay, time to get out the address book. Time to stir something up for Sunday. Another day like this will push me over the edge. I was mad at myself for being so uptight, mad at Noah for bailing on me, mad at life for putting me in this situation to begin with, and mad at Frank for being gay, leaving me, and now dying, for Chrissakes.

Judy's voicemail greeting sounded way too cheerful. I didn't leave a message because I didn't trust myself not to lay a guilt trip on her for being unavailable.

Who else could I call? Who else, who else? I didn't have that many friends anymore. My narrow little life started to close in on me, each tick of the clock getting louder and meaner.

That's when I called Margaret. Normally, I didn't intrude on her weekends, which I assumed were family time, but I was desperate. I almost couldn't talk from holding my breath when a girl's voice answered the phone. It turned out to be Deirdre. Even though she still lived at home, Deirdre was far more self-reliant than Noah's son, the helpless little punk.

And more polite.

"Hi, Susan," she said warmly when I identified myself. As if we'd just chatted the other day. "I bet you want Mama, right?"

I heard her muffled voice say, "Mama—it's for you. Susan Krajewski."

No fumbling over my last name, the way many did. Why had I never taken my maiden name back? Search me.

When Margaret came on the line, she sounded a little out of breath. And wary.

"Noah bailed on our weekend plans," I told her. "And I just took a chance that you might be looking for something to do over the holiday. No big deal if you're busy."

In the tiny pause that followed, I mentally kicked myself for calling.

"And you probably *are* busy," I added quickly. "I realize married folks use the weekends to—"

"Philippe is in Angola," she said. That figured. Her husband was the Project Manager for an engineering company, and many of his clients were in countries that didn't observe American holidays.

"The girls and I are going shopping tomorrow," she continued slowly, as if thinking while she spoke. "An end-of-summer ritual. Why don't you join us?"

"No, that's okay, I don't want to butt in."

"Please do. Claire is convinced I've lost most of my brain cells. Perhaps you can help persuade her I'm miscast in the Neanderthal role."

"If you're sure."

"Positive."

I hung up with misgivings, and by the next morning I was sure I'd made a mistake. I almost called to back out, but then I thought about Noah and what he might be doing, probably taking that spoiled brat to breakfast. No way was I going to mope around. Besides, if Margaret really hadn't wanted me to tag along, she wouldn't have invited me and "retail therapy" never failed to lift my spirits.

* * *

I met them in front of Nordstrom in the Westside Pavilion just after eleven a.m. Margaret was her usual cool and elegant self, and Deirdre, a burst of color in hot pink Capri pants and a flowered shirt, reminded me a little of Judy—not that Deirdre was heavy. She just had the same vivid complexion and dark curly hair.

Claire didn't resemble her mom or her sister. Short, slim, and pale, she looked on the verge of shattering at the slightest touch. She didn't wear any makeup that I could see, and no jewelry except for tiny gold hoops in her earlobes. Although she didn't smile when I approached, I felt an odd, protective urge toward Margaret's younger daughter.

Deirdre welcomed me with a hug. "It's nice to see you again. I'm so glad you could join us."

Claire's greeting was a simple "hello."

Not everyone had gone to the beach that weekend, judging by the crowds in the stores. We split up inside Nordstrom. Margaret and I browsed the store's Narrative department, with its mishmash selection of clothes, although she had a far wider choice than I. We were about the same height, but I had a good twenty pounds on her. Despite what my mother would tell you, I've never been truly fat, but I did inherit my father's hefty, widely spaced bones.

Deirdre bounced up to her mother with a calf-length, chiffon-y dress in a fetching blend of navy and brown swirls, a question in her eyes. Margaret held the outfit up next to Deirdre, narrowed her eyes, and nodded almost imperceptibly. Deirdre beamed.

While Margaret tried on a striking red and black dress, she asked me to find Claire so we could get her opinion. I found her in the shoe department on the first floor, wobbling around in a pair of red patent leather stilettos. She looked like a guilty little kid when she saw me and quickly sat down.

"Your mom wants your vote on a dress," I said as cheerfully as I could.

Claire shrugged and put the red shoes aside. "Okay."

On the escalator, I gave friendliness another try. "Margaret must have a lot of faith in your judgment."

She didn't take the bait, but then I remembered a vital clue: Claire was taking private art lessons after school. Margaret felt her daughter had true talent and had brought a small watercolor to one of our Friday dinners. It really was good, in my uneducated opinion.

"She's so proud of your painting," I went on. "I loved the little watercolor of the woman and the dog on the park bench."

Claire rolled her eyes, but I caught the tiniest twitch of a smile. "She doesn't act like it."

"Sometimes parents have a hard time praising their kids," I, Little Ms. Philosopher, replied. "My mom said she didn't want me to get stuck up."

"No worries there," Claire said, and by then we reached Margaret, who was modeling the dress for us.

"The color's not right," Claire told her, "and the skirt is too flow-y."

I didn't exactly know what she meant about the skirt, but I had to agree that the color overwhelmed Margaret's pale skin, and I think she felt it too. Still, she pressed her lips together in—what? Disappointment? Annoyance?

"Thanks for your honesty," she said, and her voice was kinder than her expression.

Claire shrugged again—she had the gesture down pretty good— and drifted off toward the lingerie.

Margaret eventually settled on a pink-and-gray print skirt. Meanwhile, I found a silk blouse in my favorite shade of blue, somewhere between the color of a summer sky and my favorite piece of turquoise from Santa Fe. Since it was on sale, I whipped out my credit card.

While Margaret paid for herself and Deirdre, I risked another approach to Claire. She was drifting through a display of nightgowns and peignoirs, fingering the silky fabrics and looking bored out of her mind. But, to my amazement, she smiled just a little bit when she saw me.

"See something you like?" I asked.

She shook her head. "I don't need anything."

I held up my shopping bag. "Me neither. But I always find something I want. Sometimes it's fun to get something, even something little, just *because*—don't you think?"

Claire nodded. "I guess so."

I trailed along after her. "I bet you miss your dad—it being a holiday and all."

She turned and looked at me. "Yeah. But he's gone a lot. I should be used to it." Her expression brightened. "He's supposed to come home Thursday, though. For my birthday."

"Then you *have* to get something—a present to yourself."

I pointed to a rack of bright cotton tops midway to the register where Margaret and Deirdre were watching us. "You'd look very cool in one of those."

She wrinkled her nose, then reconsidered and followed me to the display. I held up a pale pink t-shirt with scallops around the neck.

She ran her hand over the soft fabric, tested it next to her face in a mirror, checked out the size, and shrugged. "It's good," she said.

I felt immensely pleased with myself, although no one else seemed impressed with my accomplishment.

"Well, ladies," I told them, "thanks for letting me tag along. You really brightened my—"

"Oh, Susan, please come with us—we're going to lunch next," Margaret said.

I hesitated.

Claire put her frail hand on my arm. "Please."

That did it. After all, a girl's gotta eat, right?

* * *

The maitre d' at Les Nuages—"The Clouds," Deirdre translated for me with a wink—bowed and kissed Margaret's hand. "Madame Deschanels. So good to see you."

"*Merci, Georges.*"

Georges greeted both girls with a tiny bow and a smile, and when Margaret introduced me, he bestowed one of those gallant kisses on my hand, too.

The menu was definitely French-influenced but not exotic. I settled on some chicken crepes which Margaret pronounced a good choice. She and I ordered wine and Deirdre looked longingly at the golden liquid in our glasses.

"At home," Margaret whispered, "we sometimes allow her a small glass of wine with dinner."

We grinned at each other like conspirators. I thought that was pretty smart—defuse the lure of the forbidden. If only my mother had done that with chocolate, I thought, instead of hiding it like contraband in a high cupboard where I couldn't get to it.

"So Philippe comes home Thursday?" I asked.

An indifferent shrug from Margaret. "So he says. But you know how it is …"

Claire tore off a morsel of bread and flattened it between her thumb and index finger. "He'll be here."

Her faith almost choked me; I felt a twinge of recognition. Claire's belief in her father echoed my hope that Noah would, one of these days, really let me into his life. One of these days, Jason would grow up, and I'd come first. A selfish thought? Sure. But I probably wasn't the first woman to feel that way.

I concentrated on buttering my warm, crusty French bread while the girls talked about some relatives in France who were coming for a visit. Margaret jumped in with a story about one of them, her cousin Marie, and how the two of them had scandalized their parents by hitchhiking to Italy one summer when they were in high school. I assumed the tale was for Claire's benefit, to prove that Margaret had her own rebel streak, but I began to feel invisible in the midst of all that family chatter. I thought of Noah. Was he missing me? Or was he having such fun playing Dad that he didn't even stop to think of where I was and what I was doing? Was being a parent that all-consuming?

When Frank and I were married, we talked of starting a family, but somehow we never got past the talking part. Birth control pills became a staple in my medicine cabinet, and I took them as routinely as I brushed my teeth. I didn't think I was good parent material: too selfish and impatient and unprepared to be accountable for a child's welfare. When Frank and I split up, I was actually relieved that he wanted to keep Max. Too much responsibility for me.

Deirdre was an eater after my own heart. She attacked the baguette encasing her sandwich and sprinkled crumbs everywhere. Margaret shot her a reproving look but didn't say anything; she gracefully nibbled her *Cassoulet Grand-mère,* chicken soaked in a thick brown sauce that smelled of celery and onions and other things a grandmother would toss into a stew. Claire had ordered a spinach-and-scallops salad, and pecked at the scallops, taking tiny bites and chewing them without energy. Every now and then I'd catch her studying me while we ate.

We ended the meal with strong French coffee all around. I felt very continental by then. And very full.

As we went our separate ways in the parking lot, I hugged Margaret. "Thanks for rescuing my weekend."

She looked surprised. "It was our pleasure." She turned to her daughters. "Wasn't it, ladies?"

* * *

I took my time driving home to postpone the return to a silent, empty house. At least this little outing had broken up the day and taken me out of myself.

In my driveway, I checked for Zeus the cat; he was, as usual, snoozing by the garage. With plenty of warning, he roused himself, stretched and yawned, showing me his claws and fangs, then sauntered out of the way. I was carrying my shopping bag into the house when Noah's Mercedes pulled into the driveway. I froze.

He got out slowly and walked toward me. I pondered my next move. Run inside and lock the door? Pick up a rock and throw it at him? Or follow my gut instinct to hurl myself into his arms?

He didn't make me choose. His arms were around me before I saw it coming, and I dropped the bag and hugged him back.

He stroked my hair. "I missed you."

His mouth closed over mine, and I could hardly breathe because I'd started to cry.

Finally I pulled away and wiped my face. I missed a few tears, and he stroked them off my cheek with his thumb, looking sad and happy at the same time.

"How's June?" I asked

"Better. She comes home tomorrow."

"And Jason?"

"At the movies with one of his buddies. I gave him money for dinner, and his friend drove, so he'll get home okay Which means I can stay a while. If you want."

I picked up the shopping bag and let him follow me into the house.

"Coffee?"

"I'll make it," he said, and the easy way he moved about my kitchen made me smile. He brewed coffee while I modeled my new blouse.

The coffee tasted great, the way Noah's coffee always did. Something about having someone else make it, I guess. I found some relatively fresh Milanos in the cupboard; I wasn't hungry, but I didn't trust myself to talk much. Noah didn't have a lot to say either as we sat at the kitchen table sipping coffee and scattering cookie crumbs. Finally Noah set down his cup and put his hand on mine.

"You're real important to me, Susan. Do you know that?"

"Oh, I think I do. Third in line, right?"

Don't be such a bitch. He's trying.

Noah shook his head. "It's not that simple."

"Really?"

"I can't put my family out of my life just because you want me to. But you matter to me in a different way. I wish I could make you understand."

"Your family. See? That's the problem. You still think of June as your family. You've never let go."

Noah looked baffled. "Jason and June *are* my family. I can't change that. But it doesn't mean I don't love you."

Noah had never used the words "love" and "you" in the same sentence with me before, and the combination left me speechless.

"Yeah," he went on, and he kissed my hand. Two hand-kisses in one day, from two different men. I was on a roll. "I love you. You know that, right?"

"I… uh… I guess so."

So eloquent, Susan. So smooth.

He stood up and leaned over me, nuzzled my neck. I let him. Let him slide his hands over my breasts, then pull me out of the chair and lead me to the bedroom. I was such easy prey for him, but what could I do? Kick him out, and spend the night alone? Cut off my nose to spite my face, as my mother would say?

* * *

Afterward we lay together, drowsy and warm, and I'd almost drifted off when I felt him stir. Again? No, he got out of bed, and in the darkness I could hear the jingle of coins, the click of his belt buckle.

"You're getting dressed," I muttered. "I thought you said you could stay."

He murmured something in response, something that ended with the word "Jason."

I sat up. "You're going home? Now? Can't he spend one night without adult supervision?"

"It's more complicated than that."

"Really? Damn it, Noah, I want you to stay."

He sighed and sat down, his weight sinking into the bed next to me. He ran his hand over my head like he was patting a dog.

"I told him I'd be home, and I need to keep my word."

"So go check in with him and come back. I want to wake up next to you in the morning. Please."

"Don't do this. I can't."

"Won't."

"Whatever."

I rolled over, away from him. "Then go. Just remember you made your choice."

He reached across the bed and pulled me close to him, but I refused to unclench my body. He kissed the top of my head.

"Can we at least have dinner tomorrow?" I asked.

He didn't answer right away. *Ah—he'll want to be sure June is up to watching Jason. Maybe he'll make dinner for her. Mr. Responsible.*

"Maybe," he said finally. "We'll see."

"I'd really like it." Did my voice sound as whiny as I thought? *Who's acting like the spoiled little kid now?*

"I'll call you tomorrow."

I realized with an overwhelming sadness that another impromptu visit was probably the best I could expect from him. I thought of Claire Deschanels and her fragile trust that her dad would come home in time for her birthday. I sure hoped he would.

* * *

Philippe wasn't going to make it, though, I learned later that week when Margaret called to confirm our Friday night dinner with Judy. A collapsed drilling rig, people were hurt, maybe he'd get back by Monday.

"Claire must be disappointed," I said.

"Hysterical is a better word. Oh, she understands on an intellectual level, but—"

"But it's her birthday. Shouldn't you maybe be taking her out on Friday instead of seeing Judy and me?"

Bite my tongue. And never give advice to a therapist, fool!

But Margaret didn't seem to mind. "Deirdre and I are taking her out tomorrow, but she is determined to be inconsolable. So there's no use foregoing our get-together. It wouldn't make anything better, especially my mood."

From time to time I'd see this coldness in Margaret, and I didn't much like it. But I figured it came with the territory. We set a time for dinner, and I called Judy to remind her.

* * *

When I got to Don Francisco's, our favorite Mexican joint, Margaret was already there, and so was Jennifer. I suppressed my annoyance and greeted her with a big hello. Judy showed up five minutes later, out of breath, hair flying wildly around her face and still damp from the shower. Typical Judy. She didn't seem to fake her pleasure at seeing Jennifer again.

I was hoping to get some well-deserved (I thought) sympathy for the way Noah had treated me, even with Little Ms. Decorator around, but I waited until we'd ordered a round of margaritas, toasted each other, and dug into the chips and salsa.

"It was so sweet of you to let me tag along last weekend," I said to Margaret. "You saved my life—my holiday anyway."

Don't ask me why, but I felt compelled to tell Judy and Jennifer— especially Jennifer—what a great time I'd had shopping with Margaret and "the girls" on Sunday.

Judy said, "Wait a second. I thought you and Noah were going to Napa."

"He canceled. Ex got sick and he had to babysit."

"Wow, you sure know how to pick 'em," Judy said.

This was going in the wrong direction. Did I deserve that remark? Maybe, but still it pissed me off. Who was Judy, the self-described Dateless Wonder, to judge me?

"Oh, and you're the big expert. How is *your* love life these days?"

Judy had been bringing a salsa-laden chip to her mouth, and she stopped. A gob of the salsa splashed on the table in front of her, and she focused on wiping it up. The chip went onto her bread plate uneaten.

"It's none of my business," Jennifer said, "but how old is his son? I thought he was older, somehow—old enough not to get in the way—unless his dad wants him to."

"Excuse me," I said, "but you're right—it really isn't your business."

Margaret's margarita glass clunked on the table top. "I feel like I'm having dinner with my daughters, and I need a break from that. Can we please calm down and have a peaceful meal together?"

Jennifer's face had turned even paler than usual, and I felt guilty for snapping at her and for needling Judy.

"I'm sorry," I said, looking around the table.

"Me, too," Judy said.

Jennifer nodded. "Sometimes I get so caught up in my own stuff I forget about other people's feelings."

Margaret smiled at us and turned to Jennifer. "So who was that handsome young man who picked you up from work yesterday? Oh, yes, I saw him. I think you rather wanted everyone in the building to see him."

Jennifer brushed a lock of perfect blonde hair off her cheek and smiled. I decided I really did hate her, and swore to work on changing that. After all, even I remembered the heady joy of dating a New Man, when everything is fresh and new and wonderful. Colors seem brighter, music sweeter, life's tempo just a little more upbeat.

"His name is Eric," Jennifer said. "He's a trainer at my gym."

"How perfect," I said, determined to make up for my earlier bad behavior. "You can get free coaching."

I waited for Judy to jump in with her usual round of questions: so, have you done the deed? Is he as good in bed as he is in the gym? And so on. Judy could be incredibly nosy and specific when it came to sex—not that the rest of us didn't wonder the exact same things. But Judy was holding back.

I turned to her, trying really hard to be gracious. "So, are you all unpacked? Stereo still working? Still loving your new place?"

Judy rewarded me with a grin. "It's great. I'm so glad I did it."

Then she launched a monolog about how she dreaded the following week, when school would start. I knew the story by heart: the kids would be wild, the parents would be pains in the ass, insisting on special treatment and shirking responsibility, why had she chosen this career, and so on.

I could sense Margaret's laser eyes boring into me. Her mild reprimand had chilled me, mostly for its truth; I'd been acting like a bratty teenager.

Finally Judy came up for air, and I made myself face Margaret. "How's Claire? Were you and Deirdre able to salvage her birthday?"

Margaret flinched. "Claire is going through a dark phase. I've told her she can stop practicing her tragic heroine act; she has it perfected." Something sparked in the icy reaches of her eyes.

"Compared to Noah's little monster, she's an angel," I said, and I meant it as reassurance. "I just don't get his need for twenty-four-seven supervision. Noah claimed he couldn't stay with me Sunday night because—"

Judy picked up on that right away. "I thought he bailed on you for the weekend."

"He paid a surprise visit. I guess his conscience got the better of him."

Pretty lame, Susan.

The other three women just stared at me. Did I imagine the same dismissive look on each of their faces?

"Anyway, he didn't stay long after we—" I faltered. The words I was going to say suddenly seemed so trashy. *Maybe I should wiggle my eyebrows and leer instead.* "Well—you know. He had to rush home to keep Jason company."

Judy put her drink down. "So let me get this straight. You let him come in, let him have sex with you, and then after he's had his fun he leaves you and goes home to his family?"

"His son. June was in the hospital."

Judy's face radiated contempt. "He said."

Jennifer leaned forward. "It's your life, Susan, but doesn't it bother you that he just pops in and out like that?"

I drained my margarita and signaled the waiter for a refill. The conversation started to take its toll on me. Why were they so challenging?

"It bothers me, but what am I going to do? I can't exactly lock him up in my house and not let him leave. It doesn't do any good to force someone to act against their will, now does it?"

Margaret leaned forward. "You've let him treat you as a part-time lover so long, he's come to take it for granted."

I felt my face grow warm. "Thank you for the impromptu diagnosis, Dr. Deschanels. But I don't need it right now."

"I think maybe you need it more than you know." Anger flickered across her face, but I didn't care.

"I think maybe you're wrong. And maybe you're taking something out on me that belongs somewhere else."

In the silence that rose up between us, the murmur of other diners grew loud and annoying. Why did Don Francisco's have so damn many hard surfaces to bounce the noise back?

Margaret's face softened. "I'm sorry. It's the mother instinct in me coming out. He's trifling with you, and I don't like him for it. You deserve better."

"We all deserve better," I said.

The food arrived just then, thank God. It gave us something else to focus on, and we let the tasting and seasoning divert our conversation, to my supreme relief. Margaret's flash of temper had unnerved me. Did her daughters ever see that reaction? No wonder poor little Claire seemed so distant.

The thing is, Margaret was right. And I knew it. Noah would do whatever I allowed him to do. And I wasn't ready to change the rules. I didn't have the strength. Maybe someday. But not just then. Just then all I wanted was to have a few laughs with my friends. To feel happy and comfortable and safe.

To be able to take a deep breath and relax. Not so much to ask, now was it?

Chapter 7
The Birthday Present

Why didn't I just say no? I wondered for about the hundredth time as I trudged up the flagstone path to Frank and Clayton's front door. My shoes—technically, high-heeled black patent leather sandals—grew heavier with each step.

* * *

The invitation had arrived in mid-September, and I went over the list of excuses I'd started the day Frank told me about the birthday party Clayton was planning. Would "a prior engagement" sound too obviously phony? I didn't much care because, dateless or otherwise, I didn't want to spend a Saturday night hanging out with a room full of strangers—okay, a room full of gay men. What would we talk about? I didn't consider myself the least bit homophobic, but, face it, my husband turned out to be gay. It came damn close to ruining my life. So why would I want to hang out with him and his friends? Moreover, how could I help celebrate Frank's Last Birthday? I added the invitation to a growing stack of papers in my "To Do" file until I formulated the perfect refusal. Maybe I'd send a nice plant along with my regrets.

And then Clayton had called me. The conversation began a little awkwardly, although I had progressed a long way from the shrew who called him a "home-wrecking little cunt" at our first meeting, right before I threatened to run him over with my car. Once I got that out of my system, I'd been able to maintain a fairly cordial exterior. Honestly, if we'd met under other circumstances, I probably would have liked Clayton, with his infectious laugh and surfer-boy good looks. At least I hadn't lost my husband to some fat, balding slob.

"Susan?" I didn't recognize his voice, and my first thought was, *damn telemarketer.*

"This is Clayton," he said. "Clayton Selden."

"Oh. Hi." I tried to shake the lingering annoyance out of my voice. I'd struggled through a long and stressful work week, all the way to Thursday night, and had just exercised away some of my frustration at the gym. Ravenous, thirsty, and sweaty, I wanted wine, a shower, and food, in that order, and all that stood between me and my goals was Clayton Selden. I'm sure my greeting conveyed a feeling of *What do you want?*

"I was checking to be sure you got our invitation—to Frank's party?"

Oh great—where are those fine excuses I invented? Why can't I remember any one of them?

"Yes, I did. Thanks. I've been meaning to call. I'm sorry, but I won't be able to come."

I didn't sound that sorry.

During a static-filled pause, I noticed a cobweb dangling from the ceiling above the sink. I swiped at it with a paper towel, but the damn thing hovered just out of reach.

"I'm sorry too," Clayton said, and he did sound genuinely disappointed. "Frank really wanted you to come. It's pretty special."

"I know," I said, "but I have to be somewhere else." *Anywhere else.*

"If your plans change, Susan, please come, even if it's last-minute. It would mean so much to Frank. And to me."

"Definitely. Thanks."

He didn't hang up as I'd hoped he would, though. I heard him breathing.

"How are you doing?" I added, to break the silence. Maybe he wanted me to ask.

"Not well. This has been such a horrible shock."

"I know," I said again. "I still can't believe it myself."

"He seems so … some of the time, at least, he seems so healthy—and I keep thinking maybe the doctor made a mistake. Maybe he's really okay."

"I guess that's natural."

Clayton sighed. "I suppose." Another pause. *What does this guy want from me anyway?*

"Oh," he continued, "Thank you so much for going to see his grandfather. That was very kind. I've tried to convince Frank not worry about the trust—I make a good living, and Lord knows I'm not with him for his money, but—"

"I was in the neighborhood anyway, and I always liked Grandpa K. It made a good excuse to see him. Sorry I couldn't get him to change his mind."

"I appreciate the effort. If anyone had a chance, it would've been you. He adores you, Frank tells me that all the time." Another silence. "He won't meet me, you know."

"He's old—and old-fashioned. It's the way he was brought up."

"Yes. Anyway, I—"

And he started crying. Right there over the phone.

"Hey," I said as gently as I could, "Clayton. Try not to freak out, okay? Frank's gonna need you to be strong."

The sobs subsided. "I'm sorry," he said. "I …" I heard him inhale and exhale. "Susan, maybe it's not appropriate to say this to you, but somehow I think you're the only one who could understand what it's like to be losing him."

You got that right, buddy.

"Oh, I understand," I said and bit my lip when I heard the bitterness.

"This whole party thing … I know it's stupid, but I just wanted to get some of Frank's favorite people together."

Then why include me? If I'm such a goddamn favorite, why is he with you?

"And Frank actually showed some enthusiasm about it," Clayton went on. "So little excites him these days."

"I can imagine."

"He'll be so disappointed you can't come. He was looking forward to having you meet some of our friends. You know, he talks about you all the time. Susan this and Susan that. If I were the jealous type, I'd be … well, jealous."

The cobweb was taunting me, fluttering in an invisible air current in time to the refrigerator's hum. I felt my resistance dissolve like sugar in a cup of hot coffee. My sweaty workout clothes were turning clammy on me, and I wanted to get him off the phone so I could shower the day away.

"Look," I said, "if it's that big a deal, I'll move my plans around. I'll be there."

"Wonderful! It will make us both so happy. Thank you, Susan. I really appreciate it."

Yeah, yeah. Now leave me alone.

But one last detail occurred to me. *What do you give a dying man for his birthday?*

"Any gift suggestions?" I asked Clayton.

"Your being here will be present enough. Honestly. And thank you for letting me vent a little. Frank's right, Susan—you're the best."

Oh please!

I'd hung up and taken the damn cobweb down, then poured my wine and let it soothe me.

* * *

I'd thought about making a last-minute excuse, but I'm kind of superstitious, and I was afraid that if I lied about being sick, I'd get the flu, or something worse, for real. Besides, Noah was still playing Dad more weekends than he used to, and although he didn't say so, I got the feeling his ex-wife participated in some of his outings with Jason. Going to Frank's party, and then casually mentioning it a week or so later, might get his attention. Especially when I met his outrage with, "Well, you weren't around, what was I supposed to do, sit home and collect dust?" —or something equally clever and mature.

Only as I rang Frank's doorbell did I regret my choice.

I had wandered through the Internet, not to mention every store in the Glendale Galleria, before I found an acceptable birthday gift the day before the party. I clutched the brightly wrapped box, trying not to crush the ribbon, as the door opened.

The weeks had passed by me invisibly, but Frank bore their mark. He'd lost some weight, and fine little furrows had carved a home in the corners of his eyes and mouth. His posture, always erect and proud, had eroded. The backs of his hands looked like a Rivers of the World relief map. His sparkly eyes, however, were undaunted by the course of the disease.

I held up the package, and his face brightened.

"Come in," he said, holding the door wide. He took the present, admired it, and kissed my cheek. "What a beautiful package! You made the bow, didn't you?"

I nodded, rightfully proud of my work. My foul-mouthed friend Judy—of all people—taught me the odd skill of tying loops of stiff wide satin ribbon together and then yanking them into an elaborate fluffy bow, showy but effective in dressing up even the most humble gift. I'd spent a long time on Frank's package, getting it as perfect as possible.

The entry walls were lined with photographs: Clayton and Frank in tuxedos; Max at the beach with the breeze lifting his majestic ears; Frank and Max in matching Santa hats; Clayton and a cluster of children—nieces and nephews maybe? And right by the doorway to the kitchen, a young Elise Krajewski smiled out of a cherry wood frame. Frank's mother wasn't smiling at me, of course. Her face tilted up so that she seemed to be looking at the ceiling. She'd been quite a beauty in her youth, before time and trouble had etched her face with frown lines that were all too familiar to me.

I heard voices and laughter coming from the end of the hall, and Frank steered me toward the sound. The hallway ended at the kitchen, which opened at the far end into a big, airy room with sliding glass doors that let in a crimson sunset fading to pink on the horizon. Ten or so people sat in a rough circle of sofas and chairs, and the clink of ice against glass blended with the voices. Clayton was perched on the arm of a comfy-looking overstuffed sofa, and he smiled and waved.

The others ignored my arrival until Frank called out, "Boys and girls, meet Madame Susan, our new dominatrix." He bowed deeply, like the head waiter at a fancy restaurant.

Jesus! What felt like a million eyeballs turned my way, and the room got very quiet.

I put on my widest smile and turned to Frank. "In your dreams."

That must have been the right response, because it got a big laugh before everyone went back to talking. Frank poured me a drink and led me around for introductions, but I quickly lost track of names. I felt horribly out of place; the other guests all seemed to know one another.

Frank deserted me to confer with Clayton about something, so I turned to a pair of well-groomed, friendly-looking fellows whose names I miraculously remembered: Pete and Joseph. The blonder half of the pair—that would be Joseph—smiled, scooted over, and patted the sofa cushion next to him.

"The famous Susan," he said. I noticed a trace of an accent.

I accepted his invitation and slid into the space next to him, grateful I didn't have to stand alone and awkward for another endless minute.

"Don't believe everything Frank says," I replied. "I'm really not a bad person."

"No," they both said at the same time and then laughed.

Joseph continued, "Frank always says nice things about you."

"Really?" I longed to know what kind of nice things.

"I think it's so cool you guys can be friends," Pete said. "I'm not on speaking terms with any of my exes."

When Joseph's relaxed expression turned stern, Pete added, "Not that there are a ton of them or anything."

The guy sitting across from Pete and Joseph leaned forward. "Not in comparison to the population of China anyway," he said with a knowing smirk.

I remembered his name, too: Dan Fellows. A gorgeous man, but in a rugged, robust sort of way. Dark wavy hair grazed the collar of his black silk shirt; more dark hair peeked from the shirt's open neck. Pale hazel eyes behind wire-rimmed glasses. And something in his posture that conveyed a sense of ease and command. He needed a shave, I observed, or else he was growing a beard that hadn't matured yet.

"Oh, this from Mr. Celibate," Pete said.

Dan smiled.

"So how do you know Clayton and Frank?" I asked the question of all three, but Pete spoke first.

"Clayton and I went to UC Davis together."

Pete, I learned, was also a veterinarian, with a practice in North Hollywood. And Joseph revealed that he originally came from Germany but had been in the US for more than half his life. He owned an auto repair shop on Hyperion—turned out I'd driven by it many times—that specialized in cars made in his motherland. As he told me about his beloved Porsche, I had a strong urge to trade in my Honda.

Dan, however, disclosed nothing about himself, and I was beginning to feel like a fixture, wedged there on the sofa between Joseph and Pete. Then Frank summoned me to the patio and I got up and went out to join him.

He smiled and put a hand on my back. "You doing okay?" he asked.

I nodded. "You have nice friends."

I looked toward two women talking with Clayton. They were the only females at the party besides me. Both looked to be in their late twenties, one tall and slender, with long raven-black hair, and the other a sturdy brunette.

"I'm glad to see this is an integrated party," I said.

Frank laughed and then told me, "Michelle is helping us with Ralph."

I was about to ask which one was Ralph when a slimy, wet rubber ball landed on my sandaled foot, and I shrieked like a schoolgirl. No one noticed. When I saw the panting dog that had dropped the ball, I gasped.

Clayton moved up beside us. "Looks a lot like Max, huh?"

My mouth was probably hanging open. I nodded. "Could be his twin."

When Frank left me, I threatened to keep Max, even though he was legally and ethically Frank's dog—and I really didn't want him, but I wanted to hurt Frank. "You owe me that much, not to leave me all alone," I'd insisted. Frank refused, and it was the one time he fought me. He gave me the car, the furniture, the camera, and all the dishes and linens and anything else I even hinted that I wanted. He even offered up half his paycheck; at least I had the decency to turn that down.

Only with Max did he resist; he used every dirty trick in his arsenal, said every hurtful thing he could think of. Max was *his* first, he reminded me, and I didn't even like dogs that much, I just wanted to keep Frank from having what he wanted, I was being a vindictive bitch. All true. I finally relented, but I did miss Max's reassuring snores my first night alone. I used the radio as a pathetic substitute, and eventually I got used to the solitude.

"But this one is a girl," Frank said. He frowned at Clayton. "Although her name is Ralph."

"Hope you weren't the one to name her," I said to Clayton.

"She's a rescue. Someone dumped her on the porch at the clinic. When I told Frank, well, you know how he was about Max …"

He draped his arm casually around Frank's shoulder, and I tried not to let it bother me. I did know how Frank was about Max, and I didn't like sharing the knowledge with Clayton. I picked up the ball and tossed it gently across the lawn. Ralph leaped after it happily, and of course she brought it back to me like a trophy. *That's what retrievers do*, I reminded myself as I tossed it again. *Over and over. And over.*

The shorter woman called out, "Congratulations. You've been accepted into the pack."

It took me a second to figure out what she meant, and then I remembered Frank's introduction. Her name was Michelle—professional dog trainer. And her friend was … Rhonda. *Good girl, Susan; give yourself a Milk Bone.*

Ralph obviously had decided I was her New Best Friend, and I felt like everyone was watching me. I patted Ralph's head, tossed the ball a little farther, and edged back into the house.

"Be flattered," Clayton said. "Ralph doesn't usually take to people right away. She has attachment issues from being abandoned."

"She's not the only one," Dan said.

Before I had a chance to ponder what he meant, the doorbell rang. This guest let herself in, and clearly she was one of Ralph's favorites, because the dog ran to her, tail thrashing from side to side.

"Ralphie!" the woman exclaimed, squatting on the floor to let Ralph lick her face before she stood up and waved to the rest of us.

"Flo!" several people called out at once.

As she got closer, I saw a short, trim woman with a heavily made-up face and bright red lipstick. She wore flowing black pants, heels that were higher than mine, and a sheer black top over a black lace camisole. Curly auburn hair and scarlet fingernails completed the picture: a crazy contrast to the other partygoers.

When she saw me, Flo's smile widened and she held out her arms. "At last I get to meet Susie!" she said in a low, raspy voice.

Drag queen? I wondered. Nothing would have surprised me by then. I had no choice but to hug her, and it felt unexpectedly good. Despite my suspicions, I sensed something motherly about Flo under the flashy clothes and makeup, and up close I saw a woman about my mom's age. Enveloped in Shalimar, she even smelled like Mom. I liked Flo already.

"Here, sweetheart," Frank said, taking her hand and wrapping it around a tall, frosty glass.

Flo raised her glass in a toast and took a sip. "Mmmmm, that's good," she said. "Just the right proportion of vodka and ice."

She winked at me. "He could've been a hell of a bartender."

"Did you go to the hospital dressed like *that?*" Joseph asked. I could tell he was teasing.

Flo flopped down next to Dan and gave him a peck on the cheek. "You're probably the only one here who can appreciate me," she said and then turned to Joseph. "No, sweetie, I did go home and change, for your benefit. Although it was probably a wasted effort."

"Flo has a therapy dog," Frank told me. "They go visit sick kids in the hospital on Saturday afternoons."

"How come you didn't bring Ginger with you?" Rhonda wanted to know.

Flo waved long, elegant fingers. "She is *wiped out.* The girl doesn't have my stamina. I gave her a piece of rawhide and left her snoozing in front of the TV."

Ginger, I cleverly figured out, was her dog. So the puzzle started coming together. Flo had a dog, Michelle trained dogs. Clayton and Pete healed sick dogs. So where did Dan fit in? Where did I?

Flo beckoned to me. "Come here, darling. I have wanted to meet you for just about forever. Frank tells me you're some kind of corporate big shot. Come and tell me all—what's it like in the executive suite?"

I got the feeling people usually did as Flo asked, so I obeyed. My vodka tonic was long gone. I didn't want to look like a lush, so I twirled the glass and sipped the melted ice, but Flo didn't miss anything.

"Frank K, you get this girl another drink. What kind of host are you, anyway?"

Frank whisked my glass away.

"I'm no big shot," I told Flo. "Merely another flunky, I'm afraid."

"Hah," Frank said from over his shoulder. "They don't make a move without asking her first."

"That's not true," I said, but I didn't want to make myself look completely boring, so I added, "my job is to keep them out of court."

"You're a lawyer?" Dan asked.

The question annoyed me, and I wasn't sure why. "No—lawyers are for damage control. My job is to stop the trouble before it starts—to be proactive."

Flo slapped my knee. "Proactive! I like that. A good thing for a woman to be."

Frank came back with my drink. I took a sip—good, he'd made it weaker than the first. Frank remembered things like that—I preferred the first one strong enough to almost blow my head off, and the rest to take their time.

Dan smiled. "Where were you when I needed you, Ms. Proactive?"

"Trouble planning your moves?" I asked. The question sounded more challenging than I intended.

"Don't get him started," Flo said with a cackle. She drained her glass and rattled the ice against her teeth, then handed it to Dan. "Would you be a darling?"

While he was gone, I whispered, "What's his story?"

Flo shrugged. "He's a funny guy. A good heart—too good, I think sometimes. More lovers than the rest of the room put together."

"But he didn't bring anyone tonight."

"No, he wouldn't. Most of Dan's lady friends wouldn't feel comfortable here, I think."

"Lady friends?"

"Yes, of c— Oh my dear, you thought … oh, what a hoot! Susan, darling—Dan is *straight*. As an arrow."

"Oh."

"Now, don't go getting any ideas, hon. You keep away from that one. He goes through women like I go through panty hose. You deserve better than that."

"Oh, I wasn't … no, I'm kind of going with someone now anyway. Really."

"That's what Frank said. Good for you. I hope he's a good man, I hope he treats you like a princess."

"He's pretty good to me," I said. *Until lately, anyway.*

Flo shook her head. "Such a terrible thing about Frank, though. I'm so glad he has you in his corner."

"And Clayton," I said. "He's lucky to have Clayton."

"If you think Clayton's going to get through this without your help," Flo replied, "you're living in a dream world, hon. You know how men are—"

"No," Dan said, as he held out Flo's drink. "How are they?"

Flo grabbed the glass. "What took you so long?"

Dan tilted his head toward the kitchen. "The chefs are having a dispute over the hors d'oeuvres. Clayton's virgin effort."

Flo's eyebrows rose half an inch. "Clayton? He hates to cook. He *can't* cook."

"Frank's coaching," Dan told her. "I had to referee."

Flo shook her head and took a drink. "We'll be needing these," she said and pointed to her glass.

"So," I asked Dan as he sat back down, "how do you know Frank and Clayton?"

At the exact same time he said to me, "So—how *are* men?"

I laughed to cover my embarrassment and said, "Don't ask me. I probably know less than anyone else here."

"I don't believe that for a minute," he said and put his hand on Flo's knee. "Although Flo probably knows the most."

"Lord knows, I've had enough experience," she said. She turned to me. "Three husbands. Buried all of them, too."

Dan looked a little uncomfortable by her statement, like he wanted to change the subject, and I realized that most of my silly assumptions about Frank's friends had been demolished in less than an hour.

"So," I asked again, "how *do* you know Frank and Clayton?"

This time he answered. "Old neighbors—did you ever go to their place on Oakshire? I was their upstairs neighbor. And unlike my wealthy friends, I'm still there. Can't afford to move out."

"God bless rent control," Flo said, raising her glass.

We clinked glasses, and then Flo told me, "Danny's a struggling writer, you know."

Intrigued, I leaned forward to ask, "What kind of writing?"

He made a circling motion with his hands. "Anything and everything. Right now I'm writing a training manual for a van line. It's a good gig, actually pay's decent, and I can work pretty much when I want. But it'll be over in a month, and I should actually be home trolling the net for job leads, but—"

"But this is a special occasion," Flo put in.

Flushed with excitement—or fear—Clayton appeared with a tray of appetizers. I accepted a little puff pastry and took a wary bite. "This is good!" I told him, trying not to sound surprised; the meat and cheese filling tasted delicious.

"Frank's secret recipe," Clayton told me. "He's trying to teach me the basics, but I'm a slow learner."

Frank had taught me a few tricks in the kitchen, too, when we were married. My domestic skills were survival-level but adequate. Frank, however, seemed to really enjoy cooking. When he left, the responsibility for fixing my own meals had been one of the lousy side effects of living without him. Now, it occurred to me, Clayton would have to go through the same rude awakening.

Ralph was going from person to person, waiting for any morsel to fall to the ground. A Bach concerto spilled from speakers mounted on ceiling beams, and the music welded our voices together in a nice companionable hum. This wasn't so bad, I decided, glad I'd been brave enough to come to the party.

From across the room, I heard Frank laugh at something Joseph said, and for a minute I forgot he was sick, I forgot he was with Clayton. I remembered how it felt being with him, eating ice cream and watching Max chase a butterfly through the sunlight. Our lives had stretched ahead of us with all kinds of possibilities; we would always be young, strong, and in love.

Reality hit me across the face when Frank's laughter dissolved into a moist, strangling cough. Everyone pretended not to notice except Clayton, who moved to his side and patted his back. It made my own chest hurt to witness, to realize that he really was going to die. And I would have to watch it happen. *Wait. I don't have to see it. This is Clayton's problem, not mine. I can walk away.*

Clayton handed Frank a tissue to spit into, and the party went on. That's the great thing about friends: they keep you busy and distracted. Frank and Clayton circulated some more, poured more drinks, made more small talk, and eventually I saw them both head toward the kitchen again.

I tried to learn more about Dan, without acting like I was flirting with him, but the guy wasn't cooperating and I felt Flo's scrutiny the whole time. Her warning whispered through my mind. "He goes through women like I go through panty hose." Hmmmm.

Then a crash came from the kitchen, the unmistakable shattering of glass, followed by, "God damn it!"

Conversations stopped mid-syllable. Flo looked at me, her dark-fringed eyes wide. "Uh oh."

I acted out of habit rather than common sense. Everyone else seemed frozen, but I had to get up and see what was wrong. Frank and Clayton glared at each other across a mess of broken glass scattered through a purple puddle spreading across the brown tile floor.

"You are so damned careless!" Clayton yelled at Frank as I approached.

Frank saw me and didn't respond to Clayton, just squatted and started sopping up the mess.

"Yuck," I said. "Red wine. The worst kind of spill."

"Not simply any red wine," Clayton muttered. "A four-year-old Stag's Leap cabernet I'd been saving for—"

"Look, I said I'm sorry," Frank yelled. "It's not like—shit!"

He stood, blood oozing from his right index finger. He reached for a dry paper towel and wrapped it around the cut. I knelt and took over the cleanup.

"You had to go clowning around," Clayton said. His hands were at eye level for me, and I saw them clenched into fists. I looked up. His face was pale except for dark red splotches on both cheeks.

"Clayton," I said, raising my voice to get his attention. "Get a grip. It's only wine. It'll clean up, and you can buy more."

He didn't answer.

"Hey," I said, "you might want to give me a hand here before it soaks into the grout."

The wrap on Frank's finger was turning bright red, and he raised his hand above his head. "Yeah—make yourself useful. Instead of whining about what I did wrong. Again."

Clayton stalked out of the kitchen.

I kept blotting for a couple of minutes.

"Do you have any rags?" I asked. "These paper towels aren't doing it."

I held up a sopping purple mess to prove my point.

Frank was leaning against the sink with his back to me. "I'll get some."

"No, tell me where they are and—"

I think he was crying. He reached into a drawer and pulled out some terry cloth towels and bent down to help. Yep, his eyes were red and damp.

I heard a voice say, "Hey, you better put a bandage on that finger." And Dan Fellows was there with us, on his knees, mopping up wine. He looked at me and winked. A minute later Clayton returned, carrying peroxide, gauze, and a Band-Aid the size of Delaware. He tugged Frank away from us and went to work on the cut while Dan and I finished up.

"Toss me a sponge," Dan called to Clayton.

The sponge came flying and we both reached for it. As our hands touched, I felt a current sizzle down my wrist, and I couldn't have held that small piece of cellulose if my life depended on it. Dan showed no sign he'd noticed as he wiped up the last traces of cabernet.

"What a waste," he murmured, but I think I was the only one who heard. I smiled and shook my head.

I stood up and dried my hands on the last clean towel. "There," I said to Clayton. "All fixed. And last I heard, Stag's Leap was still in business, so you can always replace the wine."

I wanted to slap his pissy little face and remind him that he wouldn't be able to replace Frank, but his arms were around Frank and he was whispering something I didn't want to hear. I was already trespassing just by being there. With his uninjured hand, Frank patted Clayton's back.

"It's okay," he murmured. "It's okay. I know. Shhhh. It's okay."

Dan took my hand, and I felt that little sizzle again, like a wire short-circuiting on the surface of my skin. "Let's go," he mouthed at me.

Several people looked up when we came back from the kitchen, but no one asked what had happened. Maybe this was a familiar scene. Flo took charge.

"Hey, when's the birthday boy going to open his presents?" she called out. "And when do we get cake?"

They all started clapping like an impatient audience at a rock concert, which finally coaxed Frank and Clayton back to the party.

The birthday cake, a beautiful whipped cream and raspberry confection, had a rainbow border and "Happy Birthday Frank" written in rosy script. A single thick white candle stuck out above the "i."

Rhonda started singing "Happy Birthday to you," and for a second

I almost joined in, but no one else did. Then I figured it out: Rhonda had such a beautiful voice—as clear as ice on a winter morning—that I didn't want to pollute it. When she finished, everyone cheered as Frank blew out his candle.

Then came the present-opening. I settled down next to Flo and kicked off my sandals, which were beginning to pinch.

Some of the packages contained gag gifts, like a boxed DVD set called "Amazon Women from Mars" from Pete and Joseph. It had a lurid cover drawing of a mostly naked woman with long black hair leading a man by a dog leash. Dan's present was a compilation of the year's best American short stories, a great idea I thought. Flo gave him a CD of Yo Yo Ma playing Boccherini. Frank seemed to like my gift: a soft blue plaid flannel shirt that would complement his eyes. Flo nodded her approval when Frank held up the shirt for all to see.

Then Clayton started bussing plates and glasses to the kitchen. Ever the Little Ms. Helpful, I pitched in.

"You have some really nice friends," I told Clayton as I scraped uneaten cake into the garbage disposal.

"Yes. We've been lucky." He seemed to hold no ill will from our earlier confrontation.

"Flo is so funny. And I love her laugh."

Clayton took the stack of plates from me and loaded them in the dishwasher. "It's amazing that she *can* laugh after all that's happened to her. She is my inspiration, really."

"She mentioned she's been widowed three times—how awful."

He closed the dishwasher and wiped his hands on what was probably the only dry towel in the kitchen, after the red wine fiasco.

"That's not the half of it. Her daughter was murdered."

"Jesus!"

"Yes. And the daughter was pregnant at the time. It would've been Flo's first grandchild. Flo said it almost drove her into the crazy house, but she decided not to let it."

"Wow." What an insightful reply. "Was that her only child?"

Clayton shook his head. "Although it might have been easier. She has a son up at Folsom."

"Prison?"

Clayton looked grim. "Yep. Caught selling crack cocaine one time too many."

"Incredible," I said. "She doesn't let on about any of that."

"And she's a cancer survivor. Breast cancer."

I couldn't make any more brilliant responses, so I just took it in without speaking. That sparkly, laughing woman I'd spent the evening with had been through more tragedy than any ten people I knew, but my first impression of her had been, *This one has had an easy life; I envy her.* You never know, do you?

In the silence I heard a woman's voice, "Quit telling me what to do! I'm not one of your dogs!"

Rhonda's voice, I realized. What was going on? Clayton had gone for more empty plates. I was about to follow him when Dan came in, carrying my sandals.

"Cinderella, is that you?" he asked, handing them over. "You might want to stay in here where it's safe."

A few seconds later the front door slammed.

I bent over to put my sandals on.

"Here," Dan said, and he knelt at my feet. "Let me."

The touch of his hands felt delicious. What would it be like to kiss him? To have his arms around me? I closed my eyes and pretended I could feel his lips, their soft warmth, the intoxicating sensation of his flesh against mine.

"There you go," he said as he stood and tugged at his shirt cuffs.

I looked away. "Thank you, kind sir."

Frank came in with another stack of dishes. I heard Flo murmuring something soothing, presumably to Michelle, from the other room.

"Everything okay?" I asked.

Frank nodded and set the plates down. "In an hour she won't even remember why she was mad."

Dan put his hand on my waist, and I felt the heavenly warmth of his skin through my blouse. "I have to get going, but I really enjoyed meeting you, Susan. Hope we run into each other again one of these days."

I struggled for something brilliant to say and came up with "Me, too." *Lame, lame, lame.*

"So, old man," Dan said to Frank, "let me know when you want to go out to the track again, will you?'

I left them to their plans and went to see what was up with Flo and Michelle. One empty wine glass caught my eye, so I picked it up and turned back toward the kitchen, just in time to overhear Dan saying, "You didn't tell me how pretty she was."

I froze.

"I guess we didn't think it was any of your business," Frank responded, and then said something else I couldn't make out.

I backed away so they wouldn't catch me eavesdropping. In the most protected corner of my mind, I dared hope they were talking about me. Probably not, but a girl can dream.

* * *

The party broke up soon afterward, and Frank walked me to my car.

"Thanks for asking me. I had a lot more fun than I expected," I confessed.

Frank laughed. "Ah, Susie, we made a good team sometimes, didn't we?"

I could see him smile in the darkness.

"Yeah, Frank, we did."

He took my hand and swung it lightly between us. "I remember what a rabbit you were, back when I first met you."

"Rabbit?"

"Yeah. Scared—ready to dive back in your burrow if anything weird happened."

"Is that how I seemed? I never knew."

He quit swinging my hand and held it between both of his for a minute, then kissed it lightly and let go.

"There's a lot you never knew."

Ouch.

"Frank? Why'd you ask me out that first time? I never understood."

He looked up at the stars, like he was trying to find the answer himself.

"Because you laughed at my jokes."

"I don't remember your jokes. And that's a pretty sucky reason to ask someone out."

"Nobody remembers my jokes—but you did laugh. And you were —are—pretty, and smart, and there was something about you … something I wanted to protect. The rabbit."

"I never knew that, Frank. That's sweet."

"Yeah, but look what I did to you."

Silence. I found my car keys and pushed the remote button. The Honda's locks clicked open.

"Anyway," Frank went on, "everybody told me tonight how cool you are, and I got chewed out for not bringing you around sooner. Flo told me I was an idiot to let you go. But of course we all know that."

Another opening, and again I let it pass. "You even have nice straight friends," I said. "Dan seemed pretty comfortable there."

"Dan would be comfortable in the middle of a race riot. He's that way." Frank paused. "Be careful with him, Suse."

"What do you mean?"

"You like him—I can see it. Remember, this is me—you can't hide stuff from me. Dan is a great guy, but he … he's a busy boy."

"I'm in a relationship, remember?"

"Oh, right—what's his name again? And why didn't you bring him tonight?"

The Honda re-locked itself since I hadn't opened the door. I pushed the remote button so hard that my finger hurt and then yanked the door open. "Not your business."

"Ouch—hit a nerve, huh? Sorry."

"Hey, Mr. Part-of-a-Couple—it's not like there are tons of guys out there trying to date me, you know. Bad enough you stole my prime dating years, don't go criticizing my choice of boyfriends."

Frank put his hand under my chin and lifted my face toward the streetlight. Probably trying to see if I was kidding or not. Truth be told, I wasn't sure myself.

The night air still held some warmth, but with a chilly undercurrent of winter's approach, just enough bite to make me wish I'd worn a sweater. A slice of bright moon hovered to the west, silvering the sickly orange glow of the streetlight and bouncing off the Honda's hood. My hand rested on the doorframe for support, but it didn't help much.

"Susie, Susie," he said after a minute. "Who're you gonna blame for your troubles when I'm gone?"

He kissed my forehead to make it look like he was teasing, but he sounded serious. Dead serious.

"Anyway," I added, "I just think Dan's nice. That doesn't mean I want to jump his bones or anything."

"If you say so."

I tweaked his cheek. "Thanks for your concern. But I'm a big girl now."

"You sure are. I'm glad you came tonight, Susie."

"Me, too."

I was sliding into the driver's seat when Frank said, really softly, "I love you, you know."

I blew him a kiss. "I know. I love you, too."

On the way home, I kept seeing Frank's face and hearing the sadness in his voice.

"Who're you gonna blame for your troubles when I'm gone?"

Who indeed? And did I blame him? Maybe a little. I'd pretty much taken responsibility for my own happiness, but every now and then the snippy little whiner snuck out like she had that night, even though the last thing I wanted was to put a guilt trip on Frank.

I couldn't bear to think of what was happening to him. He'd stayed such a presence in my life, even after the divorce, even when he annoyed me the way he had that night with his smug warning about Dan.

Dan … what a charmer. I welcomed the distracting memory of his touch, the way he looked at me so intensely, like I was the only person in the room. That was probably a technique he used with all his women, but I found it spellbinding.

I got to my street and made myself put away all thoughts of Dan. *Don't be a fool. You're old enough to know better. Besides, you have Noah.*

And speaking of Noah, he'd left two voicemails, but I'd kept my cell phone off, on purpose. The first message was time-stamped eight-ten p.m.: "Just saying hi." At nine-thirty he'd phoned again to tell me he was home and that I could call him if I wanted.

"Hope you're having a good time … wherever you are," he said, but from his tone of voice I could tell he hoped I was having anything but. I decided not to call him back; if I did, I might tell him where I'd been, and I'd heard enough yelling for one day.

Chapter 8
Little Victories

Noah didn't answer when I phoned him the next morning, and as I listened to his voicemail greeting, an urgent longing grabbed me. I hadn't seen him in over a week, and I missed him. Time to try and patch things up. I had to let go of my resentment about the scuttled Napa trip. Noah was a good man, a responsible father … and an awesome lover. Why had I risked losing all that?

I tried him again half an hour later, and this time I worked up a hearty, cheerful voice and left a message at the beep. "Hey, stranger, it's me, Susan. I miss you. Why don't you come for dinner tonight? You can bring dessert, and I'm not talking about a chocolate cake. Call me, 'kay?"

He phoned about noon and sounded happy that I'd called. We agreed on six p.m. for dinner, and I scurried off to the market.

* * *

Noah showed up a couple of minutes early, with a nice bottle of sauvignon blanc. When I kissed him hello, however, I felt a definite resistance, a holding-back that was not like Noah. Was he sulking about my disappearing act the night before?

I'd chosen to deviate from Noah's favorite steak-and-potatoes menu, and as I dished up the scallops and wild rice in an improvised dill sauce, I hoped it would set the tone of a new beginning for us. Put old grudges behind and move forward; move closer.

The food tasted fine to me, and Noah's wine set it off perfectly. In the midst of congratulating myself on this culinary triumph, however, I noticed that Noah mostly pushed his food around. He'd take a bite and chew it almost reluctantly.

"Is something wrong with the scallops?" I asked him.

He looked up like he didn't recognize me. The central heat kicked on, the first blast chilly as usual, and as it washed over me, I felt naked in the revealing black halter top and clingy pants I'd chosen. Noah wore his usual jeans and flannel shirt. The shirt had a tiny rip in the right sleeve, and I suddenly wished I could sew well enough to mend the shirt because I knew it was one of his favorites—a soft gray plaid that flattered his ruddy complexion.

I realized I'd neglected my usual dim-light-and-candles routine; the bright beams from the chandelier danced over Noah's uplifted fork and blinded me for a second. The table between us could've been an ocean.

He set his fork down with a noticeable clink and wiped the napkin across his mouth in a quick, elegant gesture almost out of place with the rest of him.

"It's okay," he said. "Guess I'm not as hungry as I thought. And the sauce tastes a little funny to me, but maybe I'm just tired."

"I can grill up a burger real fast," I offered.

He smiled then, the old familiar Noah smile that always sent a ripple of pleasure through me. "It's okay, babe, honest. I think I'm too wiped out to appreciate your cooking tonight."

"The job giving you trouble?" Had he gone in to work, even on Sunday?

He shook his head, took another bite and tried to look happy about it for my benefit. I loved him for the effort.

After he swallowed, he said, "Not that. But I've been hanging out a lot with Jason—he's really into the soccer thing. First time I've seen him care so much about anything."

I fought down a rush of resentment that Jason could evoke such enthusiasm. "That's great. Maybe he turned the corner."

Actually, I was glad for Noah. Jason had been a heavy weight on him, and if a few soccer games lightened the load, I was all for it.

Noah drummed his fingers on the tabletop, and his eyes went a little out of focus. "He's really good at sports—better than I ever was."

"I don't believe that! You're so coordinated."

He waved away the compliment. "Except for swim team, I was a major klutz in Phys Ed."

"Swimming? I didn't know that."

His "yeah … well" shrug implied there was a lot I didn't know about Noah.

I got up and came around to his side of the table to kiss the top of his head. Then I kneaded his shoulders for a minute, and he relaxed into the massage and leaned back, eyes closed. He seemed so content I hated to break the spell, but I did it anyway. Don't ask me why; maybe I just wanted to prove to myself I could take his mind off Jason.

I leaned over and nibbled his ear lobe. "Did you bring dessert?" I whispered as suggestively as I could, blowing into his ear for good measure. I wasn't talking about food, and I think he understood that.

Noah reacted as if I'd doused him with ice water; he sat up straight and was about to reach back and push me away when I saw him hesitate and get control of his arm. Then he stood up, put his hands on my shoulders and kissed my cheek.

"I'm sorry," he said, and he sounded sincere. "I'm beat tonight. I probably shoulda stayed home, but I wanted to see you."

I put my arms around him but didn't try to start anything. Noah's behavior troubled me—he was *always* ready for sex.

"That's sweet," I told him. "And I understand. Honest."

Noah's face was flushed; he looked really uncomfortable. I ran my hand over his cheek and felt his forehead. Damp, but no fever.

"Want to curl up in bed and watch TV?" I asked.

He shook his head. "I better head home. Early day tomorrow."

I knew better than to argue, so I pulled him close for a fast lip-kiss. "I'll give you a rain check then."

Relief washed over his face. "Great. I'll try and be better

company."

"You're fine. Believe me, I understand fatigue. Want to get together midweek?"

He hesitated. "Maybe we better hold off 'til next weekend."

The rejection stung a little, but I fought past it. "A real Saturday-night date?"

His teeth worked over his lower lip for a second. "Fine. We can set it up in a couple of days."

"Okay, big boy. Go home and rest—you'll need it."

I meant to sound playful, but it came out more like an order.

Noah winced. "Sorry again."

"No apology required. Take care of yourself, okay?"

"I will."

Another brief kiss on my cheek and he was clumping down the porch steps. He started the Mercedes and drove away without one look back at me.

Don't go imagining disaster, I told myself. Still, I had the nasty feeling Noah was right: there was a lot about him I didn't know.

* * *

When he called me at work Wednesday morning, I cringed at the pathetic delight in my greeting. But it had been two long days and nights since I'd heard from him. And before our Labor Day tiff, he typically phoned me at least once a day, sometimes more.

"Hi!" I said when I recognized his voice. "Feeling better?"

There was a tiny pause on his end that felt disturbingly familiar.

Finally he said, "Yeah. I slept like a corpse Sunday night."

"Good—you obviously needed the rest."

"Yeah, well … look, I know we planned to get together Saturday, but I just realized I can't. Jason's team won their playoff, and Saturday's a big game. I need to be there for him."

"No problem," I said, although it was a huge problem in my book. Then I had a thought: "Hey, why don't I come along to the game? We can all go celebrate afterward, because with you and me both cheering, they've gotta win."

He didn't reply.

Oh shit. I stepped over the line.

But I didn't understand how I could have, really. I was only being understanding and supportive.

"That won't work," Noah said at last. I heard him inhale. "June's going to be there."

"Oh. Well, yeah, that might be a little tricky, but sooner or later she has to understand that you've moved on with—"

"Actually," Noah said, "you're the one who'll need to understand."

I didn't get what he meant, or didn't want to, so like a fool I went ahead and asked, "Understand what?"

A part of me already knew, of course.

"Ah, shit, Susan, I didn't want to do this over the phone, but maybe it's better this way. June and I … well, since she got out of the hospital, she's been … different. Kinder. And Jason—Jason feels it too. I see a difference in him, he's not pissed off at the world anymore. Maybe I'm fooling myself, but I'm starting to think that maybe, if June and I really work at patching things up, maybe Jason will come around."

So June, the little manipulator, was making a play to lure Noah back. Apparently she'd even conscripted Hellboy to her cause. I wanted to yell at Noah, tell him how stupid he was being. Why didn't he get it? He was smart enough, he should be able to smell a trap. Once he'd moved back in, the claws would come out again. Sure, people could change—but not that much, not that fast.

And poor, goodhearted Noah was willing to ignore that fact of human nature in the interest of saving his son. Even as I seethed with the hate of rejection, I had to love him a little for wanting to risk it.

"So you're telling me it's over between you and me?" I asked, amazed that I sounded merely neutral and curious.

I heard another noisy gulp of breath on his end. "Yeah, I guess so. I'm really sorry, Susan, I didn't expect things to work out this way."

I looked around my office for something to hold on to. Otherwise I thought I might disintegrate in a bright red flame. The desk was still there, a big chunk of oak some craftsman in Iowa had built. I'd had the desk for six years, ever since the last downsizing when some poor schmuck in Accounting had gotten the axe, leaving his office furniture up for grabs. It showed its age, but I didn't mind the gouges and worn places because it had plenty of room for my files and my clock and my calendar. A calendar that was going to have a lot more empty evenings after this phone call.

"Quit apologizing," I said, and my words came out too loud and angry. "You don't have to explain. You're an adult, and you make your own choices. I'm the one who should have seen this coming. My dumb fault for being surprised."

The train was screaming down the track and I couldn't stop it. Honestly, I wasn't sure I wanted to.

"Susan, I still care about you, and—"

"Good luck, Noah. Hope it works out."

I slammed the receiver into its cradle, then got up and calmly closed my office door. When I sat back down, the tears came, spattering the desktop. I told myself he didn't mean that much to me, he was never really there for me, he wasn't the right one. But none of it helped.

Normally I thought of self-pity as an unattractive waste of time. But that morning I let it in, big time. I kept my hand over my mouth to muffle the sobs, and I went into a hideous "poor me" litany. *Why does this always happen to me? Why do the men in my life keep abandoning me? First my father, then Frank, now Noah. What's wrong with me?*

Half an hour passed before I got tired of wallowing. I wiped my face dry, put drops in my eyes to mask the red, reapplied my mascara, took a deep breath, and opened the door. No one looked at me strangely, so I must have managed to keep my grief to myself.

I turned to my computer screen and started answering the emails that had piled up, but my concentration was still shaky. I had to talk to someone about this; I couldn't keep it to myself. Margaret. I could call Margaret. She was the best consoler in the world.

I dialed her office and got the service. Oh yeah, she doesn't work on Wednesdays. I tried her home number and to my great relief, she answered.

"It's me, Susan," I said, like there was any doubt. "I need help. Noah and I just broke up."

Damn it, I was crying again. I swiped at my face and took a deep breath, then launched into my sad story, grateful that Margaret did not even once come close to an "I told you so." In fact, I realized after I'd babbled for about five minutes, she hadn't said much of anything except "mmm hmmm"—although I was pretty sure she'd been listening.

I finally ran out of steam. Silence.

"Margaret? Say something."

I heard Margaret clear her throat, but her voice still sounded thick. "I apologize, Susan. I'm … I'm not exactly myself right now. I'm having a rather bad day, and it's difficult to talk at the moment."

This was not like Margaret. Shame flooded me. Here I came dumping my troubles on her, presuming she'd be ready and willing to help, and something bad had happened to her, something worse than my little tragedy.

"What is it?" I asked, hoping I could undo some of the damage. "Is it Philippe?"

Jeez, he worked in some pretty unstable places. What if there had been an accident? Or a political coup? Or … my imagination flexed its muscle. Then I heard a girl's voice in the background, high-pitched and angry. The words were distorted, but the tone was urgent.

"I have to go, Susan. Claire and I are having an … an argument, and I have to deal with it. I'll try and call you later."

"I'm so sorry," I said, and I truly meant it. "Let me know if I can do anyth—"

But she had hung up.

When my phone rang just before quitting time, I almost didn't answer because I didn't recognize the number on the display. But on the wild chance Noah had come to his senses and was using someone else's phone, I picked up the call before it went to voicemail.

Clayton's voice, shaky and distorted, came over the line. He was driving Frank to the hospital. Would I meet them there? "Please! We need you."

Could the day have gotten any better?

On the way to the hospital I beat myself up for not asking more questions of Clayton, but he'd been so rattled that he could hardly talk. *Can this be the end? So soon? Why else would he ask me to come there? What about Frank's mom—should someone call her? Where's Flo? What about their other friends? Why did he call* me? By the time I fought my way through westbound rush hour traffic to Burbank and found a parking place at the medical center, Clayton had managed to get Frank admitted—so he wasn't as incompetent as I feared. I found him in the Oncology wing visitors' lounge.

He stood and hugged me. "Thanks for coming."

"How bad is it?" I asked.

Clayton shook his head. "We don't know. The doctor's examining him now."

"Have you called Elise?"

Clayton's eyes finally came into focus. "No. I don't think it's time for that yet. Oh my God, I'm so sorry. You thought—you thought this was *it*, didn't you?"

It? What the hell did he mean? Frank wasn't at death's door? I didn't know what I felt more: anger or relief.

"I am so sorry," Clayton repeated. "My mind wasn't working. I thought we'd need help with the admitting desk, and Frank's always said how good you are in emergencies. And I couldn't reach anyone else. I dragged you out on a wild goose chase, didn't I?"

Yeah, and thanks for making me a last-ditch choice.

"No, it's okay. And I'm glad it's not as bad as I thought. But what happened?"

"I came home early," he told me, "thought I'd surprise him and take him to dinner." His voice trembled. "He was lying on the floor in the den, squirming around, thrashing like—"

Clayton had to stop for breath. A stranger to this kind of comfort, I put my hand on his arm and patted gently. "Did he fall?"

Clayton shook his head. "Best we can figure, his leg just gave out. And he couldn't get up because it hurt so bad. He'd been there for a couple of hours." He shuddered and rubbed his arm. "What if I hadn't come home when I did? He couldn't get to the phone, couldn't do anything but lie there and hurt."

"But you did come home. You saved him."

"This time! I wanted to call nine-one-one, but you know Frank, he wouldn't let me. Insisted he'd be fine once I got him up. But he wasn't."

Clayton's usually tan face had paled, and a thin layer of sweat rose on his forehead. "I heaved him up and into the chair, but—Susan, he could hardly move! And he hurt like hell, but he wouldn't let me call an ambulance even then, oh no, we had to drive here on our own."

"Sounds like Frank," I agreed.

"I know! God, Susan—I don't know what to do with him!"

Clayton clenched his fists in a grand dramatic gesture that didn't fool me one bit. He was scared, and his fear was contagious. I shivered and pulled my jacket closed.

A tall, burly man in a doctor's coat strode into the lounge and pumped Clayton's hand. His name tag identified him as Richard Wardell, M.D., and I surmised he was Frank's oncologist. Clayton confirmed this a second later when he introduced us, telling Wardell I was a "close family friend."

Wardell's big hands seemed inappropriate for the practice of medicine, but what did I know? He enveloped my hand in one of his paws and shook vigorously. He had a bushy mustache, curly blond hair that meandered in every direction, and a brisk if distracted demeanor.

"Sit, please," he commanded.

We sat.

Dr. Wardell didn't bother with vague preliminaries. His delivery was clinical and direct, with no room for interruption. Or doubt.

As we already knew, the tumor in Frank's lung had spread to his spine. That offspring had turned mean, had grown and was pressing on nerves and ligaments, weakening his left leg to the point where it couldn't support his weight any more. Along with that, for an extra measure of cruelty, the cancer had cranked up his pain several notches.

"We've administered morphine to make him more comfortable," Wardell concluded. "That should be taking effect by now."

He paused for air, so I jumped in. "What happens next?"

His smile was patronizing, and for a second I thought he was simply going to say, "He dies."

But he surprised me. "I want to do some tests to see how far it's progressed. We'll do an X-ray, maybe a CT scan."

"And then?"

Clayton sat with his forearms on his knees, studying the floor. He probably knew a lot of this already. If not, did he want to? No matter, I wanted to hear it from the doctor.

"If my suspicions are correct, there's little we can do beyond pain mitigation. We'll send him home."

He looked at Clayton. "You'll probably need a hospital bed. The hospice can help arrange that."

Clayton nodded but said nothing.

"We'll wait until the test results come back before making any decisions, but if I were you, I'd line up some nursing assistance. He'll probably need round-the clock care very soon."

Again the silent nod.

"You can see him now if you like," Wardell said. "But for a short time. We'll take him down to X-ray soon. Remember, he'll be a little woozy from the morphine."

A little woozy is right. Frank waved gaily at us; he knew who we were, and who he was, but he kept forgetting little things like why he was in the hospital. He didn't look bad, except for the dull morphine sheen in his eyes. A nasty looking needle was taped to the back of his hand, at the end of a plastic tube running from a bottle of clear intravenous fluid. A red and purple bruise had already spread out around the spot where the needle pierced Frank's flesh.

Feeling vaguely like an intruder, I tried to hang back, but Clayton looked so much the scared little boy that I found myself edging closer, nudging him to take Frank's free hand, forcing him to engage in conversation. *How is the pain? Are your pillows okay? Do you want to watch the television? Want some water? Need the nurse?*

Frank's eyelids finally drifted down over those drug-glazed eyes, and his breathing slowed to a deep, regular rhythm. Clayton looked at me, and I nodded an answer to the question in his eyes. Time to go.

Outside we both had to lean against the wall, inhaling and exhaling until things came back into focus a little.

"He seems comfortable enough," I told Clayton, and he nodded.

"He looks so helpless," Clayton said.

"But he's in the best place he can be right now. Go home and get some rest. Let me know what the doctor says."

We went our separate ways then, and I tried to put the sight of Clayton's pale, frightened face out of my thoughts. He was going to fold, I thought, and fold soon. He wasn't up for this at all. But then, neither was I.

* * *

A bright chunk of moon hung in the eastern sky as I made my way home. Traffic on the 134 Freeway had lightened a little by then. The 134 was once a wide-open highway, but eventually it became overburdened like so many of the roads, never empty of people in a hurry to be someplace else.

Hunger, fatigue, and fear urged me toward home, although I dreaded the quiet emptiness that waited for me. Why hadn't I ever gotten a pet? Something that cared when I came and went. Zeus was nowhere around; even my visiting cat had abandoned me.

I poured myself a glass of wine—I'd earned it, I thought. The freezer held a diet tuna casserole, two icy-looking ground beef patties, and some fish sticks. I opted for the tuna, and while I nuked that I sifted through my mail: the usual bills and advertisements ("Instant Credit! 10% Rebate!") The microwave chimed, and a second later the telephone rang.

Noah? Hope pounded in my blood as I answered.

"Susan? It's Margaret."

As if I wouldn't have recognized that voice anywhere.

"Oh. Hi." I probably sounded a little pissed off, even if I didn't want to.

"I called to apologize for this afternoon. It was … Claire and I were having a horrible fight, as you may have gathered."

"Right. I'm sorry, I didn't mean to interrupt."

"I know. And I shouldn't have answered the telephone, but I was expecting a call from a colleague, about Claire."

"Sorry," I said again, even though I wasn't. "So—are things better now?"

I heard a deep, almost endless sigh. "More or less. She has decided she wants to get married, and of course that's impossible."

"Married? Who on earth does she—"

"Her painting teacher. The man is thirty-five years old! And to think this has been going on right under my nose, and I didn't have a clue."

"Is it maybe some schoolgirl crush? Or has he actually encouraged her?"

"According to Claire, he has. I intend to confront him tomorrow and find out. Today was the first I'd heard about it, and I am beside myself trying to decide what to do. Do I send her away to a private school out of town? Do I threaten the man, or try to reason with him? I don't know where to start."

"What does Philippe think?"

"Philippe! Ah, Philippe, as usual, is somewhere in the jungle, and his cell phone doesn't work there. I left a message at the field office, but this crisis may be over before he gets it."

"Can I help?"

"No, dear friend. I have to deal with this on my own. But I wanted you to understand why I was so distracted, and to see how you're doing. I'm so sorry about Noah, but I've always felt you deserved better. In time, you'll find the right man. I know it."

"You're probably right. Don't worry about me, I'm okay, honest. I'm getting used to it already." I was also getting pretty good at lying, but this was no time to whine about my problems. "And you know what you can do—about Claire? Pretend it's not you and your daughter. Pretend you're counseling one of your clients. What would you tell them to do?"

"How did you get so smart?" Margaret said, with a tiny laugh. I could tell the idea hadn't occurred to her. Interesting.

"From listening to you."

"I'll give it a try," she said slowly. "In the meantime, please take care of yourself, and we'll talk soon. And we'll talk about you, not me. Promise?"

"Promise."

Okay, I thought, as I took the tuna casserole from the microwave and washed it down with a second glass of wine. It had been one of the shittiest days of my life. But I had survived it. Sometimes you have to be content with little victories.

* * *

I went to visit Frank after work the next night. He was propped up in bed, watching the six o'clock news on TV, a hardbound edition of *East of Eden* lying open on the pillow across his lap.

"You shouldn't be watching the news," I said as I leaned in for a kiss. He smelled like baby powder. "It'll only scare and depress you."

Frank laughed but then started to cough. His hands clutched the pillow and his face turned red. *Good going, Susan, that took you less than a minute.* I reached for the nurse's call button, but Frank shook his head and pointed to the water glass beside his bed. I gave it to him, keeping my hands around his to steady them.

He slurped some water through the straw in a big, juicy gulp and relinquished the glass.

"God," he said, "my throat gets soooo dry."

Hospitals always freaked me out: the awareness of people gravely ill, even dying, in crowded little cells off harshly lit corridors; the sharp smell of antiseptic, mixed in my imagination with the clear metallic odor of IV fluids and something else, heavy and coppery—blood maybe; and the fear of ending up there myself. I'd had one brief visit for an emergency appendectomy when I was twelve, and I never wanted to repeat the hospital experience.

Sick as he was, Frank picked up on my discomfort. "Pretty creepy, huh?"

I was ashamed. At least I could leave after a while, at least *my* body wasn't turning against me.

"It's not so bad," I lied. "How're you holding up?"

Frank shrugged. "This sucks, Susie. It really sucks."

I pointed to a basket of bright daisies and carnations on the window sill, flanked by a few get-well cards. "Your friends have been busy, I see."

"Flo brought the flowers this afternoon," Frank said.

I cringed because it hadn't occurred to me to send flowers.

"You came at a good time," he continued. "There was a whole flock of people here earlier and I think the nurses were getting annoyed. This is nice. Just you and me. We can visit. But I'm getting a little loopy, don't mind me. Had a morphine jolt a few minutes ago."

He made a twirling motion with his hand, the one with the IV needle taped to it. I shuddered and looked away.

"I probably won't be able to tell the difference," I said.

He laughed again, but carefully. No cough this time.

"I sent Clayton home," he said, and his voice was growing a little fuzzy. Good. I could hang out for thirty minutes or so, until he dozed off, and then leave with a clear conscience.

"Told him to feed Ralph and give himself a break," Frank continued. "But he won't. He'll be back later. I know it. He's been so good to me. Don't deserve it."

"Sure you do."

"Don't deserve him. Didn't deserve you either, Suse."

"Let's not go there, Frank. You need to rest."

"Don't patronize me just because I'm dying." He smirked. "Hey—sounds like the first line of a country and western song, huh?"

"Sorta."

"Yeah. Well, look—there's some stuff I want to say, and I'm running out of time. I always thought, someday I'll tell Susie, I'll find a way to make her understand how much I love her, even if I didn't act like it."

He was fighting the morphine haze by then, I could tell.

"You don't have to—"

"I know. But I need to. Let me get it off my chest, okay? I screwed up your life, and it's the only thing I really, really regret. You gotta understand that leaving you ... was the hardest thing ... the hardest thing I ever did. But I had to do it. Had to."

"I know. And you didn't screw up my life, I did that on my own. And it's not that screwed up, by the way. Look, you did what you needed to do. It hurt. I survived. End of story."

"Is it?" Frank's pupils were immense. I wanted to calm him down so he'd go to sleep and quit poking the open wound of our breakup. Sure, it had healed over, but it left a weak spot that didn't bear up well under probing, especially with Noah's betrayal so fresh in my heart.

"Yeah," I said. "And I don't blame you for anything, so let it go."

"Liar."

"Hey, I didn't drive all the way out here so you could pick a fight with me. Let's not waste the time you have being pissy with each other, all right?"

"Right," he said, and his voice was getting weak. "You're a winner, Susie. A winner …"

His eyelids fluttered. I could feel his life seeping away, and I yearned for a way to erase the past and neutralize all the bitter feelings that stuck to me like burrs on a wool blanket. I wanted to be free of my anger, but if I let it go, I might evaporate into nothing. Some people claim that all we are is the sum of our memories, and I needed those memories to keep me real.

I peeked at my watch while we sat in silence. Ten more minutes, and he'd be out. And I could escape.

Nine minutes later, Dan Fellows walked in, and I forgot all about time limits.

Frank was almost fully into Sleep Land, but my excited "Hi!" pulled him back. I was focused on Dan, but from the edge of my vision I saw Frank rouse himself, then stiffen in pain.

Dan smiled and nodded to me on his way to Frank's bedside. "Hey, old man. You look like shit."

Frank found a smile somehow and waved weakly. "No sudden moves," he mumbled. "And what're you doing here anyway?"

Dan laughed. "I was feeling noble. Thanks for noticing."

He pulled the second visitor's chair next to mine and eased into it. In that stark hospital room, he was a welcome sight: soft black leather jacket, red shirt, jeans, cowboy boots. He smelled as clean as a forest in springtime, and his beard had filled in since the birthday party. It suited him.

I grinned like an idiot when Dan turned my way.

"He behaving himself?" he asked. "Guess we don't have to worry about him goosing nurses."

"Don't be too sure," Frank said.

Right on cue, a hunky young man in blue scrubs and rubber-soled shoes burst into the room. His skin was the color of a Starbucks latte, his hair a mass of shiny chocolate curls. He smiled at Frank, showing two rows of impossibly white, perfect teeth.

"How you doing, Mr. K?" he asked. His voice had a soft Jamaican lilt.

"Hurts a little, Silas," Frank replied.

Silas's right hand went toward a little chart taped to the wall beside the bed. A succession of cartoon faces ran a left-to-right gamut of expressions from smile to open-mouthed pain grimace. Silas pointed to a face somewhere between discomfort and agony. Frank jerked his head to the right, and Silas's lips pressed together.

"I'll be back," he said.

Even though we were strangers to each other, Silas patted my shoulder as he left. Maybe it was required nurse behavior. His shoes squished away on the shiny hospital floor.

Frank wiggled his eyebrows. "See what I mean?"

To cover my embarrassment, I laughed along with Dan.

"When do you get sprung?" Dan wanted to know.

Frank's huge, dramatic shrug started a coughing spasm. A few seconds later he settled down. "That happens," he explained.

I filled Dan in on Dr. Wardell's explanation, which the CT scan had confirmed. The tumors were growing. I tried to be brief, for Frank's sake. Not that he hadn't heard it already. Not that he didn't know the prognosis far too well.

"Clayton's getting a nurse's aide lined up," Frank told us. News to me. "For when he's at work."

"I hope he's cute," Dan said. "The aide, I mean."

"Not if I can help it," Clayton said.

In contrast to Silas, Clayton had slipped up on us in thin-soled loafers that hadn't made a sound. I must have twitched when he spoke, because he patted my shoulder the same way Silas had. Did I look that much in need of comfort?

Frank's laugh was moist and strangled. "He's trying to find a sixty-year-old grandma who did time in the army."

"Don't think I won't," Clayton said.

I relinquished my chair. I'd done my duty and was ready to split.

Dan stood up, too. "Don't want to wear you out, old man."

Frank didn't try to persuade either of us to stay. He looked drained. "Thanks, Danny. Suse. Be careful going home."

We left Clayton rearranging Frank's pillow and asking about pain meds, and I felt so relieved to escape and so damn guilty that I could walk away from the suffering on Frank's face, from the hissing and gurgling machines, from the harsh clang of metal and the smell of disinfectant.

Dan kept his eyes forward on our short walk to the elevators. Even allowing for the cruelty of hospital lighting, his face was pinched and pale. It seemed to take hours for the elevator to reach us, and Dan kept jabbing the call button.

I tried to engage in meaningful conversation and offered up the brilliant observation, "It's a big shock to see him in here."

Dan puffed his cheeks and let out a loud hiss of breath. "Damn straight. Up 'til now, I could almost pretend it wasn't happening."

The elevator chimed, and the doors swooshed open. Dan put his hand on my waist and guided me into the elevator, and it was a relief to have someone take over and direct me, even in that small way. I stood near enough to catch a whiff of his cologne, so crisp and green-smelling that I longed to lean closer and inhale. But I didn't. Dan punched the lobby button, and the elevator started its lurching, noisy descent.

"They don't have a bar anyplace in here, do they?" he asked.

"No. But they should."

"No kidding."

"There's a cafeteria downstairs," I told him, "but I think coffee's the strongest thing on the menu."

He shuddered. "Hospital coffee." A few seconds later he asked, "Want to grab a cup and see if it's as bad as we think it is?"

Frank had warned me to be careful with Dan. How careful did I need to be? How could anyone hurt me more than Frank had? More than Noah had?

It's only a cup of coffee, not a marriage proposal.

"Sure," I said.

A few people sat eating dinner in the cafeteria, but there were plenty of empty tables. I grabbed a muffin to soak up the coffee, and when we got to the cashier, Dan insisted on paying.

"Well, then—thanks for dinner," I said, and he laughed. It was sort of a pathetic laugh, but at least he made the effort.

We sat by a window that overlooked floodlit tree ferns and a broad-leafed shrub I couldn't identify. The setting was deceptively peaceful, and the coffee wasn't half bad.

I liked the way Dan sat, legs thrust out, as if he felt entitled to every inch of space he wanted. Me, I'd always tried to compress myself. The Big Woman Syndrome, Margaret explained. She had some of the same issues, although her bones were finer and more closely spaced than mine.

Margaret. I wondered how she and Claire were doing, but I wasn't about to risk another call. Not yet.

"Man," Dan said, "he doesn't have long, does he?"

"I don't think they ever know for sure. It depends on so many things, on how much of a fighter he is, and …"

I trailed off because I didn't know how to finish the sentence without disrespecting Frank, but Dan seemed to understand.

"Yeah, he's always been Mr. Easy-Does-It. Man, I'm going to miss him." He stirred his coffee and seemed to be studying its dark brown depths. "He and Clayton have always been there for me, you know? One time a couple of years ago when I was in a real dry spell, really broke, they loaned me five hundred bucks to get my car fixed, and they never bugged me about paying it back. Never once mentioned it. And when I finally did repay them, they acted like I was doing them some big favor."

"Frank's always been generous," I agreed. It was true. Frank was generous with money, with his time, with his help.

"Hey," Dan said, and his right hand closed over my left and squeezed gently, "I don't mean to go on and on about myself here. This must be hell for you. Sometimes I forget that you two were … you were together, and you still have feelings for him and—"

"I do. Sure, I have feelings. But don't think for a minute I'm still in love with him."

My words came out louder than I intended.

Dan held his hand up like a traffic cop. "Whoa, don't get me wrong, okay? I wasn't implying that, I just meant that this has to be really, really painful for you, given the history. That's all."

"Sorry—I'm a little edgy tonight."

"Not to worry. I get it—you've moved on. You're with somebody else now, right?"

I took a sip of coffee and stalled for time. What difference would my answer make anyway? Part of me wanted to lie and assure Dan Fellows that I wasn't interested. And part of me wanted to see what all the warnings were about.

"Not exactly," I said and looked into those hypnotic hazel eyes, acting every inch the silly little slut.

In my defense, I wasn't myself. My emotions had been rubbed raw from seeing how much closer Frank was to dying, from Noah's defection, from Margaret's abandonment. I was ripe for distraction, any distraction. And there he was.

I held my breath and waited to see if he'd take the bait.

He did.

"In that case," he said, "would you maybe be up for dinner and a movie this weekend?"

The cafeteria was filling up. *Must be shift change,* I thought. Most of the incoming crowd wore gray-blue scrubs like Frank's nurse's. A couple of white-smocked doctors sat next to us, stethoscopes draped around their necks. Silverware clattered on Formica table tops, and the smells of soup, cooked meat, and coffee swirled around us, along with voices so intermingled they might have been bees swarming their hive.

The cup was an anchor in my hand, pale coffee-stained china, with a little chip in the handle. I raised it in a toast while I finished a slow count from one to ten.

Take that, Noah!

"Sounds great," I said.

Chapter 9
Life is Full of Surprises

Dr. Wardell sent Frank home Saturday morning. Clayton called to let me know they'd found a nurse's aide to look after Frank on weekdays. Clayton himself would handle the night shift. I made approving noises and promised to check in on Frank soon, while most of my thoughts focused on my date with Dan.

Did I feel guilty? A little. Frank was dying, Margaret and her daughter were at war, Clayton was trying to figure out end-of-life care for his lover. On the other hand, my big worries were whether my hair would look good and if I could find a new dress that wouldn't have to be altered.

The answer was yes on both counts, and by the time Dan picked me up that night, I felt as attractive as I ever had. In a cloud of perfume with a name like "Pretty Woman," I applied a layer of lip gloss as I saw his car pull up in front of my house.

His jeans had been replaced with black cords, but Dan's leather jacket felt like an old friend. His blue shirt was silk, from the look of it, and I decided the jersey knit dress I'd chosen would blend okay. I bought it mainly for the color, a cool shade of navy, and because it draped well and just grazed the top of my knees. Frank Krajewski wasn't the only man who'd admired my legs, and I wanted to show them off.

I opened the door a second after Dan rang the bell, then cursed my eagerness. But it didn't seem to matter when I saw the broad smile on his face—a smile that got bigger as he checked me out.

"Wow," he said. "Look at you. Do they make 'em any more gorgeous?"

It took every ounce of resolve not to lapse into schoolgirl giggles.

I knew Dan lived on a limited income, and I sort of expected him to drive a beat-up old jalopy, so the well-maintained if middle-aged Toyota coupe was a welcome relief. Stick shift, I noticed, and I thought, *I bet he'd let me drive* his *car if I asked.*

We ate at a tiny Italian place in the east part of Old Town Pasadena. The hostess's face lit up when we entered; she hugged Dan, ushered us to a corner table, and quickly produced a bottle of wine and two glasses.

"This just came in," she told him, ignoring me totally.

As the hostess bustled away, I tilted my head in her direction. "A relative?"

He peered at me over his menu. "No, that's Olga. I did a piece about this place for *Southland* last year, and she's been showing her gratitude ever since." He made a sweeping gesture at the menu. "Order anything you like—it's on the house. I recommend the Penne Sorrentino, though. It's the best."

He was right – the penne came in a good *arrabiata* sauce, just enough bite, with plenty of tender chicken. I chewed away with blissful abandon until I became aware of Dan's amused expression. I put down my fork and felt an uncomfortably familiar flush creep up my face, but Dan put me at ease when he grinned and said, "I like a woman who enjoys her food."

We walked to the theater, a few blocks away on Colorado. Dan had suggested a French film in black and white with English subtitles. I'd studied French in college, so I caught enough without the extra help. The film, "Mal de Mer" (literally, sea sickness), was about two people who were probably meant for each other but kept missing their connection, first on a bus, then a train, then a plane. Finally they ended up on an ocean cruise, but she got seasick.

As we strolled back to the car after the film, Dan took my hand. The night had turned chilly, and when I shivered, he put his arm around me and pulled me close. Yum. He smelled delicious, that same fresh-air scent I'd noticed at the hospital, and I felt his warmth through both our jackets.

"Well," he said, "that wasn't quite what I expected."

"I enjoyed it, though," I said, and it was true. "The French don't seem so hell-bent on casting raving beauties. Those people had interesting faces. Lived in."

Dan's laugh echoed down the mostly empty street. Mist had begun to collect on the tall lamp posts and store signs, and everything looked secretive and hushed.

He opened the Toyota's passenger door, and I paused before getting in. "This has been fun," I said.

Now. Kiss me now.

He didn't; all he had for me was a big, wide grin. "You're a good sport."

After he pulled onto the street, he explained that a friend of his had reviewed "Mal de Mer" for *Variety* and had raved about it. "But I should have known better. David's way more cerebral than I am." He paused. "Actually, I wanted to impress you."

"Me? Why?"

His eyes stayed on the road, but his right hand grazed my arm. "Frank's told me how classy you are, how smart. I couldn't exactly take you to a Vin Diesel action flick on our first date and still have you respect me in the morning."

"Actually, I like Vin Diesel," I said, fighting to keep my voice neutral. "He has a cute grin."

The drive home seemed all too short. I'd played the scene out in my head at least a dozen different ways. When we got to my place, should I invite him in for a nightcap? Was that being too obvious, too easy? According to both Frank and Flo, Dan dated a lot of women. Did I want to stand out by not giving in right away? Or would I miss the boat if I did? I really wanted him to kiss me, I wanted to feel his skin on mine, to see the body under those clothes, to touch him as much and as long as I chose.

"Susan? You didn't fall asleep on me, did you?"

Hell! I'd zoned out for a second, and I struggled to cover my lapse.

"Sorry. I was just thinking about that scene in the airport when they pass each other going opposite ways on the escalator," I lied.

"Yeah. Pretty poignant."

Poignant. I was dating a man who used words like *poignant.* I don't think I'd heard it spoken before.

"Mmmm hmmm. Anyway, what were you saying?" My heart sped up. We were almost to my freeway exit.

"Not that important—just wondering how Frank's doing. Maybe I'll stop by tomorrow." Dan was still watching the road: a very focused driver. I liked that.

"I bet he'd appreciate it," I said. "He's probably—"

"Jesus!" Dan yelled, jamming on the brakes to avoid colliding with a BMW going at least ninety as it cut in front of us. The driver was a young male with dark spiky hair, but he went by so fast I couldn't see anything else.

"Great reflexes," I said as soon as my heart started beating again.

Dan shook his head. "Damn kids. Think they're immortal. You okay? Didn't mean to give you a near-death experience this early in our relationship."

So we had a relationship. Cool.

I needn't have worried over my next move because Dan took care of that. He pulled up to my place, helped me out of the car, put his arm around me as we walked to my front door, and planted a friendly kiss on my lips, quick and light. Then he held me at arm's length.

Okay, what'd I do wrong? Didn't like the way I kiss?

"I'm kicking myself in the butt right now. I promised my niece a tennis lesson at seven tomorrow. Otherwise, I'd try and persuade you to ask me in for a nightcap, and … whatever."

And "whatever?" Hmmmm. And what a convenient little niece.

I masked my disappointment. "How old's your niece?"

"Fifteen." He smiled. "She's a real piece of work—has my brother wrapped around her little finger. And every other guy she wants, Uncle Dan included."

Okay, laugh it off.

I did. "Then I'll have to give you a rain check."

"I'm counting on it."

He kissed me again, a real kiss this time, his tongue flicking over my lips, arms pulling me to him. Nice, lingering kiss—better than Noah's, I quickly decided. Then with a huge sigh, he let me go.

I didn't know whether to be disappointed or relieved as he drove off. But there was nothing I could do about it except wait and see if he called again, or if I'd been a total wipe-out as a date.

* * *

Every time my phone rang over the next few days, I felt a wild tingling hope that it would be Dan, calling to set up another date. But no word from him. By Wednesday afternoon, I concluded that he'd had a lousy time and had covered it graciously.

I buried my head in the sand as much as possible. I'd conquered the urge to visit Frank on Sunday because it would have been a blatant move to try and see Dan again. If I knew it, so would Dan, and so would Frank. On Tuesday, I did call to check on Frank. His voice was fuzzy and sad. He said he didn't need anything, and I didn't offer to visit. My lame-assed excuse to myself was that he sounded so tired, I didn't want to wear him out. Ever polite, Frank thanked me for calling and promised to let me know if there was anything I could do. I hung up with the uneasy feeling of a job done only half right.

* * *

Lilah Cantrell returned from vacation no nicer than when she left, but at least I had Angel back. She seemed to have survived her time in Bord's lair with no visible scars, but something was bothering her, I could tell. So when she tapped on my office door Wednesday afternoon and asked in a soft voice, "Can we talk?" I wasn't all that surprised.

"Sure," I said. "Close the door."

Angel sat across from me, hands clenched in her lap. "I've been stressing out all week on how to tell you this," she began, and I felt a slow twist of dread in my guts. What could be so serious and horrible?

Angel bit her lower lip and took a breath. "When I was working for Derek, he did a couple of things that really bothered me," she began.

I relaxed, preparing for a standard-issue harassment complaint. Those I could handle in my sleep, and it would be a pleasure to lodge one against Bord.

"Go on," I said in my most encouraging voice.

"First off, he fudged a few things on his expense reports."

I knew it!

"Okay," I said, "anything big?"

The blonde curls bounced from side to side. "A few lattes on his way in to work—he said he had to stop and use the bathroom because traffic was so bad."

I almost giggled at the picture of Derek Bord explaining this to Angel.

"Yeah, well the poor guy does have a long drive in from Laguna," I said. "Too bad his bladder's as tiny as the rest of him."

Angel grinned and seemed to loosen up a little.

"It's a stretch," I said, "but probably not a huge ethical violation. That kind of thing is his call, not yours. Okay?"

Angel nodded, but her fingers were still tightly interlaced in her lap.

"What else?" I asked, because I knew there was more.

"He asked me some stuff about you."

"Me?" *Didn't the jerk have anything better to wonder about?* "Like what?"

My telephone shrilled, and by habit I looked at the ID display. Outside number, no name. *Let it go to voicemail then.*

"He was asking personal stuff, and I didn't know how to handle it," Angel said. "I mean, he wanted to know about your ex, what happened there, did you still see him, stuff like that."

I took a few seconds to absorb the news. How weird: why was Derek Bord poking around in the rubble of my marriage?

"What'd you tell him?"

"I tried not to tell him anything! I mean, at first I just said I didn't know anything, it all happened before I came to work for you. Which is true."

I nodded.

"But he kept at me," Angel continued. "He said something like, 'Come on, I know you two are tight, surely she's said something, or you've heard something.' And he … he sort of implied I owed it to him to tell him. He said … he said he was assessing everyone's strengths, trying to decide the new staffing configuration. His words, not mine."

"Meaning if you didn't give him something, you might not be part of the new 'staffing configuration'?"

"Yeah. Or you might not be."

Holy shit.

"I just said I knew there was … a third party involved, but that it'd been pretty amicable, all things considered, and that you and Frank were okay with each other now."

"A third party?" Jesus, what else did the grapevine say?

"Well, that sounds pretty harmless, Angel. You did good."

She didn't look me in the eye. *Oh God, there's more.*

"I tried. But he kept asking little questions, like were you dating anyone else, how stable was your outside life, stuff like that."

How stable? The little prick! I could file my own complaint about this.

"And you told him … what?"

"Just that I knew you were dating somebody, and it seemed really stable, and …" she trailed off. "And that's about it. The thing is, I don't think he's going to let it go at that. I could tell—you know the way he looks at you sometimes with those creepy eyes?"

I nodded. Bord's misaligned eyes could be unnerving because you never knew for sure if he was looking right at you.

"It's like he was saying, 'I know there's more. I'm not done with you yet.' And I'm scared if he doesn't get it from me, but somebody else tells him something, he'll think I was lying. And then …"

"Let's think this through. What else could he find out, and is there anything you can tell him that'll keep him off your back?"

Again her teeth scraped over her lower lip, squeezing the color out. "I don't know. I mean—I hear things. You know I don't eavesdrop on purpose, but I listen so if you make an appointment and forget to tell me, I can still put it on your calendar."

"And?"

"And *is* something going on with your ex? You've been talking to him a *lot* lately, and Noah seems to be MIA, and it's none of my business, I know, but Ginny covers my phones when I'm not here, and if *she* picked up a message or anything and figured out what was—"

"Frank has cancer," I told her. "He's dying. And, yeah, I've been talking to him more than usual. Because he doesn't have much time left. And you can tell Bord that, with a clear conscience."

Angel's expression went from shock to relief to dismay, in less than ten seconds. "That's—oh God. I'm so sorry. It must be terrible for you."

"Not as much as for Frank and for Clayton—that's Frank's … that's his third party."

Angel nodded. "I figured."

After a respectful pause, she asked, "So you think that maybe it's okay to tell Derek that Frank's … that he's sick?"

"By all means. It'll get him off your case, and I sure don't see what harm it'll do."

Angel left in a flurry of condolences and appreciation, and I retrieved the voicemail message left by the unknown caller. It turned out to be Margaret's friend Jennifer. How did *she* track me down, and what did she want?

"I'm worried about Margaret," she explained when I called her back. "She hasn't been in her office all week, and she didn't say anything about being gone. She isn't answering her phone. Do you know if she's okay?"

I hesitated. Margaret was a pretty private woman, but she was clearly fond of Jennifer.

"She and Claire were having a big fight last week. I'm not sure what all was going on, but maybe she's taking time off to get it settled. If I hear from her, I'll tell her to get in touch with you."

"Thanks," she said. Her voice was friendly and warm, and I wondered why I'd thought I disliked her. "And let me know if there's anything I can do. Her mail was piled up, so I collected it for her. I left her a message about it, but if you see her …"

"I'll tell her. Thanks. She'll appreciate it."

Hmmmm. Margaret didn't say anything about blowing off work. That was definitely not her style. Whatever was going on couldn't be good. I thought about driving over to see her, but from her reaction when I accidentally intruded on the family feud, I figured she wouldn't exactly want that.

Half an hour later, Flo called. I recognized the vodka-and-cigarettes voice even before she identified herself.

"I hope you don't mind me calling at work," she began. "Clayton thought it'd be okay."

"Of course," I said, my defenses moving into position. "Is something wrong?"

"Nothing new—and I won't burn up a lot of your work time. But I'm organizing a couple of things for Frank and Clayton, and I thought you might want in on them."

"What kind of things?" I asked, and I hoped I didn't sound as suspicious as I felt.

Flo's low, throaty laugh sounded innocent enough. "Oh, a telephone tree for one thing. You know, so Clayton doesn't have to call everybody himself if … when … there's a change, you know, or if they need something. And I'm setting up a visitor schedule so people will stop by to give Clayton a break, and cheer both of them up."

What a nice idea, I thought even as my muscles clenched. *But do you have to drag me into this? I'm not part of their lives. I don't want to be.*

"I could probably help with the telephones," I said after a guilty silence as I rummaged through my pathetic excuse list. "But I don't know if I can commit to a visiting schedule. This job—"

"I understand," Flo said. "Most of us are in the same predicament. But I want to at least give it a try."

And what are you doing that's so all-fired important, Susan Krajewski?

"That's really nice of you. I'd like to help if I didn't have to—"

"What about next Wednesday? I've got the next few nights covered, but if you could spare a couple of hours next week, I know the guys would be ever so grateful. And honestly, I don't think he'll last too much longer."

Flo sure knew how to shame a person into good behavior.

"Okay, count me in."

"You're a prize, Susan. Thank you."

I hung up feeling both noble and victimized.

By the time our conversation ended, my email inbox had registered ten incomings, so I put Frank out of my thoughts and focused on earning my paycheck.

* * *

My reluctant agreement to help out with Frank must have stirred up some good karma, though. Dan Fellows called that night as I was polishing off a Lean Cuisine pizza.

"Hey, gorgeous," he said.

Pleasure bubbled up my spine. "Hey, handsome."

Easy, girl. Play it light.

"How was your day?" he asked. No one since Frank had asked me that.

"Not bad. I earned my keep. You?"

"Same here. I got a rush assignment Monday morning and it really buried me, but I made the deadline today."

I hoped he was telling the truth. "Good boy."

"I was wondering if you wanted to risk another date with me," he said.

I've never been good at playing hard to get, but I tried. At least I made myself count to ten before I answered, and as I got to eight, Dan added, "My niece beat the crap out of me on Sunday, by the way."

"No good deed goes unpunished."

"Ha ha. Anyway, a friend of mine is in a play out in NoHo, and I thought maybe you'd like to go with me? Friday?"

"A play?" I asked, trying to sound like I had a million different options.

"Yep. It's a little theater thing—really little, equity waiver. But my friend is dating the playwright—and she's a pretty good actress, so the play probably won't be horrible."

I laughed. "Well, that's a great recommendation. Real appealing."

Dan said, "Sorry. I didn't mean it like that. Actually, Gretchen usually has good instincts for interesting stuff. I can't remember everything she said, but it's kind of a ghost story set in Manhattan Beach."

"The ghost of Joe the Surfer?"

He laughed again. "Something like that. If it's awful, we can sneak out—and I'll take you to the movie of your choice. Please say yes."

That did it. "It does sound kinda fun." I pulled a loose thread from the hem of my t-shirt and took a deep breath. "Sure. I'd love to. Thanks."

"Great!" The pleasure in his voice sounded genuine.

I'd just rinsed off my dinner dishes when another call came in. Well, wasn't *I* getting popular.

It was Judy. "Where the hell is Margaret?" she demanded without so much as a "Hi, how are ya?"

"I take it Jennifer called you?"

"Yeah. And I told her to call *you*. Then she called back and said that *you* said Margaret and Claire had a fight last week. What's going on?"

A tiny wave of irritation flicked through my concern over Margaret. Where did Jennifer and Judy get off using me as their information-gathering service anyway?

I sighed. "Don't know exactly. Margaret said Claire wants to marry her painting teacher."

"No shit!"

"And she didn't know what to do about it. She can't exactly lock Claire in her room for the next ten years."

"Not a bad idea."

"I meant to try and call her again, but I've been kinda busy. Frank took a turn for the worse, and I got caught up in that." I added this gentle reminder that I had a life and responsibilities every bit as demanding as Judy did, but I didn't mention my date with Dan.

"Excuse me? You're playing nurse to your ex, when your good friend has disappeared?"

"I'm not playing nurse! I just went to see him in the hospital. And we don't know Margaret's disappeared."

"Yeah, but it's not like her to—"

"Hey, I didn't notice *you* going out of your way to check up on her."

"With my working conditions? I don't even get a bathroom break, let alone phone privileges. But you, Ms. Junior Executive, could at least have your secretary make a few calls and see if Margaret's dead or alive."

I wanted to slam the phone down on her, but part of my brain insisted Judy was half right.

"Okay, okay," I said. "I'm sorry. I'm a terrible friend."

"Did I say that?"

"No. Look—I'll call her. If I don't get an answer, I'll come get you and we'll drive to her house and peek in the windows to be sure there aren't any bodies lying around, okay?"

I hung up and tried Margaret's home number first, not expecting much, so when one of the girls answered, all I could do was stammer my name and ask for Margaret.

It turned out to be Deirdre on the other end of the line. "Mama's not here," she said, and I heard an alarming little catch in her voice. "She and Daddy took Claire to Aunt Sophie's in Avignon."

"Avignon?" I repeated stupidly.

"France," Deirdre explained, polite as ever. She paused. "I meant to call you. Mama asked me to, but things have been so crazy, and I didn't know what to say. They left two days ago."

"Is she okay?"

Another hesitation. "Sort of. Claire—you know how *dramatic* she can be."

I didn't, but I made agreeing little noises into the phone.

"When Mama told her she couldn't see John again—that's the teacher, the one silly Claire wants to marry—Claire threatened to kill herself. I don't think she would, but Mama was worried enough she decided to get her out of town. Aunt Sophie has a big house, and it's quiet, and Mama and Daddy want to spend some time with Claire and work through this bizarre fixation of hers."

Deirdre apologized for not telling me sooner, then gave me Margaret's sister's phone number in Avignon; she said it would be all right to call, assured me that she herself was doing fine in Margaret's absence. I offered help, of course, which she politely declined.

Poor Margaret, I thought after the call. The therapist in her had to be terrified. Her own daughter … And if Philippe Deschanels took time off from his career, it was pretty damn serious.

When I called Judy to report and give her the phone number in France, she asked if I was going to call.

"I think it's the middle of the night there," I told her, "so probably not."

Truth be told, I was more than a little hurt that Margaret hadn't taken five minutes to call me herself before she left. A selfish, dumb reaction, I knew, but I thought I'd better put off phoning her until my feelings settled down.

* * *

On Friday night when we walked into the theater in NoHo—the renovated artsy section of North Hollywood—Dan gestured toward the cast photographs tacked to a cork board by the entrance. He pointed to a picture of a drop-dead gorgeous blonde. "That's Gretchen," he said.

"Yikes," I said in my usual brilliant fashion. *I wonder how he knows her. I wonder how* well *he knows her.*

The tiny theater lobby still held traces of its former retail-store life: concrete floor, big windows now darkly curtained. A small cart at one end held cellophaned cookies, a coffee urn, and Styrofoam cups. We passed on the refreshments.

Dan put his arm around me as we eased down the narrow aisle inside the musty auditorium, and I had to fight myself to keep from melting into him. Most of the ninety-nine well-worn seats were filled, but his friend had arranged two prime spots front and center for us.

"Widow's Walk" was actually a decent production. Gretchen played a widow convinced that the young man living in the other half of her duplex was her late husband's reincarnation. It had a sad ending, and Gretchen was very good. She got to scream and cry and fall down a small flight of stairs. When she came out to take her bow at the end of the play, Dan leaped to his feet and clapped wildly. I followed his lead with slightly less enthusiasm.

As the house lights went up, Dan stretched and smiled at me. "Did you like it?"

His expression was so earnest I almost laughed.

"It was great."

He looked relieved. "Yeah, I thought so, too. Little theater's always a risk. You never know."

We started up the aisle, and he put his arm around my waist again, light and casual, as a warm flush of pleasure surged up from my toes to my brain.

"Want to stick around and say hi to Gretch?"

I didn't. "Sure."

The "backstage" of the theater was a cement pad right outside the rear door, where a cluster of people were smoking and drinking coffee. I recognized a couple of the cast members. Voices blended together in an indistinct murmur.

I heard a woman call out, "Daniel!"

Gretchen dropped her cigarette and flung herself at Dan, wrapped her arms around him fiercely. "Thanks for coming."

She kissed him, firmly, on the lips. Dan kissed her back and then gently pried himself free. I wondered where Gretchen's playwright boyfriend was during all this. Dan drew me close and introduced us. Unfortunately, he didn't stop with my name.

"Remember Frank and Clay? The guys next door on Oakshire? Susan is Frank's ex-wife."

Gretchen's blue eyes widened slightly. "Oh, wow. *That* Susan."

She shook my hand with a warm, firm grip.

"*That* Susan?" I asked. I looked at Dan.

"Oh, that came out wrong," Gretchen continued. "I mean, Frank never bad-mouthed you or anything."

Was she making fun of me? It didn't matter because Dan's arm tightened around me and when no clever response came to mind, I just kept my mouth shut. For a change.

Gretchen pulled another cigarette from an impossibly tiny purse. Dan took the matches from her and lit it. She put her hand on his, lightly, to guide the match.

"So," she said, exhaling the smoke with an incredible aura of sensuality, "what are you guys up to now? There's a party at Marcia's."

Dan laughed. "There's always a party at Marcia's."

He looked at me like he was trying to make up his mind.

Gretchen tapped the ash on her cigarette and wiggled her eyebrows. "Of course, you might not want to expose Susan to *all* your friends in one night."

Dan kissed her cheek lightly. "Maybe next time," he said.

* * *

"If you want to go to that party—" I began as soon as we were out of range.

Dan took my hand and swung it in time to his steps—a casual, well-practiced gesture, it seemed. "No way," he said. "Bunch of artist-wannabes getting wasted and whining about how life is unfair. I can think of a million other things I'd like to do with you."

"Such as?"

He kissed me, open mouthed and hot. "Come home with me?"

Although I was wearing my sexiest underwear and had tucked a toothbrush and a couple of condoms into my purse, I pretended to think it over for all of five heartbeats. "Okay."

I remembered Dan's apartment building from one of my brief, tense visits to Frank and Clayton early in their relationship. Tax return time, I think. It was standard Southern California Dingbat: a cutout of a palm tree on the front of the building and "Shangri-La" in big script beneath the palm. Three-story cement box, rusted railings on the balconies and a few round patio tables with tattered umbrellas ringing a pale aqua pool.

Dan's second-floor slice of this tropical heaven was sparely furnished but comfortable and clean. I sensed a woman's touch in the décor—a vivid purple chenille throw on the hunter-green sofa, and a cluster of white pillar candles on the dining table that infused the room with a hint of gardenia.

"Would you like a drink?" he asked. "Wine? Coffee? Amaretto?" His tongue caressed the last word, made it sound so seductive that I had to go for it.

We clinked tiny glasses full of amber liquid, and I took a sip. Yum. I strolled around the living room, checked out the bookcase. A nice collection: Hemingway and Fitzgerald alongside Anne Tyler and T.C. Boyle. Bukowski's *South of No North*. And all the books looked as if they'd been read.

"Want some more?" he asked because my glass was empty.

I shook my head. "That was perfect."

Dan took the glass from me and set it down, then put his arms around me and kissed a drop of Amaretto from my lip.

"You taste as good as you smell," he whispered as he stroked my hair.

I wanted to stay there forever, his hands moving up and down my body, my breath suddenly coming in spurts, the taste of Amaretto in my mouth and the feel of Dan's lips on mine. He eased my jacket off, his hand gliding over my breasts, lingering softly. I closed my eyes and pulled his face toward me for another kiss, a long, deep one that was making me dizzy. This was going to feel so good.

That was my last conscious thought before his doorbell rang. The gentle chime yanked me back into myself. Dan stopped kissing me and looked uncertainly at the door. The bell chimed again, and someone started knocking. Hard.

A young woman was making all that racket, I saw a minute later when he opened the door. She had on a short, tight leather skirt and a snug knit top that left nothing to the imagination. Her brown hair stood up in wet-looking spikes, and she held a bouquet of red roses.

"You didn't call me," she said in the voice of a disappointed child.

Dan tried to block the doorway, but she looked past him and saw me in the corner by the bookshelf.

"Youuuuuuuu," she wailed and pushed past him.

Dan seized her arm. "Sally, don't do this. Go home. I'll call you later."

"That's what you always say! Youuuuuuuu," she shrieked again and hurled the roses at him. He raised his arm and deflected the bouquet. Sally turned and stalked out the door. I heard her high heels thunder down the stairs.

The roses had spilled out of their wrapping onto the carpet. I stared at them while I tried to figure out what to do. Dan leaned against the closed door, his face serious and pale.

"I'm so sorry," he began.

I couldn't take my eyes off those poor pathetic roses scattered across the floor.

"I'd better go."

"She won't be back."

Sally's surprise visit had clearly shaken him, though, because he didn't try very hard to persuade me to stick around.

On the way to my place, he said, "She's ... I dated her for a while, but we just didn't click. She's so intense, she was planning our wedding by the third date. I didn't call her, so she called me and asked me out, and I turned her down. I thought that would make her understand it was over, but I guess I was wrong."

"Maybe she got the message tonight."

He nodded and smiled, but he didn't look happy. "Yeah, I think so. Listen, I'm real sorry. This has never happened before, and wouldn't you know it'd be on the one night I'm with someone I really like. I hope you'll give me another chance. Soon?"

We were at my house by then, and I'd never been so glad to see it. I took a deep breath. *Well, at least the competition was another woman this time.*

My reflection stared stupidly back at me from the side window. *Serves you right,* I told her. *It's not like Frank didn't warn you this might happen.*

"I've never been good at the triangle thing," I told him. Sally might be gone, but Dan couldn't say anything to reassure me that there weren't more where she came from. A lot more.

We sat in the car for a minute. Moonlight bounced off the Toyota's hood in streaks of silver, and the neighborhood was so quiet I could hear the tick of the cooling engine. Dan's hands still gripped the steering wheel, and he was looking out the window, not at me.

"It's not usually like this," he said finally.

Meaning what? You usually do a better job of keeping your girlfriends separated?

I didn't feel like trying for a snappy comeback, so I pushed open the car door. No need for chivalry at this point.

Dan got out and walked me to my front door, but he didn't try to kiss me. He waved sheepishly after I got the door open and stepped inside, and then he walked away, head down.

What a waste, I thought as the Toyota's taillights faded down the street. Maybe he'd call me again, and maybe I'd take another chance on him. But even if we gave it a try, I knew I'd always be listening for that knock on the door. Damn.

Chapter 10
No Match for the Darkness

By Wednesday night, I was almost glad I'd let Flo strong-arm me into visiting Frank. I needed distraction from my own whiny-assed troubles. And the minute I saw Frank, I stopped feeling sorry for myself.

In the two weeks since I'd seen him, the cancer had carved trenches in his face, and his skin hung from his arms in pale folds. I was barely able to stop a hand-to-the-mouth "Oh my God!" when I saw him. Clayton bore the telltale caregiver's marks of worry and sleep deprivation.

The hospice nurse, Becky, was there when I arrived. She looked about my age and was so cheerful and pretty it seemed impossible that she dealt with death and dying on a daily basis. How did she do her job? How was she ever able to smile like she did when she shook my hand?

Flo had warned me that Frank was now set up with a hospital bed in the family room. Their big-screen TV flickered mutely in the background while Becky questioned Frank and jotted something in a slim blue notebook. I counted six prescription bottles on the table next to the bed.

Clayton motioned me to one of the easy chairs and offered coffee, which I gratefully accepted, although vodka would have been my first choice.

"He's been puking up most of his food," Clayton told me as he handed me the coffee. "Becky's going to try him on Marinol and see if that helps."

"Marijuana derivative," Frank added. "Finally, I can get stoned legally."

Becky laughed as she handed the prescription to Clayton. "If this doesn't help, we'll talk to Dr. Wardell about Compazine. And we'll start the morphine pump tomorrow, okay?"

Frank nodded. She patted his arm, then tucked her notebook into a black leather tote bag. "See you later, guys. Nice meeting you, Susan." And with another of those death-defying smiles, she left us eyeing each other awkwardly.

Ralph had been dozing in the corner, but when the door shut behind Becky, the dog got up and looked at Clayton, her tail thrashing from side to side.

Clayton patted her head. "Maybe later, girl."

Frank waved his hand at Clayton. "Hey, baby, why don't you take a break? Go to Starbucks or the bookstore or something. Take Ralph for a ride."

I winced at the term "baby" but moved past it. "Yeah, get out of here."

Actually, I was terrified about being on my own with Frank. What if something happened? *Quit being such a baby yourself!*

Clayton seemed undecided, so I put on the bravest mask in my repertoire and said, "Get it while you can, Clayton. I'll take good care of him."

"I know," Clayton murmured. "Okay, then. Let me show you a couple of things."

The couple of things included his cell phone number, the hospice number, and a "Do Not Call 911" warning attached to the phone. Any emergencies were to be phoned in to the hospice office, he explained. He also pointed to a sheet of paper taped to the refrigerator.

"It's a 'do-not-resuscitate' order," he said softly. "Just in case …"

I shuddered but nodded that I understood. If Frank stopped

breathing, if his heart stopped beating during the one hundred and twenty minutes I was responsible for him, I had to be sure nature took its course. *Dear God.*

Clayton kissed Frank goodbye and hugged me lightly on his way out the door. He took Ralph's leash from the hall closet and waved it at her, and she trotted after him, tail held high.

I sat down beside the bed. "So," I said, "how bad is it? Really?"

He blinked a couple of times. "Right now? It's okay. I just had my fix … feeling no pain. If I zone out on you, ignore me. I've been forgetting things … like my name. Don't worry about it. You want to watch the tube? That's about all I've been doing."

"Sure," I said, "unless you'd rather talk?"

He laughed: a wet, creaky sound. "Too much like thinking. Do you mind?"

Did I mind? I was relieved all to hell. This would be a piece of cake. I found a rerun of "Friends" on a local channel, and that suited both of us fine. When Frank laughed, however, he often lapsed into coughing spasms that frightened me. When the half hour was over, I scrolled through the channels and found a "Two and a Half Men" just starting. Frank didn't seem to care what we watched, so I let it play but didn't pay much attention to the storyline.

Even with the lull of the television and Frank's erratic breathing, the house seemed empty and quiet. I sat in a cone of lamplight, with darkness filling up the corners of the room. The moon's pale illumination crept in through the patio doors, but it was no match for the darkness. I kept looking over at Frank, checking to be sure he was okay. His breathing would shift to a deep, regular rhythm, and I'd relax, but then he'd wake himself up with a snort and look around like he wasn't sure where he was. Then he'd doze off again.

* * *

Funny how your mind drifts around when you're sitting and waiting for someone to come home, for something to happen. I thought about the time Frank and I drove to Santa Fe to see my mom. He'd only met her once, at our wedding, but they got along far better than I did with his mother—or with my own, for that matter. And he'd never been through the Great Southwest, so it seemed like a good way to spend our first vacation together. We took turns driving, stayed in shabby motels right off the highway, and drank icy Cokes from gas station vending machines. Then, just inside the New Mexico state line we blew a tire. Miles from anywhere, with traffic rushing by like we didn't exist, flinging desert sand in our faces.

Frank looked at the flat, shrugged, rolled up his sleeves and got the jack out of the trunk while I fiddled with my cell phone and tried to get a signal so I could call Triple-A. By the time I gave up and wondered if we'd have to flag down a car, Frank was tightening the lug nuts on the spare. I couldn't believe it. His hands weren't even dirty.

"Where'd you learn to do that?" I'd demanded.

"Don't you know guys are born knowing how to change tires?" he'd said with a huge, satisfied grin on his face. The kind of grin some men have after great sex.

* * *

Frank had always been so damn competent at everything, and remembering that car trip I started to cry. Which pissed me off. I got up for a glass of water and a tissue, and when I sat back down, Frank was watching me. The morphine glaze was gone from his eyes. They twinkled, bright and moist.

"You're a good woman," he said, nodding his head for emphasis.

Not good enough for you, though

"And you're a good man. And that and a dollar might get you a phone call in some places."

Frank smiled. "Good to see you, Suse. Nice of you to babysit."

"You'd do the same for me. Wouldn't you?"

"You bet." He motioned toward the TV remote. "Turn it down a sec, okay? I hate to ask another favor, but I'm going to."

Oh sweet Jesus, what else?

Ever since Frank told me he had cancer, a nasty little fear had lurked in the back of my brain that he was eventually going to ask the ultimate favor: pull the plug for him. And no way was I ever going to be able to do that, no matter how sick he was, no matter how bad the pain. First off, I didn't think you could ever know for sure that all hope of recovery, or a last-minute miracle cure, was absolutely gone. Second, I had no wish to go to jail. And third, I believed in some obscure way that it was far too presumptuous a thing for me to decide. But I knew Frank pretty well, and I worried that sooner or later, he'd ask.

"Okay, ask away," I said, hoping I sounded calmer than I felt.

Frank had the beginning of a five-o'clock shadow that fuzzed the outlines of his face and added to the feeling that darkness was winning the war against light. The hospital bed sat several inches higher than a normal bed, so we were pretty much eye-to-eye. The railings were down but kept me from getting right up next to him. I noticed a small rusty stain on the sheet. Blood?

Frank's eyes reflected crazy colors, weird washes of red and green, from the muted television program. His fingers played with the edge of the pale yellow blanket, fraying the binding. I realized he was wearing blue plaid pajamas, although moments earlier I could have sworn he was in a flimsy white hospital gown. Weird the things you assume sometimes.

"Will you call my mom tomorrow? Tell her ... tell her it's getting close. That it's maybe time to come say goodbye. I can't ask Clayton to do it, and—"

"Yikes, Frank, she shouldn't hear it from *me*. That's one thing you can do yourself. And you should."

Tears spilled from his eyes. "I can't. She'll start in on me, why won't I do chemo, why I won't fight har—"

His voice broke, and I felt ashamed for making him cry. I leaned forward and rubbed his arm, wiped the tears from his face.

"Hey," I said softly, "hey, cut it out. Okay, you win. I'll call her. She can't hate me any more than she does already."

"She doesn't hate you. I don't know why you always thought that."

Oh, gee, would you like a list?

I copied down Elise's phone number and stuck it in my purse.

"Thanks, Susie," Frank said, his voice little more than a whisper now.

"You okay? You need any of your meds? Water? Anything?"

He shook his head. "This sucks, kiddo. I knew it was gonna be bad, but I didn't know it would be like this."

"Are you scared?"

Another head shake. "Not any more. Mostly I'm pissed off now. I mean, why can't I just check out? Why do I have to lie around and feel my body dissolve right from under me? I hate puking, and I hate being tired, and that seems like all there is for me anymore. I want it to be over."

I didn't know what to say, so I rubbed his arm some more and took a sneaky look at my watch. *Come on, Clayton, get back here. I'm not up for this.*

Frank settled down then, put his bony hand over mine and squeezed. His eyes closed, and he drifted off to sleep, or at least he pretended to. I slipped my hand from his, turned off the TV and flipped through a couple of magazines. Dizzy relief flooded me when I heard Clayton's car in the driveway, but I made myself stay in the chair until he came inside. Then I stood up and stretched.

The merry jingle of Ralph's tags didn't disturb Frank's sleep. Clayton looked at Frank and nodded, apparently satisfied that things were as good as could be expected. Ralph settled down by the bed with a contented grunt.

"Did he eat anything?" Clayton asked. He was carrying a white paper bag.

"I didn't know I was supposed to feed him."

"You weren't. I just hoped he'd ask for something."

Clayton took a prescription bottle out of the bag. "Marinol," he said. "Pray that it helps. I don't think I can handle much more of him melting away in front of me."

And then Clayton started to cry. *Hell! If I'd known what I was walking into, I would've brought a box of Kleenex.*

"Hey," I said, patting his back.

He turned and seized me like a drowning man grabbing a life raft. "I don't think I can go through with this," he said. He held me so tight I couldn't breathe. I kept on patting his back and babbling soothing sounds until he let me go.

"Sorry," he muttered.

"It's okay," I lied. "This is hard."

I had to ask: "Aren't you a little used to this kind of thing? I mean, you must have to treat some pretty sick animals."

"It's different," he said, exhaling a big, loud sigh. "It's not *family*. And I love animals, but—"

"But it's not the same. I get it," I said. "I don't think you have much of a choice here, though. You wanted him. Now you need to stick by him."

"I know," he said.

I waited for him to add, "… and I will." But he didn't.

Clayton's meltdown shook me up so much I could hardly wait to get away. Inside my car, when I could breathe again, I realized I'd forgotten to warn him that I was calling Elise and that she'd probably descend on them like a rampaging buffalo all too soon.

What a shitty way for Frank's life to turn out, I thought as I fired up the engine and headed home. Well, I'd done my duty for the week. I wasn't sure I could handle another visit, though, and I wasn't sure if Clayton was going to hold up, either. Maybe it was just as well to unleash Frank's mother. She was never one to fold under pressure, I'll give her that much.

* * *

I called Elise as soon as I got to work the next morning. It was just after ten a.m. Chicago time, so I was pretty sure she'd be in her office, cranking the wheels of the Krajewski empire. And she was.

How do you deliver a "time to say goodbye" message without breaking someone's heart? Is there any way to temper it with kindness? I didn't like Frank's mom, any more than she liked me, but I didn't want to make what she was going through any worse.

"Hello?"

I stiffened at the sound of that voice, challenging me, questioning my right to exist. Even before she knew who was calling.

"Elise, this is Susan. Your former dau—"

"Susan. Yes. Hello."

She might as well have been saying, "Get to the point."

My fragile good will evaporated, and the telephone receiver grew heavy in my hand. I was back to feeling like an unwelcome distraction to her. We were probably sitting at similar desks in similar offices, with our day planners and computers and assistants, but to her I'd always be a trivial annoyance. An obstacle to be steamrolled out of the way.

Not this time, lady. Here: take this, you old battleaxe.

"Frank asked me to call you. He's not doing very well. The tumors are growing, and there may not be much time left. He thought you might want to come see him." I kept my voice as calm and level as a weather report on a cloudless day.

"I—of course," she answered. "It's bad then?" She sounded as matter-of-fact as ever. A little surprised, maybe, but I got no gratification from her tone. No gasp of horror, no barely held-back sobs. Not from Elise Krajewski. Not from Old Stone Face.

"Yes," I said. "I was with him for several hours last night."

I wanted her to know I'd been looking out for Frank. She'd always considered me a failure as a wife. Would she let me succeed as Frank's friend? She didn't reply, so I added, "He doesn't seem to be in a lot of pain, if that's any consolation."

"Of course it is." Her voice could have cut a sheet of glass.

"He's real tired," I continued anyway, "and Clayton says he can't eat, that he gets sick when he does. The hospice nurse prescribed something for the nausea, so we'll see."

"Clayton is … there with him?"

I stuck the knife in with a clear conscience. "Yes. For now anyway. He's having a rough time of it. So are all of us, all of Frank's friends."

Elise didn't say anything for a minute, and then the old brisk, dismissive voice came over the line. "I'll call the airlines and fly out right away. Is there a decent hotel nearby?"

Always eager to soak up more rejection, I said, "You're welcome to stay with me."

My foolish generosity stunned me, and her reply did not.

"Thank you, dear, but I'd probably be more comfortable in a hotel."

So I recommended several nearby options. I almost offered her a ride from the airport but stopped myself in time. She no doubt would be "more comfortable" renting a car anyway.

My hands were shaking when I hung up the phone. What was that all about? Partly it was the effort to rein in my anger—at her, at the whole situation. Partly it was fear, because Elise had always been able to make me doubt my worthiness. And partly it was the effort to be civilized and compassionate with her.

Anyway, I'd kept my promise to Frank. And Clayton would have more help than he knew what to do with once Elise hit town.

* * *

A few minutes later, Derek Bord summoned me. I thought I saw a smirk on Lilah's face as I passed her desk, but maybe I imagined it.

Bord had a file folder open in front of him, and as he motioned me to sit, I saw Val Desmond's name on the label. *Oh, shit.*

He flipped the folder closed and started tapping the desk top with his fancy pen. I hoped my expression conveyed pleasant poise, but somehow I doubted it.

"We've been most lenient with Ms. Desmond," he began. "She's had more than enough time to consider her options and decide whether she wants to remain on the team."

I nodded, because Val's administrative leave—with pay, I'd determined—had lasted longer than the minimum requirement. I figured Bord was buying extra time to be sure that bozo Jeff Tate could handle Val's job. *My* jury was still out on that one, but apparently Bord had decided.

"Have you spoken with her?" Bord asked.

Did he know I had, or could I safely lie? It hadn't been a work-related call, strictly speaking.

"Once," I admitted reluctantly.

"And did she give you any indication of her intentions? Is she ready to come back to work band go along with the program?"

"We didn't discuss that," I said, and put on a sincere face when I added to the lie, "I called her about something we'd been working on before you—before she went on leave."

Bord showed no sign that he disbelieved me.

"I'm going to speak with her tomorrow," he told me, "and if my suspicions are correct, she'll continue to be recalcitrant. Which means I have little choice but to terminate her."

And you're telling me this because …? You want me to warn her, or what?

"That's your prerogative," I said. No point in trying to persuade the little bastard to give her another chance. The damage had been done, and Val would probably never forgive him for humiliating her. I wouldn't have.

"And, in turn, you need to let me know if we're on solid ground, Equal Employment wise," Bord said, glaring at me as if he dared me to find fault with his thinking. "She's over forty and female."

I nodded, surprised Bord knew enough to give a thought to Val's protected-class status.

"I have documentation of her refusal to cooperate with my job enrichment initiative," he went on.

Job enrichment initiative? Give me a break!

"That's good."

Bord dropped the pen and leaned forward on his elbows. "I need more than 'good' from you, Susan. I sense that I'm dragging you along here, and I don't have time for that. A little enthusiasm on your part would be welcome."

I took a deep breath. "Val is my friend," I told him. "It's difficult for me to be enthusiastic about her being fired."

"Ah, the truth of the matter." Bord shook his head. "You disappoint me. I thought you'd be able to separate business from your personal feelings."

I took refuge in jargon, not that it helped. "I'm doing that, Derek. But I don't have to like it. I'll review your write-up on the incident to be sure it covers all the bases. And I'll look at the demographics, who else has been suspended or fired, the reasons, the ages, and so on. Make sure this doesn't stand out."

Bord relaxed a little, and I hated myself by then. *Traitor*. But I kept thinking, *Maybe I can find a reason to stop him from firing her—or give her an opening to drive a semi-truck through on her way to the Fair Employment Practices Commission.*

He handed me Val's folder. "It's all here. Get back to me before lunch."

"I will."

I stood up and had almost made it out the door when Bord added, "Is everything all right with you, Susan? You seem a bit … distracted lately. Is it just Desmond, or is something else going on?"

I paused, inches from safety. *Hell. And I told Angel it was okay to let him know about Frank. Stupid, Susan—stupid, stupid, stupid.*

"I'm fine," I said. "Of course everyone's kind of upset—the outsourcing, Val's situation. People are on edge. Not just me."

"You're the one I noticed," Bord said. "I need to know I can count on *your* cooperation."

"Of course you can, Derek."

Damn it! I needed the lousy job, but that didn't make it any easier for me to find a smile and turn it on him. *You little prick.*

The little prick smiled back, satisfied he was going to get his way, as usual. And I'd been warned.

* * *

The write-up of his confrontation with Val was obviously slanted in his favor, and I knew Val's version would differ in tone if not fact. Bord had decided, in the interest of cross-training and "intra-departmental efficiency," to move Val to the college recruitment team. Although it was a lower-rated job, he told her he was keeping her salary whole, so that was no basis for complaint. Val refused to accept the reassignment and became argumentative and abusive (he tossed in a few tasty examples, including her calling him a "pompous twit.") Although he'd given her ample time to reconsider, she'd shown no sign of readiness to accept his decision, leaving Bord no choice but to terminate her. All very rational and complete. But the tidy little document Lilah had typed did not convey the sneer I knew had been in Bord's voice when he told Val he was giving her job to that boob Jeff Tate, who barely knew how to spell "personnel."

However, I had to agree that Val had given Bord some cause for his decision. I phoned my opinion to Bord, praying Val would never find out I helped drive the last nail into the coffin that now held her career at Jacobs.

* * *

Judy called me late in the afternoon and asked if I wanted to go to dinner with her the next night. I welcomed the distraction, although as I sat in Don Francisco's lobby waiting for Judy's usual tardy arrival, Margaret's absence gnawed at me; she would have been the first one there. Then Judy came bouncing in, looking so merry that I had to smile. She'd lost a few pounds and had on a bright-red peasant blouse that lit her complexion like a Christmas tree.

After we toasted the end of another week, I thought of Margaret again. I hadn't called her, but I still blamed the time difference.

"It feels a little weird, just us two," I said, and then felt bad. Judy didn't seem to take it as a slight, though.

"I know. I actually thought about asking Jennifer, so there'd still be three of us," she said.

"I'm glad you didn't."

Judy cocked her head. "You don't like her, do you?"

I shrugged. "She's all right. I just … I don't know. She seems phony. That perfect hair, that perfect figure."

"Jealous?"

"Maybe," I said. The suggestion stung more than I'd have thought, so I sucked down my margarita and didn't say anything else.

"How's Frank doing?" Judy asked. She didn't ask about Noah. Interesting. I wondered if she'd gloat at learning he was gone again—for good. I decided not to give her the chance and answered her question about Frank instead.

"Bad. I don't think he'll last much longer. I had to call his mother yesterday and ask her to come out from Chicago."

"This would be the mother-in-law from hell?"

I laughed. Judy had a long, clear memory, and I'd shared my misery with her and Margaret many times during my marriage.

"She hasn't gotten any nicer."

"You didn't expect her to, did you?"

"Guess not."

"You can handle her."

"Fortunately I don't have to. That'll be Clayton's problem. I think she might drive him over the edge. He's pretty wobbly already."

"Frank's lucky to have you around then. You're a rock."

"Am I? I don't feel very solid."

"You are. If I was in trouble, you're the one I'd want in my corner."

I appreciated the praise but wondered where it came from. Oh, we were friends all right, and underneath the little barbs that we tossed back and forth, we respected each other. But overt compliments didn't come often.

Judy studied the menu and then looked at me. "I met somebody."

And I'd been thinking the candlelight gave her that glow, or the red blouse. I battled a stab of genuine envy at the smile on her face. Jeez, she'd even had her nails done: a vivid shade that almost matched her blouse. The murmuring voices and clanking silverware suddenly irritated me, to the point where I wanted to slam my fist on the table and yell, "Be quiet!"

"Somebody?" I said, pretending that I'd choked on a grain of salt from the margarita.

She grinned. "A guy. A cute, straight, unmarried guy."

My resentment melted in the face of Judy's elation.

"I thought they were a myth. So—spill your guts! How'd you meet him, what's his name, when's the wedding?"

She took a sip of her drink, and some of the salt from the rim scattered on the table. She picked it up with her fingertips, and the red lacquer sparkled in the light.

"His name is Ryan. Jen introduced us."

Jen?

I didn't feel capable of forming a sentence so settled for "Aha."

"He went to college with Eric—Jen's new boyfriend. He just moved here from Portland, and Jen thought we might hit it off … and we did!"

She was trying to tone down her joy, but the way Judy said his name told me plenty. Well, good for her. She deserved a little happiness.

"I almost didn't tell you," she said. "I mean, I know you're going through a shitty time, and I feel bad being all ga-ga and happy. But I thought it might give you hope. I mean, if *I* can get lucky, somebody as great as you can, too."

I blew her a kiss. "I'm glad for you. Honest."

Really, I was. And I couldn't wait to get away from her.

Chapter 11
The Blame Game

A cloud passed over the sun as I drank my Saturday morning coffee and summoned the energy to water my plants. Did I imagine it, or did the air temperature suddenly drop a little? Had Elise Krajewski's shadow just flown over my house?

I don't know who took up more of my worry time, Frank or Val. I'd heard nothing from the Krajewski-Selden household since I'd phoned to tell them Elise was on her way. *Fasten your seatbelts, guys.* Clayton had taken my call, thanked me, said Frank seemed no worse, and certainly no better. He promised to let me know if the status quo shifted.

As for Val: Bord, typically, hadn't bothered to let me in on his decision, but he'd probably gone ahead and fired her. Why not, since I'd given him a green light to proceed?

Several times I picked up the phone and started to key in Val's number, but I never finished the sequence. What could I say? What could I do to help? And I was afraid she'd hear in my voice something that revealed how I'd sold her out. *Some friend you are.* The best I could offer was a sympathetic ear; then maybe I could steer her toward some positive action. Like I was an expert on that. I hadn't had to scrounge for a job in over twelve years; my search skills were obsolete.

Sunday morning, instead of calling Val—which is probably what I should have done—I dialed Frank's number to check up on him. Clayton answered, and he sounded freaked out. His voice trembled, and I could hear his breath coming in spurts.

My first thought was, *Frank's gotten worse.*

"What is it?" I demanded. "How bad is h—"

"The pain's worse this morning," Clayton answered. "They can't get the morphine calibrated. Becky's coming by later to see what she can do. And his *mother* is here."

"She made good time."

"I won't use the word 'good,'" Clayton said, "but she's here, and … God, Susan—she is taking over *everything.*"

"You expected any different? That's what she does."

"I know. But she's just shoved me out of the way, like—"

"Like you don't exist? Like you're some annoying little insect in her way? You don't have to tell me. I know the feeling."

"I never saw this side of her before," Clayton told me. "Until now she's been pretty nice to me."

I admit to a surge of envy when he said that. I'd harbored the illusion that Frank's choice of a male lover had to have hurt Elise. *You didn't think I was good enough for him? Well, take* this!

Evidently, however, having a gay son was preferable to having one who was married to me. Ouch.

"So what's she doing?" I asked to cover my resentment. It wasn't Clayton's fault. He was a likable guy, after all. Whereas I, apparently, was utterly lacking in likeability.

I heard a huge sigh. "For starters, she tells me I should be force-feeding him if I have to, to keep his strength up. She says I have to keep looking until I find something he can keep down. As if I hadn't already tried everything in the market."

"That sounds like her," I said.

"And you should have heard her interrogate poor Becky yesterday! How does the morphine pump work? What if we need more than it's dispensing? When does he see the doctor? And get this: she wants to try another antidepressant, even after I told her the Zoloft quit working. As if this is something a pill can fix!"

Through the hot fog of annoyance, I had to acknowledge that Elise might not be completely off base with her questions and ideas.

"If it helps him get through this," I said, "maybe it's worth a shot." *Time to move past denial and despair, buddy.*

"Oh sure, it's not bad enough that Frank's so whacked out on morphine he doesn't know up from down. Let's just pump another chemical into him and wipe out any trace of his personality!"

"Ease off," I said. "I'm not the enemy here."

"Sorry. She's been at me from the minute she walked in the door. Challenging and giving orders—and making me feel like this is all my fault. I've had it."

"She's his mother," I said. As if he needed reminding.

"I don't think so," Clayton said, with another sad, heavy sigh. "I think she bought him somewhere."

"Is she there now?"

"No. She went out foraging for groceries and her favorite home remedies. Like a good dose of Echinacea will make everything right."

"Don't let her get to you. Elise is pretty hard to take under normal circumstances, and this has to bring out the worst in her."

He muttered something I couldn't make out and then said, "Oh damn, she's back. Susan, I hate to ask, but would you come over later? For moral support?"

To take some of the heat off you, you mean. If the detested ex-wife is around, maybe Elise will let up on you?

It was absolutely the last thing I wanted to do on my Sunday afternoon. But what else did I have going on? So, as often happened with me, my mouth said "Sure" while my brain was yelling "No way!"

* * *

If she hadn't been my mother-in-law, if she hadn't so obviously disapproved of me, I might have admired Elise Krajewski. She'd wrung maximum benefit from the few advantages life had given her, overcoming a dirt-poor childhood on a tenant farm in rural Illinois, making her way to Chicago and getting work as a stenographer—eventually in the family-owned Krajewski real estate agency, where she met

Frank's dad, Joe Jr. She put herself through college at night, got a degree in business, and eventually started helping Joe Sr. run the agency, even before she married his son. She kept working after the wedding, taking a short break to deliver Frank. After her daughter Zoë was born, though, Elise retired to full-time motherhood. Temporarily.

Then came Viet Nam, and Joe Jr. got drafted. Joe Jr. got killed. And Elise went back to work to fill the void of widowhood. She must have been ferocious, from what Frank and Grandpa K told me. And she was instrumental in making the agency successful. She convinced Grandpa K to turn his talents to commercial real estate, where he really hit his stride. He did the selling and she ran the business end, and they made more money than anyone had imagined, least of all Grandpa K.

Yeah, Elise had turned life's lemons into lemonade, but the experience didn't just toughen her. It hardened her, and her judgment of people was swift and merciless. I didn't measure up from the start.

Frank as much as admitted he left Chicago to get away from her, but even long-distance she bombarded him with advice and directives: be careful of those California girls, they're all tramps; take your vitamins; don't work too hard; don't play too hard. When he got a job at the printing company, she sniffed that it didn't make full use of his talents.

And when he phoned to tell her that he'd proposed to me, there was an icy silence on the line. I know because I was there, and Frank was gripping my hand for dear life.

"Where'd you meet this one?" she finally asked.

I started out as "this one" and moved up to "she" and "her." Rarely did Elise speak my name. "Why doesn't *she* want the wedding to be in Chicago?" or "How many of *her* relatives will be there?"

* * *

So these memories were churning around in my head while I showered and dressed and prepared to confront the Gorgon again. I took my time getting ready, and then I did some deep breathing and reminded myself I was older, wiser, and beyond Elise's clutches now. No longer could she use Frank as leverage to make me feel bad about myself. Yeah, right.

Elise's rented broomstick—a black Taurus—was parked in front of Frank's house, taking up two spaces. I trudged up the walkway, and Clayton flung the door open before I knocked. Ralph yipped and slobbered her own greeting.

"Thank you for this," Clayton whispered as he seized me in a suffocating hug.

I pried myself free and patted Ralph's head.

"She's in with Frank," Clayton told me as he led me into the house.

No, she wasn't with Frank. A shadow filled the kitchen doorway, and there was Elise, looking every bit as much in control as I remembered.

"What's all the fuss ab—" she asked Clayton, and then she saw me.

"Oh," she said. "It's you."

How could she do that? How could she suck all the air out of the room, even from a distance? The entryway echoed with memories, real and imagined. Elise was standing inches away from the photograph of her younger self, the one that refused to look at me, and the combination was enough to destroy my carefully crafted defenses. I almost had to reach out for the wall to steady myself.

Clayton stood behind me, using me as a shield, so close I could hear him breathe. I was glad I'd worn jeans because Elise had always scoffed at my casual taste in clothes; this would let her know she'd never won that battle. And my high heeled boots gave me a little physical leverage at least; even barefoot, I towered over her.

Elise, of course, was carefully tricked out in a navy blue suit, red silk scarf knotted elegantly at her throat. I probably outweighed her by a good sixty pounds, but she stood her ground in her sturdy little navy pumps, blocking the way to Frank's hospital bed. Not good to let her smell fear, I remembered, so I took a deep breath and stood up tall.

"Yes," I said. "It's me."

We managed a few civil exchanges like "How are you?" Even the feeble entryway lighting showed me that Elise had aged a decade in the four years since I'd seen her. The full coat of war paint on her face might have covered some wrinkles, but it didn't mask the dark half-moons under her eyes. Only her hair, a glossy chocolate color I was positive came out of a bottle, seemed untouched by age and worry.

Finally she moved aside and let me go in to see Frank. He was lying against a bank of pillows, drowsy and pale, but he waved and worked up a weak smile.

"Hey, Susie," he said.

He looked worse than he had on Wednesday, and his skin had a waxy sheen to it that I didn't like. I noticed a square black box attached to the side of the bed; a thick plastic tube snaked out of it, up to a needle in the back of Frank's right hand. That would be the morphine pump. It had a button on the side, and I knew its purpose without being told: to give him an extra little jolt of medicine when the pain worsened.

I kissed his cheek. "How are you today?"

Stupid question, but you always have to ask, now don't you?

His mouth opened and closed, but no words came out. His head rolled from side to side and he pointed at the morphine pump. "Mom's here."

"I know." How could I not? She hovered inches behind me. "You two must have a lot to talk about."

I eased into a chair beside the bed, and Clayton leaned on its back. Elise wedged her chair into the space between us and Frank. She shook her head as she stroked Frank's cheek.

"This is unforgivable," she said. "How can anyone let him suffer like this?"

"Elise," I whispered, "he can hear you."

"Someone has to stand up for him!"

She glared over my head at Clayton. "When is that nurse coming?"

"I don't know. Usually it's around four, but if she   "

"You need to call her and get her here now. I can't stand this."

Clayton exhaled heavily; his breath fluttered against my hair. "I already called and left a message. She knows we need her. She'll be here."

I tried to distract Elise. "How was your flight?"

She wrinkled her nose. "Long and crowded. Airport security's a mess."

I nodded in agreement, desperate to find common ground and keep things pleasant.

"And you found a hotel you liked?"

Another nose wrinkle. "I decided to stay here."

Poor Clayton. Poor Frank.

She smoothed Frank's hair. "Want some soup now, baby?"

He didn't respond.

"He can't eat," Clayton said. "You saw what happened last night. He puked it all up."

"That Marinol's not helping?" I asked.

"No," Clayton said. "Nothing's working."

Elise glared at Clayton. "You have to keep trying."

"There's not a lot we can do," I said, not even sure why I felt the urge to support Clayton. "It's not like he has the flu or something."

"I'm aware of that," she snapped.

Just then Frank went into a fierce coughing fit; his whole body shook until the bed rails rattled. Clayton moved past Elise and massaged Frank's chest until the spasm ended.

Frank coughed again, then sank into the pillows. Elise's hands clenched into a knot as Clayton picked up a water glass and moved the straw to Frank's mouth. Frank managed a tiny sip; some of it dribbled down his chin, and Clayton wiped it away.

Elise stood. "I'm going to make him some tea," she announced. "Some nice ginger tea."

"I don't think he'll be able to—" Clayton started to protest.

Elise turned on him like a cobra on a mongoose. "You can't just sit around and watch him suffer!"

Frank's eyelids closed, fluttered, closed again and stayed that way.

"We have to," Clayton told her. "This is how he wants it."

"I don't believe that," Elise hissed. She looked down at Frank, who appeared so small and helpless against the stark white pillow, and even though I didn't much like Elise, I ached for her.

"He needs to be in a hospital," she said.

Clayton shook his head. "This is Frank's choice. He wants to die peacefully. With dignity. At *home*."

He hit the word "home" extra hard, and Elise recoiled like he'd slapped her, but she recovered fast.

"You can't tell me this is peaceful. You can't tell me it's dignified. It's horrible, for him and for me."

I stood up between them and put my hand on Elise's shoulder. She didn't pull away. "He really does want it this way. It's terrible, but it's part of the process."

"Elise," Clayton said, "why don't you give yourself a break? Maybe take a nap? You must be exhausted from—"

"My son is dying," Elise snapped at him. "I can sleep all I want to when he's gone."

She stomped into the kitchen and put some water on to boil. Frank's ragged breathing had steadied.

"See what I mean?" Clayton hissed.

I nodded, but I wondered what harm it could do to let her try and get some tea into Frank. At least she was doing something besides wringing her hands and waiting. I had to admit, that was getting a little old.

"She's as distraught as we are, Clayton. Try to cut her some slack."

And just where did this compassionate streak come from?

Clayton moved into the kitchen and took out a heavy ceramic mug. He looked like he wanted to brain Elise with it, but he handed it to her with a tentative smile. She snatched it away. Truce wasn't about to happen there.

Before I could stop myself, I joined them. Should have known better, but discretion was never my big strength.

"I can't believe you saw him get this sick and didn't make him see a doctor," Elise said. I wasn't sure if she was accusing Clayton, me, or both of us.

"He didn't look sick," Clayton said.

I nodded. "That's right. Until a few weeks ago you'd never have known."

The water began to churn, and a small puff of steam emerged from the kettle. Elise let it boil harder.

"I would have known! He must've been coughing or something. You should have noticed."

Clayton smacked the tile countertop hard. "He always coughed! He smoked two packs a day, for Christ's sake. And when did that start, by the way? Why didn't *you* stop him instead of giving him cigarette money?"

Their voices were drowned out by the shriek of the tea kettle, and just as Elise turned off the flame, Frank cried out and started thrashing. Elise let the kettle thunk down on the burner grate and hurried to him. The smell of scalding water gave way to a dark, sulfurous stink. Frank had shit himself.

Oh, Christ, this can't be happening.

I found the tea bags Elise had bought and finished what she'd started while she and Clayton argued about how to change the bedding without hurting Frank. She let Clayton do the heavy lifting, and when they were done she shoved the smelly sheets at him.

"Make yourself useful and wash these," she hissed.

Before Clayton hurled the sheets back at her, I stepped between them and offered her the tea.

"Here," I said. "I think you need this more than Frank does."

She pushed past me without taking the mug and went to wash her hands. Clayton stomped off with the sheets and came back a minute later, pissed off and pale.

"Want some tea?" I asked.

Our relentlessly cheerful Becky arrived at that moment. Clayton and I handed her over to Elise without a qualm and retreated to the patio, where we took turns throwing a ball for Ralph.

Every once in a while Elise's voice pierced the quiet, followed by a stream of muffled words from Becky. The patio doors were open, and I heard Frank mutter replies to Becky's questions. Another coughing spasm. The click of metal instruments. Silence.

I tossed the tennis ball to the far corner of the yard, and wiped my hand on my jeans. "Come on, let's play keep-away with Ralph."

Clayton didn't move, so I tugged on his arm. He ignored me.

"Hey," I said. "Hang on, Clayton. Hang on. It's almost over."

He turned away, and I saw his whole body was quivering.

"I know," he said. "And I want it to be over." His words came out in spurts. "How can I want it to be over? I love him so much."

I patted his back and uttered reassuring lies. "It's only natural. We all want him to be out of pain, we all want his suffering to end. This is probably the hardest thing any of us will ever do."

He blew his nose. "What will I do without him?"

Oh, come on! Think about somebody besides yourself!

"Look," I said, "maybe Becky has something else in her bag of tricks to help with the pain. Let's go talk to her."

"I don't think I can go through with this."

"I'll run interference with Elise while you talk to Becky," I said.

"No. I mean, I can't *be here*. It was hard enough before, but I can't keep fighting her. She hates me."

"She doesn't hate you, she hates it that Frank's dying."

"It doesn't matter. I can't stand to watch him die. And I can't stand for her to bustle around pretending that she can do something to stop it."

"It's her way of coping. And you know what? Maybe she's right, just this one time. You have to keep trying, and hoping. Miracles happen, Clayton. Maybe—"

"Since when are you such a goddamn optimist?"

Ralph chomped down on the tennis ball. Dumb dog, no worries in the world except when her next meal was coming.

To his credit, Clayton realized immediately what he'd said, and he put his hand on my shoulder. "I'm sorry, Susan. See—that's what this ordeal has done to me. That wasn't the real me talking." He let go of me, took Ralph's ball from her mouth and tossed it across the yard. She charged after it.

"I know you're right," Clayton said. "And maybe pretending you can do something to help is the best way for her to cope, and for you to cope. Me, I can't cope. I have to get away."

Ralph offered me her tennis ball, and I took it.

I pretended not to understand what Clayton meant. "Okay, let's talk to Becky, then you and I can go out and get a sandwich, or a beer, or something."

He shook his head. "I'm not going in there. I have to leave."

The late afternoon sunlight cast leafy shadows on Clayton's face, but I could see his eyes, and they weren't joking. The smell of fresh-cut grass rose up from the lawn, and somewhere down the block I heard children laughing. The redwood fence was beginning to sag along the west wall, I noticed. One good wind could blow it down, and all the invisible monsters lurking in the night could flood in. *If Noah and I were still together, I could ask him to fix it.*

The soggy tennis ball in my hand felt too heavy. I considered flinging it at Clayton's head, to knock some sense into him. But I knew that would be as pointless as trying to cure Frank with ginger tea. Everything was creaking along according to some hideous plan, and my part in the story had turned mighty scary.

Clayton was wearing white shorts, and I saw goose bumps form on his tan, hairy legs. Those legs could take him way beyond my reach.

"Clayton, you can't!"

I threw the ball to Ralph before I succumbed to my violent impulse.

"I can't stay here," he said. His body was rigid.

I grabbed his arm and dug in with my fingernails, but he didn't flinch.

"You can't bail on Frank now. And Ralph, who's gonna take care of Ralph?" I knew my desperate babble was useless, but I had to keep trying. He couldn't do this to Frank. He couldn't do this to *me*.

"Elise wants to take over. Let her."

He pulled away and went out the side gate. Ralph stayed on the lawn with that silly green tennis ball jutting out of her mouth. I grabbed one of the uprights supporting the patio, fighting for my own breath. Goddamn Elise! Goddamn Clayton! I heard a car engine start.

I found a few ounces of courage I didn't know I had and went inside.

Becky looked up expectantly, but Elise kept her eyes on Frank, who was mumbling but appeared to be dozing peacefully.

"Clayton's gone," I said.

Becky picked up her clipboard. "Will he be back soon? I have a few questions for him."

I shook my head. "No. He's gone. He left. Not coming back."

Becky's composure dissolved, but only for a minute. "I've seen this happen when things get bad. This is very hard on the family. But he'll reconsider. I'm sure of it."

I tried to speak softly so Frank wouldn't hear. "I don't think so."

I swear I saw a smirk on Elise's face. Probably thought she'd won the war.

"Well then, let's get my son into a hospital. Now."

Becky put a hand on her arm. "No, Mrs. Krajewski. We can't do that. Frank has made a choice, and we have to honor it."

"What is wrong with all you people? My son is sick, he's in pain, and no one wants to do anything about it except stand around watching him suffer!"

Neither Becky nor I spoke. We let her rant. Finally she ran out of steam.

"I think the pain will be better now," Becky said, her voice a miracle of calm and reason. "I've increased the morphine. And please remember that this is what Frank wants. He was very specific. And I know it's terrible for you to go through this, but it won't last much longer. A few days at most, I think."

Elise's arms were resting on the bed rails, and she put her head down and started to bawl. This unnerved me more than the anger. I had never seen Old Stone Face cry, except at my wedding. I stared at Becky because I didn't have a clue what to do.

Finally the sobs subsided. Frank hadn't stirred.

Elise wiped her face with her hands and glared at me, like she was daring me to offer sympathy. "What are we going to do now, without Clayton?" she asked. "I have to sleep sometimes. You'll have to help."

Becky, bless her perceptive soul, rescued me. "I can help you find a nurse. I was going to suggest that to Clayton today anyway. They're trained for this, and although Susan would do a great job, I think she has a full-time career that she—"

"Fine," Elise said. Subject closed.

But I couldn't just scram and leave Frank alone with her, leave her alone with Frank, now could I? Besides, there was Ralph, who looked at me expectantly, like it was suppertime or something. *Oh, Clayton, you lousy coward.*

While Becky phoned nursing services for Elise, I took Ralph for a walk—more to calm myself than to exercise her. Ever the multitasker, while the dog and I power-walked down the block, I dialed Flo's number on my cell phone and told her what had happened.

"Do you know anyone who could find Clayton and talk some sense into him?" I asked.

Flo whistled softly, settling off static crackles in my ear. "Let me make a couple of calls. But honestly, I think he'll come around all by himself."

"That's what the hospice nurse said," I told her. "But I don't think so."

"He may need to blow off a little steam. But he really loves Frank. He won't desert him."

Flo promised to check around and call me back, but I didn't have much hope of Clayton doing a one-eighty turnaround, not judging by the look on his face when he left. It wasn't the expression of someone who changed his mind easily.

* * *

By the time Ralph and I got back, Becky had lined up a nurse who could start at eight a.m. the next day, so all we had to do was get through the night.

"Tomorrow I'll see about getting nurses for the afternoon and night shifts," Becky promised. I must have looked pretty shell-shocked because she hugged me and patted my back. "Hang in there, Susan," she whispered before she went out the door.

I heard a phone ring in the background, and Elise's voice rising in pitch when she answered it. I overheard her say, "Hi, darling," and figured out it must be Zoë. Good—someone to distract her.

The sound pulled Frank from his restless slumber, and Elise took the phone to him. "It's your baby sister."

"Zoo-Zoo? Hi, kid." Frank's voice was thick with pain and painkiller, but his pleasure in her call came through.

"She wanted so badly to come with me," Elise told me. "But Miles —that's their eldest—Miles had a terrible accident on his bike last week. He was in the hospital until Friday, and there's no way she could have gone off and left Henry alone with the children, especially Miles."

I've often heard it said that our choice of a mate tends to replicate our parent. In my case, I didn't have much to go on, and neither did Zoë. She was only a baby when Joe Krajewski Jr. kicked the bucket. So, in a way, I guess she was drawn to Henry Helstrom because he was everything a girl might want in a father: he was educated, he had opinions, and he didn't hesitate to tell her what to do. Me, I wanted a buddy, not a boss. But Zoë's choice, while appearing good on the surface, had taken a serious turn toward servitude, if you asked me. Elise seemed to approve of her son-in-law (more than she ever approved of me), but I wondered if sometimes she didn't regret her endorsement.

I don't think Henry ever hurt Zoë, not physically at least. But on the occasions when I saw them together, I thought him cold and demanding. The kind of man who raised a fuss, a big one, if dinner wasn't on the table at seven p.m. sharp, if the place settings weren't perfect, if the children got out of hand and made too much noise.

And Zoë—Zoë maintained a quickness of manner, a high nervous laugh that always made her seem an inch away from flying apart at the seams and dissolving into the universe with only a few specks of dust left behind. The price of marrying a good man. It always comes with a price. In a way, I thought, I was the lucky one.

"You, too, Zoo-Zoo," Frank was saying. "Thanks for calling. Here's Mom."

The morphine kept doing its work, and Frank nodded off again. His mother quickly wound up the phone call with Zoë and sat down at the kitchen table, looking pale and worn down.

"Have you talked to Grandpa K?" I asked.

Elise shook her head.

I struggled for a gently persuasive tone of voice. "He might want to be here."

"It won't change anything."

"No, of course not, but—"

She pointed to Frank "Do you want Joe's last memory to be as horrible as ours? I can't save Frank, but I can spare Joe. He's seen enough dying."

"But what about Frank? He loves Grandpa K. Don't you think he deserves a chance to talk to him one more time?"

Her mouth quivered, but even as I sensed I was getting through to her, I began to doubt myself. It wouldn't change anything, and with Frank going in and out of delirium, he might not even know Grandpa K was there. *"He's seen enough dying."* Maybe Old Stone Face was right.

"Get some rest," I told her. "I'll sit with him and call you if there's any change."

She drifted off like a zombie, without protest—or thanks. I browsed Frank's bookshelves and found a Sue Grafton mystery I'd never read, so I made some coffee, fed Ralph, and settled in on the sofa across from Frank's bed. Dusk merged into darkness, and the house settled in around me, quiet except for Frank's breathing and Ralph's snoring.

About six p.m. the doorbell rang. I must have dozed off, because the sound startled me, and I dropped the book on my foot. Hardcover books hurt when they hit you like that. Frank didn't stir, but Ralph leaped up and plunged down the hallway toward the front door. I limped along after her, praying it was Clayton, ringing the bell because he'd lost his keys.

Flo stood on the front porch, a bottle of red wine in one hand and a takeout bag from Baja Fresh in the other. "I brought reinforcements."

She handed the food and the bottle to me and knelt to pet and cuddle Ralph. Delirious, the dog squealed and squirmed and licked Flo's face. As Flo stood up, Elise shuffled into the hall. She looked rumpled but a little rested.

Flo grinned and extended her hand. "Hello, Elise. I'm Flo Campbell. And old friend of the family. I heard you ladies might need a hand tonight."

Elise retained enough good manners to smile and shake Flo's hand. In the kitchen, she bubbled over with gratitude for the food and the wine and insisted on setting the table with china and silverware for our takeout feast.

"How can I be hungry?" Elise wondered aloud.

"We all need fuel," Flo pointed out. "Especially when we're upset."

Elise thanked Flo for the meal and lamented the lack of good Mexican restaurants in Chicago. Flo let her go on. She refilled my wine glass and winked at me. The cabernet's warmth soothed my frazzled nerves; maybe I could handle this after all.

Elise kept Frank in her field of vision the whole time she talked, and finally she ran out of steam.

"I still can't believe this," she said. "Just yesterday, he was a little boy in his cowboy outfit. Learning to ride his two-wheeler. And getting his cute little words all mixed up. He used to tell people, 'We live in a nice bus-sinity,' and of course he meant vicin—"

Her words dissolved into tears. Flo stood over her, rubbing her back and murmuring "There, there" until Elise retrieved her self-control. It didn't take long.

Frank came out of his stupor as we finished eating. He was like another person, lucid and happy. No coughing. No cringing in pain. He was delighted to see Flo and asked for all the gossip on their mutual friends. Did Rhonda and Michelle have another fight? When were Pete and Joseph going to Hawaii? He didn't ask about Clayton, although I was ready with a quick excuse that he'd been called to the animal clinic for an emergency. But I never even had to trot out the lie. After about half an hour, Frank wound down and drifted back to sleep.

"Do you have children?" Elise murmured to Flo as we stood and watched Frank's chest move up and down.

Flo didn't miss a beat. "Yes," she said softly. "I have a son. I had a daughter, but she passed away."

Elise peered at her. "So you know."

"Oh, yes," Flo replied quietly and clasped Elise's hand. "I know."

I suddenly felt both invisible and unnecessary. And as if she was reading my mind, Flo looked at me and smiled kindly.

"Susan, hon, don't you have to be at work bright and early in the morning?"

"Yes, but—"

"Why don't you toddle on home then? I'll spell Elise tonight.

You've done plenty for one day, hasn't she, Elise? And aren't you lucky to have such a responsible ex-daughter-in-law?"

"Yes," Elise said, and she sounded like she meant it even though I doubted her. "Yes, I'm very lucky that Susan is here for us. But Flo's right, dear. You need some rest, and you have to work tomorrow. We'll be fine here, and tomorrow the cavalry comes. So go home and sleep. And thank you for everything."

I never thought I'd live to hear her say those words, in that affectionate voice. I was stupefied. Then I decided I'd better seize the opening and take off before anything else happened. After good-night hugs and kisses all around, I fled.

* * *

Alone in my quiet house, I refused to waste time on regrets. I brushed my teeth and crawled into bed. *This may be your last chance to sleep for a while,* I told myself. And I took good advantage of the opportunity.

Chapter 12
Remember to Breathe

Southern California burns in October—not the fiery splendor of autumn leaves turning scarlet and orange, but a literal burning of brush land that grows in the spring and crisps in the summer. Then hot, hostile Santa Ana winds roar in from the desert, and sooner or later, something ignites.

I smelled smoke even before I got out of bed, and when I flipped on the television, I understood why. The hills above Burbank, less than ten miles away, were ablaze. The perky meteorologist on Channel Four explained that a high pressure ridge over the Great Basin was responsible for the scorching wind that we'd have to endure for the next couple of days. Terrific.

I didn't worry a lot about my house; the flames would have to climb up one side of the Verdugo Mountains and down the other to get anywhere near. But the smell set my nerves on edge, and the ragged column of smoke that rose over the foothills made my stomach clench as I walked the few feet from my house to the garage. A fine layer of ash was already settling on the driveway.

The Santa Anas shoved my Honda around on the freeway, and I fought to stay in my lane. If I hadn't needed the distraction of work, if

I hadn't been afraid that Bord would seize any excuse to get rid of me, I might have given up and gone home. But that wasn't an option.

The dry winds filled every metal surface with static electricity, and when I touched the light switch in my office, a spark stung my fingers.

"Damn," I muttered. My hair lifted at the roots; I felt my pants clinging to my butt, but I didn't have a free hand to pull them away. It didn't matter, though; I was the first arrival that morning.

Or so I thought until I passed Derek Bord's open door on my way to get coffee. Surprise, surprise, the little prick was already at work. Making trouble for somebody, no doubt.

Angel, windblown and flushed, arrived a few minutes later. We bitched about the weather, and I could tell something was going on with her, more than merely the effects of the wind. I started to ask and then changed my mind. She'd tell me when she was ready, and I had plenty of my own crises to handle.

I let myself stew part of the morning away thinking about Frank. Had he made it through the night? Probably, or Elise would have phoned. Where was Clayton, and was he coming back? Should I go by Frank's after work and relieve Elise, or had she gotten help?

After an hour or so, I decided I'd done enough wheel-spinning. Jacobs wasn't paying me to obsess about Frank Krajewski, and I'd better do something to earn my keep. The phone was quiet, and so was my email. Maybe the Santa Anas had knocked everything out. Usually at least one emergency showed up on Mondays.

The wind howled around the metal window frame and rattled my frazzled nerves even more. When the noise stopped, the silence was almost as bad because I knew it wouldn't last. The best antidote was to get busy, so I tackled some of the projects I'd stuck in my "Pending" file until I had time to work on them.

I'd whittled the stack down by half when Derek Bord caught up with me.

"I have an urgent task for you," he said when I answered my phone. No polite greeting or inquiry about my welfare. No concern over whether I had time to take on any more work. And who the hell else but Derek would say "urgent task"?

"Go ahead," I said.

"Arthur Trent's secretary is retiring. We need a replacement."

And you're telling me this because Arthur's your boss and you want everyone to know?

Arthur Trent was a decent guy, if a little weak in the backbone department, and I tried not to hate him for hiring Bord. His secretary, Elaine Monroe, had been with him since before I joined the company, but she didn't look old enough to retire. What was up with that decision?

"I'm not sure how that involves Corporate Compliance," I said, trying to diplomatically remind Bord that my job duties didn't include recruiting secretaries.

He made an exasperated little "tsk" noise, and I could picture his squirrel face scrunching up.

"As you should realize by now," he began, "our roles and responsibilities are going through a transformation. I know this assignment would have otherwise gone to your friend Ms. Desmond. But as she no longer works for us, and since Jeff Tate is busy learning the fundamentals of his new position, you're going to have to pick up the slack. I believe you spent some time in the Employment area before your current position."

I absorbed the remark about Val. *Focus, Susan. Focus on what he's asking, and be careful.*

So Bord knew my work history. Interesting. I *had* pinch hit for the Employment supervisor during my time in Personnel.

"That was years ago," I told him. "And it was mostly college recruiting. Secretaries are a lot different."

I spoke the truth. Angel had been a happy accident. Before her, I'd made two dreadful choices of assistants. The first one quit after six months for a "better" job—in other words, one where she wouldn't have to actually assist someone but could do her own thing. Val helped me fire the second one after more than a year of lost documents, mangled messages, and missed deadlines. Angel didn't have the whole skill set; her typing was great, but she didn't know a spreadsheet from a bedspread when I hired her. Lucky for both of us, she was a fast learner.

"I'm sure the principles are the same," Bord said in his stiff whiny voice. "Give it some thought, and I'll expect your recommendations after lunch."

He hung up.

I had a bad, bad feeling about this. Bord was looking to clean house for sure, to mow down the resistance and fill his staff with ass-kissers like Jeff Tate and Lilah Cantrell. And that left me with only a couple of choices.

I wasn't sure which one was worse, so I stalled for time.

First I talked to Angel. It would be cutting off my right arm, but I knew she could do the job if she wanted it, and it would mean a promotion and pay raise. Her reaction wasn't quite what I expected, though. The secret that had been bubbling around before Bord's call finally boiled over.

"Oh shit, Susan, I guess this is a lousy time for this to happen, but …" She took a deep breath, puffed her cheeks, and exhaled. "I got a part in a film. A big part. I can't believe this new agent—she's amazing."

"Congratulations!" I said, and I really meant it. Angel had been working toward this all the time I'd known her; at least one person's life was going in the right direction.

"It's a Jake Larimore film," she said, as if I'd know who that was. "He's really hot right now, I'm so lucky."

"Great," I said. "I guess this means you'll need some extra time off, right?"

Angel bit her lip. "I think it means I'll have to quit. We start filming in two weeks. In Prague."

"Prague? As in Eastern Europe?"

Her blonde curls bobbed up and down. *Son of a bitch. So I'll have to go it alone, won't I?*

As sad as that made me, I was pleased for Angel, and glad she was getting out of Jacobs before things turned really ugly.

"I understand," I told her, "and I guess that answers my question about Elaine's replacement, huh?"

"Sorry! Even if I wasn't leaving, though, I don't think I'd be right for the job. But you know who would?"

"I'm all ears."

"Don't argue until you've thought about it, okay? What about Ginny?"

"No way!"

"I said, think about it first."

Angel held up her fingers and started ticking off points in Ginny's favor. One: she was a computer whiz. Two: before coming to Jacobs, she'd been the secretary for some big shot at Paramount, until he got fired along with anyone who might have the least loyalty to him.

"I didn't know that!" I said.

Angel smiled. "You've never had lunch with her."

Three: Ginny was technically out of a job, since Val was gone and Jeff Tate had his own assistant. And she needed the income: she had an eighth-grader who was showing a scary talent for playing the viola, and Ginny wanted to send him to some fancy-shmancy music school in a couple of years.

When she tried for Point Four, however, Angel got stuck.

"Her taste in clothes is hideous," I said.

"You can fix that! I'll help."

Angel had on a bizarre outfit herself: snug white leather skirt with pale pink tights that matched her blouse. But somehow she could pull it off in ways that would forever be beyond Ginny's grasp.

"I'll think about it," I promised.

Angel's idea would sure solve the problem, and quickly. Ginny was a known quantity. And if it didn't work out, well … I'd tried to tell Bord that recruiting secretaries was not my strong suit.

Then I realized that I had to call Val Desmond—get her feedback on Ginny, and any other ideas she might have for Elaine's job, and find out how she was doing without it sounding like a pity call.

"Hey," I said, when she answered the phone. "It's me. Susan."

"When'd you get the word?" she asked.

"This morning." That much was true. Bord hadn't confirmed anything until then. "I don't know what to say," I went on. "Except I'm so sorry, and I think it sucks, and I can only imagine how I'd f—"

"It's all right, sweetie. Honest. Sure, I'm pissed, and I'm scared, but I'd pretty much expected it. Besides, I gotta take some responsibility for what happened. I provoked him. Like I wanted out but I didn't have the nerve to do it directly."

"Yeah, but he shouldn't have tried to ace you out of your job."

"No, he shouldn't've. But it's kind of a relief, you know? Bord never liked me anyway, and it was so damn hard to be civil to him. Now I can move along, find a place that I like. That likes me."

"Take me with you."

She laughed. "I gotta find it first."

"Time to start networking."

"I already have. I have an interview tomorrow morning. Probably won't amount to much, but it's good practice if nothing else."

That figured. Val had never been one to sit around twiddling her thumbs.

"Great," I said. "In the meantime, I have a huge favor to ask. For me, not Derek."

I explained the Elaine situation and Angel's idea.

"Ginny could do it blindfolded," Val said. "But maybe Arthur will need the blindfold, considering how she dresses."

At least Val's sense of humor had survived.

"I know. Angel promised to help with that before she runs off to become a movie star."

I filled her in on Angel's big break.

"That's wonderful," she said. "Only now you'll have to find a replacement for *her*. Maybe you should consider nabbing Ginny yourself."

"No way," I said. "She hates me."

"Nobody hates you, Susan, except in your imagination."

Yeah, sure. "Except maybe Bord," I pointed out.

That was good for another laugh before we said "goodbye and good luck"—and I wasn't sure who needed the luck more, Val or me. After I hung up, I thought about what she'd said, that this came as a kind of relief, that she was glad to be out from under Bord and his slimy ways. So what did that say about me, that I was still hanging around?

I pulled Ginny's personnel file and made some notes while the rest of the department took a lunch break. Good thing, because at two minutes after one, Bord called me into his office.

"Well?" he said.

I put out the Ginny Loring suggestion, and he sat staring at me like I had fern fronds growing out of my head. His fancy pen tapped relentlessly on the desk blotter.

"Is that the best you can offer?" he asked.

"It makes the most sense," I said. My toes were curling with the effort it took to be civil. "She's got the company history, the skills, the—"

"Interesting you didn't propose your own assistant," he said. "And she did a fine job substituting for Lilah, by the way."

"I'm sure she did, but Angel is leaving us. She's gotten a part in a movie, and she'll be filming out of the country."

Another reptilian stare. "Really."

I nodded. "It's going to be hard to replace her, but of course Elaine's job will get first priority."

Bord rubbed his lumpy little chin. "I wonder if we need to replace Angel."

That stumped me. "Excuse me?"

"I wonder if you couldn't share an assistant with one of the other managers. It would help us get to our staffing goal. Do you really need a full-time assistant? Can't you do a lot of the work yourself?"

"I could." I fought to keep from spitting out every syllable. "But it wouldn't be the most cost-effective use of my time."

Bord squinted at me. "You still haven't grasped the big picture, have you, Susan? You're still fighting me."

"I'm not fighting you, Derek, I'm trying to point out the illogic of paying someone a manager's salary to do their own copying and—"

"It sounds to me like you want to join your friend Desmond in the unemployment line."

"Is that a threat?"

"Of course not. But I do wonder if you'll ever be happy here, Susan. Frankly, I don't see you as a team player."

Maybe it was the wind, or the smoke, or the static electricity that put a red filter on everything. Or maybe my dislike of Derek Bord, like the dry brush in the foothills, finally sparked and caught fire. My self-control evaporated. *So this is how Val felt.*

A shard of light bounced off the pen in Bord's hand and cut through the red haze long enough to restore my voice.

"I can think of worse things than unemployment, Derek. Like continuing to work for you."

The pale beige carpet of Derek Bord's office looked endless, but somehow I made it out the door and back to my office. I sat down at my desk for probably the last time. *Oh, shit, what'd I just do? Breathe, Susan. Breathe.*

* * *

"Remember to breathe, Susan."

That was one great piece of advice my late boss Paul Dumas had given me. Overcome with stage fright, I'd been about to do a presentation on fair employment practices to a bunch of cranky scientists. I tried not to show my fear, but Paul—the picture of cool confidence in front of a group—saw through my act. He always did.

"Just remember to breathe, Susan. Before you go into the room, take a deep breath and let it out. Get some oxygen to your brain. Then focus on what you're going to say."

Trembling outside the conference room, I followed his advice. After two or three breaths, damned if I didn't feel a tiny bit better.

The presentation had gone fairly well. Paul sat at the back of the room, his face without expression, but every now and then he'd grin. After my talk, one of the geologists came up and thanked me for my time.

"You helped us understand why these things are important," he'd said.

Paul had winked at me from behind the guy. That was the kind of man he'd been. He wanted his people to succeed.

* * *

I sat in my office and thought about challenges I'd overcome in the past and how Paul had believed in me, and I missed him more than ever right then. I tried to convince myself I'd survive this latest crisis. And I breathed. And breathed.

The phone rang. Outside call, no ID. When I snatched the receiver and said my name, I almost didn't recognize my own voice, but I knew the caller instantly.

"Susan, it's Elise. Can you come? Frank's asking for you. It's getting close now."

Angel was coming back from lunch when I hung up.

"I have to leave," I told her. "Frank's worse. And I think I quit my job."

I gave her my disjointed version of what had gone on in Bord's office as I grabbed random files from my desk and stuffed them into my briefcase. She nudged me out the door with a promise to do an orderly assembly of my papers.

"Call me when you can," she said and hugged me tight.

I almost started to bawl, but I didn't. There'd be plenty of time for that later.

The smell of smoke stung my nose as I rushed to Frank's. A thick gray curtain filled the western sky. Normally I'd allow myself the luxury of gratitude that it wasn't my home in danger, that I was safe from the fire, but that afternoon I didn't feel the least bit safe.

Chapter 13
Ashes to Ashes

Only one car sat in Frank's driveway: his ash-coated Beamer. The absence of Clayton's Range Rover told the rest of the story.

Elise flung the door open before I got to the top porch step. She looked like she hadn't slept since Sunday afternoon. As I walked past her, I caught a whiff of something stale and sad, something worse than the smoke.

Barely conscious, Frank thrashed and muttered in his hospital bed. Elise introduced me to Yolanda, a stately African American in a blue smock who was wiping Frank's face with a cloth. She had lovely brown eyes, a compassionate smile, and an interesting accent that I later learned came from Kenya.

The television was on, the volume turned low, and the video coverage made it seem like all of Los Angeles was on fire.

"Frankie," Yolanda crooned, "Susan is here."

I moved up to the head of the bed and squeezed his hand. "Hey, Frank," I said. He didn't respond so I raised my voice a little to be sure he could hear me. "It's Susie. I'm here."

His eyes opened. The pupils were immense and opaque, but his fingers curled around my hand and squeezed.

"Susie." The word sounded thick with mucous.

Frank's eyelids drifted closed again. I stroked his clammy forehead and tried to convince myself that the tortured human in the bed wasn't really Frank.

Yolanda slid a chair over for me.

"Just hold his hand," she whispered. "He knows you are here."

She sat down in one of the armchairs and turned toward the television, but I could see from her posture that she was paying more attention to us than to the news. I heard the clink of china and the whine of a tea kettle: Elise at work in the kitchen.

"Would either of you like some coffee or tea?" Elise asked in a voice as wispy as smoke.

Yolanda accepted a cup of tea, but I was afraid to let go of Frank, afraid he would die at any minute.

Elise brought her coffee in and sat on the other side of the bed. "He's been like this all day."

A shaft of smoky afternoon sunlight put her face in cruel focus. Red veins threaded her eyes, and her face was puffy and bare of makeup.

"Have you called Becky?" I asked.

Yolanda nodded silently, and Elise made a soft snorting noise. Her hair looked woolly, like she hadn't brushed it in days.

"She's useless," Elise muttered. "She won't do anything to help."

"She's doing what Frank wants—"

Elise's red eyes were wide and fierce. "You keep saying that, but I don't believe you! My son would not want *this*." Her hand swept over the bed. "He doesn't deserve to suffer like this."

Yolanda's face went blank. Maybe she'd learned to tune out meltdowns by grieving families.

"I know it looks horrible, but—"

"It doesn't just *look* horrible, Susan! It *is* horrible! Don't you have any feelings at all? Or are you still so angry with him that you enjoy this?"

It took every ounce of self-control not to get up and punch her. I was shaking from the effort.

Why do you always assume the worst about me, Elise? What the hell did I ever do to you, except marry your son?

Even with the hospital bed a physical barrier between us, even in her grief, Elise had the power to sting. Power I gave her. Why?

And then Frank opened his eyes, and they were as clear and alert as they'd been the day I met him. He squeezed my hand.

"Susie? You look scared."

I forced a smile. "I'm worried about you, big boy. You've been having a bad time."

He looked from me to his mother and back.

"I know. I'm dying, huh?"

He seemed to be asking for confirmation, so I nodded. "Yeah, Frank. You're pretty sick."

"Pretty sick," he echoed. "Susie, promise you won't let people come look at me when I'm dead."

"Okay," I said, to humor him along.

"Say it. Say you won't let people come—"

"I promise, Frank. I won't let people come look at you. Okay?"

I glanced toward Elise for reinforcement, but she merely stared at us; her mouth sagged open and stayed that way.

"Good," Frank said. He dozed off for a few seconds and then came back. "One more thing, Susie. You didn't mean it before … now you have to."

"Have to what, Frank?" I honestly didn't expect an answer.

"It'll eat you up if you don't, Suse. You have to … have to forgive me."

"Forgive you? Of course I do."

For what? Getting cancer and dying? Or for leaving me the first time?

Did it matter? Yeah, it did. And had I forgiven him for Clayton? Is that the kind of thing you can just *release*, like a captive bird? I took a deep breath and stroked the back of Frank's hand.

Did it really make any sense to hold on to my grudges against Clayton and Frank? They hadn't fallen in love on purpose, or to hurt me. I'd seen enough to understand that part of the puzzle.

"Swear you do, Susie. Swear it."

Elise sat up; I felt her energy gather itself. *Okay, you stubborn old witch, listen to this.*

"I swear, okay? You couldn't help it. I understand. I forgive you."

At first I meant it only to appease him, and maybe as a bonus to show Elise how noble I could be. But when the words came out, a weird thing happened: my whole body separated into a gazillion atoms, and I could feel every one of them sizzling and sparking and moving around, separating and coming back together.

The feeling passed in a millisecond, but I had to blink and swallow and hang on tight to the hospital bed with my free hand. Maybe Frank sensed it too, because his smile seemed to say, "Told ya so." And darned if I didn't feel a thousand times cleaner and lighter than I had when I walked into the room.

Frank's face relaxed, and so did I, but the afterglow didn't last.

"Where's Clayton?" he asked.

Damn. I should've seen this one coming. So much for my newfound calm.

Elise leaned forward. "He's at work, baby."

"Oh. Yeah."

He closed his eyes, and I thought he was sleeping, but then he looked over at me again. "Read to me?"

When Frank and I were married, he loved for me to read him to sleep. He didn't care what I read, or even if I started in the middle of something. Fiction, nonfiction, or an article in *Cosmo*, he'd listen for a few minutes and then his breathing would deepen, and I could see sleep cover him like a fuzzy blanket.

I looked around and saw the short story collection Dan had given him, lying on the coffee table. I flipped through until I found a story that started off upbeat and easy.

"He always woke up in a good mood," I read, and Frank relaxed and settled in for the journey. Elise stood and stretched, then disappeared down the hall. Evidently I was trustworthy enough for the moment. Yolanda, too, had moved away. I heard her rinsing dishes in the kitchen while I read.

The story grew a little darker than I would have liked; it turned out that "he" was the narrator's son, a child born with a birthmark on his face that made him the object of torment by his fellow second-graders. By the time the story ground to its semi-happy conclusion (the boy's one true friend betrayed him, although she later came around and tried to apologize, Frank had surrendered to La La Land.

Yolanda must have been listening, too, because she murmured, "You have a pretty voice."

I put the book down next to a framed photo in which Frank and Clayton smiled into the camera from what looked like a beach in Hawaii. It knocked the breath out of me when I compared Frank's image with the man in the bed, his flesh stretched so thin it might tear at the slightest touch. A crust of white had collected at the corners of his mouth.

I fled to the bathroom, locked the door, and tried to muffle the heaving sobs that poured out of me. I sat on the floor, hanging on to the bathtub's edge, and I cried myself dry—or so I hoped.

Finally I stood, rinsed my tear-blotched face with cold water, and blinked a few times to try and get my eyes back to normal. After a few deep breaths, I opened the door.

Yolanda hovered nearby, her kind eyes large and moist. She held out her arms, and I grabbed hold of her. And damned if I didn't start bawling again.

"I know," Yolanda whispered. She smelled of oranges and vanilla. "It is very hard, when you love someone. Frankie is very lucky that so many people love him, even though they suffer now too."

"What's wrong?" Elise's voice came from behind me, and I pulled away from Yolanda and rubbed my face.

"Susie is sad," Yolanda said. "I was comforting her."

Elise shrugged and went back to Frank's bedside.

The doorbell rang, and my first, if illogical, hope was that Clayton had come to his senses. But no, the afternoon nurse had arrived: Amelia, a stocky Hispanic woman about Elise's age. She listened attentively as Yolanda gave her some brief instructions on the workings of the morphine pump and the family dynamics afoot in the room. Amelia nodded and murmured "Yes, yes" several times.

As Yolanda gathered up her bag and her coat, she seemed reluctant to leave. I wondered how often she'd seen this kind of scene played out. It could never have a happy ending, and I wanted to tell her how much I admired her for sticking with it, but I could only say "Thank you."

She kissed my cheek. "God bless you, Susan," she whispered. And then she was gone, leaving that whiff of oranges and vanilla behind.

Amelia smelled more earthy, almost like charcoal, but maybe some traces of the wildfire had come in with her. The television flickered in the background, showing the fire still going strong, but the newscaster gave us some hope that it would be contained by the next day. If the whole county didn't go up in flames by then, that is.

Amelia settled down in the chair by Frank's bed, and I followed Elise to the kitchen. My nerve endings were rubbed raw, but that's no excuse for what I did next. You don't kick a person when they're down, no matter how much they provoke you.

"What you said earlier," I began, "was way out of line. No way am I enjoying this."

She turned to me, her expression tight and weary. "You want an apology? Fine. I'm sorry."

I wanted more than words, though. I wanted her to mean them.

"'Sorry' doesn't cut it, Elise. You've hated me from the start, and I've had it with you and your criticism. It's not my fault he turned out to be gay."

My voice came out low and harsh, and I was conscious of my hands curling into fists. *Don't go there, Susan; you'll hate yourself later.* Tough shit. I wanted blood. All that time, all those years, all that anger shoved out of the way. I was tired of pushing it down. Tired of watching Frank die, tired of missing him and feeling betrayed by him, tired of this woman's silent air of disapproval.

Elise put the kettle on the stove, and in the silence I heard the hiss of the gas burner.

"I never blamed you for that," Elise said at last.

"Maybe not, but you did for plenty of other stuff."

"I certainly did not."

"You never gave me a chance. To you I was some shallow little gold-digger out to glom onto your money. You never saw how much I loved Frank and took care of him, never gave me credit for earning my own way."

God, I'd been holding those thoughts in for about a hundred years. And even as I hated myself for dumping them on that poor old grieving woman, it felt so good to get them out in the light where they could bounce around and stir up dust, where I could look at them and question them and decide if they were real or the product of my damaged imagination.

"Oh, Susan." That was all she said, and those three syllables held a world of accusation and apology.

Elise poured steaming water over a tea bag and offered the cup to me. I shook my head. No truce offering now. I'd hit pay dirt. *The truth stings, doesn't it?*

"I never meant for you to feel that way," she said. "And perhaps I didn't approve of you at first, until I got to see what a good woman you are. I never wished for Frank to leave you. Especially not the way he did."

Her words sank into my brain. *"… a good woman …"*

Exhaustion flowed over me. So much anger and hurt, like a huge ball of yarn I'd been rolling around with me for years. No wonder I was worn out.

"That I believe," I said. "You didn't want that."

She nodded. "I'm sorry for what I said before. It *was* uncalled for. I know you care about him, and I really *do* appreciate your being here." She found a tiny smile for me. "Even though I may not act like it."

I held up my hand. "Truce."

"Truce," she said. "He's lucky you're more generous than some women." She shuddered. "I always thought I knew my son, but I was so wrong. I was too caught up in my own world, in how I wanted him to be, that I never saw who he really was."

"Everybody does that," I told her. "Everybody has a picture of other people in their mind, and it hardly ever fits with reality."

We went back into the family room, where Amelia was fussing over Frank and pretending not to notice us. I hoped her English skills were fuzzy enough that she'd been spared most of our conversation. And Frank still slept; he must have been dreaming because his eyes moved under closed lids. I looked at the photo of him and Clayton.

"We have to get Clayton back here," I said to Elise, as softly as I could.

"How?"

I looked at my watch: almost five o'clock.

"I bet he's at work. I'm going to give it a shot."

Elise looked down at her dying son. Her lips pressed together and almost disappeared. She nodded. I scribbled down my cell phone number and handed it to her. "I'll be back in an hour, one way or another. But call me if there's any change."

Rush hour traffic had reached full thickness as I headed north, toward Clayton's clinic, praying he was as devoted to his patients as I thought.

The smoke smell got in through my Honda's air conditioning vents, and I sat in a clot of homebound traffic, inhaling ashes. What had they been before ashes? Trees? Houses? A deer or coyote unable to outrun the flames? I tried not to think about that, to focus instead on what I'd say to Clayton when I caught up with him.

A pink, hazy darkness filled the sky as I pulled into the parking lot of Fieldcrest Animal Hospital. And there it was: Clayton's Range Rover, parked at the far end of the lot. Great. I angled my Honda behind it, so close I blocked it in. The coward would have to go through me to escape this time.

The receptionist, a petite Asian woman who looked about twelve, frowned as I came in. "We're just closing."

"Fine. I don't have a sick pet anyway. I need to see Clayton."

She looked baffled, so I added, "Dr. Selden? It's a personal matter."

She glanced down at the telephone, like it would tell her what to do. Maybe it did, because she then said, "He's with a patient."

"Okay. I'll wait."

I got close enough to read her name tag: Bambi. *Good grief.*

"But it's very important, Bambi," I said in my softest, most urgent voice. "A family emergency. Please get word to him that Susan is here, and it's very critical I talk with him as soon as possible."

Her narrow face whitened several shades, and she nodded, scribbled something on the message pad by her left hand, and went into the back of the clinic. Minutes later she returned, opened the connecting door and pointed toward one of the exam rooms.

"You can wait there," she said. "He'll be right with you." Her eyes looked huge in her tiny face, and she kept a careful distance between us.

When Clayton swooped in, white doctor's smock flapping around his knees, he looked as haggard and stressed-out as Elise. I caught a glimpse of my reflection in a mirror behind him and realized I didn't look much better. My hair was sticking out every which way, and the dark smudges under my eyes were partly fatigue and partly flaked mascara. No wonder I'd terrified poor Bambi.

"Is he—" Clayton started to ask and then faltered.

I shook my head. "Not yet. But it's close now. Clayton, you have to come back."

He turned away and fiddled with some bottles on the counter top. I heard Bambi's voice through the closed door, a quick laugh and then a telephone's trill. Other sounds filtered in, similarly muffled: a dog barked, paused, and repeated itself, probably pleading, "Get me out of here!" The overhead light had a greenish cast to it, and I smelled antiseptic, but thicker and duller than the smell of the human hospital I'd so recently visited. *Frank and Clayton met in a room like this. How unromantic.* A photo of a Doberman hung on the wall, its teeth covered with metal braces.

In his white doctor's coat, Clayton looked larger and more substantial than I remembered. Dragging him away by force wasn't an option, then. I'd have to use my brilliant verbal powers.

"I can't!" he said finally. "I don't want to remember him like that."

His voice sounded like fingernails scraping chalkboard.

"Do you think any of us do?" I snapped. "Do you think this is some picnic for his mother and me?"

He turned to face me. "It's different for you. You don't love him the same way I do. You don't understand what it's like to—"

My hand came up on its own, and I slapped him. Hard.

"Oh, I understand plenty. I understand you're a whining little weasel who was only there for him in the good times. Damn you, Clayton. You wanted him. Now stand by him."

He rubbed his cheek, and I was proud to notice a red splotch where I'd struck him. "I have stood by him! I've watched him waste away, held his head while he puked, cleaned up his shit. I've seen him in pain so bad it hurt me just to be there. And I cannot take it anymore."

"You won't have to for much longer. It's almost over."

When I said that, something inside me let go. Suddenly I felt ancient and depleted, like I'd said and done everything in the range of human experience: read every book, heard every symphony, run through every emotion. For way too long. I didn't have an ounce of energy left. I couldn't change things anyway. Who did I think I was, Superwoman?

"You know something?" I went on. "I came out here for your sake as much as Frank's. I'm pretty sure you'll hate yourself forever if you don't come say goodbye. But now I don't care if you hate yourself. You don't deserve him, you weak piece of shit. Go to hell."

I tugged the exam room door open and stomped out. Bambi was putting on her jacket, and she froze as I stormed past her and out the front door.

* * *

Frank was still hanging on to life when I got back. I told Elise I hadn't been able to persuade Clayton to come home, and she muttered, "It figures." I wasn't sure if she meant that as a criticism of Clayton, me, or both of us. *Stop being so damned sensitive.*

A short time later, the doorbell sounded. Ralph whuffed and ran toward the front door, and I hurried after her.

Flo stood on the porch, holding a Domino's box and a six-pack of Michelob.

"This is getting to be a habit," I said.

She eased past me. "I hope you like pepperoni."

I didn't think I was hungry, but the smell of tomato sauce and oregano tantalized my overwrought senses. We consumed the pizza with a surprising zeal—stress eating, they call it. Elise and I each polished off a Michelob, and I surrendered to the pleasant bubbly numbing of my dread. Flo relieved Amelia so she could eat, too, and stood watch over Frank, wiping his face and saying, "Yes, dear heart, I know," to whatever gibberish phrases he muttered.

Amelia finished off a third slice of pizza, washed her hands, and went back to Frank's bedside. Flo popped open a beer and sat down with Elise and me in the kitchen, where we had a clear view of Frank in the hospital bed, far enough away that we didn't hear every sound he made.

Flo patted Elise's hand. "How're you holding up, hon?"

Elise shrugged. She looked like she might burst into tears, but her defenses held.

Ralph had been snuggling up to us and looking for a stray crumb of pizza. I heard a noise in the hallway and she turned, whined, and loped toward the front door. Elise and I got up simultaneously to see what the fuss was about, but I was pretty sure we already knew.

Clayton crouched in the entryway as a quivering Ralph licked his face. When he saw us, he stood and dusted his hands on his jeans. Without his white doctor's coat, he looked like a scared little boy, and his face was wet. How many tears had it taken to bring him home?

Curiosity shone in Amelia's dark eyes, and I wondered if Yolanda had filled her in on his part in the drama. If not, she'd have figured it out pretty quick, because Frank came to and struggled to sit up.

"Who's there?" he croaked.

Clayton hurried to the bed and kissed him on the lips.

Frank settled down. "You're home."

"Yes," Clayton said. "I'm home."

"Would you like something to eat?" Elise asked. Her voice held no trace of reproach, only relief.

Clayton shook his head. "I'm fine." He settled into the bedside chair.

But refusals never stopped Elise Krajewski. She put some pizza on a plate, opened a Michelob, and took them to him. "You need to keep your strength up."

She stood beside him with her hand on his shoulder. Framed in warm yellow lamplight, Elise and Clayton looked almost like mother and son. Perhaps Clayton would be able to move into the painful empty place Frank would leave behind, and I was glad for them, even as I resented the sudden but too familiar sense of exclusion. Maybe, however, the time had come for me to butt out; I'd done my part.

Rather than stand and gawk, I started to clear the table, but Flo took the dishes from my hands. She put her arms around me and patted my back, and I soaked up the comfort like a sponge. At least somebody understood how I felt.

"You look exhausted, Susan," Flo said. "Why don't you go take a nap?"

Elise looked up. "Yes, dear," she said. "You can use my room. I'll call you if there's any change, I promise."

Clayton's eyes never looked away from Frank, not that it mattered to me. Sleep was irresistible.

I left the bedroom door ajar, kicked off my shoes and flopped onto the bed. The pillow smelled faintly of Youth Dew—Elise's perfume, I remembered—a nice smell, comforting and sweet. The door swung open and Ralph panted into the room and onto the bed. I didn't know if this was permissible, and I didn't care. I buried my hand in Ralph's soft fur and let her heavy breathing rock me to sleep.

$$* * *$$

What was that sound? A horrible rattling, gasping noise, like a vacuum cleaner with something stuck in its hose. I sat up in the alien darkness and tasted stale tomato sauce, and for about thirty seconds I couldn't get my bearings. Then I remembered: Frank's guest bedroom. Ralph had deserted me, and the digital clock display read three twenty-three.

I stumbled toward the door, and the terrible noise grew louder. Even though I didn't want to follow it to the source, I had to.

Flo stood at the kitchen counter, making tea. The smell of cinnamon and cloves competed with harsher, antiseptic fumes, and in the family room Frank sat upright in the hospital bed. His mouth gaped as he wheezed and rasped. A harsh gurgle interrupted the struggle, and a slender young white man in a nurse's smock wiped Frank's mouth with a cloth. I glimpsed thick strands of mucous as he pulled the cloth away.

Clayton and Elise huddled together, their backs to me. Clayton had his arm around Elise.

Flo handed me a steaming cup of tea. "We've called Becky," she said. "This can't be good."

I nodded and sat down at the kitchen table, staring at the action in the other room. Nothing I could do for Frank, I realized.

"That's Ken," Flo whispered. "He came on duty right after you nodded off. He seems to know his stuff."

"Have you had any sleep?" I asked.

Flo cackled softly. "Don't need it. I run on caffeine and alcohol."

She didn't look the least bit tired, so maybe it was true.

Becky showed up before I finished my tea, and unlike Flo she looked sleep-deprived and a little rumpled, but there was no accusation in her kind gray eyes.

"This is a part of the process," she explained. "I know it sounds horrible, but he's not in pain, honest. His body is shutting down."

I tried not to listen, but I couldn't help myself, as she went on to tell us how Frank's heart wouldn't be able to keep up the strain much longer. I wondered how long *our* hearts would be able to withstand the stress.

Ken smiled reassuringly and introduced himself while Becky checked Frank's vitals. Then she put her instruments away.

"His breathing will get better again," she promised.

On her way out the door, she hugged each of us, even me, and then we all went back to our roles: Flo puttering in the kitchen, Elise and Clayton hovering around the hospital bed, Ken swabbing the mucous from Frank's mouth, me standing hopelessly alone. How long would this horrid tableau last?

Flo put her arm around my waist. "You've been a rock for us during all this. Simply a rock. Hasn't she, Clayton?"

"Yes," he said, "she has." He didn't look at me, though. He and Elise were still focused on Frank.

Flo stretched and rubbed her back. "Well, maybe I will catch a few winks if you're up and around now, hon. I'll be right down the hall if you need me, though."

Those few feet of hallway swallowed my one ally. *Don't be ridicu-*

lous, I told myself. Clayton and Elise weren't really teamed up against me; the strain of everything fed my imagination too much fuel. I focused on Ken, the neutral party in the room. Did he know the tangled relationships around him? Would he even care?

I took a deep breath and reminded myself to be grateful for being able to breathe, unlike poor Frank. His strangled effort tore into my heart. I forced myself to slide a chair up next to the bed, across from Clayton and Elise. The IV needle was still poking out of Frank's hand, but I found a patch of his wrist to hold and stroke.

A few minutes later his breathing eased off to an almost normal rhythm. Elise's hunched shoulders relaxed, and she let out a mouthful of air.

"Thank God," she murmured. She stroked Frank's forehead and started to cry. Clayton put his arms around her and let her bawl, and I tried not to resent my own lack of comfort.

Ken cleared his throat. "Mrs. Krajewski," he said softly, "why don't you go have something to eat? You need a break."

For a flash of a second I thought he was talking to me. Then Clayton took Elise by the elbow and steered her toward the kitchen; he sat her down while he popped some bread into the toaster and poured her a glass of orange juice. She kept her eyes on Frank the whole time she chewed the toast and drank the juice, as if she was willing the rhythmic rise and fall of his chest.

I stayed put and gently rubbed Frank's wrist, hoping he sensed my presence. I felt like I was touching the root of my existence, a tiny quivering thread of life and breath. In a whisper I hoped Elise couldn't hear, I told him, "It's okay, baby. You can let go now if you want to." I didn't mean for the goddamn tears to slide down my face, but they did. "I love you, Frank."

Ken handed me a Kleenex, and I snuffled my thanks, then stretched my shoulders to unkink some of the muscles. The sky outside was changing from black to gray, with a crust of pale blue on the edges. Another day being born.

Next to me, Ken scribbled notes on a clipboard, and all of a sudden I could hear the scratch of his pen on the paper. That sound, and nothing else.

"Oh!" I said, louder than I meant to.

Frank lay silent and still. His mouth was open, and his lips pulled tight over his teeth; his thin, yellow skin stretched over the planes of his face like paper. The eyes were the worst part: a milky film obscured their blue radiance.

Disorientation flooded me. Where was I? What was happening? The railing on the hospital bed was so cold, so hard. The morphine pump was as helpless as the pill bottles lined up on the end table like defeated soldiers. The rising sun mocked the dim yellow glow of the table lamp, and some stupid bird greeted the new day. Then a plate shattered in the kitchen, and the whole world broke apart.

Ken closed Frank's eyes quickly, before Elise could see.

From the back yard, alone and forgotten, Ralph raised her head and started to howl. Maybe a distant siren set her off, but to me the piercing, mournful cry was a wail to Frank's departed spirit. On and on she howled, like she wanted to tear the sky open.

A woman's sobs drowned out Ralph, and first I thought it was Elise, until she cried out, "Oh my sweet baby!" and grabbed Frank's hand. "My sweet, sweet baby." I could barely hear her over the gasping sobs that I finally realized were coming from me.

By the time I got control of myself, sort of, Ralph had stopped howling. She bumped her nose against the sliding glass door, and I got up and let her in. I could barely feel my feet move; everything seemed blurry and unreal. *A bad dream*, I kept thinking. Ralph whined and settled down in the corner. I wanted to curl up next to her and bawl some more, but it was so hard to move that I stood like a big, useless statue on the ragged edges of the lamplight.

Elise stroked Frank's face. "I didn't get to say goodbye."

Ken patted her arm. "He didn't want you to see him go," he said softly.

Clayton was frozen in place in the kitchen. I remember thinking, *Go ahead—now's the time to show some grief. Let it out, or you'll explode.*

But he didn't. He moved very slowly toward the bed, his face a pale mask. Maybe he'd done all his wailing and moaning already so that he could be calm and together to deal with Frank's death.

Elise was another story. The woman I'd thought of as Old Stone

Face washed away in a torrent of tears. Her whole body quivered and shook so hard I could almost feel the floor vibrate, and dumb stupid me, I just watched. My own meltdown had been merely a sniffle in comparison.

Somehow, crazy as it sounds, until the instant Ken closed Frank's eyes, I kept thinking, *This isn't real, it's a dream, a movie.* It all seemed optional, like I could choose a moment to bail out, refuse to go along with the mass delusions—and everything would rewind like a movie, and Frank wouldn't be sick anymore. But when Ken's hand moved over Frank's face, when I saw the *nothingness* in Frank's eyes, reality crashed down on me. And I could no more go comfort Elise than I could fly.

Flo did it for me. Seconds after Elise cried out, Flo was up and in action, fluttering around like a little angel of mercy, enveloping Elise in her strong, thin arms while Elise sobbed and shuddered.

"There, there," Flo murmured. "I know. It hurts so much. I know."

She didn't make any fake promises that everything would get better in time. She just let Elise feel the horror of losing her son. And the selfish kid buried right beneath my grown-up façade craved that same kind of comfort. But it wasn't owed me, I reminded myself. I'd moved past that kind of involvement with Frank. Then why couldn't I stop crying?

Clayton's eerie calm prevailed as he and Ken conferred over the hard details of death. Clayton phoned Becky, and then the mortuary, while Ken disconnected the needles and tubes running in and out of Frank's body.

Ralph was still curled up in the corner by the television, nose tucked into the curve of her tail, dark eyes taking in all the noise and activity. I felt a rush of pity for the dog. Had anyone fed her or walked her lately? She looked confused, and I probably needed her sympathy more than she needed mine, but it was the one thing I could do. I got up and took her leash from the closet; her ears perked up.

"Come on, girl," I whispered, "let's get you out of here for a while."

No one looked our way as we headed out the door.

Bright blue light engulfed the sky, and I saw no trace of smoke; the brushfire had been conquered while we were watching Frank die. The street smelled of damp lawns and winter. I still wore the clothes I'd gone to work in the day before. Had it only been twenty-four hours? I couldn't run in my leather pumps, so I walked as briskly as I could, and Ralph seemed fine with that. She peed a couple of times to show her gratitude, sniffed a lot of lamp posts and bushes, and didn't protest when I turned back toward Frank's. *Toward Clayton's*, I corrected myself.

It was finally over. No more hearing Frank gasp and struggle for breath as he thrashed around in pain, dissolving into coughing spasms when he tried to talk. Now I could go home, back to my safe, familiar life. My safe, familiar, empty little life.

A white panel truck was parked in the driveway when we got back. No identifying signage, but I figured out it belonged to the mortuary. I took one more deep, ragged breath and pulled myself together before we went inside.

A man and a woman in similar dark business suits were at work in there. The guy had covered Frank with a sheet, and the woman was sitting at the kitchen table with Clayton and Elise, filling in blank spaces on a form. Nothing happens without paperwork in quadruplicate. Clayton remained placid and matter-of-fact, and Elise's composure had slid back into place.

Flo came down the hall from the bathroom, rubbing lotion into her hands. "Oh, that was nice of you to take Ralph out," she said. "How are you doing, darling girl?"

"Okay," I lied. "I'm really sad, but—"

"But you're relieved for Frank, aren't you? Believe me, I understand."

Elise's angry voice cut through the calm. "I won't agree to it!"

Clayton murmured something, but she wasn't pacified. "It's bad enough you let him suffer this horrible death, and if it wasn't for Susan, you wouldn't have even been here when he died. But I will not permit him to be cremated and buried in California."

The woman from Forest Lawn had a soft, soothing voice. "Mrs. Krajewski, I'm afraid we're bound by your son's written directive."

I wondered if this sort of thing happened often: families stuck together for the horrible parts, then split into factions when the crisis was over.

"My son was out of his mind with fear and pain! He didn't know what he was doing!"

She launched herself out of the chair toward Flo and me. "Won't you help me with this? I can't bear to leave him here!"

My first urge was to remind her that Frank was gone and that it was only a body lying there now, but I didn't entirely believe it yet myself. I had to say or do *something*, however. It was the least I could do for Frank.

"Elise, it really is what he wanted," I told her. "Remember yesterday, when he made me promise not to let people see him after he's gone?"

She jerked her head up and down but showed no other sign of agreement. "Very well—closed coffin. I can accept that. I can even accept cremation, although I don't like it much. But I want to have his funeral at home, with his family."

"Clayton's his family too," I said softly.

"I want to be able to visit my son's grave!"

Personally, I've never been much for funeral rituals. I wanted cremation myself—and then to have my ashes scattered in the ocean. Or the mall. But I understood her pain. There had to be something comforting about a visit to your loved one's grave; otherwise why would so many people come and leave flowers? And it did sound like Frank, to want his body turned to ash, and the ash returned to the ground in California, the land of perpetual sunshine.

Then it came to me: Paul Dumas' funeral. My old boss had had very strong views about death and dying, and he was usually prepared for almost anything. Despite being in supposedly good health (the heart attack was a total shock to everyone, including his doctor), Paul had written out a detailed advance directive about what he wanted done to his body when he was dead. He wanted to be cremated, and most of his ashes were interred at Forest Lawn, but he stipulated that a small portion be set aside for a symbolic scattering around the family's vacation cabin near Lake Arrowhead. It had been his favorite place in the world, his widow had told me at the funeral, and they were going up to scatter the ashes the next day. It would be very comforting to her and to their two sons, she said.

"I have an idea," I told Elise, and explained about dividing the ashes. "Then you can take part back to Chicago and have your own service with the family."

She turned to the Forest Lawn people. "Can I do that?"

Both of them nodded vigorously, and Clayton's angry mask softened.

Elise's weary, blotched face relaxed. "Oh, Susan, no wonder Frank loved you."

That was too much praise from her, so I turned away. At this rate, though, we'd be hugging and kissing like family before long. The thought made me a little queasy.

While Elise and Clayton finished up the arrangements, I put some kibble in a bowl for Ralph and added a spoonful of canned food the way I'd seen Clayton do. Ralph gobbled it down while the folks from Forest Lawn wheeled Frank's body out on a stretcher.

Flo put her arms around me. "Are you up to making a few phone calls?"

I nodded and drained a glass of water. "Sure. I have the list. But I think I'll clear out and make them from home—unless anyone needs me."

Neither Clayton nor Elise reacted, so I figured I could safely bail out.

"I'll be right behind you," Flo said. She patted my back. "I'm glad you were here. Now go get some rest."

And there: I was free.

* * *

The way home was clogged with people going to work. I sort of envied them when I remembered I was out of a job. But that was over and done with—no way to retract that scene with Bord.

I looked forward to a long, hot shower. But first I had to phone Pete and Joseph, Rhonda and Michelle, and wreck their morning. Flo's telephone tree would take over from there, spreading the sad news to

Frank's friends. Elise would call Zoë and Grandpa Krajewski. I was almost finished with Frank and his dying.

I pulled in the driveway and saw Zeus the cat scramble over the fence. Just like old times, just like nothing had changed. The trouble was, everything had.

Chapter 14
Lights Out

The phones calls exhausted me. The moment she heard my voice, Rhonda knew why I was calling, and she started to cry before I choked out the news. *What would* Flo *say? How would she tell them?*

"It happened so quickly," I began. "He just … stopped. But he was ready, and … and it was pretty peaceful." Mostly true, anyway. No sense burdening Frank's friends with the rest of the story.

Michelle had come on the line too, and I heard tears in her voice. "He's safe now."

"Yes," I agreed. "He is."

They asked about Clayton, and I did my best to reassure them, without total confidence that he and Elise hadn't found something else to fight about.

"He was real strong at the end," I said, "holding Frank's hand and—" I had to stop and take a breath "—and I know Frank knew he was there."

Okay. One down, one to go. I dialed Pete and Joseph. Joseph answered, and, like Rhonda, he sensed right away the reason for my call.

"So it's over," he said softly. "Are you all right?"

No, of course I wasn't all right, but how do you say that, when it's not about you? Sure, I was relieved of the horrors of Frank's dying. But would I ever be all right again?

After that call, I wanted more than anything to crawl into bed and pull the covers over my head, but there was one more person to tell: my mother.

Mom wasn't one of those warm and fuzzy souls who can make your hurts go away with a hug and a kiss, but she surprised me that morning with the verbal equivalent of a comforting embrace.

"Oh, Susan," she said. "Do you want me to come?"

Her reaction stopped me in my tracks. I considered the offer. Would it help to have her with me, or make things worse? An image of Mom hovering, watching every bite of food I put in my mouth, exploded in my head before I could stifle it.

"Thanks," I said, "but no sense disrupting your life, too."

I think I heard a big sigh of relief. My mother, a disciplined woman, had routines and schedules that she hated to change. The mere offer to deviate from them amazed me. Jack had mellowed her, for sure.

"All right, darling, but call me if you need anything," Mom said.

"I will. Thanks."

"Is his mother there? I hope she's not taking her grief out on you."

Mom knew my version of how Elise had treated me when Frank and I were married. And if my mother did not always approve of me one hundred percent, God help anyone else who didn't. She'd only met Elise once, at our wedding, and I could tell Mom didn't like her much even then. Maybe she recognized some of herself in Elise: the strong willed and opinionated self. They had a lot in common: single moms, forced to live by their wits and abilities. Unlike Elise, though, Mom didn't have the Krajewski bucks behind her.

"She's actually being okay," I said. "All things considered."

"Give her my sympathy ... I don't even want to imagine what it's like to lose a child."

Was that a catch in her voice? Maybe it was just the phone line.

"I will. And how's Jack?"

I heard an exasperated laugh. "He has buried himself in the show we're putting on right now. Oh, I wish you were here to see it. We call it 'Emerging Voices of the Southwest,' and the paintings just take my breath away."

The loving way that she said it was pure Mom. These were her surrogate kids now, these artists struggling for recognition. She rattled on for a minute about how gratifying it was to discover new talent, and then she remembered why I'd called and cut herself short.

I was tempted to tell her I could hop on the next plane to Albuquerque and drive up to Santa Fe for the show, but then I'd have to explain my newly unemployed state. That should be another conversation, for another day. Mom had always been proud of her "executive" daughter. I once overheard her telling a neighbor, "Susan bought this shawl for me on one of her business trips. She travels a lot for her company, you know."

To her, my career probably seemed exciting and exotic, and if you didn't factor in the likes of Derek Bord, sometimes it was. I was going to miss it.

"Give Jack my love," I said.

"I will—and he sends his right back. Take care of yourself, darling. And I hope Elise appreciates having you there. You're the one I'd want by *my* side during a crisis like this."

Me, Mom? Your chubby screw-up of a daughter who can't even hold down a job?

I was getting drowsy by then and figured I'd earned a nap, but no sooner had I dozed off than the phone rang. Val Desmond's voice dragged me out of that dark fuzzy place where nothing hurts.

"I phoned you at the office," Val said, "and Angel told me what happened."

"Yeah," I replied. "Looks like I've joined the club."

"You can't let him do this to you. You have to fight back."

"I don't have any fight in me right now," I said, and went on to tell her about Frank.

"Oh, sweetie, I am *so* sorry. I know you loved the bum even after what happened. Look, forgive me for being hard-assed here, but you gotta look past that for a minute. You still need to earn a living— unless you won the lottery and didn't tell me."

"It's too late."

"Tell me word for word what went down."

I did.

"You didn't actually say that you quit," she said when I finished. "You were just speculating. You have to go back in there, Susan. He can't fire you, and you didn't quit. Make the little bastard squirm."

"I can't. I've had enough." *I'm sounding just like Clayton. Jeez!*

"You have to. And you can. Besides, work is exactly what you need right now to take your mind off Frank."

The haze in my head started to clear. Val was right, as usual. Bord had no grounds to fire me. So maybe he wanted me gone—but he'd have to do better than make empty threats. He'd have to open the door and shove me out.

"Okay," I said. "I'll give it a shot."

* * *

After we said our goodbyes, I closed my eyes again. Sleep wouldn't come, so I hauled my butt out of bed and went for a walk. The toasty Santa Anas had given way to a cool breeze off the ocean, with a tinge of winter in it. I felt mighty damn lucky to be alive and out walking around.

I thought about Clayton, and Elise, and Mom, and the people who'd been wrenched from my life: Frank and Margaret and Noah. If only I could've wiped out the past few months; if only Frank hadn't gotten sick. I wanted him back, laughing and healthy, even if we were no longer married. And Margaret: I missed her counsel, and the comfort of knowing she saw my higher self even when I couldn't. Noah? I missed being part of a couple, sure, but he'd only been on loan to me anyway. I didn't miss the constant worry about pleasing him—even if it was purely in my imagination. Let June sweat that one out if she wanted him so much.

I came back from my walk tired enough to finally sleep.

* * *

When I walked into Jacobs' HR department the next morning, Angel almost fell out of her chair.

She gave me an extravagant hug. "Oh God, am I glad to see you!"

"What's up?" I said, looking around, scoping out enemy turf. Trying to act casual, like I'd strolled in for a normal day's work. Like I hadn't walked off the job two days earlier.

"That guy with the ponytail—the one you told me about—he's been prancing around like he owns the place."

Streitzler. My skin prickled.

"He wanted to use *your* office," Angel continued, "but I sent him away—said there were a bunch of confidential files in there."

The sweet gesture of solidarity almost got me bawling, but I held myself together.

"Smart move. Thanks."

Angel smiled and shrugged. "He's a sneaky one. Kind of oozes his way around."

"Yeah," I said. "He does. Anything else going on?"

"Derek's been huddled with Pony Tail most of the time. But, hey, Ginny interviewed with Mr. Trent yesterday, and he offered her the job."

So Bord used my idea after all. However it came about, I was glad for Ginny.

"That's great," I said. "Sometimes we win a round."

Angel grinned. "So—do you still work here?"

"I think so. We'll find out pretty soon."

I booted up my computer and got a cup of coffee, then checked my messages: twenty-seven new emails and eleven voicemails. Good signs—no one had cut off my computer access, and I still had clients out there who needed my help.

Before tackling anything else, I pulled out my personnel file and made copies of all my performance reviews. My very favorable performance reviews, countersigned by Arthur Trent himself.

Bord made his usual half-hour-late appearance, and if he noticed me at my desk, he didn't react. I was on the phone with Rollie Sanders, the Dallas plant manager, advising him about an employee absentee problem that was undermining Rollie's production goals. It seemed pretty straightforward and defensible to me, and I told Rollie that as long as nobody else got away with the same behavior, they could give the guy a couple of weeks to mend his ways or pick up his final paycheck.

Bord did not have nearly as much cause to fire me, or even Val. We both had excellent attendance and performance records. All he had to go on was resistance to changes he'd proposed to make in our jobs, changes that could be construed as unnecessary and unreasonable. And —surprise, surprise—he hadn't done anything similar to his *male* managers. *Hmmm, Derek, can you spell discrimination?*

I didn't feel solid ground underfoot yet, but it was starting to firm up as I reviewed the circumstances. And now Bord was bringing his old friend Streitzler into the mix. What was that all about? Clearly, Bord had ignored my written evaluation of Streitzler's seminar as essentially worthless. Of course, I hadn't known he and Bord were buddies when I wrote the report, but it wouldn't have changed anything. Or would it? Might I have toned down my opinion to pacify the little prick? Nah.

A few minutes later Lilah Cantrell called. "I need your account coding," she said without so much as a "Good morning."

"Excuse me? What coding? Why?"

An annoyed hiss came over the line, and I visualized Lilah coiling around the phone like a giant python.

"Mr. Bord is charging some expenses to your consulting fees account."

"Why? Derek has his own budget."

"He didn't ask me to explain it. Maybe you have some extra money in there. Technically, it's his anyway, Susan, so would you please—"

"I'll give you the coding," I said, happy that my voice came out dead calm, "but I need to know how much is being charged, and for what. So I can adjust my budget projections."

Another irritated exhale. "All right. It's for Dr. Streitzler's services, facilitating the outsourcing. The invoice is for ten thousand dollars."

I almost dropped the receiver. Ten grand! For what? So that pretentious goofball could run around exhorting everyone to shatter paradigms and exude passion for their work? And Bord figured he was going to be rid of me and my expenses, so he could bury Streitzler's fees in my budget?

Think again, Dickhead.

But I gave Lilah the coding string and hung up. *Choose your battles,* I reminded myself.

Then I got one of my dangerous brainstorms—dangerous because I might find out more than I wanted to know. I typed "Myron Streitzler" into the internet search box and waited less than ten seconds for his website to come up. His biography was almost identical to the one on his brochure, which I pulled out of my bottom drawer for comparison. His doctorate came from Kensington University. When I first saw it, the name hadn't registered.

Then something struck me as familiar, so I typed "Kensington University" into the search engine. Aha, now we were getting somewhere. A newspaper article from three years earlier: a scandal over Kensington's accreditation. Allegations of degrees bought by the highest bidder. The term "diploma mill" appeared twice in the article.

And aside from the questionable doctorate and a stint as a facilitator for a self-improvement movement called Fulfillment of the Higher Mind, good ol' Myron didn't have much to show for his forty-plus years on earth. So how had he met Bord, and even more important, how could he justify a ten grand fee for "helping" Jacobs in its time of assumed need?

One dangerous thought follows another. I didn't have access to Bord's personnel file, but I had a copy of his résumé, which Arthur Trent had thoughtfully provided each of the managers Bord was hired to supervise, so we'd know what a spectacular find Bord had been. Yeah, right. I flipped to the last page, and sure enough, there it was: Bord's M.A. had come from Kensington University.

Now why the hell hadn't Val picked up on the Kensington controversy when she did the usual reference check? Maybe the scandal hadn't been publicized enough. Or maybe she *had* noticed it but hit a brick wall when she told Arthur, who'd been so dead set on hiring Bord. Val could've turned up evidence that Bord had masterminded the Enron scandal, and Arthur might well have replied, "Wasn't that clever of him?"

I needed to figure out my next move, but no quiet time was at hand. As I put Bord's résumé aside, Arthur Trent marched into my office.

No one filled a room quite like Arthur. He was a tall man, thin and white-haired, with an air of perpetual worry about him, underpinned with a kind of mournful vulnerability that always made me want to jump in and solve whatever problem brought him to seek my counsel. That morning, however, he came not to ask for help but to thank me—for recommending Ginny Loring as a replacement for his beloved Elaine.

"I know there'll be a break-in phase, but I think she'll do fine. I would never have thought of her."

I was stunned that he knew it was my suggestion, but then I realized what must have happened. Bord didn't expect them to click and planned to blame me for the lame-brained proposal, but he had to ask Arthur to interview her, to prove they'd given consideration to an existing employee before casting their net outside. Bord probably had a friend or a relative ready to step into the job when Ginny washed out. Only she hadn't.

Thank you, Ginny.

"I can't take all the credit," I said. "It was actually my assistant Angel Fairweather's brainchild, but when I checked into Ginny's background, it seemed like a good fit."

He nodded his agreement.

"We're going to work on her wardrobe," I added.

Arthur grinned. "Yes that was my only reservation. But it's nothing a little coaching can't fix."

"That's true. I'm happy that you're happy, Arthur. Truly."

He studied my face for a minute. "Everything else going okay?"

What was up? Had he heard about my clash with Bord?

"Pretty much. I was sorry to see Val Desmond get fired. She was a valuable member of the team."

"I always thought so, but Derek ... well, when Derek makes his mind up, it's hard to change it. As I'm sure you know."

Arthur didn't make eye contact with me, and that tipped me off to a lot of things. How old was he, anyway? Over sixty, with two decades of Jacobs employment behind him, easing up on retirement. No time to rock the boat. No time to admit a colossal error in judgment. Hell, he was probably grooming Bord as his successor.

Did I take a chance anyway, even if I thought it was useless? Yeah, I did.

"Oh, yes, I've learned that Derek has firm opinions."

Learned the hard way.

I paused for a few seconds to work up the nerve. "But I've also learned he's not always right, Arthur. This thing with Myron Streitzler —have you taken a look at his background? I did. And I have serious doubts that he's the right choice to facilitate the outsourcing."

Arthur scowled. "Do you?"

I nodded. "Do you know he and Derek went to Kensington University together?"

Again, Arthur looked away, and his eyes moved from side to side as he pretended to study my bookcase, my desk, the prints on the wall. Anything but my face. Anything but the truth.

"I'm aware of that. But it's a small world, Susan. People know one another, they meet up in the strangest ways sometimes. I don't think that's grounds for challenging Dr. Streitzler's ability to help us through this difficult time. I've met with him for several hours, and he seems genuinely concerned and caring. He takes his role very seriously."

So: Arthur didn't want to see that the Emperor was buck naked. He'd chosen sides.

I felt like all the energy I'd put into Jacobs and my career there had been sucked away from me in a muddy torrent. I got a sad, terrible glimpse into the company's future, with cowards like Arthur and schemers like Bord running the show. The company was doomed. Maybe not that year, or even the next, but sooner or later it'd get a reputation as a bad place to work. And then it would attract only people who didn't care about the atmosphere, they just wanted to get in, get their share of the pie, and get out quickly.

Okay, Arthur, don't say I didn't warn you.

Arthur stood up. "Well, you keep up the good work, Susan. We need more employees like you."

Too bad, because you'll have one less if Derek Bord gets his way.

And Fate showed a sense of humor at that moment, because who should come slithering in the door as Arthur was speaking? None other than little Mr. Bord himself.

I put on a good show, shaking hands with Arthur like we were really tight friends, smiling with every ounce of sincerity I could summon. It was worth the effort to see Bord's mouth drop open. He covered his surprise pretty well, but not fast enough.

Arthur nodded to Bord on his way out. "Just expressing my gratitude to Susan for finding a fine successor to Elaine. You should be proud of her."

"Oh, I am, Arthur. I surely am," said the lying little prick.

With the tiniest look of uncertainty in his misaligned eyes, Bord sat his sneaky butt down in the chair Arthur had vacated.

"So," he said, "I'm pleased that you've reconsidered your hasty actions of the other day."

I didn't say anything because I was hoping silence would work for me, would push him into saying more than he wanted to. I was hoping he'd start to squirm. People like Bord need constant reinforcement. They fall apart when you simply stare at them, so I did. Sure enough, I noticed faint little beads of sweat appear along his hairline.

"I understand you recently lost a close friend," Bord added. "You have my condolences."

"Thanks."

"It certainly helps me understand why you flew off the handle with me. These things can be horribly stressful."

I took a deep breath. "I wouldn't characterize it as 'flying off the handle,' Derek. I made a reasonable suggestion to solve a problem you'd given me. You didn't like my suggestion. And as best I recall, you made some remark about me 'not being a team player' and suggested I might be happier working someplace else."

The squirrel face appeared. "I thought we might be able to cease the hostilities, Susan. Apparently I was wrong."

Fine, you little bastard. But don't think you're getting rid of me that easy. I'm smarter than you, and I have a few tricks up my sleeve you never even thought of.

"You know, Derek, that's the problem. You see hostility where I see a simple disagreement. Disagreements needn't be hostile. You and I disagree on many things, but I assure you, I respect your viewpoint. Which is, unfortunately, more than you do for mine, I think."

The idea came to me while I was talking. I had a weapon; all I had to do was use it. He couldn't force me out of my job. No way.

He crossed his arms in the classic defense pose. "I don't know what you're talking about."

"What I'm talking about, Derek, is a gender bias that started during your tenure in the department. This is me—Susan—you're dealing with. I keep the data, remember? And I know how it'll look if Jacobs loses two of its few women managers. And let's look at the facts: both women are—or were—in your shop. Both have superior performance ratings."

I rattled my sheaf of performance evaluations for emphasis. Bord jumped at the sudden noise, and a little shiver of triumph ran up my backbone.

I kept going. "And what happens when you take over the department? One woman gets fired because she won't roll over and play dead when you try and reassign her to an inferior job and give *her* position to a *man*, a man with no proven track record in her area of expertise. This woman is over forty, by the way, so she's in two protected classes. And I know you're familiar with the term 'protected class,' aren't you, Derek?"

He nodded, and his dark eyes were glittering hate at me by then. "Very familiar. That's why I asked you to review the documentation on the Desmond incident, to see if any potential for discrimination existed. As I recall, you assured me that we were on solid ground."

The last thing Bord expected was that I could play as dirty as he could.

"I don't recall using the term 'solid ground'—and I don't recall putting anything in writing."

His knuckles turned white from gripping the chair arms, and I noticed a vein begin to pulse in his forehead. Good.

"You're joking."

"Nope, I'm dead serious, Derek. Did you actually think I'd just pick up my marbles and go away without a fight? Then Val's not the only person you underestimated. And even if I did tell you that techni-cally you had *some* basis for firing Val, that was before you threatened *me*."

"I did no such thing!"

"Yeah, you did. Threatened my job—*and* threatened to take away my assistant. None of the *men* managers in your department have to give up their assistants, just the one remaining woman manager."

"That was a measure of economy reflecting a streamlined organiza-tion post-outsourcing," Bord said with a smug little grin. "And it has no bearing on what happened with Desmond."

"Oh, it does. And don't trot out the cost-cutting excuse. Because then you'd have to justify hiring a very expensive consultant, one with questionable qualifications, who happens to be an old friend from school—and we won't even go into the school business right now. I'll save that for another time. See, Derek? Add it all up, and it comes out to three words: pattern of discrimination."

"That's ridiculous!"

"Not really. Not when you think about the facts I've laid out. Oh, and there's one other part of the story—the frosting on the cake. Constructive discharge."

His face scrunched up again. A roll of flesh below his chin quiv-ered enough to let me know I had him on the run.

"Constructive discharge," I went on, ticking off points on my fingertips, "occurs when an employer makes an employee's working conditions so intolerable that the employee feels she has to leave."

"I know what it is," Bord snapped. "And I know how hard it is to prove."

"Yeah, it is. But do you want to risk it? Risk the distraction of a lawsuit?"

Bord's face had turned an unhealthy red by then. "Now who's making threats?"

"I'm not threatening anyone, Derek. I'm merely pointing out the potential consequences. And you may think Arthur's on your team, but when the lawyers start filing motions, he may not be standing right behind you."

Bord leaned back and crossed his legs, clasped his knee with interlaced fingers and did a lousy job of acting casual and unafraid. After the cozy scene he'd witnessed between Arthur Trent and me, he had to wonder how much I'd said to Arthur and what Arthur had said to me.

In the silent room, I heard the second hand jump around the face of my little gold-plated desk clock, the one I'd gotten for ten years of employment with Jacobs. Bord looked like a trapped rat, but I, for the first time all day, felt the walls of my office expand. A heaviness went out of the air, and I could breathe again.

"What do you want?" Bord asked in a low, deadly voice.

I counted to ten, silently and slowly, while I watched more sweat appear on Bord's forehead. And all of a sudden I knew exactly what I wanted. Hell, I'd known all along where this was going.

"I want us both to be happy, Derek," I said. "You don't much like me—and that's fine. This isn't a popularity contest. But since we disagree on so many things, and since I know you'd find it easier to work with someone who shares your ideas about how things should be done, we'd both be happier if I went to work somewhere else."

"If that's your wish, I certainly won't stand in your way," Bord said, his eyes forming squinty little slits.

"I appreciate that. You'd get what *you* want, too—me, out of the way. And in exchange, I'd need a cushion—financial consideration, to tide me over while I look for another job."

The slits got even narrower, if that was possible. "How much?"

This time I counted to twenty. *Ask for the sun, settle for a planet.* "A year's severance would be reasonable, under the circumstances. It's a bargain, really."

He uncrossed his legs and straightened his tie. "A year."

"Yes. Look what you get in return: I go quietly, and you can replace me with someone who thinks like you and acts like you and supports your point of view."

I could almost smell rubber burning inside his head. He stroked his chin and stared at the ceiling. "That's too much. I'll give you six months."

Aha. His brain hadn't shorted out on him.

Another ten-count. "Nine months."

More chin-stroking. "Six is my final offer."

Bord picked up my Brand-X ballpoint pen and started clicking it. Click, click click. He must've wanted to jab it right between my eyes, but he contented himself with the relentless noise-making.

"Six then," I said. "Including medical and dental coverage."

He nodded, and I thought *damn—I should have held out for more. This was too easy.*

So I added, like an afterthought, "And the same for Val Desmond."

I was almost surprised to hear the words come out of my mouth.

"Desmond? I didn't realize she's part of this little scheme of yours."

"She isn't. And it's not a scheme, Derek. It's a negotiation between two reasonable parties who have conflicting goals. And after all, if this is about treating people equitably, you wouldn't want to show favoritism toward one of us, now would you?"

God, I was better at this than I ever expected. My skin was prickling with excitement, and the words kept coming out. And no matter what he decided, I felt proud that I'd put up a damn good fight.

He tossed the pen on my desk. It skidded across the surface and landed in my lap. I put it back on the desktop, relieved that my hands were not shaking.

"Very well," he said. "You'll have to sign releases."

"Along with written severance agreements—with pleasure." It was all I could do to keep the glee out of my voice. "And of course we'll want good references as well."

"Of course." He spat the words out, but I didn't care.

Bord stood up. "Goodbye, Susan."

And he stomped out of my office and out my life. I made myself take a couple of deep breaths while it all sank in. Six months. Long enough to find another job. To figure out what I wanted to do. Six months. It sounded like forever, but I knew it would speed by in a blur.

I called Angel in and told her what had happened, and she looked sad but not surprised. And after all, she wasn't going to be around that much longer anyhow, I reminded myself. I outlined my severance agreement, since she'd probably find out anyhow. One of her friends was the paralegal who would no doubt draft the releases for Val and me to sign.

Then I got busy with my inbox and my outbox and all the things that a model employee does. I assumed my pardon took effect immediately, but I wanted to leave a clean desk for the next poor sucker to sit in my chair.

* * *

A few minutes before quitting time, Ginny Loring came tapping at my door. She was dressed as atrociously as ever in a bright green jumper and matching clogs. "I wanted to thank you," she said. Her freckles popped out against her pale skin.

I tried to look puzzled. "For what?"

She edged into my office like she was ready to bolt if I so much as raised my voice, so I concentrated on being friendly and calm. I motioned her toward one of the guest chairs and she sat, but on the edge. I felt a twinge of sympathy for her; was I really that intimidating?

"You recommended me to replace Elaine."

I smiled at her. "You're the best choice, Ginny."

"Mr. Bord tried to make me think he put my name in, but Angel told me the real story. It's just like him to take credit for other people's ideas."

She wrinkled her nose and I felt a surge of gratification. So Bord's true colors were better known than I suspected.

"It doesn't matter who suggested it," I said as neutrally as I could. "The main thing is to get a good assistant for Mr. Trent, and to advance the people who deserve it."

Oh, what wonderful Corporate-Speak, Susan.

"I hope the overtime won't be too hard," I added.

Ginny smiled. "Actually … I'd been thinking about moonlighting at something else—to build up some money for my son Dennis's music classes. Anyway, I want you to know how much I appreciate this. I thought you didn't like me, and—"

"I know I can be a little abrupt sometimes, Ginny. I'm sorry if I was rude."

She stood up. "I understand—and if I can ever do anything for you—say the word. Good luck to you, Susan."

I was speechless, so I just smiled at her and watched her clump away. God, Angel was going to have to get busy with the wardrobe tips.

With no further interruptions, I responded to almost every request for help and information and drafted some memos for Angel to clean up and send out the next day. Then I put out-of-office greetings on my voicemail and my email inbox, and told anyone needing my help to consult Derek Bord. *Ha, ha, one last joke on you, sucker!*

When I looked away from the computer monitor, the world outside had been transformed: rectangles of light glowed in the night. I could see a few workers in the building across from mine, and they looked lonely and stressed-out. The Jacobs offices were deserted, and no wonder: my little clock read 7:43. But I felt like I was leaving things in good shape.

The muffled roar of a vacuum cleaner got louder; the cleaning crew had almost reached my office. Time to get out of the way. I looked around, remembering my first day in that office, the giddy feeling of *having arrived!* I'd earned my position the hard way, and most of the time I'd enjoyed it. And then—just like Frank's life—it was gone in a heartbeat.

I packed my clock and my coffee mug and my day planner. Not a lot of baggage for all those years.

"So long," I said as I powered down the computer. I flicked off the lights and walked out the door, scared and elated at the same time. I thought about calling Val to tell her what had happened, but then I figured it was safer to wait, to be sure Bord delivered. I had little doubt that he'd come through, but I didn't trust the slimy bastard. I could call Flo, but she didn't know the background so she wouldn't be able to fully savor my victory. I thought about Margaret and wished I could talk to her—she, of all people, would understand and appreciate what I'd done.

* * *

I reached for the chardonnay as soon as I got home. An empty evening loomed before me. *Get used to it. Plenty more coming.*

I peeled off my work clothes and put on my pj's. Yeah, that was the ticket: climb into bed with my wine and a book and read myself to sleep. Let some time pass.

Then the phone rang, and I nearly tripped over my pajama bottoms when I ran for it. "Hello!" Jeez, I sounded pathetically eager to talk to someone.

"Susan, dear," said Margaret Deschanels' husky voice, and I shivered. I knew I hadn't conjured her up with my thoughts, but the coincidence jolted me.

"Hi! I was just thinking about you. Where are you?" *Would she call all the way from France? Yeah, she might.*

Margaret's soft laugh soothed me. "We've finally come home."

"Welcome back," I said. "How was France?"

"Exhausting! I loved seeing my cousins, but I missed everyone here so much."

Much as I craved the relief of pouring out my troubles and triumphs, I held back. After all, Margaret had been through her own brand of hell the past weeks.

"I bet. So how's Claire doing? Have things settled down?"

"They never will, I fear, with that one. But she got what she wanted. She got Philippe's undivided attention. And mine."

"No more suicide threats?"

Again the soft laugh. "Claire, like many young women, has a strong sense of the theatrical. But I think the older professor lost his appeal when she met some of our relatives in Lyons. It opened up a whole new world of possibilities for her."

Margaret actually sounded proud of her daughter for the disruption she'd caused.

"But what about you, Susan? How have you been? And how exciting about Judy's new love, eh?"

I didn't know how to respond. So what if she'd already called Judy? This was no time for jealousy. Still …

"Yeah," I said. "It's great."

"And what's new with you? Did you and Noah work things out?"

Noah. I hadn't thought of him all day. That was a new, good

phenomenon. But Margaret had obviously forgotten the details of my desperate phone call the day he dumped me.

"In a way," I said. I tried to temper the pissy edge to my voice. *Give her a break—her daughter was threatening suicide.* "He's gone back to his ex-wife. I guess she was never that ex. He said it's for the kid's sake, but … "

"Oh, Susan—forgive me. I remember you two were in trouble when all this with Claire blew up, but I didn't realize it was that serious."

"It's not," I said after another deep, calming breath. "In fact, it's the least of my troubles these days."

"That doesn't sound good. What other horrible things have happened?"

Well, Margaret, my world has pretty much fallen apart while you were romping through the French countryside.

"Got a few hours?"

I thought I kept my tone light and teasing, but I heard a gasp on her end. And that pissed me off even more. I mean, she *had* asked. Since she didn't reply right away, I blurted out the first thing on my mind, and to my surprise it wasn't the loss of my job.

"Frank died."

"Ah. You *have* been through a lot. And even though it was expected, I'm sure you're grieving for him, no?"

"Yes. I am."

I heard a man's voice in the background but couldn't make out the words.

Margaret said, "One moment," and she must have put her hand over the receiver because her voice was muffled as she spoke to whoever was with her—probably Philippe, the often-absent husband.

"My apologies, Susan. We're still trying to work a few things out here. I'm not used to sharing the parental role."

"I bet."

"As you were saying—this is a very sad time for you. And have you sought help with processing your grief?"

I thought that's what I was just trying to do. And then it hit me: she meant, had I consulted an outsider for grief therapy? Maybe good old Dr. Francis?

My fingers were starting to tingle from clutching the phone, so I switched hands. "I think I'll try to handle it on my own," I said. How had I ever imagined this woman gave a damn about me? She hadn't even said she was sorry Frank died. It was *expected?* I couldn't tell her about my job. She might say that, too, was expected, and for the best.

"Susan? Are you still there?"

I realized Margaret had spoken and I hadn't responded while I fought the hot clutch of anger.

"Yes," I said. My voice cracked. "But it sounds like you're pretty busy right now."

"I'm never too busy to talk with you, my friend. Can we get together soon? Maybe you can take a long lunch one day next week?"

"I don't think so," I said. "I'm a little off balance—feel like I've been clobbered with a two-by-four."

She sounded detestably cheerful. "You must be overwhelmed. And here I come waltzing back, assuming nothing has changed. But on a positive note, I always felt you deserved better than Noah. Now you can make a fresh start."

Margaret's placid detachment stunned me. We might as well have been discussing the lack of fresh produce in the supermarket, as if the wreckage of my life was nothing but a small pebble's ripple on an infinite pond. And to her, maybe that's all it was.

I flexed my free hand. "Well, pardon me for not being overjoyed, but I just watched someone I love suffer and die. I'm not up for a fresh start right now."

"You're angry."

"Yes."

"Because I was gone when he died? Do you think I could have changed the outcome?"

"Of course not."

"But I wasn't there for you, and you wanted me to be."

"I suppose."

I heard Margaret sigh. "Susan, you are my very good friend, and I care about you so much. But I wish you could understand that it isn't always about you."

Ouch. Did I believe that? Did I act like that?

"I do understand. I have no right to expect you to drop everything and come running when I need help. I understand your priorities. You're entitled."

The words sounded good, but I didn't *feel* them.

"Look," I continued, fighting for control of my voice, "this isn't a very good time for me. I know I'm not making much sense. And I truly am glad you're back safely, and that things are better with Claire. We'll talk later, when I'm calmer, all right?"

And I hung up without giving her a chance to reply. What had happened to my wise and sympathetic best friend? Had I dreamed her up in the first place?

"Screw you, Margaret." I gave the telephone the finger. Maybe I'd call her again, and maybe I wouldn't. Maybe I needed a fresh start with my friends, too.

The call upset me, though, and I knew I couldn't simply fall into bed and drift off peacefully. Flo—maybe talking to Flo could help me calm down. She'd managed to salvage my good spirits several times already. I was feeling a little giddy from the wine as I punched in her number.

A man's voice answered. Deep and smoky. "Hello?"

"Uh—is—is this Flo's?" I stammered. "Is she there?"

"One minute," he said. Who the hell was he?

"Hey, babe—phone call!" I heard him say.

She came on the line sounding a little out of breath.

"Hi, it's Susan. I'm sorry, it sounds like I'm interrupting. You have company, so I won't keep you."

"Company? That's not company—that's Jimmy! I didn't tell you about him?"

"Nope," I said, feeling like an idiot for assuming Flo lived alone.

She lowered her voice. "Forgive me—I just assumed you knew. And please don't let him know I neglected to mention him. He thinks I babble on about him all the time! Let's keep that a secret, shall we?"

"I swear," I said.

"So, darling girl—how are you? The last two days have been horrible, haven't they?"

"More than I expected. I don't seem able to keep things together. I feel so empty."

"That's normal, y'know. You've been through a lot. Give it time. You're tough stuff; you'll survive."

"Yeah, I will," I said. "Anyway, I didn't mean to interrupt, I guess I just wanted to talk to somebody … and you got elected."

Flo chuckled. "I'm flattered. Say, why don't we get together tomorrow? I'd suggest breakfast, but you probably have to get to w—"

"Breakfast sounds like heaven," I broke in, without explaining my unexpected availability.

"Perfect! I love a nice nourishing breakfast! Let's go to Jojo's and have extravagant omelets and good French coffee. How's around nine sound to you?"

It sounded fabulous. I jotted down the directions to Jojo's and toddled off to bed, assured that at least one person in town cared about my feelings.

Chapter 15
"What Did You Expect?"

I slept until almost seven the next morning and awoke to clear skies, a stiff neck, and a vague throbbing in my temples from the previous night's wine. I had barely enough time to swallow some aspirin, shower, and get dressed before my breakfast with Flo.

She pulled into Jojo's parking lot a minute after I did, and never had anyone been a more welcome sight. Flo hugged me with amazing strength for such a small woman, and a tide of Shalimar wafted over me. She wore a red sweater, gray slacks, and, of course, black slingback stilettos, brilliant red lipstick, and several coats of mascara. I hoped I'd look that good, that vivid, when I was her age.

As we entered Jojo's, a cheerful layer of noise surrounded us: voices and laughter mingled with the clatter of silverware and dishes being moved around with fevered efficiency. I smelled cinnamon and coffee and baking sugar. The place was packed, but the hostess greeted Flo by name and led us to a window table right away.

"I recommend the spinach omelet," Flo said as we studied vinyl-clad menus. "Unless you just want to pour sugar into your bloodstream, that is."

I went with her suggestion, and while we waited for our food I felt some of the past few days' darkness let go.

I shook out my stiff white napkin and smoothed it onto my lap. "So who's Jimmy? I'm dying of curiosity."

"Him? Oh, he's my Boy Toy."

My face must have registered shock because she laughed so loud the people at the next table looked over.

"He does have a sexy voice," I said, not sure how much to believe.

"Oh, darling girl, don't you ever tell him! He's already hopelessly conceited! No, I mustn't tease you like that. Honestly, he's an old coot like me."

"You're not."

"You're kind, but I know what I am. I let go of my illusions a long time ago. Anyway, Jimmy and I have been together for years. He's a nurse."

If the morning had needed any more brightening, Flo's smile would've done the job. Outside the big leaded windows, sunlight ignited the Sweet Gum trees lining the street. A few reddened leaves had scattered on the sidewalk to give the scene a crisp New England look despite the California heat.

"I met him when I had my mastectomy," Flo went on.

How easily she said it. *When I had cancer. When they carved up my body to keep it from killing me.* Unlike Frank, Flo's cancer had been operable, and curable. Lucky for her, lucky for Jimmy, lucky for everyone who knew Flo.

The waiter set two mugs of fragrant coffee on the table. I blew on the steam, then took a sip.

"Great coffee," I said. "This is a neat place."

"I've come here for years. Mostly by myself. Jimmy's hours—he doesn't get out a lot. He never even met Frank and Clayton. But it's all right. He's there when I need him — that's what matters."

I envied her for having someone who was there when she needed him. Had I ever had that? Had I ever wanted it? I couldn't remember.

"He's afraid to marry me, though," Flo continued. "I don't have a very good track record with husbands, y'know."

One thing about Flo—she did know how to stop a conversation dead in its tracks. Fortunately, the food arrived then, and I admired its presentation, with pretty red and green garnishes ringing the delicate white china plates. Flo poked a hole in her omelet to release some steam while I buttered my English muffin.

"So tell me how you are, darling girl. How you *really* are."

I took a taste of omelet and chewed appreciatively, stalling for time.

"I miss him," I said. "It's dumb because I hadn't seen him a lot until he got sick, but—"

"But you cared about him, and he's gone. And it's natural to miss him. To grieve for him."

Yes, Flo would know about grief. How did she keep going, with all she'd been through? How did she live with the knowledge that someone you loved could be taken from you as fast as you could snap your fingers?

"Does it get easier?" I asked, and waited for the wise nod of the head, the acknowledgment that the passing of time would blunt pain's sharp edges.

Flo's eyes became unknowable caverns. No, I realized, she wasn't going to pacify me with trite lies. The morning sun accentuated the crazy quilt of wrinkles on her face, and for a minute she looked like she was wearing an old woman's mask, with a painted-on smile. The noise around us faded, and people's shapes blurred into a muffled haze, but Flo was in sharp, cruel focus.

She's going to tell me something terrible. I shivered.

Flo wiped her mouth and a red lipstick smear came off on the white napkin. "It never gets easy," she said. "But if you keep moving and breathing and putting one foot in front of the other, you can wait out the grief. You can outlast it."

"You make it sound simple."

She shook her head, a commotion of auburn curls. "Oh, no. It's the hardest thing in the world, to keep living when you've lost someone you love. At first you have to fake it, just go through the motions. But after a while it starts to feel real. It *becomes* real."

"What becomes real?"

"The feeling that you're still alive. Still in the game."

I put down my fork. "I'm sure you're right. But it seems so hard right now."

She reached across the table and squeezed my hand. "You don't have to do it alone, you know."

"I know," I replied, thinking she meant I'd have her support.

Flo fished her wallet out of her purse, extracted a frayed business card, and handed it to me. "He kept me from drowning in my own misery," she said gently. "More than once."

In a gray-green sans serif font was printed "Leonard Doss, MA, PhD, LCSW" and a phone number in the 310 area code.

I frowned. "A shrink?"

Why was everybody trying to herd me back to the therapist's office? Did I really seem that incapable of managing my own feelings? Maybe I did.

Flo waved an elegant hand in the air. "Grief counselor. After one too many mornings of waking up and being disappointed that I was still alive, I got out the phone book and … well, it probably wasn't the smartest way to do it, but I was lucky, and I truly think Lennie saved my life."

I shivered again and rubbed my arms; Flo leaned forward and her kind eyes bored into mine. "It was the best thing I did for myself," she continued. "I hope you'll call him. I know he can help."

I nodded. "I'll think about it."

"You can keep the card—I know his number by heart."

"Thanks." I knew she meant well—but how could I explain to a stranger what it had been like to lose Frank—not just once, but twice?

"You *will* get past this sadness," Flo whispered, and then her voice grew louder. "Frank once told me that he knew you'd survive without him. It was the only way he got up the courage to go with Clayton. He knew you were strong enough to recover. I've seen what you're made of these past weeks, darling girl. Frank was right."

I swiped at my watering eyes, and my index finger came away smeared with mascara. I probably looked like a mournful raccoon at that point, but Flo didn't laugh.

"I hope so," I said, "because this sucks."

"I know it does."

I dabbed at my face with the napkin and tried another bite of omelet. It was really quite tasty, seasoned with basil and oregano and cooked to perfection. And I realized as I swallowed that I couldn't remember when I'd last eaten. My appetite had gone dormant the past few days, but the taste of that omelet revived it. *How can I enjoy food, with all that's happened?* Hunger and guilt fought it out, and hunger won.

Flo ate with determination, if not enthusiasm, and I sensed that Frank's death had affected her zest for food as well. We talked about Clayton: Flo had checked in on him that morning, and he was, in her words, "holding his own." I felt a twinge of remorse that I hadn't thought to call Clayton myself.

As if reading my mind, Flo said, "I'm surprised he didn't check on you, after all you went through together."

Yeah, that's right. The phones work both ways. Relieved of my guilt, I could be generous. "I doubt that he's thinking real clearly yet."

Then Flo distracted me with stories of her visits to the children's hospital with her dog Ginger and how the kids' faces lit up when their furry visitor arrived.

"It's tough to see little ones so sick," she admitted, "but I wouldn't give up a minute of it, really." She paused. "I wish I could get Clayton to qualify Ralphie as a therapy dog. I know *she* would enjoy it, and she's such a love. She'd be perfect. But I supposed it'd be too much for Clayton right now."

Her gaze lingered on me, and I wondered if she expected *me* to step up and get involved. She didn't say anything else, because the check arrived. We got into a friendly arguing match over who was going to pay, then agreed to split the tab, all mention of therapy dogs abandoned.

Outside the café, I hugged her again and thanked her for the support.

"You're going to be fine, darling girl," she said, with her merriest wink.

"Say hi to Jimmy for me," I called out as I got in my car. In the rear view mirror I noticed a big red lipstick smudge on my cheek, and I didn't care. I caught a faint whiff of Shalimar when I turned my head to back the car out, and it was like a kiss from an old friend.

* * *

Something's wrong, I thought when I woke the next morning. *Something bad is going to happen.* I didn't want to get out of bed. I didn't even want to wake up, but once the mental alarm bells sounded, sleep didn't stand a chance, even when I remembered that the bad stuff had already happened. A heavy sense of dread persisted as I hauled myself from under the covers and peeked out the window to see gray skies and drizzle.

Swell. I couldn't count on Mother Nature to calm the jangly pinpricks dancing over my skin. The slow drip of water from the eaves drilled a hole in my brain while I brewed coffee and studied the Help Wanted ads in the paper. Nothing leaped out at me. I thought of all the people out there in their cars, creeping through soggy rush hour traffic, and I almost envied them for having somewhere to go, needing to get dressed for work while I sat in my pajamas and robe.

When I first started sneezing, I blamed the weather, but my hot, scratchy throat told me otherwise. *Terrific. I'm catching a cold.*

* * *

Megadoses of Vitamin C and warm salt water gargles were useless against the virus, and by late afternoon I was back in bed, nose slathered in Vaseline and sinuses alternately exploding and imploding. I slept on and off for four days, too miserable to do more than stagger to the kitchen, slurp some soup and then crawl back under the covers. At one point I wondered if this was it, if I was going to sink into a black hole of illness and never come back, and for a while I didn't much care. I shivered and sweated and slept away the hours. Every cough, every sneeze reminded me of my mortality—worse, of Frank and his last agonizing struggle to breathe.

The thick drizzle kept up, muffling the outside world and locking me away in my house, alone and wallowing in a swamp of misery. I had nothing and no one to get well for. If I just lay in bed and slept forever, who would know? Who would care? Leonard Doss's business card lay atop a pile of papers on my desk, but I told myself I was too sick to even call for an appointment.

$$* * *$$

When the doorbell rang just after eleven Tuesday morning, I assumed it was some annoying but weather-resistant salesperson. Then I peeked out the window and saw Val Desmond on the porch, shaking water off her umbrella. She looked surprised when I opened the door.

"Don't come close," I croaked. "I have the mother of all colds."

"Oh my God—do you feel as awful as you sound?" she asked.

"Worse."

"Oh, sweetie, I know it's horrid. I had it too."

"And you survived. Good to know."

Val bent and picked up a foil-wrapped pot of chrysanthemums. "I didn't mean to disturb you. I honestly didn't think you'd be home. I just wanted to bring a little thank-you for what you did."

"That's so nice." I hesitated. "Want to come in and risk a relapse?"

She pulled the screen door open and handed me the chrysanthemums. "Just for a minute or two. You need to rest."

She swept in the door, so bright and *healthy* that I felt better just looking at her, and at the cheerful white and crimson flowers.

"They're beautiful," I said. "Thank you so much."

Val grinned. "The least I could do."

"Want some tea?" I asked.

"Only if you let me make it."

She followed me into the kitchen and pointed to a chair. "Sit."

I sat. She filled the teakettle and found a couple of mugs while I opened the card she'd put with the flowers. "Thanks for prying that money out of Derek," she'd written in her bold, flowing script. "You're the best."

I smiled. "What makes you think that I—"

"The bastard would never have done it on his own," she said over her shoulder while she studied my meager collection of tea bags. "Earl Grey or Orange Spice?"

We both chose the spice, and while the tea brewed she sat down across from me. "Give me the whole story. What happened? Who blinked first, you or Derek?"

Val sat and let me talk, interrupting only once or twice to express her contempt for Bord and for Arthur Trent.

"Spineless jerk! I can't believe he backed Derek."

I shrugged. "I'm past being pissed off at them," I said. "It's over. Derek and Arthur still have to be what they are. That's punishment enough."

"I can't be as forgiving as you are. Yet." Val shook her head. Her sleek brown hair swayed with the movement and made me conscious of my own tangled, dirty curls.

"Just imagine Derek's beady eyes swiveling around in their sockets," I told her. "And Arthur having to look at him every day."

That got her giggling, and me too, and we fell into sweet, cleansing laughter for a couple of minutes.

"They *will* be sorry, though," Val said. "But by then you'll have a fabulous new career."

"Speaking of such," I said, "How'd your job interview go?"

Val fanned her fingers over the table top and grinned. "You're talking to the new Director of Recruitment for Meridian Healthcare."

Pleasure flooded over me. "Congratulations. I'd hug you, but I don't want to spread any more germs."

She beamed happiness. "I got lucky."

"Lucky my ass! You're the best person for the job, and they had the good sense to recognize it."

"Thanks. And, look, I still have a pretty active network out there—I got the lead on this job from a guy I met at a conference two years ago. When you're feeling better, I'll start putting out feelers for you, okay? Who knows? Maybe Meridian even needs a compliance manager."

"That would be too cool," I said, although I felt no enthusiasm for the idea, and Val seemed to sense it.

She cocked her head. "Unless you're thinking of a career change, that is."

"What makes you say that?"

She lifted her hands, palms up. "I dunno exactly. I just had the sense that you didn't exactly love what you were doing these last few months. I know some of it was because of Derek—but even before that, I sort of felt like your talents were wasted in compliance."

"Right, I'm just an endless reservoir of talent."

"You are, Susan. Don't sell yourself short." She paused. "At least explore some other options while you have the chance, okay? Maybe take a couple of classes, or see a career coach."

She grabbed a napkin from the table and scribbled a name and phone number, then looked up. "This is the guy who called me about the Meridian job. He's gone into the headhunting business on his own, and he's incredibly connected. Call him. Tell him I referred you."

Val's concern made me want to cry, and I turned her suggestion over in my mind like a shiny coin I'd found in the street. "I will. Thanks." I started to tear up with memories of our time at Jacobs. "Hey, we made a darn good team, didn't we?"

Her eyes misted over, too. "The best." Then she looked at her watch. "Yikes. I gotta go. And you need to rest. Can I rustle you up some soup before I take off? You need anything, groceries or Kleenex or cold meds?"

I shook my head. "I'm all set," I told her, and it was almost true. "You saved my life."

She pulled on her jacket and gave me another of those megawatt smiles. "No, Susan—you saved mine. Knowing I had that severance cushion—it gave me some nice leverage when Meridian and I started talking salary. I'll be thanking you for years to come."

She blew me a kiss, grabbed her umbrella, and trotted back into the rainy mist like a delicious mirage.

* * *

I woke at two a.m. in the chilly darkness between Tuesday and Wednesday. Frank had been dead for a week.

That was my first thought. The second was, *can it get any worse?*

Oh sure, my darker self replied. *It can always get worse.*

"Back off, Princess of Gloom," I muttered, even as I realized an argument with myself was maybe the first sign of a total mental breakdown to go with my physical collapse. I clicked on the light and sat up to clear my stuffy sinuses.

My reflection in the mirror on the closet door was appalling: hair plastered to my scalp, the skin around my nose red and peeling, eyes swollen half-shut. If my ribs hadn't hurt so much from coughing, I might have laughed at the sight. And I felt the tiniest stirring of a will to live that I thought had deserted me. I had to figure out a way to get moving again, so I dragged my sorry ass out of bed, bundled up in my big quilted robe, and tottered to the kitchen, a cup of hot tea the only thing on my mind.

I was still pretty wiped out, so I took my tea into the living room and sat on the sofa, staring into dark corners and waiting for my energy to return. Wondering if this was the new normal life for me.

Memories are brutal at two in the morning, when the rest of the world is dark and asleep. It was as good a time as any to be maudlin, so I pulled out my photo album and starting going over old pictures, not just those of Frank and me that had survived my post-divorce purge, but earlier ones as well: me and Mom when I was a kid; my best friends from high school; the day I went off to college, driving a ten-year-old Chevy Malibu and feeling very independent.

And then a few wedding pictures, and our first house, and Max, the best dog in the world. Frank's face smiled up at me, mischief in his eyes and a cigarette in his hand. I puffed away in a couple of the photos, too. What had I been thinking?

The pictures pulled me into a world long gone: the furniture, the clothes, the paintings on the walls had all been discarded or lost. The people in the photos, the versions of our younger selves, seemed pathetically innocent, unsuspecting of the damage time would inflict on us all.

Margaret and Judy and I looked like a trio of carefree bachelorettes in a photo from a Cinco de Mayo party at Don Francisco's Restaurant. Appearances, however, didn't tell everything. Margaret had an absentee husband—and a drama queen daughter who was kicking up trouble even back then. I'd started dating Noah when the picture was taken— but my face didn't glow the way Judy's had when she talked about her new boyfriend. Had I yakked on and on about Noah, though, gushing the way Judy did the last time I saw her?

And there he was, on the next to last page. Our holiday get-away at Tahoe, Noah standing on the balcony with snow glittering behind him, in the pale green sweater I'd given him for Christmas. Had he enjoyed our trip as much as I did, or had he been itching to get back to Jason, and I'd been blind to it?

"'Bye, Noah," I whispered, and blew his picture a kiss. Then I closed the album and put it away.

I must've fallen asleep on the sofa, because the next thing I remember was a slice of sunlight in my eyes. A cold, half-empty cup of tea on the coffee table oriented me when I sat up and rubbed the kink out of my neck. Sunlight. I'd almost forgotten what it looked like.

I yawned and stretched and was surprised to see I'd slept past ten a.m. Good for me. Breathing came easier, and despite my early-morning trip down memory lane, or maybe because of it, I felt energized. Time to quit moping.

Shuffling into the kitchen, I tackled the sink full of dirty dishes and brewed coffee. Then I made myself an honest-to-God breakfast. The cupboard looked a little empty, but at least I had cereal—and a bag of blueberries in the freezer.

After breakfast I did a grocery inventory and started a shopping list, figuring I'd get cleaned up and head to the market. I fell asleep instead, and didn't wake until mid-afternoon. This time I managed to stay awake long enough for a hot shower, which revived me considerably, and just after I finished drying my hair the phone rang.

Yahoo, I thought, *contact with the outside world.*

"So when were you going to tell me?" Judy Fairstein demanded without even a quick "hello."

"Tell you what?" I shot back.

I heard the flick of a lighter and a sharp inhale, and I pictured a cloud of smoke when she said, her voice vibrating outrage, "I just called your office, and they tell me you don't work there anymore."

"Oh. Yeah. It just happened."

"Fuck, Susan, what is going *on* with you? Something this huge, you don't even think to mention it?"

"Like I said, it just happened. And then I got sick, and—"

"I can't believe you didn't tell me!"

"I was going to, Jude. But I got sick, and there's been a lot going on." I paused. "Frank died."

Another inhale and exhale. "Yeah, Margaret told me."

Well, then, thanks for the sympathy call. I didn't trust myself to speak.

"But aren't you kinda glad it's over? I mean, he was so sick, and—"

"No, Jude, I'm not glad. I wish he hadn't died. I miss him."

"That came out wrong. It's just that, he must've been suffering—and you guys hadn't been together for years, I just figured—"

"Figured that I quit caring for him when the divorce papers were filed?"

"Of course not! But he'd moved on, I thought you had too. Sor-ry. You hardly ever talked about him, until he got sick, and I just assumed you got sucked into all that because you didn't know how not to. You can't say no to anybody, y'know."

Is that what you think of me? I'm some sucker always being taken advantage of?

"I didn't want to watch him die, that's for sure. But he needed me, and—"

"And that shithead Noah! Margaret told me about him, too. The fucker. He'll come crawling back, I bet—and I hope you slam the door in his face."

"I think he's gone for good, Jude."

As if I hadn't spoken, she went on, "So I call you at work to try and cheer you up, and I find out you've lost your job, on top of everything else. And all this—all this has been going on and you didn't even call me. Maybe I could've done something to help."

Like what? Can you resurrect the dead? Twitch your nose and make Derek Bord disappear?

"Sorry. I needed to hibernate for a while, and there wasn't anything to do, honest. It happened the way it was supposed to."

"Are you okay? You sound all congested. You've been crying, huh?"

I bit my lip and counted to five. "Like I said, I've had a bad cold."

"I guess so! You sound awful. No offense."

"I'm getting better."

"Look, d'you need anything? Chicken soup, OJ, anything?"

She sounded almost happy to be offering help, or maybe that was my hyperactive imagination laying a guilt trip on me. After all, I realized, I'd often thought of Judy as the loser who needed rescuing. But it was sweet of her to be concerned.

"Actually," I began, "I was just getting ready to go to the—"

"Because I could come by later tonight. I mean, Ryan and I are going to dinner with Jen and Eric in a while, but the four of us could stop by *after*."

Jen and Eric? Oh yeah, that's just what I felt like doing, entertaining Judy and three people I hardly knew or hadn't even met.

"Thanks, but I'm not up for company yet."

"It's not company, Susan. It's *me*. Me and my friends, and you'd like them if you gave 'em half a chance. Hell, it might pull you out of the blues."

"Probably, but—"

"I mean, that Jen is like a party in a box. She is *sooo* funny, and you'll love Ryan, honest."

"I bet," I said, "and if I wasn't just getting over this cold, if my house wasn't a mess, it'd be great. Maybe we could do something later this week—like Friday?"

"Ummm, maybe … I'll check with Jen and Ryan and see if we have anything else planned, okay?"

"Nah, don't bother. I'd be a fifth wheel anyhow. You seemed to want to get together, so I th—"

"I do. But you gotta remember us working people only have a couple of nights a week for fun stuff, y'know."

"It's okay. Jude. You better go, you'll be late for your dinner. I'll call you in a few days, and—"

"Now you're all mad at me."

"I'm not."

I heard exasperation on her end. "Yeah, you are. I can tell by your voice. Jeez, Susan, why do you always have to make everything so hard? I'm trying to be your friend."

Somehow, I didn't believe her.

"I appreciate it, but I don't—"

"Fine, Susan. Keep wallowing. Call me if you can ever act human again."

And she hung up.

I sat staring at the phone for a long time. Was I a bad friend? Was she? Or were we just two decent women whose lives had converged for a while and then meandered off in different directions? Was I not acting like a human being? My grief felt all too human to me.

Rather than go nuts trying to answer my own questions, I got dressed and went grocery shopping.

That was probably not the wisest thing I did all day, but it made me feel less helpless. By the time I lugged the bags in from the car, my legs felt like they had lead weights attached.

Judy's words echoed in my brain as I put away the groceries. Had she always been so cold? Or was she simply showing normal feelings? No: I couldn't remember a single ounce of compassion in what she'd said. And maybe our friendship had never gone as deep as I'd thought, and I'd only seen what I wanted to see. And maybe I was just as selfish and superficial as Judy. Was it always just about me, as Margaret had said? Did I think of my friends only in terms of what they could do for me: boost my ego, fill empty hours, make me feel better about myself?

I was pretty well into beating myself up when I noticed the cheery chrysanthemums on the kitchen table. At least I'd done something to help Val Desmond. At least *she* didn't think I was a selfish, whining screw-up as a friend. And Flo: she seemed to genuinely care about me, to think highly of me. But maybe she was just a kind, forgiving woman who overlooked everyone's character flaws.

I took my doubts and remorse to bed, even though it wasn't even ten p.m.

* * *

The next morning I decided to get my butt in gear. An empty day stretched ahead of me, and I intended to make the most of it. One thing my Mom taught me at an early age: when life gets overwhelming and you don't want to think about it—clean house!

It had been weeks since I'd done more than give the furniture a cursory swipe with a cloth, and dust bunnies peeked out from under the sofa and the bed. I pulled on my heavy-duty green rubber gloves, got out the all-purpose cleaner and some rags, and went to work. I scrubbed and polished and vacuumed, and I didn't think of anything except removing as much dirt as possible from my living space. My meager collection of framed photographs sat dusty and ignored on the middle bookcase shelf, so I cleaned them up.

Then I retrieved a picture that I'd rediscovered in my late-night photo excursion: Frank and me, grinning at the camera, with our majestic golden Max-dog sitting between us. I slid the cheerful image of our younger selves into an empty frame and put it on display.

By late afternoon my back and arms ached their protest, but every surface glistened and gleamed. The sinks sparkled, and I could walk across the floor without grit crunching underfoot. Mom would have been proud.

I got through the next few days much the same way. I cleaned out my closets, filled a black plastic bag with clothes I hadn't worn in years, and took them to the Salvation Army. I replaced missing buttons and tacked up sagging hems. I polished my shoes and organized my lingerie drawer.

Time drifted around me, hours oozed past, and I started to like the quiet, isolated existence. I didn't need people, I didn't need anything. I had myself and my memories.

* * *

Then Clayton Selden called: the funeral was set for Friday morning, and he was having a reception at "the house" afterward.

"What can I do to help?" I asked.

"Nothing, thanks," he said, his voice wavering a little. "We're mourners, Susan. We're not expected to do anything but be there. Rhonda and Michelle are putting the food together. And Flo—well, she's orchestrating it as only Flo can do."

With Flo in charge, I knew it would be flawless. Although I had no idea what I could have contributed to the reception, I craved a part to play in this last sad chapter. At least I could put on my brave face and show up at the cemetery, and support Clayton and Elise.

I looked out at a bleak landscape: clouds and shadows everywhere. My house was warm, but I shivered.

"How are you holding up?" I asked Clayton, and heard a heavy gush of breath from the other end.

"I don't know," he replied. "It still doesn't seem real."

I knew the feeling, of course. And I wanted to comfort Clayton, to tell him it would be all right, that time would soothe his grief. Frank's death had ripped a huge hole in my life, and Clayton had been even closer to the epicenter. So maybe if I spoke the words, we would both believe them; maybe if I repeated them enough, they'd be true. Nah. *Change the subject, Susan.*

"How's Elise behaving?"

A pause. "She flew home yesterday. We picked up Frank's ashes, and she took her share—God, that sounds weird—took her share and left."

Oh nice. Didn't bother to say goodbye, but what would've been the point anyway? Our business was finished. A month ago, I'd have felt a slow burn of anger at her bad manners. But now I didn't care.

"Are you glad to get her out of your hair?"

"Sort of. But the house feels so empty now, just me and Ralph rattling around. Poor Ralph. She's lonely. I can distract myself with work, but Ralph—she mopes around."

I felt a surge of sympathy for the pretty dog; she'd helped me get through the horrible morning Frank died. "She misses Frank."

"Yes," Clayton agreed. "She does."

A crazy thought passed through my mind: maybe I should offer to swing by and take Ralph to the park. After all, what else was I doing that mattered? I didn't feel ready to start interviewing for a job yet. But maybe Clayton wouldn't like that, maybe he wanted to be rid of me. Maybe I reminded him of everything he wanted to forget. Then I thought of Flo's scheme to get Ralph involved with therapy dogs, and I hoped she didn't wait much longer before bringing it up to Clayton. That would ease Ralph's loneliness for sure.

After I thanked Clayton and hung up, a gush of self-pity threatened, but that routine was getting old. It was about four o'clock, and the overcast sky hadn't brightened at all. I put on my sneakers and hit the pavement. Maybe a walk would stir up those endorphins I kept hearing about but never seemed to produce. Maybe it would chase away the mournful spirits that swirled around my lonely house.

See, if you had a dog, you'd have to do this every day, I told myself as I pounded along the sidewalk. *Something that needs you. A reason to get up in the morning; a reason to keep living.*

Now there was a scary thought. Was I that far gone, that I felt I had no reason for living? I turned the notion around in my mind as I logged another mile. In the thickening darkness, lights flicked on in living room windows. Families gathered together at the end of the day. Couples kissed hello and shared stories of the day's adventures. Dads helped kids with homework. Moms put roasts in ovens, all through the world. Except at my house.

Mom had Jack. Judy had Ryan. Flo had Jimmy. And Margaret had Philippe. It felt like everyone I knew had paired up. Everyone except me. But at least I had my pride.

And I wasn't completely alone. I had friends. Flo. Val Desmond. Maybe even Margaret, once I had a chance to think more clearly about what had gone wrong between us. My future held all kinds of possibilities, if I could just quit moping and focus on the positives. I was lucky not to have to make a fast reentry into Corporate America. I had time to figure out what I really wanted to do. Trouble was, I didn't know where to start.

* * *

When I got home from my walk I was panting, and I'd worked up a decent sweat. But no endorphins arrived to magically cure me of my loneliness. I got into the shower, and memories of Noah washed over me along with the water spray. *Don't you go there!* I forced myself to consider other subjects: in the morning, I'd definitely find at least one real job lead, maybe send out my résumé. Do *something.*

I toweled my hair dry and decided I'd passed safely into the cocktail hour. The crisp, soothing wine brightened my mood a little. But it was an artificial brightener, as phony as the dye Elise Krajewski used on her hair. Elise: would it have killed her to call me and say goodbye? And why did I even care?

I had just enough time before lights out in Santa Fe to call my own mother. It had been a few days since we'd talked, and she'd want to know about the funeral.

During our last call, I'd confessed about my job, and she hadn't seemed bothered by having an unemployed daughter.

"I always thought you deserved better," was all she said. Now, where had I heard that before?

But this time when she answered, Mom's voice sounded a little strange. Her nervous laugh punctuated every sentence as she told me about Jack's latest do-it-yourself disaster. What was up?

Finally she let it out. "Jack and I are thinking of going to Italy."

"Cool," I said. "When?"

A pause. "Well, unless you want to come see us over the holidays, we thought we'd go in mid-December and stay until after the first of the year. I know, the weather will probably be wretched, but he has his heart set on going, and we usually close the gallery over Christmas anyway, so the timing would work. But if you wanted to come here for—"

"No," I said, "I hadn't planned on it."

It wasn't like I schlepped myself to Santa Fe every December. The year before, I'd been with Noah at Tahoe, and two years before that I'd gone on a cruise with Judy—to keep us both from devouring every holiday sweet lying around our respective workplaces. So we didn't have any kind of tradition.

"If you're sure," Mom said. Then she added with another of those embarrassed little giggles, "It's sort of an anniversary for us."

"Hey, that's terrific. You guys will have a ball. All that art, all those cathedrals and things."

"Would you like to come with us?"

And ruin your romantic getaway?

"That's sweet, but I'd better stay here and start job hunting. So go! Have a great time. Bring me some lavish present from Florence and take lots of pictures. But promise you'll have fun."

I hung up as soon as I could and poured another glass of wine before I nuked a frozen pizza. Pretty soon I'd be a good candidate for AA. Well, at least I'd make some new friends to replace the ones I'd alienated. As I lifted the wine to my mouth I got a good look at myself in the window glass above the sink, and I hated what I saw.

"You have really screwed it up, Susan Krajewski," I said to my reflection.

I could almost hear Mom's voice, the one she used when I'd whine about some trivial event going wrong after I'd given it a half-assed try. "Well, Susan—what did you expect?"

What *did* I expect? That Frank would live forever? That Noah would put me ahead of his son? That Margaret would value my friendship more than her family? That Judy would stay overweight and lonely just so I could feel better off than she was? What was it about me that drove people away? Even Judy dumped me.

I put the self-loathing on hold long enough to eat my pizza and polish off the wine. Then, on the premise that activity is the best antidote to wallowing, I busied myself going through my newly organized closets and putting together my outfit for the funeral. The way things were going, that would be the highlight of my social calendar for the rest of the year.

The night lurked ahead of me, gloomy, empty, and ominous. Despite my feeble efforts, loneliness gnawed at my heart. I kept seeing Frank that last day, the wasted shell of the man whom I'd loved so much, and who had loved me. He *had* loved me, even when he wasn't *in love* with me. And I hadn't appreciated that love until it was too late, until he was gone. I'd lost Frank, I'd lost my job, I'd lost my friends. I'd lost everything important. *Boo hoo, poor Susan. Poor little helpless Susan, all alone with her sadness.*

Sorrow, you know, can kill. It isn't as fast as a bullet, but it does its work without mercy. It hurts. It weighs you down with pain and loss and exhaustion so insidious that you don't even know you're drowning until the water is over your head.

I was dangerously close to the dark place where you simply lay your head on the tracks and let the train roll over you. I'd done everything I could to cheer up, and nothing had worked. No fake enthusi-asm, no pretend happiness would chase the demons away.

Flo's advice came back to me. *You don't have to do it alone.* I picked up Leonard Doss's business card. Its frayed edges beckoned me, and I heard Flo's voice in my heart. If ever I needed help, this was the time.

I picked up the phone and dialed the counselor's number. The service picked up, of course; way too late for him to be in the office. I left a message requesting an appointment, and hung up feeling like I'd done something important.

That one small act opened a pinpoint of light in the tunnel. I knew it would take several days before he could work me into his schedule, and weeks or even months before I found a way to cope with my losses. But the first step is always the hardest, and the most significant. If Leonard Doss could give me a road map, maybe I'd be able to find my way out of the darkness. I began to feel the possibility. One foot in front of the other, if you're going in the right direction, gets you where you need to be, sooner or later. I *could* outlast my grief. But it didn't hurt to have a little company while I waited.

You're never really done with therapy, now are you?

Chapter 16
"Ask for Help, and the Universe Responds"

Did my call to Flo's grief counselor set something in motion, something too mysterious for my little world to contain? I didn't think of it that way until one of Margaret's sayings popped into my head: "Ask for help, and the Universe responds."

In the interest of accuracy: that does *not* mean the Universe will send you what you think you want.

All I know is, when my phone rang Wednesday morning, I assumed it was Dr. Doss calling back to set up an appointment. But the man's voice answering my "Hello?" was familiar, and only one guy could call me "Susie Q" without getting his ear blistered.

"Hi, Grandpa K." I couldn't figure out what else to say. Who offered whom condolences? Who had suffered the greater loss?

"Are you up for dinner?"

"Dinner?" echoed the Village Idiot.

"I'm at the Biltmore."

"The Biltmore? In L.A.?"

"Unless we took a wrong turn over Nevada."

For the first time in days, I laughed. And then it hit me: he'd come for the funeral. At least one Krajewski would watch Frank's ashes go into the California earth, and by showing up, Grandpa K was acknowledging this part of Frank's world. That counted for something, big time. It would've made Frank happy.

"Let me cook for you this time," I said before I thought up too many complications. "I'll grill us some steaks."

Grandpa K didn't hesitate. "I'd like that, honey. Tell me how to get there."

As I scribbled up a shopping list and raced to the market, I wondered if Margaret's benevolent Universe had propelled me into my recent cleaning frenzy; my house was ready for company.

I kept thinking about Margaret and Judy, though, and I ached at the way things had gone wrong. Some small part of my brain kept whispering that it was my fault, that I'd asked too much of my friends. But another part hissed back that they were cruel, unfeeling bitches who didn't care about my grief. And the truth, of course, lay somewhere in between.

* * *

By late afternoon I'd gotten myself presentable and done the minimal food prep required for Grandpa K's dinner, so I stretched out on the sofa, hoping I could catch a little nap. The telephone intervened, but when I heard Flo's voice, my irritation softened.

"I'm just checking on you, darling girl. How are you holding up these dark days?"

"I'm good," I replied, and then told her about Grandpa K's arrival.

"How wonderful that he came for you," Flo said.

For me? That notion hadn't occurred to me, but I felt a warm flush of pleasure. True or not, I chose to believe it.

"He'll probably come with you to the service then. Excellent. I wanted to be sure you weren't coming alone."

What a kind woman.

"Are you sure I can't do anything for the reception?" I asked, to cover an expected surge of sadness when I thought of the funeral's significance.

"We're set, thanks. It'll be simple: light hors d'oeuvres, nothing tricky to prepare." She paused. "But I may need your help at the service—we'll all have to try and keep Clayton from getting maudlin. And don't let him spook *you*, either."

"He sounded pretty calm on the phone," I said. "Like he was frozen or something."

"Well, there's nothing like a funeral to thaw him out."

I promised to do my best and hoped I'd be able to help rein in Clayton if I had to.

Flo's call stirred up thoughts of Margaret, because I knew that she and Flo would like each other. I missed Margaret, and I still didn't understand how things had turned so toxic between us.

Tomorrow, I promised my reflection in the mirror, *I'll call her and try to straighten this out.* Maybe it was my imagination, but the lines around my mouth seemed to loosen up a little.

* * *

The sun, muffled almost to invisibility, was sinking past the Verdugo Mountains when I heard a car door slam and peeked out to see Grandpa K walking away from a dark sedan. Someone—a woman, I thought, although the features were blurred in the streetlamp's jaundiced glow—was standing by the rear passenger door. In dark slacks and a vest, she didn't look real chauffeur-y, but I got the picture.

Grandpa K had on a handsome charcoal suit and carried a bottle of wine. Old Spice wafted in ahead of him when I opened the door. Overhead in the murky sky, one small star glittered. Then his warm arms wrapped around me, and I hugged back, hoping I'd been able to shower away the stink of sorrow and despair.

"I should've come to get you," I murmured after I kissed his cheek.

He chuckled and looked over his shoulder. "Nah, Clarice likes to drive me around. Or she pretends to, anyway. One of the perks of being old and rich. You wouldn't deny me that, would you, honey?"

He gave Clarice the high sign. She nodded, got in the sedan and drove away.

"I wouldn't deny you anything, Grandpa K."

I opened the wine, a high-end Pinot Noir, then pointed to my freshly vacuumed armchair. "Get comfy while I light the grill."

Noah had installed a super-nova patio light for me the previous winter when he caught me grilling steaks by flashlight, and I sent him a mental thank you as the back yard lit up like high noon.

Grandpa K was prowling around my living room when I came back inside, checking out my photo collection on the bookcase. When he got to the one of Frank and me, he turned around and smiled. "You two made a nice-looking couple."

I nodded, swallowed a mouthful of wine, and put the glass down. What could I say? "Looks don't count for everything"?

My fake-Tiffany floor lamp, which Judy had helped me pick out when I moved into the house, lit up the right half of Grandpa K's face, and even in its gentle glow I could see he'd aged since my visit to Chicago. His face was no more wrinkled, his posture still tall and firm —but his blue eyes were tinged with red, and he clearly had to work at the smile he offered. Sadness emanated from him like heat waves on a strip of desert sand.

The room was very still, except for the far-off hiss of barbecue burners, and the slow crackle of heat-expanding metal. *I should put some music on—wonder what he likes?* All those years I'd known Grandpa K without a clue as to his taste in music. Classical? Country? Rock 'n' Roll?

His mouth opened, but he gave up on whatever he'd started to say. I took three giant steps across the room and put my arms around him. I hadn't meant to cry. I'd been determined to stay upbeat and perky, but I'd been counting on him to help out with the cheery pretense. Seeing him so quiet and sad drained my defenses. A minute later I was choking on tears, and probably smearing makeup onto his nice charcoal lapel.

"I know, Susie Q," he whispered. One hand stroked my hair, and the other wrapped tight around me. "I know."

The spasms passed, and I let go of him to swipe at my hot, wet face, pissed off that I'd broken down. But when I looked up at him, I saw moisture in his eyes, too, and that got me started all over again.

It wasn't like I hadn't cried my share of tears for Frank already. But the reservoir apparently filled up faster than I could empty it, because I had plenty left to spill. Grandpa K stood like a big strong pillar and let me bawl, and when I finally stopped for air, he pulled a linen handkerchief out of his pocket and dabbed at my face, as tenderly as if I were a child. Then he wiped his own damp eyes and blew his nose.

I took a deep breath and let it out. "Sorry."

He brushed some soggy hair off my cheek. "It's good for us to grieve," he said. "It's good to let it out, and share the sadness. When Winnie died, I didn't know that, and it took me too long to get past losing her." His mouth puckered. "Past the worst part, I mean. You never really get over it all."

"You're right." I grabbed my wine glass again and rubbed my hand across my face one more time. "Feels like I haven't done anything *but* grieve."

I went to work on our dinner, and he followed me into the kitchen and insisted on helping. I gave him some tomatoes and mushrooms to slice for our salad while I went out to put the steaks on the grill. When I came back inside, he'd taken off his jacket, rolled up his sleeves, and was tossing the salad with total concentration. I watched the bright medley of reds and greens swirl in the big cut-crystal bowl, its facets sparkling in the light, a housewarming gift from Margaret. Grandpa K looked a little more cheerful than he had before my meltdown, as if my tears had vented some of his sadness along with my own, and I took comfort in the thought that our shared grief was somehow more manageable. The hot, earthy smell of baking potatoes mingled with the smoky aroma that had followed me inside.

I wiped my hands on my jeans, suddenly conscious of how casually I was dressed compared to Grandpa K. Well, at least my sweater was clean and fairly new, and I'd put on my black leather boots instead of the fuzzy blue slippers I'd practically been living in lately.

Although I didn't do a lot of cooking, I'd always been grateful to whoever designed that kitchen. It had miles of clean white tile countertops, plenty of cabinets, and a big window over the sink that looked out on my rose garden. There'd only been two bushes when I moved in, but that first winter I'd planted six bare-root Double Delights, and they'd flourished. Even that late in the year, a few brave flowers waved to me.

I refilled Grandpa K's wine glass and then my own and pecked him quickly on the cheek, grateful for this gift from the Universe.

The steaks turned out pretty good, I thought, and judging from the way Grandpa K went to work on his, he must've agreed. I was glad I'd gone to the trouble of hauling out my good table linens and lighting tall white tapers. The atmosphere was as elegant as I could make it.

"So," he said midway through the meal, "how's Frankie's … friend holding up?"

It was a small miracle that Grandpa K could even bring it up. I chewed on my salad and tried to figure out the best answer. Would Clayton want me to assure people that he was "managing"? I tended to give that bland answer to people I didn't know well. *But this is family, remember?*

"He's really hurting," I replied. "But he's putting up a pretty good front for now."

Grandpa K nodded. "Good."

He took a sip of wine, set his glass down, and leaned forward. I'd lowered the lights (thank you, Noah, for that handy dimmer switch) before we sat down to eat, and the candles cast warm shadows on Grandpa K's face. His blue eyes glimmered.

"I've been thinking a lot about what you said last time," he told me. "And you're right, you know. I was so busy being pig-headed about Frankie's being … being *gay* that I let it blind me."

His nose wrinkled when he said the word "gay." But, by God, he said it, and I was pretty sure that was the first time.

"That's natural. You were brought up to believe it was a bad thing. But it's not. Not really."

He lowered his head, like he was looking at me over the top of his eyeglasses, except he wasn't wearing any. "I'm not gonna get into a debate with you on that one, honey. But it's true that love and commitment don't always come tied up in a nice pretty package. Sometimes they don't look like you'd expect. Hey, look at us: I love *you*, Susie Q, like you were my own flesh and blood. Now how do you put *that* in a box?"

My eyes stung. *Damn! Where do these tears come from, anyway?*

"I love you, too," I said before my voice broke.

He held his arms out wide, palms up. "There—you see! Some things you can't explain. But there they are. And our feelings are just as real as anybody else's."

"Right." I nodded and blinked away my tears.

"So I can accept that Frank loved this guy, this Clayton. I can handle that one."

I nodded. "Good, that's good, Grandpa K. Frank would be so glad."

He took another drink, and I upended the bottle over his almost-empty glass.

"When he ran off with that Clayton fellow, I just turned my back on him. That was one of the dumbest things I ever did. I missed him so much—and all those years we had together, it was like I boxed 'em up and hid 'em where they couldn't remind me. He was such a good kid. And I never once—never once—had a clue that he was ..." He looked up toward the ceiling like he needed help with the words. "That he was gay."

I knew Grandpa K had pretty much been Frank's surrogate dad. Joe Jr. had died when Frank was a little kid. But until that moment, I hadn't understood how much of a loss it must have been for him, to see his only grandson take a path so at odds with his own values.

"Frank didn't want to hurt you," I said. "He just couldn't help being who he was."

Grandpa K's hand trembled, and he set down his fork with a clank. "I know that. Hell, I knew it all along. But I was such a stubborn old fool, and I lost those years I coulda had him in my life."

Hard as I tried, I couldn't think of anything comforting to tell him, because he was right. Frank had been the light of his life for over thirty years. Grandpa K had seen him through Little League, through high school and college, had sat by Elise at our wedding. And then, in a flash, he'd lost it all. Or convinced himself that he had. I ached for him and the irrevocability of his choice.

"And if *you* hadn't come to see me, I might never have realized what a fool I was."

"I didn't do it to make you feel bad about your beliefs, Grandpa K."

"I know that, honey. But you saw me charging off in the wrong direction, and like the smart gal you are, you knew I'd be sorry later. You wanted to help. And you did. Frank's gone, but in a way it's like you gave him back to me—gave back *my* Frankie."

Had I *really*? I hoped so.

Grandpa K shook his head. "But I waited too long to realize you were right, Susie Q. I missed my chance to let Frankie know I still loved him. Whoever and whatever he was."

"He knew, though." Here, at least, I could offer some consolation.

He cocked his head and squinted like he was trying to judge the truth of my words. I hoped he didn't look too close, because I wasn't a hundred percent sure myself. But I so wanted him to believe me, and I tried to sound confident. Finally he nodded; he'd either bought into my story for real or was going to let himself pretend that he did.

"Don't you ever do that, honey," he said quietly.

"Do what?" I thought he meant my maybe-not-true reassurance.

"Don't you ever shut somebody out of your life just because they're not how you want 'em to be. And if you ever do realize you've done that, you fix it. Right away. Don't wait 'til they're gone."

"I won't. I promise."

He raised his wine glass in a toast and winked at me. "That's my girl."

For a minute or two there was only the sound of forks and knives scraping against china. I was ready to open another bottle of wine; it would have to be a mid-grade Cabernet this time. I'd started economizing in my unemployed state.

Then Grandpa K swallowed and dabbed his mouth with a napkin. "So—Elise tells me you finally got out of that hellacious job."

I nodded, imagining what Elise had *really* said. "*I always knew she was useless, didn't I, Joe? Can't even hold onto her job.*"

Then I remembered what she'd said after Frank died: "No wonder Frank loved you." She *didn't* hate me, or even hold a grudge for my marrying her son. Who was I to hang on to old resentments then? Sure, she'd left without saying goodbye, but that was her style. *She is what she is*. And she'd lost Frank, too. We had more in common than not.

"It was time to move on," I said to Grandpa K.

He picked up his fork. "So what's up next for you?"

Damn—this talk would burn a hole in my stomach if it went on for long. "I'm not sure. I got a good severance package, so I can poke around and figure out what I want to do. Maybe change direction, do something more socially responsible."

Now where had *that* come from? Was I saying it simply to get him off the subject, or had the notion been percolating all along, waiting for me to give it voice?

"Any clue what that might be?"

"To be honest, the idea just now occurred to me."

I thought about the people I knew, and how they earned their pay: Val matched people and jobs so they meshed together; Margaret healed emotional injuries; Clayton cured sick animals; Judy helped mold the minds of little kids. What had I contributed to the betterment of the world except to be sure Jacobs Laboratories kept out of trouble with the government and the law?

"You should be a lawyer," Grandpa K said with a wink. "The way you presented Frankie's case to me, that woulda won an award somewhere, I bet."

I frowned at the mental image of musty courtrooms and mountains of paperwork, the slow creak of the legal process. But damn it, I'd persuaded Clayton Selden to come home and do right by Frank, and somehow I'd convinced Grandpa K to at least question his deep-rooted prejudice about homosexuals. Maybe I had an under-appreciated talent there that I could tap.

"I already changed the trust, Susie Q," he continued. "Like Frankie wanted."

"Wow." My vocabulary abandoned me. "That's great, Grandpa K."

"But I'm still leaving *you* a chunk of change. Frankie woulda wanted you taken care of."

Speechless, I sat with my mouth hanging open. I had no clue as to how much money he was leaving me, but the realization that he counted me as part of the family almost set off another flood of tears.

"Only thing is, you're gonna have to wait 'til I kick the bucket to get any of it," he went on.

"And that better be a long time from now," I said.

He grinned. "God willing. But in the meantime, honey, you gotta earn a living."

"I know. I'll find something soon, but I need a little time to—"

"Want to come work for me?"

That question knocked the words right out of my brain. Again. "What?" I asked, thinking I might have misheard him.

Grandpa K took another bite and squinted at me while he chewed and swallowed. "I'm getting kinda tired of running the foundation all by myself. Elise has her hands full with the brokerage, and I don't trust Henry to do the right thing. I never understood why Zoë married him. Oh, he's honest enough, but he doesn't have a generous bone in his body, and it'd grate on him to give money away. He'd never be able to decide who gets what. Now you, Susie Q, you'd get it right off the bat."

My fork almost got away from me, but I held on. "I don't know the first thing about—"

"It ain't rocket science, honey. You learn real fast. And Winnie'd have been so glad. You see things the way she did, the way she taught me to see."

"But—Chicago. Wow. I don't mean to sound ungrateful, honest, but—that'd be a huge change."

"You wouldn't have to move if you didn't want to. You could run it from here, set up a—what d'ya call it—virtual office. Fly back there a few times a year. No big deal."

I studied my plate, still stunned at the proposition, trying to remember what he'd told me about the foundation. Wondering if I'd be any good at it. Wondering what made Grandpa K think I could do it.

When I looked up, he had his head cocked in that parrot-like way.

"Winnie's dad used to beat her mom up," he said quietly. "The poor woman had nowhere to go to get away from him. Winnie wanted to make it so that never happened to anybody else. And she came pretty damn close, at least in our little piece of the world. It'd be as—what's that term you used?—socially responsible as you can get."

I tried to reply, but the words wouldn't come out. I grabbed the edge of the table and forced some air into my lungs.

"Remember what I said, Susie Q. Don't let your stubbornness get in the way of what your heart tells you. Don't wait 'til it's too late."

"It's a really generous offer, Grandpa K, but I—"

He held up his hand like a traffic cop. "This is not the right time for you to make a big decision. Just think about it, maybe in a few weeks come see what it's all about, see if it feels right."

I got up and planted a kiss on his shiny scalp. "I will. Thank you so much," I whispered in his ear.

He smiled up at me. "Now finish your dinner before it gets cold."

* * *

I had a weird dream that night: I was walking through a house—nowhere I'd ever lived, but I knew it somehow. I kept trying to turn on the lights, but none of the switches worked. "I'll call Margaret," I thought, but I couldn't find a phone. Then I saw one on the wall, but I couldn't work the dial—I kept punching in the wrong numbers. I realized I was holding my purse, and I started looking for my cell phone, but all I found was a little prescription bottle. I pried it open and a puff of smoke whooshed out, and there was a tiny fire inside. I jammed the cap back on, and the bottle was so hot I dropped it into a drain in the middle of the floor. I ran toward it, and this huge lizard came out of the drain hole. I woke myself up screaming.

My heart thudded so hard I half expected it to erupt from my rib cage, and I fought for a deep breath that didn't want to come. Finally I was able to suck in some air and release it.

What the hell was that all about?

The red digits on the clock said six forty-seven. Time to get up anyway. Daybreak seeped around the edges of the bedroom curtains, a pale blue-gray line. I had the tail end of a red wine headache, thanks to that second bottle Grandpa K and I had started on the night before.

Grandpa K … what a bombshell he'd dropped. I had no exact

notion of the extent of his foundation, or why he thought me even halfway qualified to manage it. He'd explained the basics to me, but between the wine and my surprise, not much had sunk in.

What did I have to lose, really, by accepting his offer? I probably wouldn't screw it up totally, and maybe I could actually do some good. At the very least, I'd set Grandpa K's mind at ease, and it would probably be fun to work with him. Although I was in no shape to make a decision just then, the more I thought about the opportunity, the better it sounded.

First, however, I had some unfinished business with my friend Margaret. My promise to myself the day before had been underscored by Grandpa K's warning: *"Don't you ever shut somebody out of your life just because they're not how you want 'em to be."*

That's what I'd done with Margaret, cut her off just because she didn't react to Frank's death the way I wanted. I had the nasty feeling that I did that a lot. At least Margaret had been honest; she'd pretty much said "So what?"—and who could blame her? I was no longer married to Frank. I'd underestimated how much I still loved him, sure, but how was she supposed to know that? As good a therapist as Margaret was, she sure wasn't psychic.

Somehow, my friend and I had to find our way through the maze of anger and disappointment. A dose of healthy honesty might help. It couldn't hurt. Could it?

It was too early to phone her, so I made coffee and dumped some cereal in a bowl while I tried to figure out how to start the conversation. My head still throbbed, so I downed a couple of Tylenol along with the cereal.

She'd be leaving for her office by nine, and she probably had a full day, after that unplanned trip to France. But maybe I could catch her before she left for work and say my piece. At eight-thirty I dialed her number.

Luck was with me; I got Margaret herself instead of one of her daughters, or Philippe.

"Hi," I said, "it's Susan. Can you talk for a minute?"

There was the tiniest hesitation before she replied, "Of course. How are you doing?"

"I'm okay," I said, drawing out the last syllable to show it didn't mean the same thing as "fine."

"Still angry with me?"

And I was, damn it anyway.

Maybe she didn't mean the question as a challenge, but it felt like one. Despite the Tylenol, a hot red pain pinched off my good intentions. I was standing by the kitchen sink, watching the roses bob in a soft morning breeze. Sunlight filtered down on them, and drops of moisture glistened on the pink and cream petals. Even from inside the house, I caught a whiff of their perfume. My fingers clutched the telephone like a lifeline, and I made myself breathe deeply and relax my grip.

"I am," I said, surprised at my neutral tone. "That's why I called."

A deep sigh came over the phone line, and I visualized her checking her watch, tapping her foot, wanting this conversation to end so she could get on with her life. But I wasn't going to let my anger lie there between us another minute.

"Go on," she said in a stiff, quiet voice.

I took the leap. "Okay. See, when I told you about Frank, it really hurt that you made it sound trivial. I mean, sure, I knew he was gonna die, but it was more horrible than I expected, and I was really …"

I searched for the word, and she stepped into the void.

"Devastated. I realize that now. And if I came off sounding too matter-of-fact, that was my misguided attempt to make you feel better. Truly."

"Yeah, well, it didn't work. I felt like you didn't care about Frank dying."

"Of course I cared. But then I got mad—because *you* were mad. And I know I said some things that were out of line."

"And it mushroomed," I added, frantic to use the opening she'd given me.

"Yes," Margaret agreed. "You see? That's why I don't work on my friends. I'm a terrible therapist when I care about the other person. That's probably why I've been such a horrid mother."

"You're not a horrid mother. Look at Deirdre—she's perfect. And Claire will come around."

"Thank you for that, Susan."

I thought about all the years I'd known Margaret and how much her friendship had meant to me, and all the times she *had* been supportive and I'd just sucked it up like I was entitled to it.

"I miss you," I said. My breathing was shallow, but I got the words out.

I could almost see Margaret's face, those piercing eyes that saw past the surface, when she spoke. "Oh, Susan, I'm so very sorry Frank had to die, and that you had to go through it. You're still hurting, and if I could, I'd take that pain away from you. In a heartbeat."

"I know," I whispered.

"I'm cursed—the only way I've learned to deal with loss is to simply move on. That's what I was trying to get you to do. And I was wrong. Please forgive me. You are not like me—thank goodness for both our sakes. You need time to be with your sadness."

Forgive her? Was that all it took? What about my hurt feelings? Could I simply let them go? My grief and my anger had kept me going for the past few days. What would be there to take their place?

Then I remembered the magic I'd felt when I told Frank I forgave him, and I really, truly meant it.

"I was being an idiot," I said. "I'm so off-balance right now, that I—"

And damn if I didn't dissolve in tears. "I'm sorry," I blubbered, "I didn't want to make you feel bad. I want us to be friends again—I just don't know how to fix things!"

"I think you have, my friend."

I glanced at the clock; we'd been talking for less than fifteen minutes. A lot of ground to cover in a tiny slice of time. "I bet you need to get to work."

Another sigh. "Yes, fairly soon. But this is important. *You* are important to me. I hope you understand that."

"I do."

"Good. We'll get together soon, yes? Just the two of us."

"I'd love to," I said. "The funeral is this Friday. After I get through that, my calendar is wide open."

"Aha," she said. "That will be a difficult day for you."

"Yes. But Frank's grandfather's here, and Frank had some great friends who'll be there. That'll help."

"I hope so." She didn't speak for a few seconds, and then said, "Thank you for making the first move, Susan. You've been on my mind so much."

"You too, on mine," I replied before I let her go.

There: I'd pried open the door. My face hurt, and my lungs were starved for air. But I'd managed to crack open that damn door. Every now and then, I got it right.

Chapter 17
Second Chances

How many movies begin with a funeral? Somehow, the film version's misery is redeemed. Sorrow stays clear-cut and manageable.

Reality was somewhat different. Perfect funeral weather, though: not exactly rain, but a drizzle that coated everything with dreary moisture as fat gray clouds hid the sun.

When I woke, for a second I couldn't remember the season, or even the day, although I had a vague sense of its significance. Then I recognized my old friend, grief. Of course. How could I forget you?

I shuffled toward the kitchen. On the way, I passed the photograph of Frank and me with Max, and it pulled me in. I grabbed the frame and peered at the smiling fools captured inside, so unaware of the anguish ahead of them.

When tears filled my vision, I yelled "Stop it!"—shattering the morning quiet. What a loud, angry voice; it turned off the waterworks, though. I put the photo back, rubbed my eyes, and went on my way to coffee and other distractions.

"Just get through today," I told myself, more gently.

With hours to fill before the one p.m. service, I dawdled through breakfast, scanned the morning paper's news reports, and checked the online job boards without finding anything worth pursuing. And that was fine with me: I'd pretty much decided to accept Grandpa K's offer, although the thought of a new career flooded me with terror. What if I failed?

"You won't fail," I muttered. "And if you do …"

My thoughts trailed off. This day was for Frank, not me. Over the past two weeks I'd had other events claim my attention, but not that day. Reminders of Frank were everywhere.

The dreary weather seemed to have invaded my house, my body. I climbed in the shower and let hot water chase away some of the chill. As I toweled off, I tried to summon cheerful feelings, but the dread that had dogged me all morning stayed put.

Despite my feeble efforts to believe that this wretched day would mark an end to my mourning and the start of healing, I knew a darker truth: Frank's life would be finally and officially over, and my last connection to him would be broken. Forever. My rational mind knew he was already gone, but until his ashes went into the grave, somehow I didn't have to accept it.

My black suit waited at the front of the closet, and I set about getting dressed. The fabric felt scratchy and stiff; the narrow skirt imprisoned my legs. Physical discomfort aside, something about the suit seemed wrong—a nagging feeling I couldn't grasp and examine until I saw myself, fully clothed, in the mirror.

I looked exactly like a grieving widow, minus the hat and veil, but businesslike and severe.

"Who cares how you look?" I muttered at my scowling reflection. Frank *would care.*

And then I remembered something important: I'd worn this suit to Paul Dumas' funeral and had been mildly shocked to see his wife Joann in a pale lavender dress, looking more like an Easter confection than a widow in mourning.

"This was Paul's favorite dress," she'd confided to me. "Some people might not approve, but I think Paul would've wanted it."

I'd nodded agreement, surprised at the realization. It made Joann feel closer to her lost husband. Good for her.

With that notion in mind, I pawed through my closet until I

found it: not lavender, but deep purple wool, a simple shirtwaist dress with pale off-white cuffs and a soft, flowing skirt that ended just above my knees. Frank had chosen that dress for me.Hhe loved it. I'd almost tossed it after the divorce, but I couldn't—because, in truth, I loved it too. It always made me feel special.

"It probably won't fit anymore," I mumbled as I peeled off the black suit, but the dress slid over my hips and buttoned up without resistance. Let's hear it for the stress diet.

My reflection in the mirror looked better: somber and respectful but not over the top. And even in the midst of my sadness, I felt a surge of gratitude to Frank for finding that dress in the first place, and to myself for keeping it all those years.

The clock said I still had over half an hour until Grandpa K and Clarice picked me up. He'd insisted on my riding with him, and I'd accepted gladly, not wanting to face the afternoon alone. I finished applying makeup, including mascara that would no doubt be smeared all over my face before long, and then I paced the living room and tried not to think. That didn't work so well.

What if Clayton turned hysterical during the funeral? How was I supposed to control him? I wasn't certain I could even control myself. And how was I supposed to act around Frank's friends? What was my role, exactly? Did I even belong there? But Clayton *had* invited me; I was not unwelcome at the service.

My palms were sweating, and my throat was dry. I needed a glass of water and headed to the kitchen, where I looked out at the rose garden, pleased that the Double Delights had managed to stick around through that miserable autumn. They swayed back and forth, seeming to nod encouragement.

A useful idea emerged from my tangled thoughts. I grabbed my pruning shears and went outside. Although the drizzle had stopped, I felt the promise of winter in the air as I snipped off six flowers, careful to cut just above an outward-facing bud, the way the guy at the nursery had instructed.

Then I lifted the blooms to my face and inhaled their sweetness, comforting as an old friend's hug. I would share these late-season beauties with Frank as part of my goodbye.

I shut my eyes, took a breath, and tried to pretend Frank was there with me, blue eyes sparking mischief, dark curls framing his face, and a smile that brought warmth to the coldest moments. With every ounce of my soul I yearned to reach out and touch him, just one last time. My hand closed on empty space, and I opened my eyes, alone in my purple dress with the pink and cream roses.

Inside, I wrapped the flower stems in a damp paper towel as Clarice's black sedan glided into my driveway. I grabbed my coat and went out to meet them.

Up close, Clarice appeared older than I'd originally thought: furrows around her eyes and a mouth that fell into natural smile lines as she greeted me and opened the passenger door. The smile vanished quickly, though. "I'm sorry for your loss," she murmured.

Kind words from a stranger threatened to bring on another avalanche of tears, but I fought it and somehow managed a smile for Grandpa K as I leaned over and kissed his Old Spice-scented cheek. He wore a dark blue suit that afternoon; no black for him either. Good.

His eyes were full of sorrow, but he met my smile and patted my hand. "You look real pretty, Susie Q."

I held up the roses, and his smile widened. "From your garden? That's a nice touch, honey. I remember how much Frankie loved roses."

"He did," I agreed. "And Clayton—wait'll you see *his* garden. He really has a knack."

Grandpa K's smile dissolved. "Is that right?"

The sedan surged onto the westbound Ventura Freeway like a 747 taking flight. Grandpa K stared out the window, and after a minute he cleared his throat. "So this Clayton—you think he's a good guy?"

I nodded. "He really loved Frank."

He kept his eyes on the passing scenery. "Called him to express condolences. We had a good talk. He sounded decent enough on the phone."

I wondered if "decent enough" meant that Grandpa K had detected no swishy undertones in Clayton's voice, and I knew this afternoon would be a real eye-opener for him. I felt a rush of admiration at his willingness to make this journey and hoped some of his courage would rub off on me.

The Forest Lawn Drive exit came up too soon. I wasn't ready for this, damn it. *Yes, you are, you coward. It's not Frank we're burying. It's only ashes … only ashes,* I kept repeating as I tried to persuade myself that the real Frank was somewhere else. Somewhere better.

There were several cars already in line at the gates of Forest Lawn Cemetery, and Clarice pulled in behind a vintage Mercedes. A few more cars arrived, and we waited in silence until Clayton's Range Rover moved away from the curb. The rest of the procession followed, and the lack of hearse and coffin felt wrong somehow. I wanted pageantry and spectacle to mark this final separation. But Frank had requested a simple ceremony, and I had to accept it.

As we pulled up to the gravesite Clayton had chosen, Grandpa K touched Clarice lightly on the shoulder: a sign, I guess, that she didn't need to leave the car. He opened the door and got out, then turned and held his hand toward me. I needed all the help I could get, so I grabbed it.

Pete and Joseph emerged from the Mercedes in front of us, coat collars rolled up against the chill. Right behind them I saw Flo, and I filled Grandpa K in on their friendship with Frank as they approached.

"Flo was a real help to all of us. Frank adored her—you'll see why when you meet her."

Grandpa K squinted toward them. "Nice looking lady."

Flo came up and extended a black-gloved hand toward Grandpa K. "You're Frank's grandfather," she said. "I'd've known you anywhere. There's a marvelous family resemblance."

I made quick introductions of Flo, Joseph, and Pete.

"How kind of you to escort our Susan," she said to Grandpa K. "She was such a comfort to Frank and to Clayton at the end."

Grandpa looked at me and winked. "She's pretty special."

I groped for an offhand reply to the compliment but came up blank.

Then Clayton appeared. Flo took his arm and turned to Grandpa K.

"Joe—may I call you Joe?—this is Clayton Selden. Clayton, this is Frank's grandfather, Joe Krajewski."

Was I the only one who noticed Grandpa K's posture stiffen a little? But he held out his hand, and Clayton clasped it.

"I so appreciate your being here," he said. "It would have meant the world to Frank."

What do you say to something like that? Grandpa K looked shocked, then his eyes narrowed and his lips pressed together. I wondered if he was about to tell Clayton who had the most right to be at Frank's funeral.

Flo leaped gracefully into that awkward moment and turned it around. "We've all suffered a dreadful loss," she said, straightening her hat as the wind threatened to lift it by its wide black brim, "but somehow, sharing it muffles the hurt a bit, don't you think?"

Harmony restored, we walked together up the slope, toward a lectern that held a round white ceramic urn. *Frank's ashes.* I saw Dan Fellows in the crowd, next to Rhonda and Michelle. He wore his leather jacket, and even with a somber expression, he looked every bit as handsome as I remembered, and every bit as unreachable. Michelle smiled at me and blew a kiss, and I blew one back, hoping at the last minute Dan wouldn't think it was for him. *We're burying Frank's ashes,* I reminded myself. *Who gives a damn what Dan thinks of you, especially now, today?*

Just the same, I had to look away.

Griffith Park loomed to the east of Forest Lawn; pine trees and oleanders and manicured lawns spilled out all around us, cloaked in a sparkly, evergreen-scented dampness that reminded me of childhood. I breathed it in and hoped Clayton's composure would last another hour.

* * *

The service was mercifully short. The minister, a woman in a long white brocade tunic, had actually known Frank; instead of the usual abstract platitudes about life and death, she gave us anecdotes of Frank's sense of humor and reminded us how much he had loved plants and animals and children, although not necessarily in that order.

It was all true, and right. She went on to assure us that Frank's soul was at peace now, and we were not to mourn too deeply, for …

I couldn't stop myself from crying—discreetly, I hoped. Grandpa K and I sat in the front row, and without turning my head I tried to check on Clayton, to my right. Tried to be ready if his emotions ran wild. Ready to do what, I didn't know.

Grandpa K took hold of my hand and squeezed, and I absorbed the warmth and courage from his strong old flesh. He'd gone through this before, several times. So had Flo.

"… *if you keep moving and breathing and putting one foot in front of the other, you can wait out the grief. You can outlast it.*"

How do you keep going, one foot in front of the other? And what if you don't outlast your grief? What if it wins?

My free hand clutched the Double Delights so tightly that a thorn pierced my thumb. I almost welcomed the painful distraction but tried to relax my grip. The roses' fragrance drifted up, faint and powerless against the afternoon gloom.

Grandpa K's hand left mine, and I let the grief wash over me, stifled and gasping, until his arm went around my shoulders and he pulled me gently against his wool jacket. I clung like a child as the minister finished with a prayer, her words unintelligible to me until the group collectively intoned "Amen," and a clearing of throats made me straighten in my chair. I pulled a wad of tissues from my purse and wiped my face. Looking down, I realized I had crushed one of the roses; its petals lay bruised and tattered in my lap.

I struggled and failed to summon good memories of Frank. Instead I kept seeing his ravaged face in that hospital bed, flesh stretched thin over his cheekbones, eyes clouded by pain and delirium. And his hands: those lovely elegant hands, morphed into claws with yellowed fingernails, and welts where needles had pierced the ruined skin.

I shut my eyes and let my breath shudder in and out. At least I could breathe. I tried to picture Frank before he got sick, that expression of wry amusement in his twinkling eyes. If he were alive, he'd saunter up to the cluster of mourners, fold his arms across his chest, and say, "Well! Why the glum faces, everyone?"

But of course he wasn't going to do that. I had to acknowledge the facts: death is never far away; life is never safe. And Frank was really, really gone. Love couldn't bring him back. Neither could sorrow.

Nothing had prepared me for the physical part of grief, the feeling that my guts had been twisted into a thousand knots, that my chest had been bruised by a million sobs. My face felt raw and hot; enough tears can corrode anything.

"And now," the minister concluded, "Clayton would like to say a few words."

Pale and tense, Clayton stood and turned toward the mourners. I braced myself to intervene if he freaked out. The sun poked through the clouds and lit up his face, his eyes that were the same shade of blue as Frank's. Had I ever really looked at Clayton before? His handsome face bore the marks of loss in the lines around his mouth. A breeze disturbed the tree branches, sent a shiver up my spine, and ruffled Clayton's hair. I noticed a gleam of silver at his temples.

The wind whispered of winter, dark and cold. I smelled damp earth and freshly cut grass. Clayton wore one of Frank's sweaters, gray and navy plaid, under his dark jacket, and why not? Why not hold on to a tangible memento, no matter how sad? I wondered if Frank's cologne lingered on the sweater, giving Clayton comfort as well as warmth.

Another gust washed over us and set my earrings jingling. The sun retreated as quickly as it had come, and for a moment all I heard was the distant whine of freeway traffic. Then Clayton started to speak.

"Our beloved Frank's suffering is over, and this is a day of mourning for our loss."

Hoarse at first, his voice strengthened as he spoke. "But this is also a day to celebrate his life and to remember Frank, not with sorrow, but with gratitude for the time we had with him. This is a day for reflecting on the man he was."

Wow, Clayton, you're really good.

I couldn't see Flo, who sat behind me, but I bet she shared my surprise. Clayton's voice wavered a bit, but he kept talking.

"He was a man who lived life to the fullest; he knew how to have fun. He was a man who defied plans and schedules; he was always in the moment, and he savored each and every one of those moments. He was a man who wasn't afraid to feel; and when he saw something he wanted, Frank pursued it with his whole heart and soul."

And don't we know that better than anyone, Clayton? As spiteful as the thought was, I allowed it to linger. I felt the weight of all that baggage I carried around, the remnants of my relationship with Frank, even though I had to acknowledge that Clayton spoke the truth. He managed to evoke the parts of Frank I wanted to remember, and without any effort on my part, those good memories flickered to life in my head.

"I loved him for that," Clayton continued. "I loved him for his determination, his vision, and his laughter. I loved him for knowing how to fix our leaky faucets and jump-start my car when I forgot and left the lights on."

And I *saw* Frank, clear as day, on that New Mexico highway, smiling and dusting off his hands after he'd changed our flat tire. I saw the Frank I wanted to remember, to keep in my memories and in my heart.

"I loved him for being so brave and so funny," Clayton went on, "even when he knew he was dying, when each new morning was a miracle and a blessing. At the end of his life, Frank taught me so much. He taught me how to move past pain into grace."

I plucked the bruised rose petals and ground them together between my fingers. *At least he taught one of us.* And even as that cynical thought bubbled up, another awareness replaced it. Clayton *had* really, truly loved Frank, maybe even more than I had. He'd given his heart unconditionally to Frank, and now he was paying the price, and with more courage than I imagined was humanly possible.

"This may seem like the end of our relationship with Frank," Clayton continued, "but I for one don't believe it. I believe there is an afterlife. I believe Frank's lovely spirit is in a wonderful place right now, a place that will beckon to each of us one day. And I believe in my heart that I will see Frank again."

I didn't have Clayton's unshakable faith, but his words had brought

Frank to life for me, and maybe that's what he meant. I *was* seeing Frank again, if only in my thoughts. If it just didn't hurt so damn much, I'd have been grateful.

Clayton could barely speak by the time he got to the last words, but he made it. And it sounded like most of the people behind me were getting out their tissues and handkerchiefs by then. Emotional? Sure. But beautiful, too. And far better than what I expected from Clayton. Far better than I could have done, dumb Susan who'd persuaded herself that she'd made peace with Frank's death. Wrong again.

Clayton scrubbed at his face and sent the tiniest of smiles out to the mourners; I heard approving murmurs among them. Damn it, he'd done it—and done it exactly right. I could almost hear Frank applauding.

And then things took a weird turn.

Clayton cleared his throat and said, "Does anyone else want to share their thoughts and feelings about Frank?"

And in the gap of silence that followed, it felt to me like the earth stopped spinning for a millisecond and we were all frozen in place. Then Grandpa K nudged me, ever so gently, in the ribs.

"Speak for both of us, will you, Susie Q? We knew him longer and better than anyone here."

Oh, God, no, I don't want to do that. I can't. Yes you can, you big coward. For Grandpa K. For Frank. I raised my hand.

Clayton's blue eyes turned my way, I nodded, and we traded places.

As I faced those people, all eyes on me, my chest tightened, and I fought for breath. I was terrified I would fall to my knees, self-esteem in shreds, my grief the public spectacle Flo had feared, but from a different source.

My mouth turned desert-dry, and a familiar paralysis seized me as I fought to swallow, to find some moisture for my stiff, parched tongue.

Remember to breathe, Susan. I could hear Paul Dumas' voice inside my head, and that hard-won lesson he'd taught me. I took a deep breath, prolonging the silence that probably lasted just seconds but felt like eternity. There. Another breath, while I tried not to ponder my folly.

Not only was I totally unprepared, clueless about what to say, any words would sound ridiculous in the aftermath of Clayton's moving eulogy. But there I was, and I had to say *something*, if only for the sake of Grandpa K, who gazed at me with total confidence that I knew what I was doing. I focused on his friendly face, and that helped.

Acutely aware that this was my last chance to explain what Frank meant to me, I started to talk. "Most of you know that Frank and I were married," I began, and I had to squeeze out those first words, but once I started, I managed to breathe and speak in rhythm. "And I completely agree with what Clayton just said. Frank brought out the best in everyone. He saw beauty in everyday things that some of us might overlook. And he made everything special, just by being there."

I saw a few heads nodding, and that gave me courage. Some of my words were pure babble, but Grandpa K smiled at me, and that mattered more than worries about looking foolish.

"He was such a complex man," I continued, "And he had so many talents. You might remember our dog Max? One time Max had hurt his leg, and when Frank knelt down and rubbed Max's leg for a minute —just like that—Max was fine again. That was Frank's gift: he could work miracles with the touch of his hand. But did you know that Frank could also sing almost any Broadway show tune?"

A few people laughed at that, and I guessed I wasn't the only one who'd heard Frank belt out "Ol' Man River" after a few cocktails, changing the words to silly things like, "He don't plant onions, or rutabagas."

"Frank loved his family so much," I continued, and Grandpa K pressed his lips together as something like regret clouded his expression. I didn't want that, so I hurried along. "He loved his friends. And I'm thankful he loved me; I'm honored to have shared his life."

From the blurry corners of my vision I saw more nods of agreement. Encouraged, I kept going. "And I need to tell you something *I* just realized when Clayton was talking. Frank really isn't gone, and our relationship with him isn't gone. It's *changed*, but it's still there. It's in our memories. I don't know about an afterlife," I confessed, and then pointed to my heart, "but I know Frank will always live in my heart."

Grandpa K had kept his eyes dry, but when I said that, tears streamed down his cheeks, and I was crying too as I choked out those last words. Rather than make a total ass of myself, I shut up and sat down.

Trembling, Grandpa K put his arm around me. "That was beautiful, honey," he said.

I looked over at the trees, where a couple of sparrows hopped around in the shadows of their branches. One of the birds lifted its wings and flew away, and I ached at the sight of that tiny body as it became a dark speck in the endless gray canopy overhead.

The minister ended the ceremony then. Grandpa K let go of me, and we stood along with the others. My legs felt numb; if I'd had more faith in them I might have started running, away from all that sadness. Instead, I forced myself to turn toward the cluster of mourners behind us.

And the first person I saw was Margaret Deschanels.

I felt a weird sense of disconnection. What was she doing in this context? My mouth fell open as we made eye contact. Only after an awkward few seconds was I able to speak.

"I didn't know you were coming."

Margaret wore a silvery sweater, almost the color of her hair, over a black tunic and slacks, and with her arms folded across her chest she looked cold and tired. And sad. The entire landscape behind her seemed muted by the overcast, the green lawns faded and dull.

She took a step toward me, arms held open wide, and her smile lit up her face and everything around her. I grabbed hold of her and didn't care how foolish I looked. I only cared that my friend had come to Frank's funeral, without my having to ask. With Margaret's strong arms around me, I felt so protected, so comforted that I wanted to stand there forever.

"How could I not be with you on this day?" she said.

I cried like a baby. A big baby who had no right to be even more out of control than I'd been up to then. I was an idiot; an emotional wreck of a woman who hadn't been able to move on with her life while everyone around her had made the shift.

Finally I was able to release her and stand on my own. Grandpa K was right beside me, concern filling his face, already etched with grief. I reached for his arm.

"Grandpa K," I said, "this is my friend Margaret Deschanels. My good friend."

Grandpa K shook hands with Margaret. "Any friend of Susie's is a friend of mine," he said.

* * *

One last ceremony remained. Michelle held a cluster of Peruvian lilies, which she handed out for mourners to drop into the hole where Frank's ashes were being buried. As I passed her, I held up the remains of my Double Delights; most of them were still intact. They might be lost in the splendor of the other flowers, but I didn't care. I kissed the roses softly and inhaled their fragrance before I tossed them into the grave. *Rest in peace, Frank.*

Margaret followed me, and then Grandpa K. When his turn came, he nodded his thanks to Michelle for the flower, and his lips moved as he bowed his head and dropped the lily in with the rest. His body sagged like he was about to collapse, and I worried that the day had demanded too much from him. He drew himself up, however, and moved away from the grave. I saw tears on his face and, to my horror, I started to cry again.

I didn't sob out loud, but I felt the hot salt on my cheeks, and my eyes were so blurry I couldn't see where I was going. Hands clenched, I dug my nails into my palms to try and stop the tears, but it didn't work.

There. It was over. Through the blur I saw Flo approach Grandpa K and link arms with him. She patted his hand and although I couldn't hear their words, I imagined they were talking about other loved ones they'd lost and how they got through it before and could do it again.

Everyone started moving down toward the cars, and I lost track of

Margaret. My heels sank into the grass, and I had to walk carefully to keep from stumbling. I focused on avoiding the obvious grave sites as my ankles wobbled on the uneven turf. Then a hand gripped my elbow, and there was Margaret again, guiding me down the slope. I tried to smile, and failed.

"That was a lovely service," Margaret said. "And your eulogy was very touching. I know that was incredibly difficult for you."

I nodded because I couldn't talk yet.

"Are you all right?" she asked.

I shook my head. "I don't know. Just when I think I've got it licked, I lose control. I'm so confused, I don't know what to think. What to feel."

"That's very normal, you know … except when it happens to you."

"Yeah, it sure doesn't feel normal. You'd think I could at least get a handle on my feelings. It's not like—"

"It doesn't have to be like anything. You've suffered a horrible loss, and you have every right to grieve," Margaret said. "You loved him as much as anyone did."

"Yeah. Yeah, I did."

We made it to the cars without either of us falling. Blades of wet grass clung to our shoes. I made a halfhearted try at wiping mine with my hand but just managed to smear wet grass on myself.

Margaret handed me a tissue to clean my hand. "I'm sorry I wasn't there for you. When he died. And right after."

"I didn't expect it." *No, wait.* "Well, maybe I did, a little. But I had no right."

"You had every right to *want* it. We're friends, and friends support each other."

"Yeah, but you had other stuff going on. The thing with Claire."

"No excuse for abandoning you when you needed me. I am so sorry."

"It's past. You're here now. And I didn't know until I saw you how much I needed you today."

Her smile warmed me on that chilly afternoon, and a huge weight lifted from my heart. I'd lost Frank, but I still had my friend Margaret.

We stood without speaking for a moment, until I asked, "Will you come to the reception at Clayton's?"

"Of course."

Flo and Grandpa K were still talking as they made their way slowly down the slope, and I smiled at the sight. They made a nice-looking pair. *Jimmy better watch out.*

"Frank's grandfather is quite impressive," Margaret said. "And how wonderful of him to be here."

"It took a lot of guts," I replied.

"And for you, too. To be here. I know Frank would have been pleased: all his loved ones coming together."

"Too bad it didn't happen while he was alive to enjoy it."

"Still, he knows, I think."

"You believe that?"

"I do. I have to."

Grandpa K noticed us and waved. Time to go. Time to finish the ritual.

I turned to Margaret. "You know how to get there?"

"I'll follow you," she said.

And she did.

Chapter 18
Back on the Bike

Grandpa K and I didn't talk much during the ride to Clayton's. We absorbed each other's quiet solace as Clarice guided the big sedan through afternoon traffic. The Los Angeles rush hour starts at noon on Fridays, so she had her work cut out for her.

When we were almost there, Grandpa K took out his handkerchief and blew his nose. "That Clayton—what he said—he really did love Frankie, didn't he?"

I nodded. "He still does."

"Yeah. I figured that out." He puffed out his cheeks and blew.

He picked up my hand and kissed the back of it, then pressed it between his own. "God bless you, honey."

I didn't know what to say so I leaned into him and put my head on his shoulder, and we rode like that the rest of the way.

Flo was already there to greet us. She led Grandpa K in to meet the rest of Frank's friends. I watched him move through the crowd, smiling and shaking hands, Flo's arm linked companionably with his. And for a minute or two, I felt more alone than I ever had. Frank was gone, Grandpa K would be flying home soon, and everyone else would pick up the threads of their lives. Then I pushed the feeling away and went looking for Margaret.

I found her in the kitchen, helping Rhonda arrange tiny sandwiches on a ceramic platter. I washed my hands and went to work alongside them, filling bowls with chips and salsa and carrying them to the dining room table, checking the liquor stock at the makeshift bar and stopping to accept condolences from strangers. After the first few times, I stopped being surprised that so many people knew who I was, and how much I'd lost. Some of them seemed to understand it even better than I did.

On my way back to the kitchen, I met up with Margaret, outbound with a tray of cheese. I swiped a wedge of brie.

Her steely eyebrows went up. "You've dislodged my perfect symmetry."

I feigned remorse, and Margaret's smile betrayed her pretense.

"Take a piece yourself then," I said. "Restore order to the universe."

Margaret rolled her eyes in a "What am I going to do with you?" look. She swept off with her cheese tray.

Behind her, in the kitchen, Rhonda stopped stirring a vat of guacamole long enough thank me for pitching in. "I need more help than I thought," she said. "You and your friend are lifesavers."

"Glad to do it," I replied. "It's actually a relief to have stuff to *do*."

Rhonda wiped the back of her hand across her forehead. "I know. God, I miss him. I didn't realize how much until he was gone."

She teared up, and I went over and hugged her. "Me too," I said.

Holding an ice bucket, Michelle breezed into the kitchen. "I hope we got enough ice," she said, "I thought with this cold weather we wouldn't—"

She broke off when she saw me embracing her girlfriend and for a horrifying second I was afraid she'd think I'd made a pass at Rhonda. I started to back away, but Michelle's raised eyebrows came down and her expression softened almost immediately.

"Aw, yes—it still hurts, huh?"

And she wrapped her arms around both of us.

These women really cared about Frank, I thought. *And they care about me,* I realized with a jolt. Rhonda and Michelle were my friends too, now.

Rhonda let go first and turned back to her guacamole, wiping her damp cheeks with her apron hem. Michelle peered up at me; until that moment I hadn't noticed that I towered over her. She had lovely gray-green eyes, even if they were rimmed in red at the moment, and I saw a world of concern in them. Her dark hair curved around her face like a heart-shaped picture frame.

"You doing okay, Susan?" asked Michelle. "I know this is even tougher for you."

I shook my head. "Every now and then I feel like I'm coming apart," I confessed, "but mostly I'm maintaining."

"Frank's grandpa is a doll," Rhonda said as she handed me the bowl of guacamole.

"Isn't he? I'm so grateful he's here. It would've meant a lot to Frank."

"And it means the world to Clayton," Michelle said. "He always felt bad that he'd come between Frank and his grandpa."

Rhonda pulled a bag of ice from the freezer. "I wonder what changed the old guy's mind?"

I shrugged. "Sometimes love is stronger than you'd expect, I guess. And he really did love Frank."

"And he's pretty darn fond of you," Michelle said with a giggle. "Flo was teasing him—at least I think she was teasing, I hope so for Jimmy's sake—and he got all bashful and then said something about you being his best girl and he didn't want to make you jealous."

That got me laughing enough that I could go back out among the guests without worrying about another meltdown. I put the guacamole by the chip bowl and meandered around, looking for more work to do. Everything seemed under control.

The family room bore no trace of Frank's dying, but I shuddered when I passed the spot where his hospital bed had been. Did some part of his spirit linger in the air there? I couldn't feel it.

I'd stuck with water and juice up to then, but I needed a *real* drink, so I mixed a vodka-tonic and soaked up the voices, the thick press of bodies all around. I saw Margaret, an empty platter in one hand, laughing at something Grandpa K said while Flo beamed up at him, and I thought, *most of the people I care about are here in this house today.*

The liquor sizzled in my brain, and I splashed in some more tonic before I took another sip. The last thing I wanted was to start seeing double and end up puking and passed out in the bathroom. That'd be a lovely last view of the grieving ex-wife.

An arm circled my waist, and there was Dan Fellows, holding a frosty beer bottle. He raised it in a toast, and I clinked my glass against the beer. People moved past us; someone's elbow grazed my arm, and I let Dan steady me.

Despite my earlier "who cares?" attitude, my feelings still zigzagged all over the place, and I felt the physical pull of Dan's presence. He stood so close I could smell his fresh-air cologne and see the individual hairs of his beard. If I wanted to, I could reach up and stroke his face; I could kiss him. I could melt into him, let him sweep me up and take me home with him, and maybe I could pretend there'd never be another old girlfriend banging on the door. Maybe I could.

The vodka was making mischief with my thoughts. I pulled away and set down my glass.

"Ready for a refill?" he asked.

His hand on my waist had felt delicious.

"No, thanks. I better not." My voice sounded hollow and unconvincing.

He cocked his head, and those adorable crinkles at the corners of his eyes chipped away at my resistance.

"Why not? I can't think of a better time to get sloshed. You earned it. Hey—if you drink too much, I'll drive you home. Or take you home with me."

Was he kidding? I pretended to believe he was, to brush off the suggestion.

"Thanks, but no."

"It might be good for you, you know—a little distraction," he said, with that killer grin. And, for just a few seconds, I was tempted.

A vision of my future rose up, a lifetime of men like Noah and Dan, men who'd love me for the moment, until someone else called to them. I'd never come first for them. *But Frank had put me first,* I thought—*until Clayton came along.* Except for Elise, I had been The Woman in his life. And see where that had led. Maybe this was the best I could hope for. Trophy boyfriends, a pretend-happy life, blot out the loss and fear and knowledge of my own mortality. But it wouldn't make me safe, not *really* safe. I'd always be waiting for the phone call, the knock on the door. Waiting to be abandoned again.

"I appreciate your concern," I said, as lightly as I could. "But honest, I don't need anything from you."

I had the immense satisfaction of watching him register surprise and disbelief, and for just a flash of a second I wondered if I was missing out on something I should accept. *Nah. I really don't want that. I deserve more.*

"Hey, is somebody moving in on my girl?"

Grandpa K appeared at that very instant, and it took all my self-control to keep from physically pushing him between Dan and me.

He thrust his hand toward Dan. "Joe Krajewski. Frank's grandpa."

Dan's grin lost some of its confidence as he shook Grandpa K's hand. "Dan Fellows. Family friend. It's a pleasure to meet you, sir. My condolences on your loss."

Grandpa K nodded his acknowledgment and put his arm around me. "You be careful with this one, young Dan. She's had a rough time."

Had he heard our exchange? How much did he know, or guess? I didn't care. Between Grandpa K and Dan, to me it was no contest. Out there in the world, somewhere, was a younger version of Joseph Krajewski Sr. I just had to help him find me.

The sky must've cleared up, because a ray of warm purple-orange light fell in through the sliding doors and swept across my face. I stepped back out of the glare and raised my empty glass in a toast to Dan.

"Thanks for coming today," I said. "Frank would've appreciated it."

Dan gave a half-salute and blended into the crowd.

"That Flo is a pistol," Grandpa K said, winking at me.

"She's spoken for, Grandpa K," I told him.

He threw back his head and laughed. "So she told me. But you gotta admire me for even having thoughts like that, Susie Q."

"Oh, I admire you plenty, Grandpa K. You have no idea how much."

I kissed his cheek and whispered, "Thanks for rescuing me."

He winked again. "My pleasure. Hey—and your pal Margaret. What a lady! French, no less!"

"She's a good friend," I agreed. "We had a falling out a while ago, but, thanks to you, we patched it up."

"Thanks to *me*?"

I nodded. "I almost lost her. We had a huge fight—but remember what you told me? About not shutting people out just because you disagree with them, because they're not the way you want them to be?"

He rubbed his chin like he was trying to recall that conversation. "And that happened between you and Margaret."

"Yeah. But thanks to your wise counsel, we straightened it out. You saved our friendship."

"Seems to me like it was well worth saving, honey. You have some real nice friends."

And I realized he was talking about the other people at the reception, too.

"People care about you, Susie Q," he added. "You have no idea how much."

I didn't know if he was consciously parroting my words, but it made me giggle.

He drifted off to socialize some more, and I caught up with Margaret as she carried an armload of used plastic cups to the trash barrel on the service porch.

"You have charmed Frank's grandfather beyond belief," I told her.

"He's wonderful! What a life he's had! And to come all this way for the services." She leaned close to me. "He did it for you, Susan. He absolutely worships you, you know."

"The feeling is mutual," I murmured and then decided to confide my big secret. "He's offered me a job."

She studied my face for a moment without speaking and I remembered I hadn't told her about my leaving Jacobs.

Margaret nodded solemnly. "Judy told me you quit your job," she said. "She took it very personally that she only found out when she tried to call you at work." Her lips curved into a smile. "She was quite angry with you."

"Yeah," I replied, "I think Judy and I have moved past each other."

"Good."

My mouth dropped open in surprise. Margaret pressed her lips together, like she was trying to gather her thoughts to say something unwelcome.

"She's not your friend," she said at last.

And a ton of guilt fell away.

"I know. When it's not all about her, she gets nasty." I lowered my voice in my best Judy impersonation. "'Fuck, Susan, what is going on with you? Something this huge, you don't even think to mention it!'"

So it may have been mean-spirited, but we both laughed anyway. I felt like a high school kid sneaking a smoke behind the cafeteria.

"I should've told you, though—about the job," I said. "I'm sorry."

She patted my arm. "It's not as if you haven't had a few other issues on your mind. But I do want to know what happened, and what you plan to do next."

I filled her in on the important parts, ending with Grandpa K's unexpected offer to run his charitable foundation.

"But that's marvelous!" Margaret said.

"I'm not so sure. It's a huge change in direction. And what if I screw it up?"

"You won't! You'll be wonderful."

"You're prejudiced."

"Possibly—but Joe isn't. He's a smart guy. He wouldn't have made the offer if he didn't know you could do it."

"You really think so?"

"Absolutely!" Margaret replied, with a firm nod. Her expression turned to concern then. "The only thing is—I wish you'd allow yourself a little time off, just to enjoy life for a while before you plunge back into the working world."

"I will. But I don't want to take too long. I'm afraid I'll forget how to work."

"You'll be fine," Margaret replied. "It's like riding a bike—you never forget."

My mom had taught me to ride my first two-wheeler. We used the parking lot at the supermarket down the street early one Sunday morning. She ran behind me at first, holding the frame to keep me upright, and I didn't even realize that she'd let go until I looked back and saw her grinning and waving as I pedaled forward on my own. I felt wind in my hair and this incredible feeling of freedom, almost like flying. My breath came in jagged gushes, wonder and amazement and terror flooding over me all at once.

Did I fall down? Sure. Lots of times. Scraped elbows and skinned knees. But always I got back on the bike. Always I gave it one more shot, and I made it through until the next crash, as they got further and further apart.

That must've been hard for Mom, watching me pedal away from her like that. Knowing it was the first of many separations. But when I recalled her face that Sunday morning, I didn't see loss or regret; I saw pride.

"I'm so glad you're here today," I told Margaret.

"When things are dark, we need to know that people care," she said. I cringed at the memory of my own selfish reaction when she'd been having trouble with Claire.

As if she'd read my thoughts, Margaret continued, "When Philippe and I took Claire to France, it was such a relief to know you were just a phone call away from Deirdre, if she needed help while we were gone."

"Deirdre? She sounded totally in control when I talked to her."

"Yes, that's her way. Still … she told me how reassuring it was to have you nearby. I knew without having to ask that I could count on you. I always have."

And before either of us could start sniffling, I led her back to the kitchen. Still reeling between emotions, I was starting to believe life could be good again, someday. Margaret's presence eased my grief and the jagged empty space Frank had left behind. Eased but could not erase. I knew I had to sit with my sorrow a while longer; how long, I couldn't control.

So I went in search of more busy work. Then I saw Ralph, sitting on the patio, nose pressed to the sliding glass doors. Of course it made sense to keep her outside; not everyone enjoyed the swipe of a big wet dog tongue. The sight of her brought a heart-stopping insight: how much of my life had I been like Ralph, watching from the other side of the glass? I could see the world around me, I could hear it and sometimes feel a little vibration from it, but I hadn't really been *in* it; I'd merely observed.

Ralph leaped up at me, tail thrashing, as I slid the glass panel open and stepped outside.

I squatted and rubbed the dog's chest. "Hey, girl. You're lonesome today, huh?"

Her sloppy pink tongue lapped at my hand, and she whined softly. Poor thing, she didn't have a clue what was going on. Or maybe she did. I shivered at the memory of her desolate howl right after Frank died. I found her tennis ball and tossed it across the yard. She raced after it, cares forgotten. If only I could let go of my troubles that easily.

Ralph retrieved the ball and dropped it at my feet; her head tilted up, and I thought I saw affection in her dark brown eyes. I knelt, put my arms around her neck and buried my face in her soft amber fur. She didn't try to get away.

I heard footsteps behind us. "Oh, good," Clayton said. "I was hoping she'd get some attention."

"She's real lonely," I told him.

"Yes. She is. And she seems to have gotten quite attached to you."

I shrugged it off. "Better than being by herself, I guess."

"No, seriously. She isn't this lively with anyone else lately. Even me. But then I'm not much fun for her."

I threw the ball and stood up. "It'll get better."

"I know it will   eventually." He looked up at the sky and sighed. "Meanwhile, there's this *now* to get through. But you know that as well as I do."

"Afraid so."

"That was wonderful, Susan, what you said this afternoon. You captured my feelings exactly."

Ralph brought the ball back again, huffing for more.

"Thanks," I replied. "But you get the credit. You brought Frank back for me."

"Do you think he heard us?"

I tossed the ball for Ralph. "I'm gonna let myself believe he did."

Clayton swiped tears from his cheeks. "Sorry."

Ralph returned with her toy, and she must have sensed I was tiring of the game, for she started batting the ball around with her front paw, like a cat would do.

"You're allowed," I told Clayton. "I expect we'll both be doing a lot of that for a while. But it *will* stop hurting so much. I hope."

"Me too."

For a few awkward moments, we watched Ralph play.

"So," I said, to break the silence, "what are you doing to keep your spirits up? I've read that we're supposed to make plans, things to look forward to."

"Actually," Clayton said, "I'm going to take a trip. A long trip, to get away from the memories."

"Oh. Sounds like fun."

He made a sour-lemon face. "Maybe. But I'll have to board Ralph while I'm gone."

I spoke without thinking. "How cruel."

Clayton's laugh was brittle. "Don't hold back, Susan."

"Sorry. But she's had a loss, too. You can't just ship her off and pretend she doesn't have feelings."

"You sound like Frank."

I ignored the comment. "Can't one of your friends keep her while you're gone? Rhonda, or Flo, or—"

He cocked his head and narrowed those lethal blue eyes. "Actually, I was wondering if you'd take her."

"Me? I don't have time for a dog! What would I do with her?"

Ralph came back and sat at my feet; her gaze focused on me, like she knew what we were talking about. *If she could talk, what would she say?*

"She's a good dog," Clayton pointed out.

A ton of excuses chattered in my head: I'd be busy learning a new job, learning a new me. What about those trips to Chicago? My house wasn't set up for a dog. I had no dog door, and I …

"If it didn't work out," Clayton said, "I'd take her back."

And there, he'd nailed it, the one Big Excuse. It *would* work out; Ralph and I were meant for each other. But what if Clayton changed his mind? I couldn't handle getting attached and then having her yanked away. I'd lost enough.

Clayton turned mind reader on me. He put his arms around me, intent on a hug whether I wanted it or not. "But only if you asked me to. I promise."

I kept from crying that time, and when he let go I crouched next to Ralph again. "How about it, girl? You think we'd make a good team?"

She yawned, licked my hand and picked up the tennis ball, tail swaying.

"That's a yes if ever I heard one," Flo said.

I hadn't heard her come outside, and I felt silly down there on the ground, interviewing a dog.

"You're one lucky girl, Ralphie," said Flo.

"You didn't warn me Clayton was going to spring this," I told her.

Flo chuckled. "Would you have given a different answer?"

I stood and put my hands on my hips in fake protest. "I haven't said yes."

Flo and Clayton traded a look that said it all.

"Dogs are wonderful companions," Flo pointed out. "And you'll meet the most interesting people when you take Ralphie out for walks."

"Speaking of interesting people," Grandpa K said from the doorway, "seems like they're all meeting out here."

"Joe," said Flo, holding out her hand, "come meet Susan's new dog, Ralph."

Grandpa K strolled over to Ralph and bowed. "How do you do, Ralph? Pleased to make your acquaintance."

Ralph dropped her tennis ball and responded with a soft "whuff." I swear she smiled at him.

Grandpa K turned to Clayton. "Frankie always loved dogs, didn't he? I got him his first one, when he was just seven."

"Duffy!" Clayton said. "I remember—he told me about that."

Frank had told me, too, but I kept my mouth shut.

Grandpa K's expression went distant. "He loved that mutt. They were inseparable." Then he came back to us and patted Ralph's head. "You are a cutie—you make me wish I had a dog myself."

Flo seized the opening. "I can make that happen in a flash, y'know."

"Watch out, Grandpa K," I told him. "Before you know it she'll have you up to your eyeballs in dogs."

I giggled at the image of Grandpa K surrounded by a flock of Goldies, their fur covering his elegant wool suit, and him loving every minute of it.

"What is so funny about *that*?" Flo asked in pretend indignation. Then she started to laugh, too.

Laughter is contagious, and it spread to Grandpa K and Clayton, so cleansing and healing that I didn't want to stop, and I didn't care if I sounded like a donkey braying, or a hen cackling, or anything else. Laughing in the face of the day's significance felt life-affirming, and right, and I imagined I heard Frank join the chorus.

Margaret came onto the patio just then, holding a plate of cookies.

"These will help you keep laughing," she said. "Courtesy of Rhonda, and fresh from the oven. They're *magic*."

Flo took a cookie and passed the plate around. "Rhonda is a culinary *artist*," she told us.

And she was right. The warm rush of sugar and butter and oatmeal and chocolate chips flooded my senses. If these weren't comfort food, nothing was.

Around a mouthful of cookie, Grandpa K said, "You came at exactly the right time, Margaret. We were just congratulating Susie on her new dog. Or maybe it's Ralph who gets congratulated?"

Margaret's voice rippled with pleasure. "Must be something in the air. Deirdre brought home a dog from the shelter while we were in France—some kind of collie. She's very sweet."

Margaret had never been a dog person as far as I knew, so Deirdre's rescue must have been a *real* charmer.

"I can't imagine life without a dog," Flo said, her eyes issuing me a challenge.

"Deirdre and I can share new-dog-parent stories then," I told Margaret.

She sighed. "Yes, I'm sure there'll be plenty. Daisy—that's what Deirdre named her—isn't nearly as well behaved as Ralph here."

Margaret was right, I realized. Ralph had stayed placidly in place, not jumping up or trying to steal a cookie, while we discussed her future.

Clayton leaned forward. "You should talk to Michelle. She's a fabulous trainer. She's the reason Ralph is so good. Well, part of the reason."

Her face alight, Margaret turned to me. "You have the *best* friends," she said.

"Yeah," I agreed. "You included."

The last rays of sunset fell across us then, illuminating Ralph's copper coat as if it were a campfire, and we were explorers, gathered around the flame for companionship and warmth. She gazed up at me with perfect trust in her soft brown eyes. *I have to come through for her,* I thought. *I won't let her down.*

Grandpa K looked tired, though. He was probably still on Chicago time.

"Are you okay?" I asked. "Need a nap or anything?"

He put his arm around me. "I'm fine, honey. With you as my date, I can dance all night."

And so could I.

A couple of stars glittered in the darkening sky. A chilly breeze whipped my hair back, but it was the same wind that had blown the clouds away, so I didn't mind.

Michelle came to the doorway and peered out at us in the gathering darkness, her curly brown hair backlit so that she resembled an angel. My friend? Yes, she was. A gift from Frank. I envisioned her and Margaret bonding over Deirdre's dog, expanding their worlds, and Deirdre's. And mine.

"Does anyone know where Susan is?" asked Michelle.

I took a step forward, drew in a deep breath, and waved to her. "Yes," I said. "Here I am."

Acknowledgments

Writing a novel is a lonely pursuit—at least until you get the words on the page. Then, if you're lucky, you can share your work with other writers who help you mold your words, sentences, and paragraphs into something worth reading.

I have been more than lucky in meeting up with some of the most perceptive, sensitive, and honest fellow writers in the world. Irene Bowers, Tim Bryant, and Tracy London were there at the birth of this novel, and they gave it shape and direction. Then came Heather Ames, Gayle Bartos-Pool, Terry Carr, Jackie Houchin, Miko Johnston, Rosemary Lord, and Jacqueline Vick—all accomplished writers who were generous in their counsel and support. They didn't always like what I wrote—and thank goodness for that, because their feedback gave Mending Dreams a focus and depth I could not have achieved on my own. Their encouragement kept me writing through those times when I questioned my ability to complete this novel, not to mention my sanity for even wanting to try.

Folks, I couldn't have done it without you.

Book Group Questions
Discussing Mending Dreams

1. Did you like Susan when you first met her? Did you get a sense of her anger, even before you knew its source?
2. Were you surprised to learn about the reason for her divorce from Frank? Did you get a sense of her real feelings for him—the ones she hid from herself? Could you relate to these feelings?
3. How did the circumstances of the divorce affect Susan's self-image?
4. When Susan decides to try and heal the rift between Frank and Grandpa K, she sets something else in motion. Did the end result of this surprise you? Did you expect to see Grandpa K's further involvement in her life?
5. What did you think the book was about?
6. Did you enjoy reading the book? Why or why not? At what point did you decide if you liked it or not? What influenced this decision?
7. Did you learn something you didn't know before in reading this book? After you read it, did you see anything in a different light?

8. What did the book's title mean to you? What dreams are mended? Does Susan do it on her own, or does she have help?
9. Susan says, at the end, "Here I am." What is she really saying here?
10. The themes of courage and forgiveness run through the book. Who is braver: Susan or Frank? Or Clayton? Do you think Susan *really* forgave Frank?
11. Who was your favorite character? Why? Your least favorite? Why?
12. Friendship plays an important role in Susan's life, but she eventually realizes that she has to let go of one friendship. Have you ever outgrown a friendship? Were you able to let go of it?
13. If you could change something about the book, what would it be? Why?
14. How did you feel about the book's ending? Did it satisfy you as a reader?

Preview

Read an excerpt from Bonnie Schroeder's next novel, *Write My Name on the Sky.*

Setting the scene...

The Summer of Love began in San Francisco, California, in 1967 and launched a social, cultural and political movement that is unrivaled to this day. Young people wearing bright patterned clothes, often with a joint or a hit of acid in their pockets, called themselves hippies, or flower children. Espousing peace, love and freedom, they gathered at Love-Ins, on grassy park hillsides, to celebrate freedom from convention, listen to the music of Jesse Colin Young or Joan Baez, and give themselves over to the dance, arms outstretched.

Their movement spread to Los Angeles, otherwise known as the City of Angels, although those who really knew the town called it City of Fallen Angels. There, by the summer of 1968, peace and love experimented in the Los Angeles air.

Write My Name on the Sky
Chapter 1 • July 1968

Where the hell was Arlene?

Kate Prescott scanned the crowd of sweaty strangers, searching for her co-worker, who had coaxed Kate into driving to the Griffith Park Love-In on a hot Saturday afternoon. As soon as they arrived, Arlene had moseyed off with a fellow wearing a crown of flowers in his long black hair. Kate feared she'd seen the last of Arlene for the day; it was impossible to pick her out in this ocean of bodies and noise and blinding colors.

People jostled past, and the summer sun singed Kate's skin. Had she ever felt more out of place?

A grubby man approached, dirt-caked hand extended. He grinned, revealing two rows of yellowed teeth. "Here, sister."

Kate backed away, shaking her head as her silver earrings jingled. No way in hell was she going to take the brownie he offered; her stomach clenched, and she was sure there was more to that brownie than eggs, butter and baking chocolate.

"Don't get all uptight, Blondie."

"My name isn't Blondie—it's ...Alice. And you need to back off!"

With his free hand, the man stroked his sparse beard; his disheveled auburn hair looked like it hadn't been washed in a month.

He squinted red-rimmed eyes at her. "Come on, then, Alice. This will help you get where you want to go."

Behind Brownie Man, the hills of Griffith Park had turned summer beige, rising to meet a fair blue sky, oak and Manzanita branches puncturing the shimmering canvas. More revelers oozed past, giving off odors of perfume, incense, and cigarette smoke. Pucci prints swirled against glistening bare skin.

The scruffy guy took a step closer.

"Alice," said a voice behind her, "there you are! We've been looking all over for you."

Kate turned, baffled because she didn't recognize the man who'd spoken, but he seemed to be talking to her. *Who are you?*

In worn jeans and a blue shirt, he still looked cleaner than Brownie Man. Curly brown hair, a little on the long side. And eyes the color of dark chocolate.

He held out his hand. "Come along, Alice. The Wonderland Express is leaving."

He winked at her, and time stopped. She was no longer alone in a sea of frolickers who all knew something she didn't. Drums and voices faded as she took a step toward this man she didn't know but somehow *recognized,* the two of them apart from the crowd.

She took his hand: strong, with spatters of blue and green paint along the back.

He nodded to Brownie Man. "It's cool, we're already trippin'."

"Thanks," she murmured to the man who held her hand.

He pointed toward the shade of a nearby eucalyptus. "My friend over there says he knows you, but he was too stoned to help you out."

When he released her hand, Kate wished he hadn't. She squinted through the sunlight at a long-haired fellow leaning against the eucalyptus. Then she made the connection: Leonard Ryder, from Bright Street. They'd been neighbors until high school graduation. But he looked so *different* that afternoon.

She remembered Leonard as acne-scarred and pudgy, but this guy was slender, and a beard camouflaged his pitted cheekbones.

"Little Katie Prescott," he said, "fancy meeting you here."

Speechless, Kate groped for a greeting. In their senior year,

Leonard had discovered music, playing his guitar and singing folk songs in coffee houses, using only his last name.

"Hello, Ryder," she replied eventually. "Thanks for sending your friend to save me."

Ryder's smirk and his indifferent posture triggered memories of summer afternoons on Bright Street, playing hide and seek with other kids on the block. Ryder always lost; he was too slow and too chubby to find good hiding places, but he always pretended not to care.

"My friend," Ryder said, "*wanted* to save you. But did you need saving?"

"Probably," Kate replied. She turned to Ryder's companion. "I'm Kate Prescott."

"Jack Morrison." He extended that wonderful, paint-spattered hand again. "And what brings you here, Kate Prescott?"

Kate forbid herself to prolong the handshake. "Curiosity."

"Which killed the cat," Jack Morrison pointed out with a slow grin.

"But satisfaction brought it back."

Jack looked at Ryder. "You didn't tell me she was smart."

Kate studied his profile for a moment; he was quite handsome.

"I came with somebody from work," she continued, "but she ditched me."

Ryder sat down, cross legged, and motioned her to join him. "Work? I thought you were a college girl."

Kate sat, fanning her sundress around her knees. "You haven't been home lately, have you?"

Ryder flinched. "Shit, that's right. Man, what a bummer about your dad. I really liked him."

Kate started to tell him more when a line of dancers snaked past in a wild swirl of bright colors. Tambourines and voices drowned out any chance of conversation, so she leaned back and breathed in the thick, minty fragrance of eucalyptus, mingled with incense and another, sharper smell.

Jack Morrison eased down on the grass next to Kate and raised his voice above the racket. "You stick with us. Pretty girls shouldn't run around here on their own. Too many stray wolves hunting."

Kate shivered. "Thanks for the cheerful thought."

He smiled, and the world turned brighter.

Ryder reached in his shirt pocket and produced a thin cigarette. *Weed*, Kate realized, as Ryder lit it, inhaled and offered it to her. Kate shook her head.

"Come on, Kate—join the party," Ryder said as he exhaled.

Reluctantly, Kate put the joint to her lips and took a careful puff, unable to suppress the urge to look over her shoulder.

Jack's laugh came out low and throaty. "Don't act so nervous. Pretend it's a cigarette. Breathe in. Good."

The smoke tasted strangely sweet. A cough rose in her throat, and she swallowed it away, then handed the joint to Jack.

Their hands touched, and she felt a sizzle along her skin, as if she'd brushed a live electric wire. Did he feel it too? He gave no sign but inhaled deeply and held the smoke in his lungs for an impossibly long time as he passed the joint to Ryder.

Through a stream of exhaled marijuana smoke, Jack asked, "So what were you doing before you got lost?"

"I wasn't lost," she told him.

"We're *all* lost, but some of us don't know it."

"Be careful of him, Katie Girl," said Ryder. "He's a mad artist."

He turned away to gaze at the people flowing past, tapping his thighs in time to the drums. Kate watched the collision of colors, reds and greens and golds and blues, merging and separating. She felt drab in comparison, a wren among flamingoes and peacocks.

The chain of dancers circled back. Bangle bracelets jingled as they beckoned. Ryder pinched out the roach, swallowed it, and rose in one graceful movement, as if defying gravity, brushing leaf fragments from his jeans.

"C'mon, folks, let's groove." He swayed and clapped in time to the tambourines' tempo.

Kate shook her head. "I'm a terrible dancer—don't you remember?"

"Nobody cares. C'mon."

"Let her be," Jack said. "She can keep me company."

Ryder cocked his head and started to say something, but a woman whose breasts were falling out of her orange tank top grabbed his arm and pulled him into the crowd.

Jack took out his Marlboros and offered her one. Kate studied the pack, and he laughed—a soft, teasing sound.

"They're plain old cigarettes," he told her, so she accepted and cupped her hands around his as he struck a match flame and touched it to the tip of her cigarette. Kate's flesh tingled again.

"Thanks," she said, breathing smoke into the pristine summer air.

Jack blew two small, perfect smoke rings and poked his finger through one as it drifted skyward. Kate giggled.

"So, did you like that weed?" he asked.

Kate considered her answer. "I guess. Don't feel it all that much."

"Give it time," Jack said.

She reclined on her elbows and waited.

"You have good skin," he said.

"Me?" Kate tried not to look surprised.

"I've started noticing the models' skin in drawing class," he said, as if that explained the off-the-wall compliment. "You don't go out much in the sun, do you?"

She shook her head. "I burn." She looked down at her bare arms. "I'll be sorry I wore this dress today."

He motioned her closer, into the deeper shade of the eucalyptus, and she scooted toward him.

"You'll be a beautiful old woman when the rest of them are wrinkled crones," he said.

Kate felt the blush on her nineteen-year-old cheeks. "I have a long wait."

Silence descended. *Say something!* Kate admonished herself. Here she was with a good-looking man who paid her *compliments*, and she was totally tongue-tied. She'd never had this kind of trouble talking to men before; had she lost the ability to flirt? Her vocal cords were tight, her muscles as taut as her mother's back-yard clothesline, her brain slow and useless.

Finally a few feeble words came to her. "How do you know Ryder?"

Jack rubbed the tip of his smoldering Marlboro into the grass to extinguish it. "Roommates," he replied.

"At college?"

His smile held a touch of something she didn't understand. "Yeah. Off campus."

"Which college?"

"You've heard of Chouinard?"

She had. "The art school? Ryder's in *art school*?"

Jack smirked. "Not any more—but don't tell his folks, okay? They're under the illusion he'll make more money as an artist than as a folk singer. Which I suppose he could, if he got a teaching credential."

"Is that what you're working toward?" Kate asked.

In answer, Jack pulled a folded paper and a pencil from his jeans pocket and began to draw. A few minutes later, he held up a remarkably flattering sketch of Kate herself. She took the drawing and studied it, unable to keep from grinning. He'd made her look prettier than she was, her hair smoother and longer, her nose straighter.

"Very nice; I wish I looked like that."

"You do. Very Alice in Wonderland, except for your green eyes."

He'd noticed her eyes. She'd have to be careful with this guy.

When she offered to return the drawing, he said, "No—keep it. A souvenir."

Kate folded the sketch carefully and tucked it in her pocket. "Thanks." After a pause while she searched for clever words and failed to find them, she asked, "Are drawings your specialty, then?"

He clicked his tongue. "Mostly paintings, but they're harder to carry around. Someday maybe I'll show you, though."

Kate fought more embarrassing shyness. "I'd like that."

"So you know Chouinard."

Kate nodded. "My dad went there."

"Your dad's an artist?"

"To me he was. He was an animator at Disney."

"Was?"

Pain, the non-physical kind, stabbed through her. "He died last year. Drunk driver ran into him."

He put his hand on her bare calf. "I'm sorry."

She should have expected the tears, but they took her by surprise and she swiped at them, mad at herself for acting maudlin. *Time to grow up, get used to it. Get over it.*

He didn't question her tears, and she was grateful for that. Kate couldn't explain why, but she cared what Jack Morrison thought of her.

"And you," he continued. "You've had more education than most, haven't you?"

Kate mimicked his way of putting out a cigarette but found herself empty-handed; she waved toward the mountains surrounding the park. "I almost did."

"Almost?"

"A year at UC Santa Barbara—liberal arts stuff. Nothing you can earn a living with."

"Is that why you quit?"

"Sort of. When my dad died, the money ran out."

"Ouch."

She shrugged. "Life's a bitch sometimes."

He smiled, and again there was that touch of something the exact opposite of mirth. "Right."

Then he lay back on the grass, staring up at the eucalyptus canopy. His eyes drifted shut, and Kate thought he might have fallen asleep, but she didn't mind. Somehow being next to him made her feel safe.

A woman in a vivid emerald gown glided up to them, a matching green scarf around her shiny black hair. Her skin was the color of dark chocolate. She held out her hand, fingers long and tapered. In the middle of her palm was a small white pill.

"One to grow on," the woman said, then threw back her head and laughed. She had immense white teeth.

Kate shook her head and echoed the polite refusal she'd heard Jack use. "Thanks, but we're already trippin'."

The woman laughed again and frolicked off.

Jack sat up. "You learn fast," he said.

Kate watched the woman move away. "What *was* that?"

He pursed his lips. "Acid, probably. LSD. You know LSD?"

"Of course. I didn't just fall off a turnip truck."

What a stupid thing to say. But he seemed to accept it. Kate began to feel like Jack Morrison would accept almost anything she said, or did. He had her father's attitude of competence and comfort in his skin.

"And you know better than to take candy from strangers," Jack said, and Kate felt a glow of pleasure.

That one hit of pot had begun to muddy her thoughts and perceptions, and the voices around her became an incoherent buzz. The air reeked of burning marijuana and incense; her pulse throbbed in sync with the bongos.

Then she heard other sounds: a whistle's shriek and an amplified voice. "THIS IS THE LOS ANGELES POLICE DEPARTMENT!"

Panic seized her. She'd seen news reports of uniformed officers, faces hidden by reflective shields, wading into crowds of unarmed hippies, cracking clubs against skulls and hauling scores of people off to jail—all for the bad luck of being in the wrong place at the wrong time.

The crowd began to disperse like stampeding cattle. Kate scrambled to her feet, and so did Jack.

"We have to get out of here," he shouted above the commotion.

"I know a back way," Kate yelled. "What about Ryder?"

Jack shook his head. "No time. Besides, Ryder always lands on his feet."

She felt a momentary flash of protectiveness for her old neighbor, always the butt of childish jokes, always the one left behind. She wanted to try and find him, and her co worker Arlene, but the pandemonium made it impossible. She took Jack's hand and pulled him toward a parking lot above the carousel, away from the field where people churned in noisy confusion.

Kate knew the way by heart; she and her dad had hiked every trail in Griffith Park at one time or another. The parking lot ended in a rough strip of asphalt, ringed by a low stone wall topped with a chain link fence. And there, right where she remembered, was the slash in the fence some impatient hiker had cut years ago. Kate squeezed through, Jack followed, and she led him up a bridle path, around the parking lot, above the melee playing out in the park.

Sirens wailed in the distance, and she heard screams and shouts and whistles.

Jack patted her back. "Nice going, Girl Scout. But now what? We can't camp out here all night."

"We don't have to," Kate told him. She pointed to her left. "That takes us down to the road. My car's half a mile from here."

He rubbed his chin. "Well, I'll be damned. Looks like I picked the right person to rescue."

I sure hope so.

"Can you give me a lift home?" Jack added. "I came with Ryder."

Well, well. Maybe the universe is finally giving me a break.

About the Author

 Bonnie Schroeder was bitten by the writing bug in the fifth grade and never recovered. Among her published short stories are "The Go-Between," "A Losing Game," "Vigilantes," and "Fault Lines." In the nonfiction arena, she wrote a weekly column in *Drama-Logue* on the subject of "survival skills" for actors and other theater professionals and has written e-newsletters for a chapter of the American Red Cross.

She has also completed two feature-length screenplays, one of which, *Smoke and Mirrors,* was a semi-finalist in the Monterey County Film Commission's competition. Long-form fiction, however, remains her first love, and *Mending Dreams* is her first published novel.

If you enjoyed *Mending Dreams,* please post a review online. Visit BonnieSchroederBooks.com for more on Bonnie.